THE SEXY SCIENTISTS SERIES

BOOKS 1 - 3

RAMONA GRAY

EK PUBLISHING INC.

Edited by:
L. Nunn Editing

Cover art by
EK Designs

THE CHEMIST

VOLUME ONE

THE CHEMIST

He knows how to use his beaker...

Sophie

I love my boss. Liam Whitby is brilliant, funny, and makes a lab coat look sexy. He's also completely uninterested in me.

Until one late night at work changes everything.

Now, we can't keep our hands off each other, and the sparks could cause fiery chaos in the lab.

Liam

I don't date coworkers. At least not since my messy breakup with my lab tech. I'm determined to stick to my vow, even if I'm constantly imagining what my fellow chemist, Sophie looks like in nothing but a lab coat and heels. Sleeping with Sophie is a mistake, but I can't resist her sweet kisses or our explosive chemistry.

Even though I only want a casual relationship, our bond is elemental. Is that why I can't stay away from her?

CHAPTER 1

Sophie

"Sophie, don't take this the wrong way, but that's a stupid idea." My best friend Hattie sipped at her coffee and took a bite of the carrot cake muffin.

"Mrs. Galath always said there was no such thing as a stupid idea," I said.

"Look, our second grade teacher was a real sweetheart, but trust me, even she would say that's a stupid idea," Hattie said.

"Lots of people move to new towns, get plastic surgery, and assume new identities," I said. "It happens all the time, Hattie."

"No, it doesn't."

Hattie's pragmatism was a real downer.

"Honey," Hattie's gaze was sympathetic, "I know this week has sucked really hard -"

"Just like me in that video! Heyo!" I held out my fist, but Hattie shook her head.

"I'm not fist bumping something that is upsetting you."

"I'm using humour to overcome the humiliation," I said. "Since the 'change my identity and my looks' option is not viable."

Hattie's continuing look of sympathy didn't make me feel any better. "Don't feel sorry for me, okay, Hatts? I have no one to blame but myself."

Her sympathy became fierce disapproval. "Don't even start with me on that bullshit, Sophie. This is one hundred percent that cocksucker Cody's fault. He uploaded the video to PornCentral, not you. He sent the copy of the video to your coworkers, not you."

"Ugh." I stared at my coffee and my uneaten piece of banana loaf. I'd lost my appetite sometime around Tuesday when Cody sent the email, and it had yet to return.

"Why did he have to send it to everyone at work?" I asked. "Why?"

"Because he's an asshole," Hattie said. "An asshole with an inflated ego and a ridiculously tiny dick. Now I know why you faked your orgasms with him. Although the one on the video was real, yeah?"

"No," I admitted. "It's fake."

"Huh. Your faking ability is impressive, girl."

"Thanks," I said morosely. "I had a lot of practice."

"I never understood why you dated Cody for so long, anyway. I mean, not that sex is everything, but if he couldn't even make you cum, why stick with him?"

"Well, because like you said, sex isn't everything in a relationship, and I kind of thought that I could teach him how to make me cum eventually, you know?"

"Not with a dick that small," Hattie said.

"It's not about the size," I said, "it's how they use it. Besides, Cody is average size, and you know it. Although I appreciate you trying to make me feel better."

"I'm sorry it's not working," Hattie said.

"Honestly, I'm not sure there's anything that can help," I said. "Not when every person at Optimum Pharmaceuticals was emailed a copy of my sex tape with my ex-boyfriend."

"Any luck getting the porn site to remove it?" Hattie asked.

"Not yet. Honestly, the real damage was sending the video to my coworkers, and Cody knew that, you know? How they look at me now is... well, it's awful and embarrassing."

"It's only been three days," Hattie said. "The novelty will die off, and they'll treat you the same as they did before."

My blonde hair was in its usual ponytail, and I tugged absently on the end of it. "Did I tell you that Cody replied to my text?"

"Shit, no. What did he say? Did he tell you why he did it?"

"Yeah. Says he knows it was me who ratted him out to Liam, and that's why Liam fired him."

"Are you kidding me? You didn't tell Liam about Cody's mistake!" Hattie's look of outrage was kind of adorable. "That fucking cunt. Seriously, I hate that guy so much. You were the one who fixed his mistake! And if you were going to rat him out for the fuck-up, you would have done it three months ago when he broke up with you."

"Honestly, I should have reported his mistake the day it happened. Liam gave me so much shit on Monday about not reporting it. I thought he was gonna fire me too," I said.

"It's been over four months since Cody fucked up. Do you know how Liam found out?"

"No, but I suspect it was Erica. Liam didn't say who told him, and he was so pissed that I didn't want to push. I'd be heartbroken if I got fired just as we started the pre-clinical development stage. It feels like it's taken us forever to get here."

Hattie smoothed back a strand of her dark hair that had already escaped her braid. "I'm proud of you, Soph. You do important work."

"So do you," I said.

She scoffed and took another sip of coffee. "I was paid to pretend to be someone else. That's not important work. You're creating a new drug that could help epilepsy. *That's* important work."

"That isn't who you are anymore," I said. "And you haven't been that person for a long time. What you do now is important."

"I fix cars," she said.

"People need their cars," I said.

"Yeah, I know."

"You okay?" I asked. "I thought you loved being a mechanic."

"I do," she said. "I seriously love it, but lately, I've just been restless. I'm looking for…."

"Looking for what?" I asked when she didn't continue.

She shook her head. "I don't want to talk about it. At least not right here in the middle of Brilliant Beanz where anyone can overhear us."

I looked around the crowded coffee shop. I recognized about seventy-five percent of the faces, which happened when you lived your entire life in the same small town.

"All right," I said, "but we are circling back to this, Hattie."

"Yeah, yeah. Right now, let's focus on your crisis, okay?"

"Do you think Barb looked at me funny when we ordered our coffee?" I asked.

Hattie glanced at the silver-haired woman standing at the till and smiling at a customer. "No, why?"

"Because she gave me an, *I've seen you sucking your boyfriend's dick* look," I said. "And Walter at the Super Save last night definitely gave me an, *I watched you taking it from behind* look."

"Oh, Walter has absolutely seen your sex tape," Hattie said. "He asked me on Thursday night if you and I had ever hooked up and recorded it. Said if we had, we could load that to PornCentral, and he'd even pay to watch it."

"What a gentleman." My voice was thick with sarcasm and embarrassment. "Sorry you're getting dragged into this, Hattie."

"Honey, you know I don't care. Besides, there are, like, four videos of me on PornCentral right now."

"Yeah, but none of them are actually you," I said. "Just incredibly impressive look-alikes."

She shrugged. "People believe it's me. Or want to believe it is. It's what happens when you're a moderately successful actress."

Moderately successful was total BS. My best friend had become the star of a very popular sitcom at the age of eleven. Everyone knew her name, but few people knew why she'd quit the show and returned to Willowdale as soon as she turned eighteen.

It'd been seven years since she'd quit, but thanks to the show's popularity, syndicated reruns, and the antics of Hattie's mother, Hattie hadn't faded into obscurity as she'd hoped. Paparazzi occasionally showed up to our small town of Willowdale to stalk and snap pictures - usually whenever her mother did something stupid - and Hattie bore it all with a quiet stoicism, no matter what they wrote about her in the tabloids.

"Anyway," Hattie said, "I promise this will die down, even with your coworkers."

"I'm working with him today," I said.

"Liam?" she asked.

I nodded, my stomach churning up the small amount of coffee I'd managed to drink. "Yeah."

"Okay." Hattie's voice turned brisk. "So, the guy you've been crushing on since you started at the lab has seen you banging another guy. It's not ideal, but it's not that big of a deal in the grand scheme of things because…."

"Because Liam is gay and probably more into watching Cody in the video than me," I said.

"Bingo." Hattie gave me finger guns and ate another bite of muffin.

"Finger guns, Hattie?"

"I'm bringing them back. Making them cool again."

"They were never cool in the first place."

She just shrugged before smiling at me. "Look, I know it's embarrassing that Liam saw you naked and doing nakedy things in the video, but you're a twenty-five-year-old woman who doesn't need to be ashamed that she had sex with her boyfriend. You did nothing wrong, honey."

"I know, but it's just…."

"What?" she asked.

"It's bad enough that I'm crushing on my gay boss and have been for what feels like forever. Now I have to deal with the fact that he's seen me naked, even if it does absolutely nothing for him. My boss saw me having sex with a co-worker, Hattie. It's so embarrassing."

"One, it's not like it was a secret that you and Cody were dating, and two, Liam had his own drama with dating a co-worker, remember? He's probably the most sympathetic out of everyone at the lab."

"That's a good point," I said. "Dayton did kind of lose his mind when Liam broke up with him."

"Honestly, I'm surprised that HR didn't mandate a 'no dating your co-workers' rule after that fiasco," Hattie said. "Dayton destroyed the entire lab."

"You know that's only gossip and rumours," I said. "He just broke some beakers and smashed his fist through the fridge glass door."

"Just," Hattie said with a roll of her eyes. "My point is, Liam had his own co-worker drama at the lab, so he gets how embarrassed you are. He hasn't brought up the video, has he?"

"No, but I haven't seen him since Cody emailed the video. But that ends today. We're working together this afternoon, and, even worse, Finn will be there for part of it."

"Finn?" Hattie immediately perked up. She'd had a crush on Liam's older brother since the moment she'd seen him at the company barbecue I'd dragged her to last month. She'd peppered me for details about him, but unfortunately, I knew very little about Finn beyond he was a biologist at the lab, he was at least a decade older than Liam, and he intimidated the hell out of me.

"Why don't you like Finn?" Hattie asked after a few seconds of silence.

"It's not that I don't like him. I barely know him," I said. "I don't like working with him."

"Why?"

"Because he's intimidating, and he's as smart, if not smarter than Liam."

"So?" Hattie said. "You're not exactly a dumb-dumb, Sophie. You have a Ph.D. in chemistry, for God's sake."

"I know, but trust me - Liam and Finn are both brilliant and hot as fuck, and when you put them in a room together -"

"The ladies start to spontaneously combust?" Hattie said.

I laughed. "Not in the lab, we're all way too busy, but I imagine out in the real world - yes. It's like both of them are the Hollywood version of what a chemist and a biologist look like."

"Don't remind me. I'm still dreaming about how Finn's ass looked in his jeans," Hattie said. "Why aren't you interested in Finn? He and Liam are pretty similar in looks, and Finn's not gay, right?"

She ruined her casual tone by immediately biting at her fingernails, an old and familiar indication of her nerves. My best friend had it bad for Finn Whitby, no matter how hard she tried to pretend she didn't.

"As far as I know, he isn't gay. But he doesn't do it for me," I said. "Sure, he's good looking, but he's gotta be in his forties, and he has a very 'you will do exactly what I say when I say it' attitude that's a little off-putting. I don't need to be told what to do, thanks."

Hattie continued to chew at her already ragged fingernails. "So, he's a dick, is what you're saying."

"No," I said. "He isn't. At least, I don't think he is. He just has very high expectations. Also, it's super obvious he likes to be in control, and I'm not interested in my dude telling me what to do and how to do it, day in and day out. Could you imagine how he'd be in bed? He'd probably be like a drill sergeant barking out orders. Spread your legs! Get on your knees! Show me that pussy! Suck my dick!"

I laughed at my own joke, but Hattie's face had gone pink and sweaty, and she practically gnawed on her fingernails. I reached out and tugged her hand away from her mouth. "Hey, stop that, honey. You're about to start eating your flesh."

She stared blankly at her hand before muttering a curse and tucking both hands under her legs.

"Why are you so flushed?" I asked.

"I'm not," she said.

"You are. You turned red and got all sweaty the minute I started talking about Finn and his control." I stared silently at Hattie for almost thirty seconds. "Oh my God."

"What?" Hattie practically vibrated in her chair.

I glanced around to make sure no one could overhear, then lowered my voice anyway. "You like the idea of Finn telling you what to do in bed."

"Keep your voice down," Hattie said with a scowl.

"It already is," I pointed out. "Admit it, Hatts. You like being told what to do in bed."

Hattie pressed her lips together and looked around the coffeehouse before leaning across the table. "I have certain preferences in bed, yes. Which I am not about to explain or share in this damn coffee shop, so don't even ask."

"That's fair," I said. "I have to get to work anyway. But we're definitely talking about this in detail later. Although before we leave, I want to know why you've never mentioned this before to me."

I wouldn't admit this, but I was a little hurt. We'd been best friends since kindergarten, and Hattie knew everything about me. Up until now, I thought I'd known everything about her.

Hattie sighed. "It has nothing to do with you and every-thing to do with me. I didn't want you judging me for my... kink."

"You know I wouldn't do that. Besides, is being bossed around in bed even a kink or more of a preference?" I asked.

"It's more than just being bossed around in bed," Hattie said.

"Okay, that's it. We're both calling in sick to work, and you're telling me everything," I said.

Hattie smiled, the flush on her chest and face finally fading. "Neither of us can call in sick. Whenever an employee calls in sick on a Friday, their boss thinks they're lying. Look, I have a Saturday off for a change, so I'll come over tomorrow, and we'll talk, okay?"

"Sounds good," I said.

We both stood, and I wrapped my banana bread in a napkin and stuck it in my purse. Maybe my appetite would return by lunch. I picked up my coffee and followed Hattie outside to our cars in the lot. She kissed my cheek. "Love you, Soph. Today will go better than you think. Just remember, Liam doesn't have any interest in seeing you naked anyway."

I made myself smile and wave at her as she climbed into her car and drove away. I slid behind the wheel, placing my coffee in the cup holder and my purse on the seat beside me. I knew that Hattie was only trying to help, but the reminder that Liam would never be interested in me only depressed me more.

I might have been a little hurt by Hattie keeping a secret, but I'd been keeping a doozie of a secret from her.

I wasn't just crushing on my boss, Liam. I was utterly and hopelessly in love with him.

CHAPTER 2

Liam

"You should have told me about the video, Liam."

Finn stalked into the lab, a scowl on his face and his dark hair sticking up like he'd been running his hands through it.

"Good afternoon to you too, Finn," I said. I stepped back from the microscope and leaned against the lab counter, crossing my arms across my chest.

My older brother scowled at me. We had different mothers, and Finn was fifteen years older than me, but we both favoured our dad in looks, so it was easy to tell we were siblings. His blue eyes, the same shade as mine, had narrowed and a muscle ticked at his temple. "Why didn't you tell me about the video?"

"Because Cody was my employee and my problem," I said. "Besides, it's been four days since he emailed it. Did you seriously only find out about it today?"

"Just now,' he said. "And only because I got trapped in the goddamn kitchen with Luther, who took great delight in sharing every detail with me. He even tried to show me the link on PornCentral on his fucking phone. When the fuck is it appropriate to show a co-worker a porno at your place of business?"

"Honestly, I'm surprised it took this long for you to find out about it. It's all anyone's talking about," I said.

"Maybe because I'm working and not gossiping?" Finn said. "Christ, am I the only one who works in this fucking lab?"

I rolled my eyes but didn't reply. Finn's car, a 1957 Chevy Bel Air and his one true love, was having mechanical issues, and it had put him in a real mood for the past two weeks. There was no point in poking the bear when he got like this. It would only make him even harder to deal with. I loved my brother, but sometimes there was nothing to do but keep your head down and wait out his mood.

"Did you go to PornCentral and watch the video?" I asked.

"Christ no," Finn said. "How many times did you watch it?"

"I didn't," I said.

That got a reaction from my usually unflappable brother. "You're kidding me."

"Nope. I had about four employees texting me before I even opened my email," I said. "You really didn't watch it?"

"I'm not interested in seeing the woman my brother is crushing on, naked," Finn said.

"I'm not crushing on Sophie," I said.

"Bullshit."

"She has no interest in me. She thinks I'm gay," I said.

"Everyone in the lab does," Finn said. "Because you haven't told anyone you're bi."

"None of their fucking business," I said.

"Agreed. Why did Cody send the video?" Finn asked.

"Cody blames her for being fired. He thinks Sophie told me about his fuck up."

"You told me Erica shared Cody's mistake with you."

"She did, but Cody believes it was Sophie."

"Did you set him straight?"

"So he could then upload a video of Erica to PornCentral as well? Erica came to me crying on Tuesday morning, saying that Cody had recorded them having sex too, and practically begged me not to tell him it was her," I said. "Which I won't because one of my employees being violated so horribly is enough, thanks."

"Wait... Cody was fucking Erica?"

I nodded. "He started fucking Erica the day after breaking up with Sophie."

"Jesus wept," Finn said. "It's like a fucking soap opera at this place."

I knew he didn't mean anything by it, but I cringed inwardly anyway. A year ago, my personal drama had lent a certain soap opera-ish atmosphere to the lab, so I could hardly call Cody out for fucking his way through our roster of chemists.

But I could and *had* fired him for making such a colossal fuck up, even if said fuck up was four months ago.

You should have fired Sophie for not telling you about his mistake.

Yeah, I should have. But I hadn't. I couldn't. Sophie was one of my best chemists, and while it'd been easy to get rid of that fucker Cody, even the idea of firing Sophie had made me sick to my stomach.

Because she's so good at her job or because you desperately want to fuck her?

"Why did Erica tell you about his mistake?" Finn asked.

"Cody was cheating on her with Alanna, and she found out."

"Alanna, our receptionist?" Finn's eyes went wide.

"Yep."

"Does he just let his dick hang out all the fucking time?"

"Probably. Anyway, Erica told me about his mistake. I verified it happened and then fired him on Monday. He sent a company-wide email of his and Sophie's sex tape on Tuesday morning. I had IT pull it from the email server, but at least eighty percent of the employees saw it."

"Fuck, what a shitshow," Finn said.

"Yeah." I rubbed at the back of my neck. "I haven't talked to Sophie since the video was emailed. But she'll be working with us this afternoon."

"I can't make it," Finn said but didn't give a reason. Not surprising. My brother rarely gave explanations for anything he did or said.

"All right," I said. "There's a good chance we'll be working late, though. Can you check on Alina tonight?"

Finn nodded. Our younger sister didn't need to be 'checked on,' and we both knew it, but old habits died hard.

"It's my fault," I said. "The video being released."

"It's not your fault," Finn said.

"It is. Most of our coworkers have seen Sophie naked, and it's because of me. If I hadn't fired Cody -"

"If you hadn't fired him, he'd still be here potentially making another huge and costly mistake," Finn said. "The only reason we even made it to the pre-clinical development stage after what he did, is because Sophie worked a goddamn miracle and fixed his error."

He glanced at his phone when it buzzed. "Does she realize that's the only reason she wasn't fired right along with Cody?"

I didn't reply, and Finn gave me a hard look. "Did you clarify to her that what she did should have gotten her fired, Liam?"

"She's basically a genius. I'm sure she already knows."

"You're letting your feelings for her get in the way. It's the same thing that happened with Dayton and -"

"Don't, Finn." My voice went uncharacteristically sharp, and I stood up straight, my fists clenched and my spine stiff. "Don't you fucking act like I haven't learned my lesson since Dayton. I have, and you fucking well know it."

For once, it was my brother who backed down. "I know. I let my temper get the best of me, and I shouldn't have said that. What happened with Dayton wasn't your fault and -"

"It was," I said, "but it's never going to happen again, and I don't need you throwing it in my face, asshole."

"Watch your mouth with me, Liam," Finn said.

I glared at him, but Finn met my look with a cool calmness that made me feel like I did when I was a little kid, and he'd caught me stealing a candy bar from Walgreens. I didn't look away, but I took a deep breath and said, "I won't let what happened with Dayton happen again. You don't have to worry about that."

"I'm worried about your tendency to take everything onto your shoulders. Not every bad thing that happens is your fault, Liam."

"You're seriously getting pissed because I'm taking responsibility for my actions?" I asked.

"It isn't your fault that Cody emailed that video," Finn said.

"I still need to apologize to Sophie," I said.

Finn shrugged as he glanced at his phone again. "Shit, I have to go. Look, apologize or don't, whatever. But make it clear to Sophie that she can't be keeping these types of mistakes from you again, or she will be fired."

The soft gasp behind him indicated I wouldn't need to talk to Sophie.

Finn closed his eyes, a *fuck me, why won't this day end* look on his face, before opening them and turning around. "Hello, Sophie."

"Hello, Finn," Sophie said stiffly.

After a moment, Finn glanced back at me. "I'll text you tomorrow." He walked out of the lab, shutting the door behind him.

Her face pale, Sophie joined me at the counter. Her blonde hair was pulled into its usual ponytail, and I itched to pull out the elastic and bury my hands in the silky-looking strands. Her lab coat hid her perfect tits and firm ass, but the memory of how she'd looked last month at the company barbecue was still burned into my mind. It was the first and only time I'd seen her in a dress, and while the dress had ended modestly at her knee, I'd gotten a fucking boner just seeing her bare shins and the hint of thigh when she'd sat down.

Having those legs wrapped around my waist as I buried myself in her tight pussy had been my number one fantasy for months now.

Her pale skin was soft pink with embarrassment, and her gorgeous dark brown eyes studied me. She occasionally wore glasses when working at the lab, but she wasn't currently wearing them. Probably for the best. I also tended to get boners when she wore her glasses.

She took a deep breath and straightened her shoulders. "If you believe I should be fired for not telling you about Cody's mistake, you should fire me. I'd rather be fired than work for a boss who believes I'm incompetent at my job."

"You're not incompetent," I said. "You fixed Cody's mistake, remember?"

Her chin lifted a little higher. "But you think I should be fired anyway."

"No, my brother thinks you should have been fired. But he's not your boss, is he?"

"No," she said.

"I owe you an apology," I said.

Cute little lines appeared in the smooth skin between her eyes. "An apology?"

"Yes. It's my fault that Cody released the video. He believed you told me about his mistake, so he sent the video in retaliation."

"I know," she said. "But did Cody tell you that he blamed me when you fired him on Monday?"

"No, he didn't," I said.

"Then how is it your fault?"

"I didn't tell him who came forward with the knowledge of his mistake."

"You shouldn't have," she said. "I'm sure he has a video of him and Erica having sex, and he would have done to her exactly what he did to me."

My jaw dropped. "You know it was Erica who told me about his mistake?"

"I suspected. I don't know how she found out, but it makes sense she would want revenge when she realized Cody was cheating on her with Alanna."

"Christ," I said. "What a dick."

"Yes. For what it's worth, I wish I'd told you about the mistake when it happened, and I'm sorry I didn't. I let my personal life affect my work life, and it won't happen again. You have my word on that."

"He shouldn't have sent out the video to everyone. I'm sorry he did," I said.

She shrugged and tried to sound nonchalant, but embarrassment practically radiated off of her. "Yeah, well, I shouldn't have let him record us."

I frowned. "This is in no way your fault, Sophie. He's the asshole for violating your trust."

She just nodded and stepped away to peer into the microscope. I waited for a beat and said, "I didn't watch the video."

Her body jerked, and she straightened, staring at me with a mixture of relief and embarrassment. "You didn't?"

"No," I said. "I didn't."

"Thank you. I appreciate that."

I nodded, and she turned back to the microscope. I told myself for the hundredth time that I'd learned my lesson about fucking a co-worker, and even if I hadn't, Sophie most definitely had.

CHAPTER 3

Sophie

"Christ, I'm going cross-eyed over here." Liam sat down on a stool and rubbed at his eyes.

I straightened, wincing when my back cracked, and rubbed at the base of my spine. "I've been bent over this microscope for so long, I'm pretty sure I've done permanent damage."

Liam didn't laugh at my joke. "Do you do stretches? Some really simple ones make a huge difference. With how much we're sitting and hunched over, you really should do stretches."

"I'll look into it," I said as Liam's stomach growled loudly.

"I'll send you a link to the ones I use." He glanced at his watch. "It's almost six, and we have at least another couple of hours of work. We should order some food."

"Sure," I said. It wasn't the first time I'd worked late with Liam. Hell, it wasn't even the tenth time, but tonight felt…

strange. He had weird energy, and everything felt slightly off-kilter between us.

Unlike his brother, Liam had an easy-going nature and was good to work for. Not that we were friends or anything, but we'd always gotten along well in the lab. Until Monday, I'd never given him a single reason to be unhappy with my work.

Yeah, well, you fucked that up, didn't you? Big time. That weird energy is how it will be between you two from now on. He can't trust you anymore.

"How about A Taste of Thai?" Liam said. "I know we always order from there, but it's my favourite."

"Mine too," I said.

"You want your usual?" Liam had already pulled out his phone.

"Yes, please." I rubbed at my spine again as Liam tapped away on his phone. Fuck, what if I'd permanently screwed up my working relationship with Liam? My stomach tightened, and I could barely breathe through the pinhole that my throat had become.

Relax, and take a breath. Everything's fine. At least he hasn't seen you naked and screwing Cody, right?

A colossal sized wave of relief washed over me. Somehow, Liam not watching the video made me feel like I could put up with my coworkers' side looks of judgment and the awkward silences when I walked into the lunchroom. Hell, I could even find a way to laugh it off when one of our lab techs, Darren, *joked* that I could benefit from a boob job for the third day in a row.

I mean, he wasn't wrong, right? My tits were pretty tiny.

"Food'll be here in about thirty minutes," Liam said.

"Great, thanks." Ignoring my aching spine, I bent over my microscope again.

Thirty-three minutes later, there was a knock on the lab door. A guy carrying a large paper bag with a Taste of Thai logo stamped on it stood in the doorway. "Hey, the dude at the front desk said I should just bring this back here."

I glanced at Liam. He was in his office at the far end of the lab, typing on his laptop and deep in his own world. I doubted he'd even heard the guy knock.

I grabbed my wallet from my purse and headed over to the door, taking out fifty in cash and handing it to the guy. "Keep the rest for a tip."

"Hey, thanks," he said. "That's really...."

He paused, holding the bag in front of him as he took a good look at me. Up close, I could smell his BO, and his long, greasy hair and wispy mustache practically screamed creeper.

I reached for the bag, tensing when the guy refused to let go of it. "I know you."

"No, I don't think so," I said.

"I'm pretty sure I do. I never forget a face," he said.

"We probably went to school together," I said. "It's a small town."

"Nah, I just moved here a month ago. I grew up in Marketville. You been there?"

"A couple of times," I said shortly. "Thanks for the delivery. Have a nice weekend."

He refused to relinquish his hold on the paper bag. He peered at me, and dismay rippled through me when recognition lit up his muddy brown eyes. "Holy fuck. I watched you get railed on PornCentral last night."

My face turned bright red. Could the asshole talk any fucking louder? Praying like hell that Liam was still wrapped up in his work, I said, "No, I don't think you did."

"Oh, I did," he said as his gaze skipped down my body.

"You had a hot little body and took that dick like a champ, didn't you?"

His eyes lingered on my tits. "Tits are kind of small, but the rest of your body ain't too bad. You really sucked down that dude's dick."

"Give me the food and leave," I said.

"Okay, no need to be prickly." He handed over the bag but took my arm when I started to turn away.

"Let go of me," I said.

"What are you doing once you're finished here?" he asked. "You wanna get a drink or something?"

"No," I said. "This is your last chance to let go of me."

He rolled his eyes but dropped his hand from my arm. "C'mon, girl, have a drink with me. We can go back to my place, get comfortable, and you can show me how good you are with that mouth of yours."

"Fuck off," I said in a low voice before walking away.

"Prickly bitch," the guy said.

I kept walking toward the far end of the lab. By the time I got to Liam, my hands shook from adrenaline, and I felt sick to my stomach. The tiny thread of hunger I'd felt had disappeared, but I set the bag on Liam's desk and plastered a smile on my face. "Dinner's here."

Liam looked up in surprise. "Already?"

"Yep."

"I didn't even hear the guy. Did you pay for the food?"

I wanted to say who else would have paid for it but didn't. I was just upset about what happened, and taking my feelings out on Liam was a dick move.

"I did," I said.

"Shit. Make sure you expense it, all right?"

"Will do. The food smells good." It didn't, at least not

anymore, but I could fake being hungry. I was exceptionally good at faking. Just ask Cody.

"It smells fucking amazing." Liam reached into the bag and pulled out a container. "You good with eating in my office? We can't eat in the lab, but I don't feel like walking to the break room."

"Here's fine," I said.

"I'll get us a couple of sodas from the vending machine out... hey, you okay?" Liam stared at me, a container of noodles in one hand and napkins in the other.

"Fine," I said.

He studied me silently. His usual clean-shaven jaw had a five o'clock shadow, and his gorgeous full lips had thinned out with concern.

I made myself smile at him. "I'm a little tired. And hungry."

I got the distinct feeling he didn't believe me, but thankfully, he didn't push. He handed me the container of noodles. "You want a Sprite?"

"Yes, please," I said.

"I'll be right back."

"Sure, okay." I made that stupid smile even larger, not dropping it until Liam had left the lab. I slumped against his desk, rubbing at my temples and wishing not for the first time that I'd never dated Cody.

Why did you? You love Liam, remember?

Yeah, I did, but I also knew he would never feel the same way. Dating Cody, sleeping with Cody, was my attempt at getting over Liam. Sitting alone, night after night and pining for a man I would never have wasn't healthy. So, I'd put myself out there, went on dates, tried to forget my love for my boss, and find my happiness.

Only I'd chosen poorly and ended up with an idiot with a

vindictive streak. Even worse, I'd let him record us having sex.

I sighed before taking out the rest of the containers and lining them up neatly on Liam's desk. What was done was done, and I couldn't change the past. I needed to let it go and look for someone who a) I didn't work with and b) wasn't an asshole.

What's the point of dating? You'll only wish they were Liam when you're with them. You'll have to close your eyes and pretend they're Liam in bed if you want even a chance of cumming.

A flicker of anger surged through me. No, I wouldn't have to. Just because I had to fake ninety-five percent of my orgasms with Cody and the few I did manage to have, were because I pretended it was Liam touching me didn't mean I'd have to do that with every man I dated.

I just had to find someone who made me feel the way Liam did. I didn't believe in soulmates or that there was only one person out there or any of that stupid bullshit. There was a guy in the world for me who wasn't Liam. I just needed to find him.

"I THINK I'VE DONE EVERYTHING I CAN DO TONIGHT," I SAID.

Liam didn't even look up from the microscope. "Okay, see you Monday."

"You sure there isn't something I can help you with? I don't mind staying longer," I said.

He waved distractedly. "Nah, I'm all good here. I'll be finishing up in the next half hour or so. Go home, Soph."

Some of the tension in my stomach loosened when he said

my nickname. Which was stupid because it didn't mean anything, but my mind tried to pretend it did. I puttered around my lab station for another five minutes, tidying the already clean area and trying to think of a reason to stay with him.

Which was pathetic because it was after nine on a Friday night, and what twenty-five-year-old wanted to spend their entire Friday night at a lab? I should be out at a bar getting wasted and making bad choices, right?

I think you've made enough bad choices for a lifetime.

Lord, wasn't that the truth. Besides, I'd never been much for bar hopping or socializing the way most people my age were. I was an introvert, and the idea of spending my evening in a crowded bar made me shudder.

I needed to leave. Spending time with Liam when I didn't have to wouldn't help me fall out of love with him anytime soon.

I slipped into my jacket and grabbed my purse. "Good night, Liam."

He didn't respond, too absorbed in his work to even hear me. I would have been mad, but I loved seeing this side of him. How seriously he took his job and the effort and the intensity with which he worked was a huge turn on.

I left the lab and headed for the front foyer. It was a long walk. Optimum Pharmaceuticals was housed in a large sprawling building on the outskirts of town. The pharmaceutical company had been in Willowdale for over thirty years. Until the auto manufacturing plant, Hudson Automobiles, had built their factory here two years ago, Optimum was the most significant hiring force for our small town.

My heels loudly click-clacked as I walked down the silent hallways. This late on a Friday night, no one was left but Liam and me and the janitorial staff. Honestly, the empty hallways were a little eerie when they were typically packed with people.

I reached the front foyer, pulling out my keys from my purse when I realized the security guard, Arnie, had left for the evening. I'd never understood why they had him work until nine every evening anyway. Sure, there was expensive equipment in the lab, but they had security cameras and building alarms, and it's not like Willowdale was a hub of criminal activity.

I locked the door behind me and briefly considered texting Liam to remind him to set the alarm before dismissing the idea. He was a grown-ass man who worked late hours a lot. He wouldn't appreciate a reminder from his employee to set the alarm.

I headed toward my car in the employee parking lot, ignoring my aching spine and sore feet. I was having a hot bath the minute I stepped foot in my home. I'd pour myself a glass of wine and watch a mindless action movie to take my mind off the fact that most of the damn town had probably watched me on a -

"Hey there, cutie."

I froze a few steps from my car before turning slowly to see the Taste of Thai delivery driver standing behind me. Adrenaline sang her sweet song in my veins as I swallowed hard. "What are you doing here?"

He shrugged, shoving his hands into his pockets before smiling at me. "I got off work early. Thought I'd swing by and see if you'd changed your mind about that drink."

"I haven't," I said. "Good night."

"C'mon now," he said. "Don't be so hasty to say no. I'm Dave. What's your name?"

When I didn't reply, he took a few steps closer. I backed

away until my ass hit my car. "I'm not interested. Fuck off, Dave."

He frowned and moved forward until he stood only inches away. "Why are you being such an uppity bitch? You think you're too good for old Dave? Is that it?"

I took a deep breath, inhaling the scent of his BO mixed with weed as he reached out and touched the end of my ponytail before grinning at me. "C'mon, cutie, why don't we take a ride back to my place?"

Fuck me sideways.

Liam

MY PHONE BUZZED AGAIN IN MY POCKET, AND WITH A muttered curse, I stepped away from the lab counter and yanked the phone out of my pocket. I glanced at the screen before answering the call.

"What's up?"

"Well, hello to you too, bunny."

I could tell immediately from Nick's voice that he was drunk.

"You're drunk," I said.

"Fuck, yeah, I am. How'd you know?"

You couldn't be best friends with someone for fifteen years without knowing their drunk voice.

"Where are you?" I asked.

"I'm at the Brewhouse. Get your ass over here and drink with me," Nick said.

"Can't. I'm working."

"You're always working," Nick said.

"Because what I do is important."

"Hey." Nick's voice turned indignant. "I'm a physicist. I do important shit too, you know."

"Hmm, let's see." I leaned against the counter. "I'm creating a new drug that may help drug-resistant epileptics. You're creating a car that runs on electricity."

"I'm saving the planet, man," Nick said.

I laughed. "Yeah, that's fair. But I can't join you."

"Sure you can," he said. "It's better than being alone at your lab on a Friday night."

"I'm not alone," I said. "Sophie is …" I looked around the empty lab before glancing at the clock on the wall. Shit, I didn't even remember saying goodbye to her.

"You fuck her yet?" Nick asked.

"Shut up," I said. "You know I haven't, and I won't."

"You should. Life's too short to not fuck the ladies or men you want to fuck, bud."

"I learned my lesson about fucking an employee," I said. "Christ, are you so drunk you've forgotten about Dayton?"

"Like I could forget about that fuckwad," Nick said. "Also, you maybe shouldn't talk about fucking an employee in front of an employee."

"She left," I said. "I think."

"You think?"

"Yeah, she did. I remember her saying she was leaving."

"You let her walk out to her car alone?" Nick said. "It's like ten at night, dude."

"It's nine-thirty," I said. "And it's Willowdale. She's perfectly safe."

"I'm telling your brother you let a girl walk to her car late at night," Nick said.

"Don't you fucking dare, Nicky," I said. "She's fine. She's probably halfway home by now."

"Maybe," Nick said.

"Fuck. I gotta go," I said.

"You going to check on your girl?"

"She's not my girl, but yes, I'm going to check that she made it safely to her car in the town of Willowdale, where the biggest crime spree we've seen since moving here was when that gang of teenagers went on a cow tipping rampage last spring."

Nick roared laughter. "Teenagers are the fucking worst. Get your ass to the bar after you make sure she's safe, yeah?"

"No," I said. "I'm finishing up here and going home. It's been a long day. I'll call you tomorrow."

"Fine. Later, asshole."

"Bye, dick for brains."

I ended the call and shoved my phone back into my pocket before leaving the lab. I jogged down the empty hallways, nodding to Edith, who pushed her cleaning cart down the hallway.

"You working late again, Liam?" she asked.

"I am. Did you see Sophie leave?" I paused by the door to the break room.

"Haven't seen her," Edith said. "Have a good night."

"You too, Edith."

Even though I was confident that Sophie was fine, confident that she'd be in her car and halfway home by now, I couldn't ignore the trepidation that slowly settled over my body.

She's fine, I repeated to myself as I entered the front foyer and jogged over to the door. *She's perfectly fine. Don't let Nick get into your head.*

I peered out the door, cupping my hands around my face to cut the glare as I looked toward the employee lot. I froze for a few seconds, the noodles in my stomach threatening to mutiny, when I saw the man standing near Sophie.

I unlocked the door and stepped outside, running toward them before the door even closed behind me. I had no idea who the guy was, but when he stepped closer and touched Sophie's ponytail, the fear on her face sent real anger rocketing through my body.

I raced forward, the anger turning to rage when the man crowded Sophie, his body pressed up against hers. To my surprise, Sophie immediately punched him in the face and then kneed him in the balls. I stopped behind them as the man screamed and sank to his knees, grabbing his balls before falling over onto his side on the pavement.

"I told you not to fucking touch me," Sophie spat before she kicked him in the ass.

He squealed, one hand grabbing at his ass, the other still cupping his balls. I burst into laughter, and Sophie gave me a startled look.

"Liam? What are you doing here?"

"I came to make sure you were okay." I studied the crying, moaning man at our feet before nudging him in the leg. "Buddy, get the fuck up."

"My balls, man," he groaned before retching. "My balls."

"Get the fuck up," I repeated as I reached for my phone.

"Who are you calling?" Sophie asked.

"The police."

She shook her head as the man staggered to his feet. "No, don't call them."

"Soph, he attacked you. I'm calling them."

"I didn't attack her," the man whined as he backed away, his hands still holding onto his balls. "I was just being…."

"You were being a fucking asshole," I said. "And you're getting arrested."

Before I could dial 911, the man turned and, considering that his balls were probably somewhere near his esophagus, ran surprisingly quick across the parking lot to a car parked near the road.

"Let him go." Sophie reached for my arm, stopping me from going after him. "I know where he works."

"What? How?"

She grimaced as she rubbed at her hand. "He was the delivery guy from earlier."

"Fuck me," I said.

Still rubbing at her hand, she said, "Yeah. I'll call them and let them know what he did. I doubt they'll fire him, though. He didn't do anything to me beyond saying some gross shit and touching my hair."

"The police need to be involved," I said.

"If we call the police, I'll most likely be arrested for assaulting him," she said. "You know that."

I muttered a curse before taking Sophie's left hand. "C'mon."

She balked. "Where are we going?"

"Back to the lab. You need some ice for your hand, and I want to check you over, make sure you're okay."

"I'm fine," she said. "Liam, I'm okay."

"Let me take care of you, Sophie. Please?" I asked.

Her face softened, and she let me lead her toward the building.

By the time we made it back to the lab, some of my anger had receded, and I no longer thought I might simply punch through a wall. As long as I kept the image of that guy touching Sophie out of my head, anyway.

Still holding hands, we walked through the lab to my office. I pointed to my chair. "Sit for a second, Soph."

She sat down, and I crossed to the tiny bar fridge shoved into the corner. I opened it and reached into the freezer for the ice pack I kept in it. I didn't suffer from headaches like Finn did, but it was nice to have something cold for the occasional headache I got while working.

I returned to my desk. Sophie had stood, and when I gave her a disapproving look, she sat her butt on the corner of my desk. "It feels weird to sit in your chair."

"Why?"

"Because it's your chair, and you're my boss," she said.

I took her hand, studying the knuckles already swelling a little. "Shit, I hope you haven't broken your hand."

"I haven't." She flexed her hand carefully and grimaced.

"How do you know?"

"I know what a broken hand feels like, and this isn't it," she said.

"You've broken your hand before?" I placed the ice pack across her knuckles, holding it in place as she stared up at me.

"The one and only time I climbed a tree," she said.

I laughed, and she smiled, but her face was pale, and her entire body trembled. I moved closer, cupping her face and rubbing my thumb along her cheekbone. "You okay, Soph?"

She nodded, closing her eyes briefly when I used my other hand to knead the back of her neck. "Wh-what are you doing, Liam?"

"Checking to make sure you aren't hurt," I said.

Fuck, I was a liar. I closed my eyes so she wouldn't see the rage in them. I wanted to touch her. I needed to touch her soft skin. Needed to reassure myself that she was okay. Because the memory of that asshole touching her made my urge to punch the wall return with a fury.

"Liam," Sophie's voice was soft, her breath warm on my lips, the heat of her inner thighs burning against my legs.

"Yeah?" I kept my eyes closed. My rage had died as quickly as it returned, leaving only desire and an all-consuming ache to fuck the woman sitting in front of me.

"Look at me."

I took a deep breath. I couldn't look at her, couldn't let her see the need barely simmering below the surface. "Sophie, I…"

"Please," she said.

I opened my eyes, staring into those gorgeous brown eyes, my hand already sliding to cup the back of her neck to tug her head back and give me access to those beautiful lips.

"Liam, do you…" she swallowed hard, her gaze roaming over my face, surprise written all over hers, "do you want me?"

"So much," I groaned before pressing my mouth against hers.

CHAPTER 4

Sophie

The touch of Liam's mouth against mine left me frozen in shock.

Liam was kissing me.

Liam was sliding his tongue between my lips.

Liam was… oh fuck… he was sucking on my bottom lip.

I moaned, my paralysis broken by the pull of Liam's mouth on my lip. I dropped the ice pack on the desk and pressed up against him, immediately frantic for his touch and kisses. I didn't know what fucking rabbit hole I had fallen down, but I didn't care. I didn't want this to end.

I returned his kiss, slipping my tongue into his mouth. We kissed eagerly, our mouths devouring each other's, our tongues twisting and turning. I yanked at Liam's lab coat, and he shrugged out of it before stepping back long enough to pull his t-shirt over his head.

"Holy fuck," I breathed as I stared at his upper body. His chest was gorgeous with a light layer of dark hair, and I traced my hand over his visible six pack, making him shudder and groan.

He reached for my jacket, pushing it off my shoulders before grabbing the hem of my shirt. He paused. "This okay?"

"Yes." My voice was impatient as I lifted my arms over my head. Liam pulled my shirt over my head and had my bra unhooked and on the floor before I'd even unbuckled his belt.

He cupped my breasts. I was embarrassed that they were barely a handful for him but lost my self-consciousness when his fingers started playing with my nipples. My tits might have been nothing to be proud of, but I had nice nipples. They were large and… oh fuck me… sensitive as hell.

I moaned when Liam pinched my right nipple. He made a low growling sound. "Fuck, your tits are amazing."

I was too busy unbuttoning his pants to reply. I shoved my hand into his briefs, and wrapped my hand around a dick that was most definitely not too small. I stroked him firmly, watching his face as pleasure washed over it, and he groaned.

He pushed his hand under my skirt, spreading my thighs open roughly. Fresh wetness flooded my pussy. He rubbed me through my soaked panties, a smug grin crossing his face. "My girl is so wet for me."

I shuddered all over. Being called Liam's girl while he touched my pussy was almost enough to make me cum.

He pushed the crotch of my panties to the side and stroked one finger across my wet pussy lips.

"Liam," I whimpered, my hand tightening around his dick, "please."

He groaned again, his hips pumping against my hand. "Fuck, you're gonna make me cum before I even get into your,' his finger sank deep into my pussy, "tight, hot cunt."

I forgot all about his dick the minute he rubbed my clit

with his thumb. I released him and gripped his shoulders, pulling him closer, rocking my hips against him as I reached for my release.

"Not yet, sweet girl," he said, pulling his hand away from my sopping pussy. He licked his finger, grinning at me as I made a low moan of frustration. "You taste so good."

"Liam, I need you to fuck me," I said.

A part of me was so certain he would stop or remember who he was and who I was that I was frantic to cum before it happened. Selfish, I know.

He pulled a condom out of his wallet and shoved his pants and briefs down his legs. I stared at his perfect, fat dick, my mouth watering and my pussy practically begging to be filled with it.

"Skirt up," he said as he rolled the condom onto his dick.

I hurriedly shoved my skirt up to my waist, but before I could push down my panties, Liam had crowded up close and pulled them to the side again. "Hold them," he demanded.

I wrapped my fingers around the wet fabric, holding my panties in the crease of my thigh. Liam pressed the head of his dick against my opening, and I cried out when it slipped in.

"Shh, Sophie," he said as he wrapped his arm around my waist and made another slow push. "Take my dick like my good girl."

"Oh God," I said.

He grinned and pushed again, sliding his dick deep into my pussy until his balls slapped against me. "Fuuuuck. Such a tight pussy, Soph. Put your arms around my shoulders."

I did what he asked, moaning when his chest brushed against my sensitive nipples. He thrust in and out of me, gripping my hips to keep me still as he took my pussy with hard and fast strokes.

I clutched at his shoulders, burying my face in his neck as he moved faster. Each stroke sent me spiraling higher and higher. His grunts and groans grew louder, his pace more frantic, and when he reached between us and rubbed my clit, my orgasm washed over me in a shower of light and raw pleasure.

He moaned my name, his hands digging into my hips before he thrust so hard the desk scraped across the floor. His body shuddered, and he groaned one last 'fuuuuuck' as he came inside me.

I clung to him, my body quivering, my pussy still milking his cock as we came down from our high. He rubbed my back in slow circles, his breath stirring the ends of my ponytail.

His dick had softened, and he pulled out, holding onto the condom before taking it off and tossing it in the trash can. He pulled up his briefs and pants, and I straightened my panties and slid off his desk, yanking my skirt down.

The entire office smelled like sex and regret, and my orgasm high disappeared almost immediately. Feeling sick to my stomach, I quickly finished dressing as Liam did the same. When he stayed quiet, I couldn't take the uncomfortable silence a minute longer.

"That was unexpected," I said, massaging my sore hand. I hadn't even noticed the dull throb while Liam and I were fucking.

When Liam just continued to look at a spot over my shoulder, I blurted, "Because you're gay."

"I'm bi," he said.

"Oh. Ohhh… uh, well, good for you," I said.

That made him smile, and enough of the awkwardness disappeared that I could breathe again. "Liam, I'm -"

"Sophie, I shouldn't have -"

We both stopped, and I made a go on gesture. He rubbed a hand through his hair. "I shouldn't have done that."

"You?" I said. "You weren't the only one in the room."

He took a deep breath. "*We* shouldn't have done that. I'm your boss, and while there isn't a rule against coworkers dating, I think we both know from experience that it's a bad idea."

"Why did you fuck me?" I asked.

"Because I've wanted you for a long time." He hesitated, his look uncharacteristically shy. "Why did you fuck me?"

"Because I've wanted you too."

He didn't say anything, and I grabbed my coat, wincing when my hand knocked against his desk. "I should go."

"Sophie, wait."

I paused with my jacket halfway zipped. Looking incredibly uncomfortable, Liam said, "It's not that I don't like you. I do. You're a fantastic employee and a nice person, and -"

"I don't need the 'you're a nice person, but I don't want to date you' speech, Liam. I'm aware of why our dating isn't a good idea."

"I've already dated a co-worker, and then everyone watched our relationship implode right here in the lab," Liam said. "I won't let that happen again."

"I get it," I said. "I dated a co-worker, and now everyone at the company has seen me naked and with a dick in my mouth. Trust me, I understand. I'd appreciate it if you stopped acting like I'm an idiot or giving you sad puppy dog eyes because you fucked me and now won't date me. I don't want to date you either. We made a mistake tonight, and we won't let it happen again. Simple as that."

I pushed past him before he could see the lie on my face. I'd always been terrible at lying.

"Sophie, wait."

"I have to go, Liam. It's late, and I'm tired, and I'd like to get out of here before one of the cleaning staff comes in and realizes we just fucked on your desk."

"Wait, Sophie." Liam's voice had turned hard, not the easy-going tone I was used to.

I stared at him over my shoulder, turned on all over again by the intensity of his gaze.

"I need to shut down my computer, and then I'll walk you to your car," he said. "You're not leaving the building without me. Is that understood?"

I nodded, my traitorous pussy pulsing with need and my body practically screaming at me to push Liam to the floor and ride him like a pony. I turned away quickly, staring out at the lab.

Why did I feel like I'd just made the biggest mistake of my career?

CHAPTER 5

Sophie

"Okay, so I have a theory about why you want to be bossed around." I sat cross-legged on the couch and took a huge bite of my tomato sandwich.

"I told you, Soph," Hattie's voice was a little exasperated, "it's more than just being bossed around."

I couldn't blame her for being annoyed. She'd spent the last hour pouring her heart out to me about what she needed and wanted, and I was boiling it down to a simple 'be bossed around'.

"Yeah, you're right. I'm sorry. I'm simplifying it too much. Pretty sure my theory is still a good one, though. Depending, of course, on how you answer my next question."

Hattie ate a bite of her sandwich. "What's your question?"

"You said you're looking for a partner who takes control in bed. Someone who tells you what to do, and if you don't do it, punishes you with spankings or floggings, or whatever, right?"

"Yes." Hattie's face was pink again.

"Hey, what did I tell you earlier?"

"That I don't need to be embarrassed," Hattie said.

"Exactly. You like what you like in bed, and I will never ever judge you. You know that, right?"

"I do. But hearing it out loud from another person makes it more real. Until now, it's always been a fantasy for just me."

"Sure, but we've already established that this is a fantasy you want to come true. Some fantasies are just that - fantasies. But you're looking to turn this into the real thing. A guy who'll take control, make you call him Daddy... wait, do you have a daddy kink?" I asked.

"I don't think so," Hattie said thoughtfully. "I mean, I'm not against calling him Daddy if that's what he wants, but it doesn't feel like a personal kink."

"Okay, cool. Anyway, so you crave control in bed. Do you want him to tell you what to do outside the bedroom?"

"Sort of, but not really," Hattie said. "It's complicated."

"But you are looking for someone to take care of you," I said.

Hattie laughed. "I've been taking care of myself since I was a kid, Sophie. I don't need a parent. I need a partner."

"A partner can take care of you without being a parent," I said. "Look, here's my theory - you like being bossed around," I held up my hand when Hattie started to protest, "I know, I know, it's an oversimplification but just go with it. You like being bossed around because you never had that. Your mom was a total selfish flake who constantly put her own needs ahead of yours. You have never had someone take care of you, look after you, or worry about you other than me. Right?"

"Yes," Hattie said.

"You've always had to make all the decisions, so it's no

wonder you want to give that up in the bedroom," I said. "It would be so freeing to not worry about when you'll cum or how you'll cum. You do enough worrying outside of the bedroom."

I sat back and took another huge bite of my sandwich as Hattie stared at her half-eaten sandwich.

"You're right," she said. "I mean, I already knew that's why I wanted to give up control, but it's nice to hear someone else say it too."

"Good. So, all we need to do is find you a Dom," I said. "And you think Finn might be one."

Hattie's face went an even deeper pink. "It's just a feeling I get."

"A feeling," I said. "From meeting him once at a company barbecue?"

She nodded, poking at her sandwich with the tip of her finger. "Yes. I stood next to him in the food line, and there was this moment where…."

"Ooh, you had a moment!" I said excitedly.

Hattie huffed out a laugh. "I don't really know. He looked at me, I mean, he *really* looked at me, and there was something between us. It's hard to explain."

"A 'he's picturing you naked and tied to his bed' something?" I asked.

"No, nothing like that. More of a 'he could see right to the center of me and immediately knew what I needed from him'. Like he could tell I was submissive just from looking at me and he…."

"He what?" I asked.

"He liked it." Hattie's voice had dropped to almost a whisper.

"So, why haven't you asked him out?" I asked.

"He's out of my league," Hattie said.

"Are you fucking kidding me? You've looked in a mirror recently, right? You're drop dead gorgeous. You're brilliant. You're Hattie *fucking* King. You're a goddamn movie star."

"TV star, and that was a long time ago. Now I'm a broke mechanic living in a single wide trailer," Hattie said.

"It's not your fault your mother blew through all of the money you made when you were a kid. Nor is it your fault that she screwed up your chance to get residuals from What About Julie reruns."

"Yeah, well, I'm still a loser with seventeen dollars in my bank account," Hattie said.

"You're not a loser. And why won't you let me give you a loan? I want to help, Hattie."

"Don't, Soph," Hattie said. "I don't want your charity."

I scowled, but we'd had this argument many times, and I'd never won. I loved Hattie, but she could be stubborn as hell when she wanted to be.

I brushed the sandwich crumbs off my shirt. For whatever reason, my appetite had come roaring back this morning. Maybe Liam had fucked it back into me last night. I grimaced and took a drink of water. Thinking about what I did with Liam last night was a terrible idea.

"What's wrong?" Hattie asked.

"Nothing."

"You have a look."

"I don't have a look."

"You totally have a look."

"So, are you asking Finn out or not?" I said.

Hattie shook her head. "I don't know."

"Is it the age difference?" I asked.

"No. I don't care that he's in his forties. In fact, it makes him sexier to me. I like older men. You know that."

"He is in pretty good shape for his age," I said. "It's weird

48

that there's such an age difference between him and Liam, though. Like, why did their parents wait so long between kids?"

"No idea," Hattie said.

"You can find out if you ask Finn on a date," I said.

"The thing is," Hattie said, "if he is a Dom, I think I want to have a little more experience under my belt as a submissive before I ask him out."

"You gonna put out a call on Facebook for an experienced Dom to teach you some shit?" I asked and then laughed.

When Hattie didn't laugh with me, I said, "Wait, you're not doing that, are you?"

"Not exactly. But there is a club in Havenport. It's called Sapphire."

Havenport was a midsize city about twenty minutes away. It's where most of us went when we couldn't find what we needed in Willowdale.

"Okay, so this Sapphire club is what? A sex club?"

Hattie nodded, and I almost fell off the couch. "Seriously?"

"Yeah. I mean, it's a particular kind of sex club."

"Meaning what?" I asked.

"Well, the main part of the club is, like, a normal club, you know? Drinks and dancing and what have you. Anyone can go to it. But there's a second part of the club that's exclusive and by invite only."

"And that's where all the sexy times happen," I said.

"Yes. That part of the club is all about sex. There are shows, uh, flogging and spanking demonstrations, private rooms, that sort of thing. The club brings in Doms each night. They're looking for submissives to play with, and if you're not one, they politely escort you back to the regular section of the club. I'm considering going to the club and asking one of the Doms to teach me some stuff."

"Okay, so you know someone who's a regular and can get you an invite? Someone you trust?" I asked.

"No. But in the main club area, they have spotters whose job is to observe clubgoers and invite them to the club's VIP section if they think they might be a good fit."

"That's a little sus," I said.

"It isn't," Hattie said.

"How do you even know about this club?" I asked. "You're more of an introvert than I am."

"I belong to some submissive groups online. They talk about it all the time. Many of them have been there, and they all say it's fantastic. That it's the best place for a new submissive to learn what they do and don't like with a Dom they can trust. A Dom who knows what they're doing, you know?"

"I don't like the idea of you going to some club and putting it all out there in hopes of being picked to join the sex club," I said. "It's risky."

"It'll be fine. I want to do this, Soph. I *need* to do it."

I studied my best friend. She'd spent most of her life never doing what she wanted to do and being forced to live a life she'd never wanted to live. I wouldn't be the one to tell her she couldn't go for her dreams now.

"I'll go with you," I said.

Hattie nearly dropped her sandwich. "What?"

"I'll go with you," I repeated. "To the club."

"I can't ask you to do that. You're not submissive. And if we do manage to get an invite to the sex part of the club, it's kind of an expectation that you'll be fucking the Doms."

I shrugged. "Like I can't handle a little slap and tickle or play pretend sub for the night. You're not going alone, Hattie."

"Soph, are you sure?" Hattie would never admit it, but I could see the relief in her eyes.

"Positive," I said. "Besides, maybe I'll like it, right? Maybe I'm a submissive too and don't realize it."

"Maybe," Hattie said, "but I doubt it. Most subs know pretty quickly that they're one. But the subs in my online group who've gone to the club all say that the Doms are amazing at making them cum. After having to fake it with Cody for so long, it'll be nice to have a real orgasm during sex, right?"

"Right," I said. My mind immediately flashed back to last night in Liam's office. It'd been one of the best orgasms of my life, and I doubted that any of the sex club Doms could make me cum harder than Liam had.

"You have that look again," Hattie said.

"No, I don't."

"Yes, you do. Spill it, Soph."

I sighed. "Today is about you, Hattie. I'm not going to start going on and on about me when -"

"We've talked plenty about me. Tell me what's got you acting so weird today."

"I fucked Liam last night in his office."

This time Hattie did drop her sandwich. It sat forgotten on the floor as she stared wide-eyed at me. "What the hell? You and Liam had sex?"

"Yep. On his desk. And it was hot."

"I thought he was gay," Hattie said.

"He's bi."

"Oh." Hattie leaned forward on the couch. "Tell me everything, Sophie."

CHAPTER 6

Liam

"Finn, if you don't stop sulking, Alina and I are leaving you here to sulk while we get ice cream." I sat back in the kitchen chair and didn't let my gaze waver from Finn's, even when he looked like he'd cheerfully murder me.

"I am not sulking," Finn said, scraping his chair back and standing. He took our plates and stuck them in the dishwasher as, behind his back, I thumbed my nose at him before crossing my eyes and sticking out my tongue.

Finn wasn't the only one in a mood today. Our sister, Alina, smiled at my antics, but it was for show. Although Alina tended to go inward, becoming even quieter than she usually was, while Finn stomped around like an angry buffalo, barking out orders like he was the Godfather.

"Your car still isn't fixed, huh?" Alina said.

Finn shook his head as he rolled up his sleeves and filled the sink with water and dish soap. He submerged the pan and started scrubbing at it. "No, that idiot over at Under the Dash didn't know what the fuck he was doing. Gretchen's been acting worse since I got her back from that shitty garage."

"You realize that naming your car is super weird, right?" I said.

"Give it a rest," Finn said. "I know how you feel about how I feel about my car, and I don't fucking care. Gretchen is important to me."

I laughed, and this time Alina's smile was much more natural. "She'll be okay, Finn. You just need to find the right mechanic to look at her."

"Thanks, kid." Finn's gaze softened when Alina stood and limped her way to the sink to join him. "Sit down and rest your leg. Liam will dry the pots and pans."

"I can help," Alina said.

"You made lunch. And your leg is sore today," Finn said. "Go sit down."

Alina made a face but returned to her seat. At twenty-five, she might have been a grown woman, but she still did what Finn told her. Hell, so did I. We'd been like that our entire lives, and I didn't see it changing anytime soon. It wasn't just the fact that at forty-five, he was fifteen years old than me and twenty years older than Alina. Finn was a natural leader, and he'd been a control freak for as long as I could remember. He liked being in charge, and neither Alina nor I had a problem with it.

Our dad was a good man, but he'd never done well with the whole 'being a dad' thing. He'd always been more concerned with his career and whatever woman currently shared his bed than his three kids. The car accident that had killed my and Alina's mother and seriously injured Alina hadn't made our dad any more of a hands-on dad. If anything, it had driven a deeper wedge between him and us.

Finn had taken over the father role for both Alina and me

without any fanfare or fuss, and I still worried that we were the reason he and Melissa had divorced or why he'd never had kids of his own.

The accident had been a decade ago, and Finn had spent most of the last ten years making sure I didn't blow up my life because of my grief and being a caretaker for Alina as she'd gone through multiple surgeries and physiotherapy to learn to walk again.

Melissa had left him about a year after the accident, and while Finn denied it had anything to do with Alina or me, I knew my younger sister felt as much guilt as I did. We hated that Finn had lost the person he loved because of how much we'd needed him.

Finn's phone buzzed, and he dried his hands before pulling the phone from his pocket. He glanced at the number and headed out of the kitchen. "I need to take this."

When he was gone, Alina said, "I'm worried about him. He's sad."

"He's okay," I said. "Just busy at work and upset about his car."

"It's more than that," Alina said. "He's lonely. Just like you are."

"I'm fine," I said.

Alina leaned forward, her cool hand cupping my face. "You aren't. And neither is Finn. Hell, neither am I."

She sat back. "We're all broken, Liam."

"Hey," I said, taking her hand and squeezing it. "We're not broken. We're the three musketeers, remember? All for one, and one for all."

That brought a ghost of a smile to her lips. As a kid, she'd been obsessed with the Three Musketeers book and begged Finn and me to dress up as the Porthos and Athos to her Aramis for three Halloweens in a row. Unable to resist giving our baby sister whatever she wanted, we'd donned the giant feathery hats, the stupid tights, and carried the plastic swords.

"We'll be okay," I said. "All three of us."

She nodded, although her face suggested she didn't believe a word of it, and I squeezed her hand again before releasing it. "Hey, Finn and I are going to the Copper Bistro and Grill tomorrow for lunch. Why don't you join us?"

"It's too far to bike," Alina said.

"Finn and I could pick you up in my car," I said.

Her face paled, and she shook her head.

"Honey," I kept my voice gentle, "it's been two months since you tried last. Maybe you should try again."

"It won't help," she said as her voice wavered and tears gathered in her lower lashes. "You know I can't, Liam. Please stop asking me."

"We just want what's best for you." Finn had returned, and he sat on the other side of Alina, taking her small hand in his large one. "Your therapist said you needed to keep trying, remember?"

She nodded. "I know. But not tomorrow. It's… it's been a bad week."

Finn studied her pale face before wiping away the tear that had escaped her lashes to slide down her cheek. "Okay, kiddo. Not tomorrow."

He kissed her forehead and then stood. "Liam, help me finish the dishes."

What are you doing, idiot? This is a terrible idea.

My inner voice was right, but it didn't stop me from turning down Sophie's street and driving toward her house.

I'd left Alina's place, more shaken by her broken

comment than I wanted to admit. I also didn't want to admit that yeah, I was lonely since Dayton and I had broken up, or that last night with Sophie had been the first time I'd felt truly happy in the last year and a half.

What did it say about me that I'd stayed for another six months in a relationship with a man I no longer loved? Was I that desperate to be with someone I would ignore the dozens of red flags Dayton had thrown my way?

I was almost to Sophie's house, and I pushed thoughts of Dayton and my brokenness out of my head. I was stopping by her place only because I wanted to double check that we were okay. She'd said we were okay last night at the lab, but it wouldn't hurt to confirm, right? Sophie was my best chemist, and I didn't want her looking for another job because I was a horny asshole who couldn't keep my hands to myself.

I parked on the street, my heart plummeting to my damn feet when I saw Sophie on a ladder in front of her townhouse. I practically fell out of my car and ran up the sidewalk, stopping at the bottom of the ladder and holding on to it.

"What the hell are you doing, Sophie?"

Sophie screeched, and I'm pretty sure I went into heart failure when she almost slipped off the ladder. She grabbed at the ladder with both hands before glaring down at me. "What the fuck, Liam? Are you trying to make me break my neck? I'm on a ladder in case you haven't noticed."

"I noticed!" My voice was weirdly high. "Do you know how dangerous it is to be on a ladder with no one holding it? Jesus Christ, Sophie, what the fuck are you doing up there?"

"Cleaning out the gutters," she said as if that was a perfectly good reason for her to put me into cardiac arrest.

"Your gutters? You're cleaning your fucking gutters," I said.

"Yes." She used her gloved hands to pull out a mess of

leaves and unidentifiable goop and dropped it into the bucket she had placed on the roof.

"Sophie," I tried to keep my voice calm, "You cannot clean out your gutters."

"Uh, yeah, I can."

"Your hand," I said. "You hurt your hand last night punching that dickhead, and you can't safely grip the ladder with it."

She laughed and held up her gloved hand, flexing it a few times. "It feels a lot better. Barely hurts, in fact. Why are you here, Liam?"

She scooped out another handful of gunk and dropped it into the bucket.

"I wanted to talk."

"Okay, so talk," she said.

"Please come down off the ladder," I said.

"These gutters need to be cleaned. So, unless you're gonna come up here and do it for me…." She stared down at me with one eyebrow raised.

"I'm afraid of heights," I muttered.

She nodded. "I get it. I'm claustrophobic. I wouldn't make my boss clean out my gutters anyway."

"Sophie," I tried to stay calm but watching her up there, swaying on the ladder as she stretched to her right, made me want to vomit, "please come down."

"It's fine," she said. "I'm almost done."

She stretched again, and when the ladder creaked, and the wind blew her blonde hair around her face, I couldn't take it anymore. "I'll eat your pussy, Sophie."

She froze with one hand buried in the gutters. "What?"

"If you come down off the ladder, I'll eat your pussy."

"Right here in the front yard? Because I'm pretty sure that'll get us arrested," she said.

"In your house," I said. "If you join me here on the nice, solid, safe earth, I'll take you inside and eat your pussy for as long as you want me to."

"Ooh, you have yourself a deal." Sophie slung the bucket handle over her forearm and climbed down the ladder to my immense relief. When she was safely on solid ground, I took the bucket from her, setting it down and hoping she didn't notice how my hands shook.

"Your hands are shaking," Sophie said.

I glared at her. "Maybe because you just scared the shit out of me by standing on a ladder in very unsafe conditions."

She laughed. "Take it down a notch, Safety Dan."

"You can't do shit like this. It's dangerous," I said.

"They need to be cleaned out," she said.

"Then hire someone to do it."

She gave me an indignant look. "Why would I waste my hard earned money paying someone to do something I can easily do myself?"

I wanted to spank her. I wanted to kiss her. I wanted to bury my dick deep inside her perfect, wet cunt.

"Look, were you fibbing about the pussy eating or what? Because if you were, one - that's not cool, dude, and b) I need to finish cleaning out those gutters," Sophie said.

"I wasn't lying," I said.

"Great." A gorgeous grin lit up her face. "Come on in."

CHAPTER 7

Liam

My hands still shaking, I followed Sophie into the house, taking off my shoes and hanging my jacket on the coat tree. Sophie kicked off her shoes and led me down the narrow hallway to the kitchen. She took off her gloves and tossed them into the attached mud room/laundry room before washing her hands at the kitchen sink.

"How did you know where I lived?" she asked.

"It's Willowdale," I said. "It's not that difficult to find out where anyone lives."

She laughed. "Good point. Did you grow up in a small town?"

"No. I was born and raised in Havenport."

"Cool. So, you and your brother moved here for your jobs at Optimum?"

I nodded. "And because we thought it might be better for our sister."

She stared at me in surprise. "You have a sister?"

"We do. Her name's Alina. She's twenty-five."

"Same age as me," Sophie said. "There's a big age gap between you and Finn, huh?"

I nodded. "He's our half brother. He was twelve when his dad married our mom and fifteen when I was born."

"Ah, that explains it," she said.

"Do you have any siblings?" I leaned against the counter as she took out two glasses from the cupboard and a water jug from the fridge.

"Nope, an only child. But I was super close to Hattie King growing up. She's basically like a sister to me."

"She's the former TV actress, right?" I asked, accepting the glass of water from Sophie. "You brought her to the company barbecue."

"That's right," Sophie said. "We kept in touch even after her mom moved her to Hollywood for that stupid TV show."

I sipped at my water as Sophie took a big drink of hers. She had a small dirt smudge on her forehead that I found weirdly adorable. "So, how's your Saturday going?"

"Fine. Yours?"

"Good. I had lunch with Finn and Alina."

"Nice. So, why did you come by my place?"

"I wanted to make sure we were okay after last night. Work wise, I mean. That you're not saying you're okay but secretly planning on quitting your job on Monday."

"I'm not the type to say one thing when I mean something else," Sophie said. "But if I reassure you that I'm not quitting my job, does that mean you won't eat my pussy?"

"I'll still eat your pussy," I said.

"A man of his word. I like that." She stared at me over the rim of her water glass. "We're fine, Liam. Really. I'm not quitting my job, and I'm not going to act weird on Monday because we've had sex. Are you going to act weird?"

"No," I said.

"You sure? Because you just offered to eat my pussy to get me to stop cleaning out my gutters. That's kinda weird."

"It's not weird," I said.

"It's so weird, man," she said.

I laughed, and she grinned at me before taking my water glass and setting it on the counter. "C'mon, weirdo, let's go to my bedroom."

I followed her up the stairs to her room. "I like your place."

"Thanks," she said. "It's small and needs some repairs, but I bought it myself with my own money, and I'm proud of that."

We were in her bedroom now, and I studied the double bed smothered in pillows. "Hey, Soph?"

"Yeah?" She had already taken off her socks and was unbuttoning her jeans.

"Do you think you have enough pillows on your bed?"

She paused with her hands on her zipper. "I like pillows. They make me happy. And they're comfy cozy."

"Right," I said.

"Stop worrying about my pillows and get naked," she said.

I laughed and finished undressing as Sophie peeled off her jeans before moving to the bed in her t-shirt and panties. She shoved most of the pillows onto the floor before reaching into the nightstand and pulling out a condom. She placed it next to the lamp as I joined her beside the bed.

"What?" she said when she caught sight of my face.

"I thought I was eating your pussy," I said.

"You are." Her hand reached for my half erect dick, and she pumped it lightly. "But I won't take and not give. That's not very nice of me, is it?"

"Hmm," my head fell back as she moved her hand up and

down my shaft in a twisting motion, "maybe not. Christ, that feels good, Sophie."

"I'm glad." She kissed my chest before licking at one flat nipple.

I sucked in a breath and stepped back, gently tugging her hand free from my dick.

"Sorry," she said. "You not into nipple play?"

"I like it," I said hoarsely. "But this is about you first."

She smiled, her teeth pulling coyly at her bottom lip. "You're making an excellent second impression, Liam."

"Good," I said. "Especially considering my first wasn't that great."

"Are you fishing for compliments?" she asked.

I laughed. "No, it really wasn't my best performance last night."

"Crap," she said, "then I'm in trouble because the orgasm I had in your office last night just about blew my head off."

"Is that right?" I reached for her shirt and tugged it over her head. She wore a soft pink cotton bralette under her shirt, and I could already see those magnificent nipples pressing against the fabric.

I bent my head and sucked on her right nipple through the fabric. Sophie made a harsh moan before clutching at my head. I teased her through the material for only a few more seconds before lifting my head. I was dying to see Sophie's sweet little tits again.

I pulled the bralette off of her, trying not to look too eager when her tits were bared to me. I kissed between her breasts, then cupped her left one and circled her puffy nipple until it tightened into a hard point.

"Oh God," she breathed when I sucked it into my mouth. "Fuck, that's good, Liam."

"I love your tits." I kissed her left one.

She laughed. "Sure, you do."

I straightened and pulled her up against me, gripping her ass through her panties and squeezing it. "I'm being serious. They're perfect."

"They aren't," she said with another laugh. "No guy I've slept with has ever thought they were even good, let alone perfect. They're ridiculously small, and the right one is noticeably smaller than the left."

I palmed her left breast. "More than a handful is a waste, right?"

"They're not even a handful for you," she said.

"I have big hands."

"And a big dick," she said.

"And you have small and perfect tits with the most gorgeous nipples I've ever seen." I leaned down and kissed the right one. "I love how sensitive they are."

"They are pretty good nips," she agreed before tugging on my head until I looked at her. "But, seriously, Liam, I know what this is between us. You don't have to be complimentary about my body, okay?"

"I like your body, Soph. I like it a lot. And I'll be disappointed if you don't let me tell you how much I like it."

She laughed. "So, you're a talker in bed, is that what you're saying? I would never have guessed that."

"You think I just grunt like a caveman when I have a beautiful woman in my bed?" I leaned down and sucked on her nipple.

"Technically," Sophie's hands clutched my head again, "you're in my bed. I'm gonna cum if you keep doing that, Liam."

I guided her back toward the bed. "If I make you cum without touching your pussy, you know I'll tell everyone, right? Because that basically makes me a god in bed. The people need to know, Soph."

She laughed as she relaxed on the bed, running her hand down my chest when I stretched out beside her. "I'm enjoying the nipple sucking, but I distinctly remember something about pussy eating."

"So bossy," I said but started kissing my way down her body. I stopped to investigate the small pink birthmark on her ribcage, licking it lightly as Sophie's hands threaded through my hair.

She pushed on the top of my skull, and I laughed. "Man, you really are impatient for the pussy eating, aren't you?"

"It's been a while," she said.

"For me too," I said.

"I hope you haven't forgotten how to do it," she said.

I laughed hard as Sophie grinned down at me. Based on how quiet she was at the lab, I hadn't expected Sophie to be so open and honest in bed. It was a real fucking turn on to see this side of her.

"I'm pretty sure it's like riding a bike," I said before tracing a circle around her navel with my tongue.

She pushed on the top of my skull again. "How will you know if you don't get down there and start licking?"

I laughed again before kissing her hipbones and settling my body between her smooth thighs. I kissed her inner thighs, then kissed the patch of blond hair at the top of her pussy and inhaled deeply.

Sophie had propped a few pillows beneath her head, and she stared down at me. "Swear to God, Liam, if you say you love the smell of pussy in the morning, I'm kicking you out of bed. I don't care how horny I am."

"It's afternoon," I said.

She burst into laughter, and something that felt a little like love washed over me. I scoffed inwardly. You didn't fall in love with someone because of their laugh.

I buried my face in Sophie's pussy while she still laughed. Her giggling died an abrupt death when I licked at her pink clit peeking out from between her lips. I cleaned away her delicious cream before concentrating on her clit again with soft, slow licks.

"Oh fuck," Sophie moaned, her legs falling open and her hands sliding into my hair. She ground her pussy against my mouth and gasped when I slid one finger into her opening. Fuck, she was tight. My dick throbbed with need, and I rubbed it against the bed as I finger fucked her and sucked on her clit.

Sophie's moans grew louder, her sweet pussy humping my face faster and faster until she came all over my mouth with a harsh cry. I sucked on her clit as she came, her cunt squeezing hard around my finger. I couldn't wait to fuck her.

When she collapsed on the bed, panting loudly and her hair sticking to her face, I sat up and wiped my face on the sheet before rubbing her thigh. "Well, what's the verdict? Am I still good at riding the bicycle?"

"Buddy, you could be in the Tour de France," she said breathlessly.

I grinned and reached for the condom, rolling it onto my dick as Sophie watched. "God, you have a nice dick."

"Thank you," I said. "You good with being on top?"

She nodded and sat up, straddling my waist when I stretched out on the bed. I cupped her tits, teasing her nipples with my fingers as she ran her hands over my chest. "You have a great body."

"So do you," I said.

She smiled and reached behind her to grip my cock. She guided it into her wet, hot pussy, and I groaned loudly at the feel of her slick tightness surrounding my dick. "Fuck, that pussy."

"That's the idea," she said with a small laugh.

I gripped her hips, helping her rise up and down until she'd taken my entire dick.

"You're so damn thick." Her voice was low and heavy with desire, and it made me want to fuck her hard and fast.

"You good?" I asked. I could hear the barely controlled need in my voice. Sophie must have as well because a flash of smugness crossed her face before she nodded.

"Fuck me, Liam."

I didn't need to be told twice. I thrust into her, groaning when she braced her hands on my chest and met my thrusts. She bounced hard on my cock, her cunt gripping me so tightly I knew I wouldn't last even five fucking minutes. Her fingers toyed with my flat nipple, and I shuddered with pleasure.

"You feel so fucking good," I gasped out.

"So do you. You cool with me touching myself?" Sophie asked.

"Fuck, yeah."

She smiled, and I eagerly watched as she rubbed at her clit. It made her tighten exquisitely around me, and I groaned, trying desperately to hold off on blowing my load as she circled her clit with her fingertips. I made shallow thrusts as the base of my spine started tingling.

"Soph, baby, I need you to cum," I groaned out.

"Sure, no problem." Sophie's voice was breathless and distracted as she worked her clit furiously with her fingers. I thrust harder, knowing that I couldn't stop even if she didn't cum before me. It was too fucking late. Sophie's pussy had me losing my fucking mind and my stamina.

"Soph… Soph… oh fuuuuck!" I thrust hard into her, my

dick practically exploding cum into the condom, barely registering how Sophie cried my name as she climaxed, and her
cunt squeezed hard around me. I thrust repeatedly until every
last bit of pleasure was wrung out of me, and I collapsed on
the bed.

Sophie fell onto me with a soft thunk, her blonde hair
everywhere, her perfect tits pressed against my chest. I
rubbed her back in slow circles as our breathing slowed and
my cock softened inside her.

After a few minutes, Sophie climbed off of me, and I sat
up. "Bathroom?"

"Down the hallway, second door on the left."

"Be right back." I eased the condom off and carried it to
the bathroom. By the time I'd cleaned up, used the wash-
room, and washed my hands, Sophie was fully dressed and in
the hallway outside the bathroom. She smiled and brushed
past me to go into the bathroom, shutting the door behind her.

Feeling a little disgruntled and annoyed, I returned to the
bedroom and dressed before meeting Sophie in the kitchen.
She poured a glass of water and handed it to me, doing a
double take when she saw my face. "What's wrong?"

"Nothing," I said. "Thank you for the water."

"You're welcome." She watched me drink it all in four
giant gulps. After a moment of awkwardness, I set it on the
counter and said, "I should get going."

"Yeah, okay." She smiled at me. "Thank you, Liam, that
was a lot of fun."

"It was. We shouldn't do it again, though. It's not a good
idea with our history of fucking coworkers."

"I know," she said. "I don't want to be the girl fucking the
boss any more than you want to be the boss fucking his
employee."

"It's not that I don't care about you because -"

Her laughter sent a flush of heat to my cheeks. "Liam, seriously. It's fine. I knew what this was, okay? I'm cool with it."

She didn't seem upset by that, and it pissed me off that she wasn't, which was stupid because she was right. "Is that why you so obviously want me to leave?"

Shit, I sounded like a bratty little kid. Sophie leaned against the counter, staring at me like maybe my brain had slipped a cog or two. "You don't *have* to leave, Liam. I just assumed you would want to. You got what you came for, right?"

"I didn't just come here to…." I sighed and scrubbed my hand through my hair. Sophie was right, I had gotten what I came for, and it was time to leave before I made an even bigger idiot of myself.

"Liam? Why are you upset?" she asked.

"I'm not." I plastered a smile on my face. "I should get going. I'm meeting Nick at the Brewhouse."

"Okay, have fun." She walked me to the door, and I stepped outside, pausing when I saw the ladder leaning against the house.

"Don't go back up on the ladder without someone here to hold it, okay, Soph? Promise me."

She hesitated, and I resisted the urge to take her hand. "It's not safe."

"Yeah, you're right. I'll ask Hattie to come by and hold the ladder."

"I can stop in tomorrow and -"

"Nah, it's all good," she said with a cheerful smile. "See you Monday, Liam."

She closed the door before I could say goodbye, leaving my stomach in knots and my feelings all twisted up like a fucking slinky.

CHAPTER 8

Sophie

"Ooh, this one's pretty." I clicked the pictures on the Etsy listing, making it bigger to see all the little details of the embroidery. "Hattie would love this one."

My voice was too loud in my living room. Usually, I loved my house, but it felt too quiet and too empty ever since Liam had been here yesterday. Which was ridiculous because he'd been here for less than two hours. I shouldn't have felt the absence of his presence, but I did. And it was seriously bumming me out.

"Don't be stupid," I told myself as I resumed scrolling through Etsy. "You and Liam can't be a couple. He's been clear that he doesn't want that."

And you did a great job of pretending you didn't want that either.

I really had. I was almost proud of how well I'd lied to Liam yesterday. Immediately getting out of bed and getting dressed after the best fuck of my life had required herculean strength. I'd wanted nothing more than to lie in bed and wait for Liam to return so we could cuddle.

Instead, I'd dragged my ass out of bed. It would be easier to sell the lie that I was perfectly fine with an afternoon of casual fucking if I wasn't in bed and begging him for more while he tried to leave.

And aside from a bit of weirdness in the kitchen, Liam had been ready to leave. So, I'd made the right decision. As much as I loved him - and now that I'd been with him, I couldn't even fool myself into thinking it was just a crush - I wouldn't beg him for something he didn't want to give me. That wasn't fair to him.

It's not fair to you to keep fucking him, knowing that it means nothing beyond a good time to him. You need to protect your heart, Soph.

Yeah, I did. But I couldn't regret yesterday, even if the memory of Liam in my bed lingered for years. It hurt now, but it would become a sweet memory in a few years, one that I would always cherish.

A few years? Girl, stop this. You need to get over Liam and move on.

I made myself concentrate on my laptop screen. Hattie's birthday was next month, and I wanted to get her something unique and hand crafted. Since I was in no way talented with arts and crafts, I was doing the next best thing - scouring Etsy.

I clicked on a different seller, and the first listing on her page immediately caught my attention. It was an embroidery of a beach landscape, and I clicked through the pictures on the listing, marveling at how the artist had captured all the different blues in the ocean and mimicked a crashing wave with nothing more than some darker blues and white. Holy fuck, this artist was crazy talented.

I knew this was the one for Hattie. My best friend loved the ocean, and on our last vacation together, we'd driven twelve hours to the nearest coastal town and spent the entire four days at the beach. I couldn't keep Hattie out of the ocean despite how many times I brought up the possibility of being eaten by a shark.

I checked the listing price. It was expensive, but Hattie was worth it. Besides, with the amount of time and effort the artist put into her creation, it was more than a fair price. I checked the artist's bio, reading aloud to myself.

"A. Manning has been dabbling in different art mediums since childhood. She enjoys all forms of expression through art but especially loves the fibre arts. She's been embroidering and cross-stitching for over a decade, and her love of traveling inspires her work."

There was a picture of her with her bio. She had long dark hair and a pretty face with bright blue eyes. They were the same shade as Liam's eyes and -

I huffed out an annoyed breath and added the listing to my cart. Christ, if everything in my life started to remind me of Liam, I would go insane. Forcing Liam's face out of my head, I grabbed my credit card to pay for the listing.

"Ooh, a local seller." I immediately clicked the free local pick-up offer under the shipping choices and wrote a note in the message section for the seller about arranging a pick-up time, then paid for the listing.

I tucked my credit card into my wallet and stared blankly at my phone. Sunday loomed ahead of me, full of nothing but boredom and loneliness. I could call Hattie and ask her if she wanted to come over and hold the damn ladder while I finished cleaning out my gutters. Or I could text Liam and see if he wanted to have an afternoon of casual sex. He'd gone down on me, and I hadn't gone down on him. That didn't seem at all fair, right? There was no harm in asking him if he wanted the favour returned.

Sophie, no!

My inner voice practically screamed at me as I scrolled to Liam's name in my text messages. I hesitated, my thumbs hovering over the keyboard. This was a mistake. I knew it, so why was I even considering it?

My email dinged, and I checked my messages. The Etsy seller had replied to my email, offering this afternoon as a pick-up choice along with her address. I replied and hit send.

There. Now I had plans this afternoon.

I would pick up Hattie's birthday gift, and I wouldn't think once about stupid Liam or his stupid beautiful thick cock.

Liam

"You look different today." I studied my sister as she leaned against her kitchen counter.

Alina touched her hair, giving me a weirdly nervous look. "No, I don't."

"Yes, you do." I peered closer at her. "Are you wearing makeup?"

"Maybe," Alina said.

"Why?"

"I have a client picking up an embroidery," she said.

I scowled at her. "You know you're supposed to call Finn or me when you do a local pick up. It's not safe for you to be here alone with a stranger."

"She didn't have to call. We're here, aren't we?"

Nick's voice was muffled, but that wasn't surprising,

considering he was lying on his back on the floor with his upper body inside the cabinet under the kitchen sink.

"No comment from the peanut gallery." I tapped Nick on the leg with my foot.

"He's right," Alina said. "I didn't say anything because I knew you and Nick would be here."

I rolled my eyes as Alina squatted and peered under the cupboard. "Nick, you don't have to do this. I can call a plumber."

"He's a physicist," I said, "who fancies himself a plumber."

"Nah, it's a basic repair," Nick said as he flipped me the bird with his free hand. "Besides, I'm done. Hold on. I'm turning the water back on."

There was a squeaking sound, and then Nick said, "Liam, turn on the tap."

"Sure." I reached over and turned on the tap. Alina gasped, and I laughed when water sprayed out from under the cabinet, soaking Nick's shirt and undoubtedly his face.

"Fuck!" Nick shouted. "Turn off the goddamn tap, Liam!"

I turned off the tap, and Nick slid out from under the sink. I laughed harder, and he scowled at me as he climbed to his feet. Water drenched his upper body, and his dark hair was completely soaked.

"So," I said. "How'd that go?"

"Apparently, I forgot to tighten one of the drain couplings," Nick said as water dripped down his face.

"I'll get you a towel," Alina said.

"Thanks, Alina."

She limped out of the kitchen. Less than ten seconds later, the doorbell rang.

"Liam, can you get that? It's my client. Tell her I'll be right with her," Alina called.

"Sure." I left the kitchen as Nick stripped off his shirt and wrung it out in the sink.

I walked to the front door as Alina headed to the kitchen with a towel. I opened the door and stared in surprise at Sophie standing on the front porch.

"Sophie? What are you doing here?"

She stared blankly at me before blurting, "I'm not stalking you. I bought something… a local seller… embroidery… what is happening right now?"

I grinned at her, happier to see her gorgeous face than I should have been. She stared suspiciously at me. "Do you secretly embroider and pretend your name is A. Manning?"

I laughed. "It's my sister, you dork. She uses our mom's maiden name for her Etsy store."

"Oh! That makes sense because in her picture, she…."

"She what?" I asked.

"You guys have the same eye colour." Sophie turned a little red and cleared her throat. "So, I didn't know you lived with your sister."

"I don't. We're here helping her with a leaking pipe. Come in."

She stepped inside, and I closed the door behind her, resisting the urge to stick my nose in her throat and breathe her in. God, she smelled so fucking good.

"We?" Sophie said. "Is Finn here too?"

"No, my friend Nick."

"He's a physicist, works for Hudson Automobiles, right?"

"That's right," I said. "Do you know him?"

"I've seen him when he's stopped into the lab to see you. Brown eyes, dark hair, super cute?"

"Not that cute," I said as jealousy wormed into my stomach.

"Pretty cute," Sophie said.

I scowled at her, and she reached up and pinched my cheek. "You're adorable when you're jealous."

"I'm not jealous."

"Really? Because you're so green, you could be the Hulk right now."

"I had a questionable burrito at Fiesta Mexico for lunch," I said.

She laughed, and it took every ounce of my willpower not to kiss her.

"I can't believe you keep going there after Jody got so sick from that taco. She puked all over the lab counter, remember?"

"It was an epic amount of puke," I said. "But I like to live life on the edge."

"Is that right?" Sophie said with a cute grin.

"Yep." I backed up a few steps before I did something stupid like asking her to let me fuck her again. "Come into the kitchen. The plumbing repair isn't going as planned, and Alina's mopping up Nick and her kitchen floor."

Sophie

I COULD CONFIDENTLY SAY THE LAST PERSON I EXPECTED TO see when I picked up Hattie's birthday present was my boss. But as I followed his perfect ass down the narrow hallway of his sister's house, I couldn't deny I was thrilled to see him again. And for once, I was happy for small town coincidences.

Liam stepped into the kitchen, and I joined him. I stared at Nick and Alina, who stood near the kitchen sink. Liam was right. Nick's admittedly fine-looking upper body was soaked in water, as was the floor around him.

Nick was shorter than Liam. If I had to guess, he was right around the 5'10 mark, but he still towered over Liam's sister. If she were 5'2", I would have been surprised. Alina was using the towel to dry Nick's bare chest, and I could practically see the sexual tension surrounding them.

They hadn't noticed Liam or me, which wasn't that surprising. They couldn't stop staring at each other, and damn if I didn't recognize the look on Alina's face. It was the same one I had whenever I looked at Liam. The girl was in love.

Nick's hands slowly reached for Alina. As they curled around her narrow hips, Liam said, "Nick? What are you doing?"

Nick stepped back like Liam had set him on fire, snatching the towel from Alina and roughly drying his upper body. "Nothing. Just, uh, getting the towel from Alina."

Liam studied them both, and the look of confusion on his face was all kinds of adorable.

Alina stood near the counter, her face red as she stared at Nick and then at Liam. She looked uncomfortable and embarrassed, and feeling sorry for her, I crossed the room and held out my hand. "Hi, I'm Sophie Clark. You're Alina, right?"

"Hi, uh, yes." Alina shook my hand, her gaze flickering to Nick and his naked chest before back to me. "It's nice to meet you. Sorry, I…"

She cleared her throat, and I mentally cheered her on when she took a deep breath and composed herself. "My apologies for the mess. I'm usually a little more professional when a client picks up a piece."

"It's no problem," I said. "I know both your brothers. I work with them at the lab."

"Oh, that's cool," Alina said.

"Small town, am I right?" I asked.

Alina nodded, her face still red as the tension and awkwardness lingered. I turned to Nick. "Hey, Nick. I'm Sophie. I've seen you at the lab, but I don't think we've ever officially met."

"Hi, Sophie," Nick said.

In the silence that followed, Liam said, "What is going on with you two?"

"Nothing," Alina said as Nick studied the floor.

"Alina, tell me the truth," Liam said.

Alina's gaze caught mine, and even though I'd just met her, I couldn't help but react to the silent plea in her eyes.

"Hey," I said, "What do you call a room full of cynical plumbers?"

"What?" Nick said in confusion.

"A skeptic tank," I said.

Nick stared at me before bursting into laughter. Alina grinned, and Liam groaned. "That was so bad."

"Um, so good, you mean," I said. "What do plumbers have when they fall asleep?"

"What?" Nick said, grinning.

"Pipe dreams."

"Nice." Nick held up his hand, and I high-fived it.

Liam shook his head. "We should not be encouraging this type of behaviour."

"Hey, zip it, mister, or I'll start bringing out the chemist jokes," I said.

"Hit me with a chemist joke," Nick said.

"Oh no," Liam said.

"What do you with a sick chemist?" I asked.

"What?" Nick said.

"If you can't helium, and you can't curium, then you might as well barium!"

Nick laughed until he had to hold his flat stomach. Alina laughed too, but I think it had more to do with seeing Nick laugh so hard than my jokes. Still, the awkwardness and tension were gone entirely, and Liam seemed to have forgotten that Alina hadn't answered his last question.

"You're funny," Alina said to me. "I can see why my brother likes you."

"Alina." Liam glared at her.

"What? You obviously like her. You haven't stopped staring at her butt since she walked into the kitchen."

"This is the last time I'm helping you with home repair, you little knobhead," Liam said as I tried to hold in the giggles.

"You didn't help. Nick helped," Alina said.

"I helped," Liam said. "I handed him the tools and looked really pretty doing it."

I couldn't hold in my laughter any longer, and Liam grinned at me before turning to Nick. "I think I have an extra shirt in my car. I'll grab it for you while you fix the sink for real this time."

"Your hoop is in my studio," Alina said to me. She glanced at my shoes and then the puddle of water I stood in. "I promise you won't have to stand in water in my studio."

"Show me the way," I said with a small grin.

I followed Alina out of the kitchen. She had a fairly pronounced limp, and it took us almost five minutes to navigate to the back of the house where her studio was.

"Sorry," Alina was slightly out of breath, with thin pain lines drawn around her mouth. "I'm having a bad leg day."

"It's fine," I said. "Go as slowly as you need."

"This is my studio." She pushed open a door, and I joined her in the room, staring in delight at the bright and cheery room.

"I love it," I said. "What a great space."

"Thank you." As Alina moved to the far table, I studied the hoops on the wall. Each one was a landscape, and all of them were strikingly beautiful.

"Did you make all of these?"

"I did," she said.

"You are seriously talented," I said. "I have no idea how you make such beautiful things with just thread, a needle, and some fabric."

"Thank you." Alina showed me the hoop I bought. It was even more gorgeous in person, and I told her that.

Alina blushed softly. "You're very kind."

I wandered around her studio, staring at the hoop art on the wall and some of her WIPs as Alina carefully placed the hoop in a flat box with tissue paper. She added her card and tied a ribbon around the box.

"Have you ever considered giving lessons?" I asked.

"I'm not sure there would be much interest," Alina said.

"I think you'd be surprised. I'm terrible at this sort of thing, but I bet my friend Hattie - I bought this as a birthday gift for her - would love to learn. Your studio is big enough that you could teach a few students here or do one-on-one. Or you could do some online teaching. Then you could teach people from all over the world."

Alina smiled and handed me the box with the hoop in it. "Thanks for the idea, Sophie. I appreciate it."

"Let me know if you decide to do it, and I'll mention it to Hattie."

"I will."

"So, Liam and Finn are your brothers, huh? I bet that's... something."

Her smile widened. "They're good brothers. A little over-protective sometimes, but I love them."

"I'm an only kid, but I'm pretty sure it's a brother's job to be overprotective," I said. "Nick's super cute. You two are into each other pretty hard, yeah?"

Alina glanced at the open door before shaking her head. "No, of course not. He's Liam's best friend. I've known him since I was little. We're just, uh, we're... I mean, I don't even... we're just friends."

"Oh," I said. "My bad. I thought I saw a thing between you."

"What kind of thing?" Alina's face had gone pink, and she looked both excited and terrified.

"Nothing," I said. "Forget I said anything. What do I know, right? I should probably get going."

"Okay, well, thank you again," Alina said as we slowly made our way back to the front door. "I appreciate your business."

"Thank *you*," I said. "I know Hattie will love this."

I peeked in the kitchen as we walked by, but it was empty. Masking my disappointment, I opened the front door and waved to Alina. "Thanks again. It was nice to meet you, Alina. Tell Liam I'll see him on Monday."

CHAPTER 9

Sophie

It was almost ten when my doorbell rang. I sat up from the couch and brushed the chip crumbs off my tank top before muting the television.

I'd never been afraid of living alone, but I wasn't dumb enough to answer the door at ten o'clock at night. I sat back on the couch and shoved another chip into my mouth. I took a swig of soda straight from the two-litre bottle before burping so loudly I was surprised the windows didn't vibrate. I ignored the doorbell when it rang again.

I wasn't usually the type to snack at night, but I was a little bored and a little depressed, and there was nothing wrong with a girl eating her feelings for a night. Seeing Liam at his sister's today had been great, but it also reminded me that I'd never have a real relationship with him.

Which, frankly, was depressing as fuck.

"Yeah, well, that's what you get for falling in love with your damn boss," I told the empty room.

Hearing the words out loud didn't make me feel any better.

My phone buzzed, and I snagged it from where it had gotten stuffed between the couch cushions. I read the message and nearly fell off the couch in my haste to stand up. "Holy fuck. Oh shit. Oh shit. Oh shit."

I gathered up the chips and soda and put them on the kitchen counter before running to the half-bathroom in the hallway and staring at myself in the mirror.

"Fuck me," I said before wiping the chip crumbs off my face. My hair was piled on top of my head in a bun. Not one of those cute messy buns but a scraggly bird's nest kind of bun - good lord, how did I get chips in my hair? - and I had a stain on my tank top, and I wasn't wearing a bra, and, *Christ,* I wasn't wearing underwear underneath my pajama shorts either.

I peeked out into the hallway, staring at the front door. Liam stared back at me through the side window next to the door. "I can see you, Sophie. Let me in." His voice was muffled but perfectly understandable.

"I'm not wearing a bra," I hollered.

"Definitely let me in then," he said.

"I look terrible. I was eating chips, and somehow they got in my hair!" I shouted.

"I like chips," he said. "Let me in, Soph."

I made one last attempt to brush the chip crumbs out of my hair before walking to the front door and opening it. Liam grinned at me. "Hey, I like your outfit."

I pulled self-consciously at my tank top. "What are you doing here, Liam? It's ten at night."

"Can I come in?" he asked.

"Yeah, okay." I stepped back, and Liam came inside, shutting the door and taking off his boots and jacket. Without saying anything, he walked toward the kitchen.

I followed him, watching as he ate a chip from the bowl before pointing at the soda bottle. "Can I have a drink of that?"

"Yes, but you should know I drank straight from it," I said.

He laughed and poured himself some soda. "I've had my tongue in your mouth and your pussy. I'm good with sharing the same soda bottle."

I shivered as my traitorous nips turned hard just remembering how it felt to have Liam's face in my pussy. Liam grinned, his gaze dropping to my small tits and the unmistakable outline of my nipples against the thin fabric. "Your gorgeous nipples make me so fucking hard."

My throat was suddenly bone dry, and I had to work to swallow. "Why are you here, Liam?"

"I came over to talk to you about Alina and thank you for being so nice to her, but now," he studied my tits again, "I'm distracted by how much I want to sink my cock into your tight cunt."

"We said we couldn't do this anymore, remember?" My voice practically dripped with need.

"We did," Liam said. "But I can't seem to stay away from you, Soph. Feel free to tell me to get the fuck out, but what do you say we make it one more night? Round out the weekend."

"Well," I pretended to think about it, "it does make sense that we should have sex tonight. I mean, we did have sex yesterday and Friday. If a person is going to fuck their boss on the weekend, they probably should fuck their boss on the *entire* weekend, right?"

"I could not agree more," Liam said.

"Plus, I do kind of owe you a dick sucking," I said.

Liam set his soda down with a thump. "You don't owe me anything, but I'm not going to argue if you want to suck my cock."

I smiled and held out my hand. "I want, Liam. I want very much. Come to the bedroom with me."

He took my hand and followed me to my bedroom. We were barely inside the room before he pulled my tank top over my head and cupped my breasts, gently teasing my nipples as he kissed and nuzzled my neck. I leaned back against him, grinding my ass against his cock as he slid one hand inside my cotton shorts.

I giggled at the surprise in his voice when he said, "You're not wearing panties."

"Is that a problem?" I asked.

"Never," he said. "In fact, you should probably not wear panties at the lab."

"I think there's some kind of rule about going without underwear in a lab," I said.

He rubbed my clit, kissing my shoulder when I moaned and arched into his hand. "Is that right?"

"Pretty sure," I gasped. "I can Google it if you want."

"Later." He tugged on one swollen nipple until I thought I might go crazy with need. "Right now, I need to taste your pussy again."

I immediately pulled his hand out from my shorts and pushed away from him.

"Sophie, what's wrong? What did I say?" Liam asked.

I waggled my finger at him. "Stop trying to distract me. It's my turn to go down on you."

He grinned, the concern on his face melting away. "I really want you to sit on my face."

"Oh my God," I said. "Is there no level to which you will not stoop to get what you want?"

He laughed, but I danced away when he tried to pull me into his embrace again. "C'mon, Soph, you know you want to sit on my face."

"Yes, sitting on your face would be entirely enjoyable," I said as I sat on the bed, "but tonight is about my mouth and your cock, so get over here."

"Yes, ma'am," Liam said.

He stood in front of me, and I stared at his cock, my mouth already watering. It was leaking precum, and the head was a dark red. I gripped the shaft, stroking lightly before leaning forward and kissing the neatly groomed patch of dark pubic hair.

He groaned when the head of his dick brushed against my chin, and his hand palmed the back of my skull. "Sophie, suck me."

"Soon," I said before licking from the base of his cock to the tip like he was a lollipop. Liam's second groan was louder, more urgent, and his fingers were already digging into my skull.

I teased the head with the tip of my tongue, cleaning off the precum and tracing around his ridge as Liam panted harshly. I cupped his balls, testing their heavy weight, and gave them a gentle tug before sucking hard on the head of his dick.

He moaned my name, sliding his other hand into my hair and holding me tight as I took more of him into my mouth. I set a rhythm of long, slow sucks, using plenty of tongue and spit until Liam's hips were pumping and he was fucking my mouth.

"Oh fuck, Soph," he made another drawn out moan, his burning gaze staring down at me as I sucked him hard. "Oh fuck, that's so good. You're gonna make me cum if you keep doing that, baby. Fuck, we should stop."

I sucked harder. I wanted Liam to cum in my mouth. I wanted to watch his face as I took everything he gave me.

Liam cried out. His hips thrust faster, and he gripped my head so tightly I couldn't have pulled away even if I'd wanted to. I reached between my legs and rubbed at my throbbing clit. I was so wet my fingers could barely find the friction I wanted. I stared up at Liam, letting him use my mouth the way he needed as he moaned and panted and whispered my name.

"Soph, baby… I'm so close."

I was close to cumming myself, but I yanked my hand out from between my legs and slipped them between Liam's. I wanted this moment to be about him. I wanted nothing distracting me as I watched him cum. I stroked his balls before reaching further back and pressing hard on that smooth spot behind them.

Liam made a strangled cry, his hips surging forward and his hands clamping down on my skull as he shot his load straight down my throat. I swallowed and swallowed again, loving the taste of his salty sweetness. Liam moaned, his entire body shaking as he pumped gently in and out of my mouth a final few times. I gripped his softening cock and cleaned off the head, making Liam jerk and pull away.

"Sorry," he gasped out. "Sensitive."

I smiled at him as he smoothed my hair back from my face. "You okay?"

"Fucking incredible," he said. "I'm sorry I didn't ask you if I could cum in your mouth. It surprised me, but that's a terrible fucking excuse."

I laughed and kissed his flat stomach. "It was fine. I had no problem with it."

"Christ, you're amazing," Liam said.

"Thanks, I am pretty good at - oh my God, Liam!"

Liam had picked me up and tossed me further back on the bed. I started to sit up, and Liam pushed me flat on my back before throwing my legs over his shoulders and burying his face in my pussy.

"Fuck!" I grabbed his head, pleasure spiraling through me as he licked up my slit and then sucked hard on my clit.

He pushed two thick fingers into my opening and fucked me with them, his lips and tongue working my clit as I dug my heels into his back and ground my pussy against his mouth. It took less than a minute for me to climax, the pleasure exploding in my lower belly and pelvis and my entire body quivering as Liam lapped gently at my wet pussy lips.

My legs slid from his shoulders, and Liam raised his head and kissed my thigh before wiping his face off with the sheet. My body still shook, and I was grateful for Liam's help when he moved me around on the bed and slid me under the sheet and quilt. He stretched out beside me, and I curled into him, resting my head on his chest as I waited for my breathing to return to normal.

I kept my eyes closed, listening to the solid beat of Liam's heart under my ear as he rubbed my back. After a few minutes, Liam said, "Do you want me to go, Sophie?"

"No," I said before my stupid brain could make the 'right' decision. "Stay the night."

He didn't reply, and cursing myself for being so dumb, I said, "You don't have to. I mean, only if you want -"

"I want to," he said.

I smiled up at him, and maybe he saw my love for him on my face, or maybe he'd finally noticed the chip crumbs in my hair, but he looked away quickly. "Because it's late, and I'm pretty tired."

"No, I know," I said, forcing a smile to stay on my face. "Why else would you stay?"

He didn't answer. Feeling stupid, I started to turn over, but Liam grabbed me and plastered me against his body again. "Cuddle for a little longer with me."

I rested my hand against his stomach, making my voice light and teasing. "I had no idea you'd be so into cuddling."

He laughed. "I've always been a cuddler. When I was a little kid, I loved snuggling with my mom on the couch. When Alina came along, I was super jealous and constantly tried to get in Mom's lap before she did."

"That's cute," I said. "Are you still close to your mom?"

His body tensed, and I could hear the sorrow in his voice when he said, "She died in a car accident when I was twenty, and Alina was fifteen."

"Oh, honey." I sat up, pulling the sheet up around me and smoothing my hand across Liam's forehead. "I'm very sorry."

"Thanks." He sat up and leaned against the headboard as I reached over to the nightstand and grabbed a water bottle. I took a drink and handed it to him.

He drank a few swallows before picking absently at the paper label. "Alina was in the car with her, and she nearly died too. She was in a coma for two weeks, and when she woke up, she was paralyzed from the waist down."

"Oh my God," I said.

"Her right leg was basically shattered. The doctors told us it would need to be amputated, but there happened to be this brilliant New York surgeon in Havenport as a conference keynote speaker. He heard about Alina and asked to look at her chart. He said he thought he could save her leg and believed it was worth trying. We agreed to let him operate. It took multiple surgeries, and at one point, we had to fly Alina to New York for him to do a surgery, but he saved her leg. It was a damn miracle."

I rubbed his arm, and he put it around me and pulled me in close. "She kept her leg because of him. Finn and I send him a bottle of whiskey every year on the anniversary of Alina's first operation."

"I'm glad he could help her," I said. "You said she was paralyzed when she woke up?"

He nodded, rubbing his thumb repeatedly over the water bottle label. "Yeah, because of swelling. The doctors thought that's what it was and that it wouldn't be permanent, but it took a while for her to get any feeling back. When she did...."

Liam's eyes were red, and I wiped away the tear that slid down his cheek.

"It was another miracle," he said hoarsely. "Alina is a walking, talking miracle."

I kissed his cheek. "It must have been so difficult on all of you."

"It was hard," he admitted. "Our dad checked out early on. He's a good guy but not much of a dad, and he was grieving the loss of my mom pretty hard. If it hadn't been for Finn...."

He cleared his throat. "I wouldn't be where I am today if Finn hadn't stepped up the way he did. I know he comes across as bossy and controlling, but he was there for Alina and me when we needed him most. He's still here for us. Every day."

"He sounds like a great brother," I said.

"He is. Alina is struggling with some trauma from the accident, and he's done everything he can to make her life easier. He was the one who suggested that we move to a smaller town to make it easier for Alina to be independent, and he bought Alina's house for her. She pays him rent every month, which he hates, but she's insistent."

A small smile crossed Liam's face. "He puts the rent money into a separate account every month and never touches any of it. He says it's her rainy day funds. She'll be pissed if she ever finds out."

I smiled. "She does seem pretty independent. She's an incredibly talented artist."

"She is," he said. "She's limited in what she can do work wise because of her leg and her trauma, so when she started selling her art online, Finn and I encouraged it. We knew she'd do well, but we didn't imagine how well she'd do. She's not swimming in money or anything, but she makes enough from selling her embroidery to cover her rent and other expenses."

"That's fantastic," I said.

"It is. She likes the small-town life, and she's made a really good friend here. A woman named Bryce who doesn't seem to care about Alina's... quirks. To a certain extent, small-town living has been a rough adjustment for Finn and me, but it's worth it to see Alina happy," Liam said.

"So, Alina said something about knowing Nick since she was a little kid," I said. "Nick lived in Havenport too, I assume?"

"He did. He and I have been best friends since high school. When Hudson Automobile opened here in town, Nick interviewed for a job. He said he was tired of big city living and wanted to try small-town living since we seemed to love it so much."

"You must have been happy to have your best friend here with you," I said.

"Yes. I missed him a lot even though Havenport isn't that far away," Liam said. "He helps with Alina too, which takes some pressure off Finn and me. We know that Alina is an adult and doesn't need to be checked on, but we worry."

"Understandable," I said.

"Anyway, Nicky checks on Alina when we can't, which we appreciate."

"They seem pretty close," I said.

Liam glanced at me. "Nick and Alina?"

I nodded, and he shrugged. "I guess so."

"Maybe Nick helps her because he likes her," I said.

Liam laughed. "God, no. She's like a sister to him. Trust me, he's not interested in her like that, which is a good thing."

"Why?"

"I love Nick, but he's a player. He's had one serious girlfriend the entire time I've known him. He isn't the relationship type and can be a little selfish sometimes. Alina needs someone who will make her a priority, who'll understand what she's gone through, and help her when the past becomes too much for her."

"Well, maybe Nick has changed," I said. "People change."

"They do," Liam said. "But not to that extent. Nick is a great guy, and I'm not trying to make it sound like he isn't. He just isn't the right guy for Alina."

"Okay," I said.

He kissed my forehead. "It doesn't matter anyway because they only see each other as siblings. I guarantee it."

I took the water bottle from him and drank a few swallows before setting it on the nightstand.

"You grew up here, right?" Liam said.

"I did. Born and raised. Which can be great but also really, really bad when your ex uploads a sex tape of you to a popular porn site. Thanks to small-town gossip, I'm pretty sure eighty percent of the town has now seen me buck naked."

He pulled me close and kissed my forehead again. "I'm sorry this happened to you, Soph. You don't deserve any of this."

"Thanks." I rested my head on his chest. "Why didn't you watch the video?"

He tipped my head up until I looked at him. "Because it's not something you shared voluntarily, Sophie. It was a horrible invasion of your privacy, and as much as I wanted to see you naked, I didn't want it to be that way. I hate what that asshole did to you. If there were a way I could get the video removed from the porn site, I would."

I studied him for a few seconds before cupping his face and kissing him. "Thank you, Liam. That means a lot."

He returned my kiss, and I wanted him again despite how late it was getting. Especially since this was it for us. I could sleep later, right? Tonight, I wanted Liam.

"I want you," I said to him. "I know it's late."

He cupped my breast in one big hand. "I want you too, Sophie."

"Good." I tipped my head back and closed my eyes as Liam kissed a gentle path down my throat.

Thoughts of this being our last night tried to worm their way into my brain, but I shoved them out viciously. I wouldn't think about tomorrow and how I'd never have Liam in my bed again. I would concentrate on this moment, right here and right now.

CHAPTER 10

Liam

"What the fuck?" I glared at my computer screen before shoving my hands in my hair and leaning back in my chair. "What the hell do I have to do to get a fucking laptop that actually works around here?"

Finn walked into my office. "I see your bad mood hasn't improved."

"I'm not in a bad mood," I snapped.

"The fuck you aren't." He dropped into the chair across from my desk. "You've been in a horrible mood for the last week and a half."

"Is there something work related I can help you with, Finn?" I asked.

"Nope."

"Then leave."

"Don't be a dick," Finn said.

I glared at him, but Finn just stared calmly at me. "Tell me why you're being such a fuck to be around."

"I'm not."

"You are. Even Alina said something to me about it, and she thinks you walk on fucking water most of the time."

My scowl deepened, and I reached for my phone. "Fuck. Is she upset with me?"

Before I could call her, Finn said, "She's fine. She's worried about you but not upset with you. Even if you're being a dink."

"Enough with the name calling, okay?" I said. "Today isn't the fucking day."

Finn's face softened, and he leaned forward. "Tell me what's wrong, Liam."

"Nothing's wrong. I did something stupid, and now I regret it."

"What did you do?"

I glanced at the open door. Sophie wasn't in the lab. She'd left for the day, but I still didn't want the few lab techs still working to overhear what I had to say. Finn pushed the door shut before leaning back in his chair. "Tell me."

"I slept with Sophie," I said.

"What the fuck, Liam?" Finn rubbed his hand across his jaw. "You said you'd learned your lesson with Dayton."

"I did," I said. "This was casual, nothing more than a weekend of fun. But now…"

"Let me guess, now Sophie wants more."

"No," I said. "She hasn't said a word to me about anything not work related in the last ten days. She doesn't want more."

"Then what's the problem?" Finn said.

"I don't know," I said, my voice rising. "I know I can't date another fucking employee, and I know that my reputation has already taken a hit here at the lab, but I can't…."

Finn waited for a beat. "You want more."

"No… yes. I don't fucking know. I know that I miss her

like crazy even though I see her every fucking day. In fact, seeing her every day makes it that much worse."

"You're in love with her," Finn said.

"No."

"Yes."

"Finn, I'm not in love with her."

"Then why do you have an 'I'm in love with her' face?" Finn asked.

"I don't have a… my face is my face, you jackass."

"This is a real mess you've gotten yourself into, bud," Finn said.

"Tell me something I don't know," I said.

I waited for Finn to keep lecturing me, to tell me all the reasons why I had fucked up and how I should have listened to him. To my surprise, he gave me a sympathetic look and said, "You could transfer her. Put her with Crayton and his research team."

"No," I said. "I won't do that to Sophie. She's a big reason we even got to the pre-clinical development stage, and I won't take her off the project because I can't control my dick around her."

Finn stood and stretched the kinks out of his back. "Okay. It was only a suggestion."

"I'm thinking of asking her if she wants to do something casual," I said.

"Something casual," Finn repeated.

"Yeah. Friends with benefits."

"Is that what you want?"

"Anything more is a bad idea," I said.

"That's the fucking truth," Finn said. "You think she'll go for it?"

"I don't know. I hope so, but the way she's acted this week, I don't have my hopes up," I said.

"You should walk away from this girl," Finn said. "It won't end well."

"I didn't ask for your opinion," I said.

A rare grin crossed Finn's face. "No, you didn't, but when has that ever stopped me?"

I laughed. "Hey, let's do movie night at Alina's on Friday instead of Saturday."

"Can't. Already have plans for Friday night," Finn said.

"You always have Friday night plans. You ever gonna introduce her to us?" I asked.

"It's not a woman," Finn said.

"Sure it isn't," I said.

"It's not. Talk to you later, Liam." Finn walked out of my office.

I stared at my phone, still on the fence about texting Sophie. What good would it do? She'd been fine with the casual weekend, but I doubted she'd want to continue the casual fucking. But it was all I could offer her. I'd made that mistake of dating an employee once before. I wouldn't do it again.

Sophie

"I HATE SEEING YOU SAD," HATTIE SAID.

"I'm not sad. I'm tired," I said. "Do you have any sevens?"

"Go fish," Hattie said. "You're sad, Sophie. It's a Wednesday night, and you're making me play Go Fish. Do you have any nines?"

"Go fish. What does that have to do with anything?" I asked.

"We only play Go Fish when you're sad and want to feel better," Hattie said.

I laid my cards down on the table. "That's not true."

"Yes, it is." Hattie took a sip of lemonade. "You should text him, honey."

"What for? He's just going to turn me down."

"You don't know that. You said the weekend you spent together was great, right? Maybe he's pining for more too."

"He isn't," I said. "He acts completely the same at the lab. He doesn't even look at me like he might want to see me naked again. The weekend was enough for him."

"Or, he's being professional at work," Hattie said. "Didn't you say that until Dayton lost his shit at the lab, most people had no idea he and Liam were dating?"

"Yes, but -"

"There's no harm in texting him," Hattie said.

"There's plenty of harm - mostly in the form of him rejecting me soundly."

"So what? You'll never get what you don't ask for. If he says thanks, but no thanks, you chalk it up to a learning experience and move on."

"I'm already moving on," I said. "I have a date on Sunday afternoon."

"What?" Hattie let her cards fall to the table.

"Hey! You had a seven!" I said.

"Whatever, you know I cheat at Go Fish," Hattie said. "Who are you going on a date with?"

"I rejoined Tinder. Some guy messaged me, and he could spell, and he didn't send me a bunch of dick pics, so I said yes to a date," I said.

"Sophie," Hattie gave me a look, "Tinder is just a place to hook up."

"That's all I'm looking for," I said. "It's perfect."

"Yeah, you're only looking for a hook up because you're in love with Liam," Hattie said.

"I can't spend the rest of my life pining after him, okay? If that means distracting myself with casual sex until I stop loving Liam, then that's what I'll do. I don't want to be alone forever, Hatts."

"I know, honey," Hattie said. "But I think falling out of love with Liam will take longer than you think."

"Yeah." I poked at the cards on the table. "I'm thinking of asking to be transferred to a different project."

"Oh, Soph." Hattie's look of sympathy made the backs of my eyelids sting. "But this project means so much to you."

"It does," I admitted, "but it's also changed. Instead of coming into work every day and being excited about helping people with epilepsy like my Aunt Sarah, I spend the entire day moping about Liam and dissecting every look he gives me like I'm a fucking teenage girl. It's depressing as fuck."

"Maybe give it a few more weeks," Hattie said. "I'm not saying you'll fall out of love with Liam that quick, but it might get easier, right?"

"Maybe," I said.

"C'mon," Hattie reached across and squeezed my hand, "let's make some popcorn and watch *Queer Eye*. The new season is out."

"Sure," I said. I made myself smile at her, even though all I wanted to do was crawl into bed and cry.

I stood and grabbed the popcorn from the cupboard as the doorbell rang.

"I'll get it," Hattie said. Carrying her lemonade glass, she left the kitchen. I tore the cellophane off the popcorn package and placed it in the microwave. Before I could hit start, I heard Hattie return to the kitchen. I turned around. "Hey, who was... Liam?"

Liam stood next to Hattie, holding my work cardigan in one hand and looking extremely uncomfortable. "Hi, I should have texted first. Sorry."

"That's okay," I said. "Uh, how are you?"

"Fine. How are you?"

"Good," I said. "You remember my friend Hattie?"

"I do." Liam smiled at her. "How are you, Hattie?"

"Living the dream," Hattie said.

"Good, that's, um, good," Liam said.

There was an uncomfortable pause, and then he said, "I'm gonna go. You have company and -"

"No, it's fine," I said.

Hattie set her glass on the counter, kissed my cheek, and grabbed her purse. "I was just leaving. Good to see you again, Liam. Soph, text me tomorrow, yeah?"

"I will," I said. "Bye, Hattie."

"Later." She walked out of the kitchen.

I waited until the front door shut before saying, "Have a seat. Did you want something to drink?"

"No, thank you."

I sat down across from him, and when Liam didn't say anything, I said, "Why are you here?"

"You forgot your sweater." Liam placed my thin cardigan on the table.

"My sweater," I said.

"Yeah. At work. I was leaving, and I saw it on the stool. I thought you might need it tonight, so I brought it over."

"It's my work sweater," I said.

"What?"

"It's the sweater I keep at the lab in case I get cold," I said.

"Oh."

Liam was starting to look pretty sweaty. He grabbed my

sweater and stood. "Okay, sorry. I should go. I'll bring your sweater back to the lab in the morning."

"Liam, wait."

He hesitated and then sat down, the look on his face a mixture of hope and need.

I knew it was a mistake and knew that I was only causing myself further heartbreak, but, fuck, I'd missed him. I missed him so much, it made me feel sick. One more night with Liam wouldn't hurt, right?

"Did you come here to bring me my sweater, or did you come here because it's hump day, and you can't stop thinking about my outstanding sexy time skills?" I grinned at him.

Relief washed over Liam's face, and the smile that crossed his face made any lingering doubts I might have had disappear.

"I'd like to try to convince you it's because of the sweater, but arguing would waste valuable face sitting time, so in the interest of having you sitting on my face for as long as possible... I missed your outstanding sex skills."

"Knew it," I said with a smug grin. I stood and held out my hand. "Come on, Dr. Whitby. It's time for you to put your money where your mouth is."

He took my hand and followed me down the hallway. "Whatever you say, Dr. Clark."

CHAPTER 11

Sophie

"Thanks for letting me stay the night." Liam sipped at his coffee. The sun had just risen, and the light filtering through the kitchen window made his dark hair gleam.

I leaned over and pressed a kiss against his forehead before pouring myself another cup of coffee. "You're welcome."

Liam reached out and stroked my bare thigh below my nightgown. "Maybe I should join you in your shower, help you wash your back."

I laughed. "As much as I would love that, it'll make you late for work because I won't let you leave without having steamy hot shower sex. You still need to go home, shower, and change your clothes before going into the lab."

Liam stood and pulled me into his embrace. "I'm the boss. I'm allowed to be late for work, occasionally."

"True," I draped my arms over his shoulders. "It is one of the perks of being the boss."

"I had a great time last night, Soph," Liam said.

"I did too." I studied Liam's face before deciding to go for it. Last night was amazing, and not just because of the sex. Sure, we'd had sex and lots of it, but we'd also talked and cuddled, and it felt more like a relationship last night than the entirety of my relationship with Cody. Liam was a fantastic guy, and he felt more for me than lust. I know he did.

"What are you thinking about?" Liam asked.

This was my chance.

"Well," I smoothed down the tiny soft hairs on the back of his neck, "I was thinking about how awesome last night was."

"It was pretty great," Liam said with a smug grin that made me laugh.

"Yes, the sex was incredible," I said, "but it wasn't just that. It was everything. I liked the talking and the snuggling and being with you."

The look on his face changed, but I hurried on before he could say anything. "We're good together, and not just because of the sex. I'd like more, Liam. I'd like to date you if you're interested?"

Liam's body tensed against me. Shit, that wasn't a good sign.

"I thought you didn't want people to know at work," he said. "You've had a bad experience dating a co-worker."

"Isn't that the truth," I said. "But you're not like Cody. Besides, everyone at work - hell, everyone in town - is already talking about me. So, what does it matter? I like you a lot, Liam. I'd like to see where a relationship could lead."

"I like you too," he said, "you know I do, Soph."

My stomach dropped at the cautious look he gave me as he eased out of my embrace and put some space between us.

"I dated an employee, and it didn't go well," he said.

"I know. But I'm not Dayton."

"I know you're not," he said. "But because of what happened with him, the way people see me at the lab has changed. I worked hard to gain their respect, and I lost it all in an instant because of a relationship with an employee. I can't let that happen again, Sophie."

"I'm not going to do to you what Dayton did," I said. "Why don't you believe me?"

"It isn't about that," he said. "It's about being smart and not being in a relationship that my co-workers can watch unfold in front of them in real time. I also don't want your co-workers thinking you're getting special treatment because you're involved with me."

"They won't," I said. "And even if they do - fuck them. I don't care what they think."

"I do," he said. "I care about what they think about you and what they think about me."

"So, this is it for us, then?" I asked. "Or are you going to wait another week and then find some other stupid excuse to come by my house?"

He winced. "No, I... look, I wanted to talk to you about a friends with benefits relationship."

My chest tightened, and it felt like an eight-inch knife had been driven into my sternum. "So, I'm not good enough for a relationship, but I'm good enough to fuck on the down-low?"

"That's not what I meant," Liam said.

"That's how it sounds," I said.

Liam muttered a curse. "I know. I'm sorry."

"It's fine," I said and was proud of how steady my voice was.

"It isn't. Forget I said anything, okay? I shouldn't have -"

"Can I have a couple of days to think it over?" I asked.

Liam stared cautiously at me. "Sophie, I don't want you to -"

"You put this offer on the table. Are you taking it back already?" I asked.

"No, but -"

"Then give me a couple of days to consider it, and I'll let you know," I said.

Liam's face suggested he was happy to argue with me all day. I glanced at the clock. "I need to jump in the shower, and you need to go home and shower, or we'll both be late. I'll see you at the lab."

"Sophie -"

"Bye, Liam."

His face grim, Liam grabbed his phone off the table. "Bye, Sophie."

I stayed in the kitchen, and when the front door shut, I collapsed in one of the chairs and buried my face in my hands. What the fuck was I thinking?

Liam

THIS WAS HELL.

I was in fucking hell, and I had no one to blame but myself.

I leaned back in my chair, staring out into the empty lab. It was after five on a Friday night, and everyone was gone, including Sophie. I'd held out some hope that she might be ready to talk to me when she hadn't left at four-thirty with most of the other chemists and lab assistants, but that hope had died when she'd walked out of the lab with Jody a few minutes ago.

I leaned forward and rested my elbows on the desk, burying my face in my hands. Why had I asked Sophie to consider a friends with benefits deal right after she asked for a relationship? It was a horrible thing to do to her, and I was a complete fucking asshole for even suggesting it.

But the thought of never being in her bed again had me blurting it out. The look on her face... fuck, I was such an idiot.

You really are. Just date her. You like her - fuck that, you love her - so be a man and tell her.

I couldn't. As much as I cared for Sophie, the idea that my co-workers would know I was dating another employee made my stomach seize up. I'd made a fool of myself once in front of them. I wouldn't do it again, no matter how much I liked Sophie.

Love, you idiot. It's called love. What will you do if Sophie says no to the casual sex? Will you forget about her and move on?

That would be impossible. If she didn't want to be friends with benefits, I'd agree to a relationship. I couldn't not be with her, not when -

"Liam?"

Sophie's soft voice made me jerk so hard I almost fell out of the chair. I sat up straight, staring wide-eyed at her. "Sophie! Hey, uh, I thought you left."

She shook her head. "No. I mean, technically, I did leave, but it's because I didn't want Jody thinking the two of us were here alone together when she knows there isn't anything we need to work late on."

"Oh, okay," I said. "So, um, how are you?"

"Fine. You?"

"Good. Listen, about what I asked, I shouldn't -"

"Yes," Sophie said.

"What?"

"My answer is yes. I'll do a friends with benefits, casual sex thing with you."

I stared silently at her, and Sophie flushed, her hand pulling at her jacket collar. "Unless you've changed your mind?"

"I haven't," I said. "But…"

"But what?"

"This isn't what you want, so I didn't think you'd say yes."

She shrugged. "I did a lot of thinking about what you said and decided you're right. It's a bad idea for us to date. But there's no harm in us having a fun casual time together a couple of times a week, right? The sex is fantastic, and I don't know about you, but it's been a long time since I've had sex this good."

"Are you sure, Sophie? Because I…"

Say it, Liam. Tell her you want more.

"Because?" Sophie said.

"Because I want to make sure we're both clear what this is," I said.

Coward!

"I'm clear," she said with a brittle smile. "I'm not harbouring some fantasy that sex with me on the regular will eventually convince you to start dating me. I'm good in bed, but I'm not *that* good, amirite?" She grinned at me, and while it was much more natural than her previous one, there was a falseness that she couldn't entirely hide.

"I don't want to hurt you, Sophie," I said.

"You won't," she said. "So, are you busy tonight?"

"I'm having dinner with Alina," I said. "But I could come by around nine if that works?"

"Actually, would it be work if I come to your place

instead?" Sophie glanced at her phone. "Text me your address, and I can be there at nine."

"Sure," I said. "I'd like that."

I wasn't lying. The idea of having Sophie's scent in my sheets, of her spending the night with me in my bed, was an intoxicating one.

"Great. I'll see you at nine. Enjoy your dinner." She waved and left my office. I watched her leave the lab before slumping in my chair and staring at my computer screen.

Sophie was giving me exactly what I wanted, so why the fuck was I so depressed by it?

CHAPTER 12

Sophie

"I like your place." I poked my head into the living room. "Is that a guitar? Do you play guitar?"

"I do," Liam said with a grin. "I can play a couple of songs for you if you'd like."

I'd love nothing more than to have Liam play the guitar for me, but that was too much like a relationship. When I'd decided to accept Liam's offer of friends with benefits, I'd promised myself I would focus less on the friends and more on the benefits.

You can't let yourself do anything with Liam that isn't about the sex, I reminded myself. *Ever.*

It was the only way to keep myself from hoping he would eventually want more.

I smiled at Liam. "Maybe another time. So, show me that bedroom of yours."

Liam laughed and took my hand. "Follow me. How was the rest of your evening?"

"Good, thank you. How was -"

Shit! I closed my mouth before I could ask him how his dinner with Alina went. Man, this keeping it to sex only would be more difficult than I thought. But I didn't need to know about his personal life to have sex with him. Just like he didn't need to know mine. Hell, I was still going on my date on Sunday. Would I have sex with the guy? God, no. But a date with someone else would help reinforce the idea that I could never have a relationship with Liam. Besides, maybe the guy would turn out to be awesome and help me forget all about Liam.

Liam had stopped in the hallway and studied me carefully. "Everything okay tonight?"

"Great," I said. "No complaints. This doesn't look like your bedroom, though."

"If you've changed your mind, Soph, you can tell me that. You know that, right?"

"I haven't changed my mind." I dropped his hand before he could feel how sweaty mine was getting. "But I would prefer bed sex over hallway sex."

My smile felt too large and too fake. Liam looked tense and uncomfortable. Fuck. I was screwing this up big time.

I stepped closer and put my arms around Liam's waist, kissing his chest through his t-shirt. "Sorry, I have a bit of a headache, so I'm a little off."

Relief crossed his face, and he put his arms around me before pressing a tender kiss against my forehead. "Why didn't you say something? I can get you some Advil or an ice pack."

I pushed away my guilt at lying to Liam. "No, no, it's not that bad."

"Are you sure?" Liam led me into his bedroom. "We don't have to have sex tonight. I'll give you a back rub to help you relax."

Maybe it wouldn't hurt to let Liam in just a little. What harm was there in that? Boyfriend Liam was even hotter than regular Liam.

Yes, he'll make some other man or woman very happy someday.

Reality washed over me like an ice water bath. I needed to stick to the plan, and if I couldn't, I needed to leave. Immediately.

"You're very sweet," I tugged his shirt over his head and dropped it on the floor, "but I'm looking for you to make me cum so hard, I can't see straight."

I kissed his chest before tracing his flat nipple with my tongue. "Is that a problem, Dr. Whitby?"

He moaned and shook his head, his fingers digging into my hips. "Not at all."

"Good. Then get those clothes off."

He grinned and quickly stripped as I did the same. I reached into the pocket of my jeans and pulled out a condom, placing it on the bedside table before dropping my jeans on the floor with the rest of my clothes.

Liam laughed. "I have condoms, Soph. You didn't have to bring your own."

I shrugged. "I don't like relying on someone else for my personal safety."

He pulled me into his embrace, his erect cock rubbing against my stomach. "That's fair."

He smoothed my hair back from my face before cupping my jaw and placing another tender kiss against my mouth. "You're so beautiful, Sophie."

"Thank you."

He grunted in surprise when I pushed him back on the bed and straddled him. I didn't want this to be about tenderness, compliments, or feelings I'd rather not feel. I wanted it to be purely about sex, just Liam and me making each other feel good.

I leaned over and kissed Liam hard, sliding my tongue into his mouth and letting him feel how much I wanted him. Liam smiled at me when we broke for air, his fingers toying with my hair. "Someone's eager tonight."

"I like your dick. What can I say," I said.

He laughed. "He likes you too." He tucked a strand of my hair behind my ear. "Your hair is so soft, Sophie." His fingers traced down my throat and along my collarbone. "Your skin is soft too, and -"

"Hey." I wrapped my fingers around his dick, stroking him hard and fast. "Are we talking or fucking tonight?"

He groaned, his hips pumping against my hand. "Fucking. Definitely fucking."

"Good." I kissed his chest again before releasing him and straightening. Liam sat up, sliding his hands around my waist and pulling me in snug against him as he kissed between my breasts before sucking hard on my left nipple.

I groaned, desire shooting through me like fireworks. My nipple tightened into a hard peak, and Liam made a low sound of approval before switching to my other nipple. I arched my back, rubbing my pussy against his dick. The head bumped along my clit, and I sucked in a harsh breath before reaching down to grip Liam's cock. I rubbed the head back and forth against my clit, teasing myself and bringing me closer to the peak.

"That's so fucking hot." Liam leaned back and watched me use his cock to get myself off.

"Hmm," I said, closing my eyes and concentrating. Just a little bit more, and I would be there. Just a few more...

"Liam! What the hell?" My eyes flew open when Liam lifted me off his lap and tossed me onto my back on the bed.

The loss of delicious friction against my pussy made me glare at him as he grinned and leaned over to kiss my stomach.

"You're adorable when you're pissed off."

"I was close," I said.

"I know." He traced a path of kisses around each of my tits. "But I want you to cum when I'm inside you."

"What does it matter?" I slid my hand between my legs, scowling at Liam when he pulled it away and pinned it to the bed.

"I like how your little cunt squeezes my dick when you're cumming. And," he pressed a kiss against my ribs, "I want to fuck you missionary tonight."

"Boring," I said.

"Not when it's done right," he said with another wicked grin. "Don't touch that sweet pussy, Sophie."

He released my hand, and when he was satisfied that I wouldn't slide it between my legs again, he reached for the condom on the nightstand. He rolled it onto his dick and knelt between my legs, pushing them open before sliding his big hands up and down my inner thighs.

"God, I love your pussy," he said. "She's so fucking pretty."

"If you don't give her your dick in the next ten seconds, she's taking her pretty self the fuck out of here," I said.

Liam laughed so hard the bed shook. I started to giggle as well. As much as I wanted this to be about sex only, I couldn't help being delighted by how natural our connection was. I loved that Liam didn't take sex seriously all the time, that he could be a little silly and appreciate some silliness in return.

My giggles turned into a low moan when Liam leaned forward, and the head of his dick pressed against my entrance. He reached down and rubbed my clit, making me squirm and cry out. "Oh fuck, Liam!"

When he stopped, I clutched his arm. "No, don't stop!"

"Shh, Soph," he said as he gripped the base of his dick and pressed the head against my entrance again. "I wanted to make sure you were wet enough."

"You should probably check again," I said. "Do a little more rubbing, just to be on the safe... oh! Oh fuck, that's good."

I clenched around Liam as he slid into me. Liam muttered a curse, propping himself up on his hands above me. "Soph, honey, relax."

"I thought you liked it when I squeezed," I said.

He bit down on his bottom lip, the cords in his neck already standing out. "I do, baby, I do. But I need you to relax and let me in."

I relaxed, both of us groaning our pleasure when Liam slid deep into my pussy, his heavy balls slapping against me. I clutched at his waist, the delicious feel of my pussy stretching around his width a now familiar sensation.

"So tight," Liam muttered.

I braced my feet on the bed, sliding my hands around Liam's waist. "Fuck me, Liam."

"Yes, Sophie," he said in a low voice.

Our bodies found our natural rhythm quickly and easily, like they were meant for each other. When Liam lowered his body and rested his forearms against the bed, I slung my arms around his shoulders and buried my face in his neck. Our low moans grew louder, and our bodies slapped together in a quickening rhythm.

Liam groaned my name before whispering, "Touch yourself, honey."

I slid my hand between our bodies and rubbed at my

aching clit. It skyrocketed my pleasure, made me cry out, and squeeze Liam's cock until he groaned into my ear.

"That's so good, honey," he said. "Make yourself cum. Let me feel you squeeze my dick with that pretty pussy."

I cried out, rubbing harder and faster as Liam thrust in and out of me. I came hard with a low cry, pleasure drenching every nerve ending as I buried my face in his throat and let it consume me.

Liam moaned my name, his hips pumping, his hot breath blowing against my neck as he reached for his release. He found it with a bellowed curse and two hard thrusts that made me bounce against the mattress.

I clung tight to him as he rocked back and forth, his body trembling and twitching as he came down from the high of his climax. He was heavy, but I didn't mind. I fucking loved it, in fact. He kissed my throat, and I let go of him as he eased out of me. He sat up on the bed and took off the condom, tossing it into the wastebasket by the nightstand before lying back in the bed beside me.

When I didn't curl into him, he turned on his side to face me and pulled me close, kissing my forehead and rubbing my lower back. "How's your headache?"

"Gone," I said. "Thank you, Liam."

He smiled and kissed my forehead again. "You're welcome."

It was nice to lie with Liam in his bed, to feel the heat of his body against mine. A girl could get used to this every night.

Time to leave, Sophie.

I wanted to ignore my inner voice, but she was right. If I stayed any longer, I would spend the night, which was a terrible fucking idea.

I sat up and slid out of bed. "Bathroom?"

"Right there." Liam pointed at the door next to his dresser.

I used the bathroom and washed my hands, staring at myself in the mirror above the sink. I looked pale and sad. Muttering a curse under my breath, I pinched my cheeks a few times and then practiced smiling until it looked mostly natural and unforced.

"You can do this," I said in a low voice before walking out of the bathroom.

Liam frowned and sat up when I grabbed my clothes from the floor and started to dress. "Soph, what are you doing?"

"Getting dressed," I said. "It's getting pretty late."

"Stay the night," he said.

"I can't," I said. "But thank you for the offer. And thanks for tonight. I had a great time."

"Sophie." Liam climbed out of bed. "Did I do something wrong?"

"Of course not." I slipped my shirt over my head and smoothed my hair out of my face. "I had an awesome time."

"So did I." He slipped his arms around my waist and pulled me closer. "So, stay the night with me."

"I really can't," I said.

He wiggled his eyebrows at me. "I'll eat your pussy."

I laughed and gave him a quick kiss before stepping away. "Let's rain check the pussy eating for next time."

"Sophie, you don't have to leave," Liam said. "I thought you would spend the night."

"Sorry," I said. "I'll talk to you later, okay?"

I wouldn't ask him if he wanted to get together tomorrow night. This was a casual thing, and people in casual relationships didn't plan like it was a damn date or something.

"What about tomorrow?" he said. "I have a movie night with Finn and Alina, but I'm free in the afternoon."

"I'm hanging out with my parents tomorrow afternoon," I said.

"What about Sunday? I'm free in the evening," Liam said.

"I have plans on Sunday." My plans were in the afternoon, but as much as I was trying to embrace this new casual sex lifestyle, I couldn't go on a date in the afternoon and then fuck Liam that night. I just couldn't.

Liam scrubbed a hand through his hair. "Well, shit."

I smiled at him. "I'll see you on Monday at the lab."

Liam looked like he would ask me to stay one more time, and afraid I would break down and say yes, I said, "I can let myself out. Bye, Liam!" I waved and hurried out of his bedroom.

By the time I got to the front door, I was almost running.

CHAPTER 13

Liam

I smiled at the server when she set down my coffee. "Thank you."

She nodded and glanced at the empty seat across from me and the menu on the table. "I'll give you a few more minutes."

I took a sip of coffee, studying the other people in the restaurant. The Copper Bistro and Grill was one of the most popular restaurants in Willowdale, and it wasn't surprising that nearly all the tables were full on a Sunday afternoon. I people-watched for a few minutes, sipping again at my coffee. I checked the time, frowning when I realized that Finn was almost fifteen minutes late. Finn was *never* late.

My phone buzzed, and I hit the answer button. "Finn, you'd better be on your way."

"Gretchen keeps stalling." Finn sounded more pissed off than I'd heard him in a long time.

"Didn't you just get her back from the second mechanic this week?" I asked.

"Yes," Finn spit it out. "I'm not going to make lunch."

"You could take an Uber," I said.

"I'm not in the mood for lunch," Finn said. "I have to go."

He ended the call, and I quickly texted Alina.

Finn's car died again, and he's pissed. I wouldn't call him today if I were you.

I watched the three bubbles appear before Alina's text came through.

Uh oh. Poor Finn. Thanks for the heads up.

I placed my phone on the table and drummed my fingers next to it as I took another sip of coffee. I felt bad for Finn, but his canceling meant I could call Sophie and ask if she wanted to hang out.

She said she had plans, remember?

That was true, but she hadn't said when her plans were. Maybe she was free this afternoon. It wouldn't hurt to text her and ask.

She's acting weird. She couldn't leave your place fast enough after sex on Friday night, and she took forever to respond to your text yesterday.

Yeah, okay, but it was only a stupid meme about chemistry. It's not like I even required a response. I just saw it and thought she would find it funny.

I picked up my phone and scrolled to Sophie's name in my texts. My thumbs hovered over the keyboard. Maybe this was a mistake. As much as I wanted to deny it, Sophie was acting strangely, and I had no idea why.

Maybe because you're an asshole who only wants her for sex?

She agreed to it. I was clear and upfront about what this was, and she said okay.

Well, aren't you just Prince Fucking Charming?

I closed my eyes and took a deep breath. I was being

stupid. Sophie and I were friends, and friends hung out on the weekends. There was no harm in texting her. If she were busy, she'd say so.

The bistro door opened before I could text her, and Sophie walked in. Happiness washed over me. God, she looked good. Her hair was in a loose braid, and she'd painted her lips with bright red lipstick. I had half a stiffy just thinking about how those red lips would look wrapped around my cock.

She wore a mid-thigh length dress that showed off her slender legs and clung to her small but delectable ass. She looked amazing.

My jaw dropped when the man who'd walked in behind her put his hand in the small of her back before leaning down to speak directly into her ear.

Hot jealousy flared to life, and I clenched my hand around my phone as Sophie nodded and laughed at whatever he'd said. The man's gaze dropped to her tits, and I immediately wanted to punch the table. Or him.

What the fuck was going on?

She's on a date, moron.

No, she couldn't be. She was… we were…

I took a deep breath as the hostess led Sophie and - I refused to call him her date - toward their table. Their path would lead them right by my table, and I debated only half a second before calling Sophie's name as they walked past.

Sophie froze, and the man almost walked into the back of her. She stared at me in surprise as I stood and gave her a tight smile.

"Hello, Sophie."

"Hi, Liam."

There was a moment of silence before Sophie said, "What are you doing here?"

"Having lunch with Finn, but he had to cancel."

"Oh," Sophie said.

I stuck my hand out to the man. "Liam Whitby."

The man shook my hand as Sophie flushed and said, "Sorry. Um, Liam, this is Brad. He's my, um...."

"Her date," the man said before placing a proprietary hand on the small of Sophie's back again. "How do you know Sophie?"

Had I ever wanted to punch someone so much in my life? Pretty sure the answer was no.

I clenched my jaw and forced a smile. "We work together. How did you and Sophie meet?"

"Tinder," the man said cheerfully. "Isn't that how everyone meets these days?"

When I didn't reply, Brad glanced at Sophie. "Well, it was nice to meet you, but we should probably get to our table, right, Sophie?"

"Yes," Sophie said. "Uh, see you at work tomorrow, Liam."

"Bye, Sophie."

I watched them follow the hostess to their table. My blood was hot lava in my veins, and the sound of my pulse in my ears drowned out the bistro noise. I looked up at the server when she stopped by my table again.

"Still waiting for your friend or...."

"He had to cancel," I said.

"Oh, okay. Do you want to order now then?" the server asked.

"Yes," I said. Jealousy had made me lose my appetite, but there was no way I'd leave Sophie alone with some random shithead she met on fucking Tinder.

Sophie

"Hey, are you going to eat that?" Brad pointed to the half a chicken sandwich on my plate.

I shook my head. "Go ahead."

"Cool, thanks."

I forced a smile, telling myself for the thousandth time not to glance over at Liam before I glanced over at Liam. He was staring at me, just like he'd been doing all through lunch, the soup and sandwich in front of him completely untouched.

He was pissed. I could see it in his face and his stiff body. I looked away as Brad took the sandwich off my plate and took a big bite. His appetite hadn't been affected by seeing Liam. Why would it?

You've done nothing wrong, Soph. You and Liam aren't a couple. You're allowed to date other people.

That was true. So why did I feel so damn shitty?

"You don't eat a lot, huh?" Brad said around a mouthful of sandwich.

"Depends," I said.

His gaze dropped to my small tits again. I suppressed the urge to reach out and push on his forehead until he met my gaze. Why did Liam staring at my breasts make me feel desired and sexy, but Brad staring at them just made me feel gross?

Because Brad is gross? Because you've spent the last forty-five minutes listening to him drone on and on about his gaming prowess, and he hasn't asked a single question about you?

Okay, so yeah, Brad wasn't the one, but I wasn't expecting him to be, right? Tinder wasn't about dating. It was about scratching an itch.

You have Liam for that.

I cringed inwardly. I don't know why the fuck I thought having casual sex with other people would curb my desire to sleep with Liam. Going out with Brad was a mistake.

"I don't mind that you don't eat a lot," Brad said, chewing noisily. "It's why you got such a tight little body, right?"

"Right," I said.

"Your body is amazing, by the way," Brad said. "You've got great nipples. You like them sucked on, huh?"

My stomach dropped. "Excuse me?"

Brad grinned. "Don't be shy, Sophie. You weren't shy in that video."

As Brad wiped his mouth with the napkin, the blood drained from my face. "I liked watching you in that video, sweetheart. What do you say we finish up here and go back to your place? My dick's a hell of a lot bigger than that dude in the porno. I guarantee you I can make you scream."

I grabbed some cash from my purse and threw it on the table before standing. "No, thanks."

Brad stood, grabbing my arm when I started to walk past him. "Hey, where are you going?"

"Date's over," I said. "Don't text me again."

"Stuck up little bitch," Brad said as he dropped my arm. "You think you're too good for me?"

"I know I am." I walked away, keeping my back straight and my head high despite the embarrassment and the nausea swirling in my stomach. I kept my gaze on the door. I couldn't look at Liam unless I wanted to start crying.

I pushed through the door, sucking in a deep breath of warm air before walking to my car at the far end of the parking lot. I had barely gotten it unlocked before I heard Liam call my name. I had an intense urge to dive into my car and get the fuck out of there before Liam joined me.

Instead, I plastered a smile on my face and turned around as Liam jogged up to me. "Hello, Liam."

My expectation that he would ask if I was okay, maybe comfort me a little, died a messy death when he scowled at me. "What the hell, Sophie?"

"What?" I asked.

"What do you mean *what*? You were on a date with some guy."

"So," I said. "What's your point?"

He raked a hand through his hair, frustration turning his face bright red. "You think it's okay to cheat on me?"

"Cheat on you? Are you kidding me?" The sheer audacity of what he'd just said brought laughter bubbling out of my chest.

"You're with another man, Sophie!"

"We're friends with benefits only, Liam. Casual sex, nothing more. You made that clear," I said.

"We didn't talk about whether we'd date other people," Liam snapped.

"We didn't need to. Casual means we can date other people. I didn't realize we had to define every rule in the casual handbook."

"So, you're just gonna fuck me and date and fuck this Brad asshole?" Liam said.

"I'm not dating or fucking him," I said.

Relief crossed Liam's face. "So, we agree then. We won't see other people."

"No, I'm not agreeing to that," I said.

"You want to be with other people?" Hurt replaced the relief on Liam's face.

"No, what I want is to find my person. You've made it clear that's not you. Unless you've changed your mind and want to turn this friends with benefits into something more?" I asked.

My flicker of hope snuffed out when Liam swallowed hard and said, "I don't want more."

"Then stop telling me I can't date other people," I said.

"So, you're going to date other people while you're in my bed?" he said.

"Yes," I said. "I am."

Liam's face twisted. "Then I don't want to be friends with benefits anymore."

"Fine." My stomach flip-flopped like a fish on a line and the half a sandwich I ate tried to mutiny. "I'll see you at work tomorrow."

I unlocked my car and climbed in, refusing to look at Liam as I started the engine and drove out of the parking lot. I made it nearly three blocks before I had to pull over. My hands shook, and my face burned, and I could barely see through the hot tears that threatened to fall.

I put the car into park, buried my face in my hands, and sobbed.

CHAPTER 14

Liam

"Oh, Liam." Alina took one look at my face before pulling me into a hug. "Honey, what's wrong?"

"Nothing. Everything," I said.

"Come into the kitchen," Alina said. "Did you eat dinner?"

"I'm not hungry." I followed my sister into the kitchen. She limped severely, and I pushed away my self-pity. "How much does your leg hurt tonight?"

"It's okay," she said. "Sit down, and I'll make you some tea."

"No, you sit down, and I'll make the tea," I said.

I ignored Alina's protests and pulled out a chair, making her sit down before grabbing a pillow from the couch and dragging a second chair close. I placed the pillow on the chair and propped Alina's foot on it. Her ankle and foot were swollen, and I grabbed an ice pack from the freezer and placed it on her ankle.

"It's really swollen, Alina. Maybe you should make an appointment with Dr. Scholar."

"It's fine," she said. "I biked over to the Walmart and back today. It's why it's so swollen."

"Alina," I scowled at her as I popped a tea pod in the machine. "How often have Finn and I told you that that's too far for you to bike. Let us know what you need, and we'll pick it up, or you can use their delivery service."

"They charge extra for delivery," Alina said. "It's not worth it."

"Your health is worth it," I told her as I set the mug of tea in front of her and popped a second pod into the machine. "Besides, you know Finn and I are happy to drive over there for you."

"Finn doesn't have a car right now." Alina sipped at her tea.

"Fuck, his mood is something else. He made someone cry at work this morning," I said.

Alina made a disapproving sound. "I hope he apologized."

"When does Finn ever apologize?" I sat in the chair beside her.

We sipped our tea silently for a minute or so before Alina reached out and took my hand. "Not that I don't love an unexpected Tuesday night visit but tell me what's wrong."

I stared into my tea, my hand tightening on Alina's. "Do you remember that girl Sophie? She bought one of your embroideries."

"I remember." Alina squeezed my hand. "The co-worker you like."

My stomach threatened to heave up the tiny sips of tea I'd drank. "I do like her. I like her a lot, and I fucked things up with her so bad, Alina. She hasn't been to work in two days, and I'm terrified that she's never coming back. That I'll never see her again."

She squeezed my hand again until I looked at her. "Tell me what happened, honey."

"WELL?" I ASKED WHEN ALINA REMAINED QUIET. "I completely fucked up, didn't I?"

Alina drank the last of her tea. She'd listened carefully for the last twenty minutes, and unlike Finn, who was always quick to tell me exactly what he thought I should do, Alina was a little more thoughtful in her approach.

"Just tell me the truth," I said.

She sighed. "You fucked up, honey."

I groaned and pushed my tea mug away. "Fuck, I know I did. I lost my mind when I saw Sophie with that guy. She'd been so standoffish on Friday, not staying the night and acting like she was too busy to see me again on the weekend. It messed with my head. I don't know. I just thought maybe we were...."

"Dating?" Alina said.

"No," I said, "not dating. I told you that. Friends with benefits."

"Right. You want to sleep with her but not date her," Alina said.

I winced. "Can you make me sound any more of an asshole, Alina?"

"You told me to tell you the truth," Alina said. "Right?"

"Yeah."

"You're being an asshole. Obviously, you want more from

her, but you refuse to give *her* more. Instead, you made her think the only way she could be with you was by following your rules. Which, by the way, are not the rules of a friends with benefits relationship. You asked her to follow dating rules, even though you refuse to date her. Then, when she refused to agree to them, you threw a temper tantrum and ended it."

"Christ," I said, "you've been spending too much time with Finn. You're supposed to be the nice sibling, Alina."

"Honey, I love you, but honestly, I am so damn mad at you right now."

"Why?" I asked. "Look, I get that I screwed up, but you don't understand that -"

"I understand we only have a limited amount of time to be with the ones we love, and you're being an asshole who's fucking wasting that time we're given."

I blinked, shocked into silence by the anger in Alina's voice. She rarely got angry, barely cursed, and never raised her voice to Finn or me.

"You love this girl, right?" Alina said.

"Well, love is a strong -"

"Liam!"

"Yes, I love her. Okay? I love her," I said. "But I loved Dayton too, and look what happened with him. I'm a laughing stock of a boss because of my relationship with Dayton."

"So what?" Alina said. "What do you care what your employees think of you? At the end of the day, does it matter what they think of you?"

"It matters a little bit," I said.

"More than what I think of you? Or Finn and Nicky? Or what Sophie thinks of you?" she asked.

"No," I said.

Alina leaned forward, taking my hand in hers. "Life is short, Liam. It is fleeting and precious, and all that matters is being with the people you love. Spending time with me, Finn, Nicky, and Sophie is what matters. Don't be like me. Don't throw away your chance at happiness because you're afraid."

"Alina, you're not afraid. You're strong and -"

She shook her head, squeezing my hand until I shut my mouth. "This isn't about me, Liam. This is about you. Be brave, honey. Tell Sophie how you feel before it's too late."

"I think it already is," I said.

"You don't know that."

I sighed and ran my hand over the two-day growth of my beard. "I do. Before I left work tonight, I got an email from Dr. Crayton. Sophie asked for a transfer to his lab project. If I approve the transfer, I won't see Sophie again."

"You'll still work at the same company," Alina said. "Maybe this is a good thing. It'll be easier to date if she's not working directly with you, right?"

"Yes, but this research we're doing means a lot to Sophie. She has an aunt with epilepsy. Besides, she's asking for the transfer because she hates my guts now."

"Or she doesn't want to be around the man she loves day in and day out without knowing he loves her back," Alina said. "Liam, tell her how you feel."

"I don't know if I can," I said.

Alina sat back with disappointment on her face. "Then I guess you'll lose her."

Sophie

I STORMED INTO THE LAB, NOT CARING ABOUT THE STARTLED looks that Jody and the four lab techs gave me. I grabbed the paper out of my laptop bag, dropped my bag on the counter, and stalked to Liam's office, not bothering to knock as I wrenched open his door and stepped into his office.

I slammed the door shut behind me, glaring at Liam when he looked up from his computer. "What the fuck, Liam?"

"Hi, Sophie." Liam stood up behind his desk. "Welcome back. Are you feeling better?"

"Don't give me that bullshit," I said. "You know I wasn't sick. I just needed some time off from seeing you."

Telling my boss I'd faked two sick days was a potentially career-ending move, but I didn't give one fuck. Not when Liam was actively trying to fuck me over.

I slapped the paper down on his desk. "Sign the transfer, Liam."

"Can we talk for a minute," he said.

"No. Dr. Clayton told me this morning that you refused to sign the transfer. I'm here to tell you that you're signing it or I'm quitting."

"Okay," Liam held up his hands, "I know you're upset with me, and you have every right to be. How I acted on Sunday was fucked up, and I want to apologize for -"

"Stop it," I said. "You made it clear that you don't want to be involved with me in any capacity outside of a boss employee relationship. So, stop bringing up shit that doesn't involve the lab or this damn transfer. I don't want to work for you anymore, Liam. I don't want to see you, I don't want to talk to you, and if that means I have to give up on my dream project, then so fucking be it."

My voice caught on the last word, and I berated myself in my head.

I wouldn't show any weakness around him.

I wouldn't show him how much he hurt me when he so easily walked away.

I wouldn't show him how much I still loved him.

"Sophie, I'm so sorry," Liam said.

I pushed the paper toward him. "I'll give you half an hour to sign this. If you don't, I'll hand in my resignation. I mean it, Liam."

I turned and stalked toward his office door, my hand freezing on the door handle when Liam said, "I love you, Sophie."

Joy and sorrow and surprise jumbled up inside of me. I turned around, the look on Liam's face casting aside any doubt that he didn't love me. I could see it in his face.

But I kept the barriers up that I'd built around my heart. "That's great, Liam. Really great. Because you know - *you fucking know* - that I love you too. But what good does that do us? I don't want to hide my love for you. I can't. So just sign the damn transfer, and we can stay out of each other's lives."

I walked out of his office, shutting the door behind me. I headed toward the counter as Jody said tentatively, "Sophie, are you okay?"

"Yeah," I said. "I need a minute."

I heard Liam's office door open. The temptation to run out of the lab was almost overbearing. As much as I wanted the transfer, the thought of not seeing Liam every day made me -

"I love you, Sophie."

I froze with my hand in my laptop bag, staring at Jody as she turned to stare at Liam.

"Sorry, what was that, Liam?" Jody said.

"I love Sophie," Liam said. "I am in love with her. I want

to date her. I want to marry her eventually, and I want her to have my children. I can't live without her."

"Um," Jody looked at the lab techs, a smile crossing her face. "Okay. Congratulations? Does Sophie know you're in love with her and planning your wedding?"

I turned to face Liam, my cheeks red and my hands shaking. "What are you doing, Liam?"

"I love you, and I want everyone in the lab to know. Hell, I want everyone in the fucking building to know," Liam said.

"You want me to send out a company email?" Byron, one of the lab techs, said. "I can do that."

Jody laughed. "Shut it, Byron, you're ruining the moment."

Byron made a zipping motion across his lips as Jody said, "Go on, Liam."

Liam walked up to me and took my hand. "I love you, Sophie. I don't want to hide that. I don't want to pretend that you're not the most important person in the world to me because you are. You matter to me, and I want everyone to know that in the lab and elsewhere. Please, will you forgive me for being such an asshole?"

I swallowed hard. "Yes."

Liam pulled me into his embrace and kissed me. When he ended the kiss, I said, "You kissed me. In front of everyone."

"I did," he said. "Because I fucking love you."

"I love you too," I said.

"Thank God." He rested his forehead on mine. "Please don't transfer, Sophie. I know how important this project is to you. I promise my personal feelings won't interfere with either of our jobs. After today, I'll be completely professional here in the lab."

I grinned and pulled him closer to whisper, "That's a

shame because I'm already picturing being fucked on top of your desk after hours, Dr. Whitby."

Liam laughed and kissed me again. "Whatever you want, Dr. Clark."

Keep reading for "The Biologist", Book Two in the Sexy Scientists Series.

THE BIOLOGIST

VOLUME TWO

THE BIOLOGIST

He can unzip my genes.

Hattie

I had the picture-perfect life. A hit TV show, a healthy bank account, and celebrity friends. But the perfect life was a perfect lie. Now I'm determined to stop pretending and take what I want.

And what I want is local biologist, Finn Whitby.

His quiet confidence and natural bossiness bring out a secret side of me I've always ignored. As it turns out, Finn can give me exactly what I need in bed, and I'm determined to prove we belong together.

Finn

Relationships are messy, complicated, and filled with half-truths and lies. I'm content with casual hookups.

Until Hattie King shows up in the last place I expected.

As a biologist, I know how hard it is to suppress your nature. I've spent months quelling my attraction to her. She's too young and innocent for someone like me. Then again, I'm the perfect man to give her what she craves.

Now, I'm fighting my instincts to claim her. We're not meant to be forever. So, why am I envisioning a life with us together?

CHAPTER 1

Hattie

"Hattie?" My co-worker, Samesh, tapped me on the shoulder.

"Yeah?" I eased out from under the hood of the Toyota Camry I was working on. I glanced at the clock on the wall. It was almost five. Ten more minutes and I could go home and soak in a hot bath.

Samesh gave me a weird look. "You need to go out into the lobby."

"What? Why?"

"Just do it," Samesh said before walking away.

Frowning, I wiped the grease off my hands and walked past the two bays and down the hallway toward the lobby's back door. My boss, Sung-Ho, was in his office, but he was on the phone and didn't look up as I passed by.

What was going on? If it'd been any co-worker but Samesh, I'd say I was being pranked, but Samesh didn't mess around at work. I opened the door and stepped into the lobby, the noise from the shop's industrial fans muting to a distant hum when the door closed behind me. I walked down the hallway and past the bathrooms, my jaw clenching as soon as I heard Craig's voice.

God, I hated that guy.

Most of the mechanics who worked here hated him. He wasn't a team player, he never shut up, and he had an off-the-charts arrogance level. It was fortunate for him that he was one of the best mechanics in the shop. Otherwise, I'm certain Sung-Ho would have fired his ass years ago.

I stepped into the reception area, glancing at our receptionist, Monica. She rolled her eyes and made a wanking motion when she caught my eye. I grinned before turning my gaze to Craig and the man he was … oh holy shit.

Craig was talking to Finn Whitby.

The man who had a starring role in all of my fantasies.

Him and his car.

I flushed, but it's not like my inner voice was wrong. Finn's lean, muscled body, blue eyes, and dark hair with threads of silver through it were more than enough to get me all worked up. Add in his imposing and bossy nature and a 1957 apple red Chevy Bel Air, and I was a fucking goner.

For some reason, Finn looked even grumpier than he usually did, and I wasn't sure what this said about me, but I just found him even hotter because of it. Of course, I'd only really seen him up close once, so maybe he always looked this grumpy.

I might have had a massive crush on Finn, but it wasn't like I had much chance to indulge in it. We didn't exactly run in the same social circles. Even though Finn's brother was dating my best friend, my selfish hope that it meant I saw Finn more often hadn't panned out yet.

Finn was a brilliant biologist working at Optimum Pharmaceuticals, and I was a mechanic. And while we did good work and Sung-Ho prided himself on our honesty with customers, Quick Start Mechanic wasn't exactly a shop a man like Finn would bring his car to.

Speaking of which… why was Finn here?

I stopped focusing on Finn's lips and concentrated on what Craig was saying to him. The conversation immediately pissed me off.

"Look, Mr. Whitby, you can get Hattie to take a look at your car, you can even let her tinker a bit under the hood, but I guarantee you that she'll come to me for help anyway. A car like yours needs a good mechanic, and I hate speaking ill of my co-workers, but that's not Hattie. What woman is, you know? We both know that girls aren't meant for this line of work. Sure, we all love Hattie, but it has less to do with her abilities and more to do with how she fills out a pair of coveralls," Craig said before laughing.

I'd never actually thought it was possible for a person to 'see red' before, but damn if the world had suddenly taken on a distinct red tinge. I would fucking kill Craig for what he'd said.

"She's a nice girl, okay," Craig said, "but she's not experienced enough or smart enough to handle your car. I'm sure the person who recommended her to you meant well, but if you want your car fixed properly, you need to let me look at it."

That motherfucker. He knew the Chevy Bel Air was my dream car and knew that the chance of me ever seeing one up close, let alone working on one, was slim to none. I took a few steps forward, ready to punch Craig in the balls, despite it meaning losing my chance to work on my dream car and my job, but Finn's deep voice stopped me in my tracks.

"Tell me, Mister…?"

"Henson. Craig Henson." Craig held out his hand. Finn stared at it until Craig dropped it back to his side.

"Tell me, Mr. Henson, do you always talk shit about your co-workers?" Finn asked.

Craig cleared his throat. "I just want what's best for your car, Mr. Whitby."

"No, you want me to believe that Hattie King is bad at her job because you're an arrogant prick trying to overcompensate for his, most assuredly, small dick."

Monica's gasp of surprise rivaled my own.

Craig's mouth worked, but nothing came out. I'd never seen him speechless before.

Finn looked him up and down, the disdain practically radiating from him in thick waves. "Men like you are a dime a dozen, Mr. Henson. You make yourself big by making others small, and I'd rather set my car on fire before letting a man like you touch it. Now, get out of my face before I get you fired."

Craig's face went bright red, and his hands clenched into fists. He turned and walked past me, his face turning nearly purple when I grinned at him and said, "See you later, Craig," in my sweetest 'fuck you' voice.

He stomped down the hallway toward the shop, and I wiped my sweaty hands on my coveralls as I approached Finn. Already my knees shook, and the butterflies were starting up in my stomach. Just being close to Finn Whitby did weird things to me.

"Hello again," I said.

"Ms. King." Finn held out his hand, and I shook it, trying not to moan out loud at the feel of his hard hand. "Sophie Clark recommended I speak with you about my car. Is this a good time to talk?"

Oh my God, I was full-on kissing my best friend the next time I saw her. *With* tongue.

"It is," I said. "Why don't you show me your car first, and then we'll chat."

That wasn't routine, but, honestly, I wasn't sure what I wanted to see up close more - Finn's naked body or his car.

Finn nodded and stepped back, allowing me to walk in front of him. I would have hoped he was studying my ass if I hadn't been wearing my shapeless coveralls. When we reached the lobby's front door, Finn reached out from behind me and pushed open the door. His chest brushed against my shoulder, and it took everything in me not to drop the coveralls and invite Finn to fuck me right there in the parking lot. Preferably against his car.

Girl, keep it together.

Right. Keep it the fuck together.

The sight of Finn's car drove the naughty thoughts right out of my head anyway. Trying not to show my excitement, I pulled a clean rag out of my pocket and wiped my hands again before gliding my fingers along the driver's door.

"Did you restore this yourself?" I asked.

Finn shook his head. "I bought it restored."

"Is it a Blue Flame inline-six engine?"

"Super Turbo Fire V8," Finn said.

I blew out my breath. "Sweet. They offered the V8 in the '57 models, but I know there aren't many restored ones that have them."

I walked around the car. That candy apple red paint gleamed in the sun without a single scratch or dent to mar the colour. I studied the chrome strip that ran from the headlights back to the rear quarters before opening up into large chrome wings. "I know it's considered a bit gaudy by today's standards, but I love the chrome. I saw a restored one online that didn't do the chrome, and it just wasn't the same, you know?"

Finn nodded but didn't say anything.

I opened the passenger door and studied the interior. The tan leather had custom stitching, and the three-spoke steering wheel had matching tan leather covering it. The power window switches had chrome window surrounds. The dashboard was painted the same candy apple red, and - my heart actually skipped a fucking beat - there was an original style radio in the center stack.

I studied the back seats, a little surprised by how roomy it was, before ducking out of the car. My urge to sit in it was overwhelming, but no way would I risk transferring even a hint of grease or oil from my coveralls onto the leather.

I closed the door and ran my fingers along the chrome strip one last time before turning to face Finn. "This is a beautiful car."

"Thank you, Ms. King."

"Call me Hattie."

"Your friend Sophie tells me that you've worked on old cars before, as she calls them." A faint smile crossed Finn's face, and fresh liquid soaked my panties. I'd never seen him smile before.

"I haven't worked directly with the Bel Air, but I have worked on quite a few classic cars," I said. "Sung-Ho, the shop owner, knows I have a special interest in them, so if we get the classics, he usually assigns them to me. I'm currently restoring a 1956 Lincoln Continental Mark II."

"Is that right?" Finn said.

"Yes. The 1957 Chevy Bel Air is my dream car, and I've been shopping around for one to restore, but I can't find one in my price range. But the Lincoln is giving me lots of practice for when I finally get the Bel Air."

I sounded like an eager little kid, and I reined it in. Finn was at least fifteen years older than me, probably more, and if I wanted any chance of dating him, I needed to sound confident and mature.

I cleared my throat. "So, what issues are you having with the car?"

"She won't idle," Finn said. "Stalls out on me. The first mechanic said it was a clogged EGR valve. When that didn't fix it, he said it was a bad spark plug. When she still stalled, he said I needed a new fuel pump."

"You replaced the fuel pump?" I asked.

He nodded. "When she continued to stall, I took her to a second mechanic."

"What did they say?"

"It became apparent rather quickly that he was bullshitting about being a classic car expert," Finn said with a scowl. "I didn't let him touch Gretchen."

"Gretchen?" I grinned at Finn. "You named your car Gretchen?"

"Yes," Finn said without even a hint of embarrassment. "What do you say, Ms. King? Are you willing to take a look at her?"

"Absolutely," I said. "Tomorrow is booked, but I have some openings on Saturday. If you leave her with me, I can look at her then."

Finn studied our parking lot. "I prefer that Gretchen be in the garage overnight. Will that be a problem?"

"Not at all, "I said. "I'll make sure she's in the garage before we close for the day."

"Good," Finn said.

"If you follow me back to the shop, I'll have you fill out some paperwork," I said.

Ten minutes later, the paperwork was completed, and we

were back outside. An Uber idled in front of the shop, and Finn handed me his car keys. Keeping the excited grin off my face, I said, "I'll call you as soon as I've taken a look at her."

"Thank you."

He walked away, and I said, "Finn?"

Hattie? What are you doing?

He turned to face me, and I said, "Would you like to have dinner with me this weekend?"

Abort! Abort! What the actual fuck, Hattie?

The look on Finn's face made me want to die. It was part surprise and part - fuck me, I was such an idiot - horror.

I clenched the keys in my fist and kept the pleasant smile on my face by sheer willpower alone as Finn cleared his throat and said, "No."

My face turned bright red, and I nodded. "Right, okay, well, um, I'll call you then."

He didn't say anything, and my face only seconds away from bursting into flame, I said, "About the car. I'll call you about the car. Not for a date or anything. I'm not going to start stalking you or something. I just thought dinner might be good, but, yeah, no, I…."

Please stop talking, Hattie. Please?

I closed my mouth and made a sort of half-smile, half-grimace in Finn's direction. After a few seconds, he said, "Talk to you soon, Ms. King."

"Bye, Mr. Whitby, uh, I mean Dr. Whitby. You're a doctor, right? Sophie said you had a Ph.D. in biology. So, uh, that makes you a doctor."

Hattie! Shut the fuck up. I am begging you.

I shut the fuck up, silently watching as Finn turned and walked away, climbing into the Uber. Keeping that smile plastered to my face, I made a stupid wave as the Uber drove away, then slumped against the side of the shop when the car turned the corner and disappeared.

Oh my God. Could that have gone any worse?

CHAPTER 2

Finn

"What is going on with you tonight?" My best friend Gabe leaned back in his chair and sipped at his beer.

"Nothing." I pushed my plate away. I'd been looking forward to having dinner with Gabe, but I'd lost my appetite after seeing the look on Hattie's face when I'd rejected her date request.

"Bullshit," Gabe said. "Tell me what's wrong."

"I'm still having issues with Gretchen."

"That car, man. She's a beauty but a real troublemaker," Gabe said with a grin.

"Yeah, I know. I took her to a new mechanic today."

"Oh yeah? Was he competent?"

"She," I said, "and I don't know yet. She'll look at Gretchen on Saturday and get back to me."

Gabe studied me for a moment. "What's the mechanic's name, and how bad do you want to fuck her?"

"What's that supposed to mean?" I cleared my throat and took a drink of beer.

"You have that look on your face."

"What look?"

"The same one you get at the club when you see a particularly tasty sub."

"The mechanic isn't a sub," I said.

"You have no way of knowing that," Gabe said. "You don't have magical Dom powers that tell you if a woman is a sub just by looking at her."

"I talked to her," I said.

"About your car," Gabe said.

I sighed and picked at the beer bottle label. "The mechanic is Hattie King."

"Hattie King… why is that name familiar?"

"She used to be in that sitcom called -"

"What About Julie!" Gabe said with a grin. "She played the mom, right? She's gorgeous."

"She played Julie," I said.

He blinked at me. "The kid?"

"She was a teenager then, yes."

"How old is she now?"

"Twenty-five," I said. I knew way too much about Hattie King, thanks to some late night Googling.

"You've played with subs in their twenties at the club," Gabe said.

"She's not a sub," I said.

"Look, I know you were burned by dating a younger woman before, but -"

"Gabe, don't," I said. "Not tonight."

Gabe's look was exasperation mixed with sympathy. "You deserve to be happy, Finn."

"I do. But a former actress with a reputation for being a spoiled little princess is not the key to my happiness."

"She's a mechanic," Gabe said. "They don't come across as the spoiled princess type."

"How many mechanics do you know?" I asked.

"Fair point. So, why isn't she acting anymore, and why does she live in this backwater little town?"

"Just because you couldn't imagine living in a small town doesn't mean other people hate it," I said.

"True. So, why did she move here?"

"She's from here," I said.

"Yeah, but that doesn't mean she has to live here again. Why not live in Havenport? It's not exactly a bustling metropolis like LA, but it's a mid-sized city with stores open past six pm on a Sunday night."

"I think she's trying to avoid attention," I said.

"Why? Wait…" Gabe gave me a thoughtful look. "Is she the actress who quit at the height of her career? She was supposed to do a film with Spielberg, right?"

"That's right," I said. "The sitcom had one more season of filming, and then she was moving on to film work. The rumours were that she'd met with Spielberg, and it was pretty much a given that she'd be working with him, but before they could sign the paperwork, she quit the sitcom and left Hollywood."

"Anyone know why?"

I shook my head. "No. She hasn't given a single interview since she walked away. Her mother was her manager and is now somewhat of a D celebrity. She's on some reality show right now about finding love."

"So, Hattie left a successful career in Hollywood to become a mechanic in Willowdale?" Gabe said.

"I guess so."

"That's fucked up," Gabe said. "But this doesn't explain how you know she isn't a sub."

"She partied a lot, had a reputation for being difficult and combative on set and off," I said. "She doesn't like being told what to do. You remember who Sophie is?"

Gabe nodded. "Yeah, Liam's new girlfriend."

"Hattie is Sophie's best friend. Last summer, Sophie brought Hattie to a company barbecue, and I met her then. I only talked to her for a few minutes, but my initial instinct was that she was a sub. Until I Googled her and found out more about her."

"You like this girl," Gabe announced.

"No, I don't," I said.

"Oh yeah, since when did you start Googling women?" Gabe asked.

"I Googled Hattie after Sophie recommended I take Gretchen to her."

I didn't lie to Gabe ever, but Gabe knowing just how obsessed I was with Hattie, wouldn't help the situation. He didn't need to know that I had been actively looking for any and all information on Hattie since the day I met her.

"Just because she's combative doesn't mean she isn't a sub," Gabe said. "Hell, I had a subbie last week at the club who gave me a shitload of attitude. It wasn't until I had a collar on her and spanked her that she gave me her submission. Some subs like to push the limit. You know that."

I did know that, and while I'd repeatedly told myself that Hattie wasn't submissive, I knew for a fucking fact that it was complete bullshit. Like Gabe, I wasn't one for believing that a man could look at a woman and tell right away if they were submissive. Doms who boasted they could were assholes on a power trip as far as I was concerned.

But I knew in my damn soul that Hattie was submissive.

The way she'd looked at me at the barbecue… there'd been an immediate connection between us. I'd felt the pull as strongly as she had, and there was no doubt in my mind that she knew I was a Dom.

It was why she'd asked me out today, despite our obvious age difference.

She would never know how fucking difficult it'd been for me to say no.

"So, are you in such a miserable mood because you want to fuck this Hattie, and she's not into you?" Gabe asked with his usual bluntness.

I should have lied again to him, but our history, or maybe it was just my damn ego, wouldn't let me. "She's into me. She asked me to have dinner with her this weekend. I said no."

"Are you not dating her because you're afraid she'll tell Liam about the club?" Gabe asked.

"I'm not dating her because she's twenty years younger than me, and she's not into the same kink that I am," I said.

"You think she isn't," Gabe corrected. "But would you worry about her spilling the beans to Liam?"

"Maybe a little," I said.

"You know this isn't something you need to hide, right? Liam and Alina love you, and neither of them would judge you for -"

"They don't need to know," I said, my voice sharp and irritated. "My private business is my own, Gabriel."

"All right," Gabe said, keeping his tone mild.

I took a deep breath. "It's been a long day and an even longer week."

That would be the closest I'd get to apologizing, but after years of friendship, Gabe wouldn't take it personally.

"You still going to the club tomorrow night?" Gabe asked.

"Yes, I'll be there." Despite how tired and out of sorts I was, I needed to go to the club. Needed the release only it could give me.

"You need me to pick you up, or will you Uber in and stay at my place for the night?"

"No, I finally gave in and pulled the Benz out of storage. Who the fuck knows when Gretchen will be running again."

"Okay." Gabe checked his watch. "Listen, I hate to cut this short, but it's getting late, and I have early morning surgery to add some fake balls to a Mastiff."

"What?" I asked.

"You heard me," he said. "We convinced the asshole owner to neuter the dog, but he needs fake balls put in his dog's sack, so his toxic masculinity isn't offended by his dog's lack of testicles."

"Fucking hell," I said.

"Tell me about it. I'm so glad I became a veterinarian to help other dudes feel better about their small dicks," Gabe said. "Christ, Friday night at the club can't come fast enough."

I laughed. "For you and me both, Gabe. You and me both."

Hattie

I FIGURED I HAD MAYBE ANOTHER HALF HOUR BEFORE THE music at the Sapphire club gave me a pounding headache or left me with permanent hearing loss. Holding my drink, I pushed through the crowd of people to the far end of the club, where the music at least felt like it was a little quieter.

I sipped at my club soda, adjusted my skin-tight dress, and tried to look like I was someone who wanted to be asked to join the sex club directly under her feet.

So far, it hadn't worked, and I'd been here for almost three hours. Maybe it was time to call it a night.

Yes, it is. What do you think Sophie would do to you if she knew you came here alone?

I didn't have to think. I knew exactly what she'd do. Straight up murder me.

But while Sophie had volunteered to come to Sapphire with me, that was before she started dating Liam. I could hardly ask her to go to a club now where she'd be spanked and fucked by a stranger.

Or more. Flogged, maybe. Hands tied behind your back, maybe a collar around your neck, or a spreader bar to keep your legs wide open while you're being fucked.

Lust hit my nerve endings, making them light up with what felt like an audible zing. A few months ago, I'd stopped feeling embarrassed or ashamed of what I wanted in bed and started actively looking for ways to fulfill it.

I tried to pretend I didn't know the catalyst for it, but that was a huge lie. It'd been that damn day at Sophie's company barbecue when I'd stood behind Finn Whitby in a lineup for potato salad and soda, and he'd looked at me.

Which sounded stupid when I thought back on it, but he'd looked at me, and I'd looked at him, and for thirty seconds, nothing else existed. Just me and Finn and the intuitive knowledge that he wanted to spank me, and I wanted to let him.

It had made me feel powerful, made me feel sexy, made me feel alive in a way I hadn't for an incredibly long time. I'd gone home that evening and masturbated my way to three insanely good orgasms just by thinking about Finn and his thirty-second look.

It gave me the courage to start looking online, to seek out more information about what I wanted and needed in bed, and it was because of Finn and his look that I'd stumbled onto the Sapphire club. On the outside, it was just one of many nightclubs in Havenport. Not one of the most popular clubs, but in a good part of town with a variety of people partying. But for the people in the know, for people like me who frequented BDSM groups and forums online, we knew what was below the club. A second, smaller club, meant for people like us... dominants and submissives.

The Sapphire club wasn't the only BDSM sex club in Havenport. Hell, it wasn't even the only secret one. But it did have the best reputation for sexy and reputable Doms, and they were welcoming to the LGBTQ community. I liked the idea of a club that didn't discriminate based on antiquated views on sex and gender.

I took another sip of my drink and ignored the way my feet ached. These stilettos weren't meant for standing or walking for hours. They were meant to be worn while your feet were in the air and you were being pounded by a hard cock.

Finn's hard cock?

Goosebumps erupted on my skin despite the club's heat, and I made the abrupt decision to go home. Being soundly rejected by Finn yesterday drove my decision to come to the Sapphire tonight. I needed to give up on my silly Finn fantasy and find someone else to give me what I wanted. But I was tired and a little depressed by my failure to be noticed by the people who counted.

The surety that I would be picked out of the crowd and

invited downstairs fairly quickly had been nicely shattered. I'd assumed my looks, maybe even the fact that I was once considered a celebrity, might have worked in my favour.

Which was ironic because I'd spent most of the last seven years trying desperately not to be noticed.

I made my way toward the closest exit, trying not to wince with every step. I wanted to get these stupid shoes off, have a hot bath, and maybe some time spent with my vibrator.

Why? So you can fantasize about Finn some more?

Nope, I'd find some spanking videos on Porn Central with guys that looked nothing like Finn and get off to that instead. My fantasizing days about Finn Whitby were finished.

"Excuse me." A tiny woman with long dark hair tapped me on the arm. She wore a dress as tight and short as mine with a discreet Sapphire Staff tag pinned just above her left breast. "My name is Cynthia. I work for the club. I'd like to extend an invitation to you to join us in the VIP section of our club."

My heart climbed into my throat, and I stared dumbly at her for a moment. Was this actually happening?

"Miss?" The woman prompted with a smile.

"Oh, um, yes. Yes, thank you. I'd like that very much."

"Excellent. Please follow me."

I followed the woman toward a narrow hallway near the exit door. My feet throbbed as I hurried to keep up with her brisk pace. She turned down another hallway that branched off from the original, and I breathed a sigh of relief as the music dulled to a faint hum.

Cynthia stopped in front of a door and smiled at me. "What's your name?"

"Oh, I'm Hattie," I said.

Cynthia knocked briskly on the door. At the muffled 'come in', she opened it and ushered me into the room. It was a small office with a bookcase, a desk, and an elegant looking Black woman sitting behind the desk. Behind her on the wall were two rows of screens, and each screen showed a different section of the club.

"Ms. Mordell, this is Hattie."

"Hello, Hattie, I'm Sylvia. It's nice to meet you. Please sit down."

I sat in the chair she pointed to, my relief at being off my aching feet outshining the slight touch of weirdness I felt.

"Thank you, Cynthia," Sylvia said.

Cynthia left the office, closing the door behind her. Sylvia sipped at a glass of wine. "Would you care for a drink, Hattie?"

"No, thank you," I said.

Sylvia tilted her head at me. "You're not much of a drinker, are you? Neither my people nor I have seen you drink anything stronger than club soda this evening."

"No," I said shortly. I wasn't explaining why I didn't drink with a woman I didn't know. "I don't mean to be rude, but Cynthia told me I was invited to the VIP section of the club."

"You are," Sylvia said. "I manage the VIP section, and before we allow our customers to become VIP members, we like to do an interview of sorts. To ensure that you're... the right fit."

"Because it's a BDSM club," I said.

Sylvia's smile widened. "Yes. I see you've heard of our club downstairs."

"I have," I said.

"Good. It makes it easier," she said. "I'll give you a brief explanation of the club, and you can choose whether you'd like to tour the club this evening and consider becoming a VIP member. If you decide yes, there will be some paperwork to fill out, and then we'll take you downstairs. How does that sound?"

My stomach churning with nerves, I took a deep breath and said, "That sounds good."

CHAPTER 3

Hattie

E*verything's cool, Hattie. Just be cool. There's nothing to freak out about. You are not freaking out.*

I was freaking out.

And not in a cool way.

I sipped at my club soda and then bit at my nails for a few seconds before making myself stop. Biting my nails was my worst habit but one I couldn't seem to quit, even when I had chewed them ragged like they were now. I tapped my fingers against the gleaming mahogany bar to keep them from my mouth before tugging at my dress. Sitting down had made it ride dangerously high, but after walking twice around the central area of the VIP club, my feet couldn't take the stilettos anymore.

At least that's the excuse I told myself for why I sat on a barstool instead of mingling or watching the live show currently playing out on the small stage on the far side of the room.

It most definitely wasn't because I was freaking out, or

completely overwhelmed, or thinking I maybe made a teensy, tiny, infinitesimal mistake in coming to the club.

The moans from the woman being flogged on the stage grew louder, but I kept my gaze on my drink. In the porn videos with flogging, I'd always gotten a little turned on by it. The sound of the flogger, the person's moans, and how they always came like a damn fire hydrant at the end was sexy as hell.

But seeing it up close and in person... I swallowed hard. It was a whole different experience. The redness of her skin, the real pain etched into her face, and the way her body jerked and twitched with every strike... it became much less sexy.

Of course, as the woman's moans turned into undeniable shrieks of pleasure and there was a smattering of applause from the crowd, it was obvious that it wasn't just pain the woman felt. Back in my safe, warm bed, the video playing on a loop while I used a vibrator to bring myself to orgasm, I'd been confident I would enjoy that type of play too. Yet here I was... freaking the fuck out at my first in-person sighting of an actual flogging.

Take some deep breaths, Hattie. You've never even been spanked beyond a couple of butt slaps from previous boyfriends. I think you'll want to work up to flogging. And if you don't like it, so what? Just because your kink is impact play doesn't mean you want to try every kind of impact play.

My inner voice was right, but I was still on the verge of just walking out of the club. The non-disclosure agreement and the paperwork absolving the club and its members of any wrongdoing if I happened to be hurt had sent the first tendrils of unease into my belly. Which was stupid because I'd known from my online groups that these documents were required to enter the club. But it had made it so much more real to me.

Or maybe it became real when I'd walked into the underground club and been immediately greeted by a man in a collar being walked around the club by a leather-clad woman holding a leash connected to his collar. That alone had been enough to make me stare in wide-eyed wonderment, but the weird leather and steel contraption he had on his dick had completely thrown me for a loop.

I'd stared like an idiot as they walked by me, my gaze glued to the steel cage his dick was in, a small gold lock at the top of the cage. Nothing I'd Googled had prepared me for that.

Nor was I prepared for all the casual nudity. I was one of the few submissives fully clothed, and despite how short and revealing my dress was, I felt weird and self-conscious. Maybe I needed to go to the ladies' room and ditch the bra. Maybe that would help me feel better. Maybe that would encourage someone to talk to me.

I'd once again arrogantly assumed I'd be popular in the sex club. While I hadn't put much thought into my appearance since I'd quit acting, I did know I was considered beautiful by society's stupid standards. It was one of the reasons my mother had forced me into acting, despite my introverted nature and lack of desire to be an actress.

My looks and body had always garnered plenty of attention, and I'd assumed it would be no different here at Sapphire's. After over an hour in the VIP section, I'd quickly discovered how wrong I was.

A bald man in skin-tight leather pants and his naked upper body covered in tattoos sat down on a barstool at the far end, resting a fabric pouch on the bar. A curvy blonde woman immediately kneeled at his feet with her back arched, her thighs spread wide, and her hands resting palms up on her thighs. A cat ears headband held her hair back from her face, and she wore a pair of panties and elaborate looking nipple clamps and nothing else.

Well, almost nothing else.

I stared at the long fluffy tail poking out from the hole cut into the ass of her panties. The tail must have been attached to her underwear somehow, but I couldn't figure out how for the life of me. As I watched them, the man took a sip of the drink the bartender placed in front of him before reaching down and petting the woman's long hair. She smiled up at him, and he reached into the pouch, produced a small tan-coloured chunk of food and fed it to the woman.

"It's called pet play." A low voice spoke into my ear.

I turned my head and stared at the devastatingly attractive man standing next to me. He wore a dark grey Henley that clung to his flat stomach and a pair of jeans that highlighted muscular thighs. Silver threaded through his brown hair, and there were fine lines around his dark brown eyes. A closely trimmed beard with more silver in it covered his lower jaw, and he had full lips and a quiet confidence that immediately reminded me of Finn.

I took a deep breath, pushing Finn's face out of my head as quickly as it appeared. The guy was in his forties, he was about the same height as Finn, and he was obviously a Dom at the club… that's the only reason he reminded me of Finn.

"Pet play," I said. "Right."

He smiled and sat next to me on a stool, his thigh brushing against mine. "Do you know what pet play is?"

"Yes," I said. "She's pretending to be his, um, kitten."

"That's right." He took a sip from his drink.

The tattooed man fed her another piece of food from the pouch, and my hand stilled with my drink halfway to my mouth.

"What's wrong?" my new friend asked.

"Please tell me he isn't feeding her cat food."

The man's grin revealed even white teeth. "He is not. Mandy is plant based, so what Blaine's feeding her is a nut and seed concoction she bakes herself."

"Thank God," I said. "Can I ask you another question that's probably incredibly stupid?"

"You may," he said.

"How is the tail attached? Is it sewn into her panties, or is she wearing some kind of contraption under her panties?"

The man picked up my hand, examining my chewed and ragged nails before smiling again. "The tail is inserted anally."

"Inserted... oh! It's a butt plug," I said.

"It is," he said.

"So, he just shoves that up her butt and then they walk around the club together," I said.

His smile grew bigger, but it was a kind one and didn't make me feel stupid. "Blaine doesn't just 'shove it' up her butt, but yes, that's the general concept."

"Right," I repeated.

"So, this is your first time at the club," the man said.

"How can you tell? Is it all the clothes I'm wearing, or because I didn't know there are butt plugs with tails?"

His low chuckle sent warmth zinging across my body and made my pussy pulse pleasantly. Oh, this was good. This was very good. This was a man I could play with, and maybe not even picture Finn in my head while we played.

"There are several factors contributing to why you're easy to spot as a newbie," he said.

"Do, um, the Doms here not like newbies? Is that why no one's talking to me?"

"It's not that they don't like newbies," the man said, "but teaching and guiding a new submissive is a large responsibility and not one to be taken lightly. Many Doms don't have the desire or the knowledge to work with a new sub."

"Oh," I said.

"Why did you come to the Sapphire?" the man asked.

"I want to be spanked." I blushed immediately. "Sorry, was that too blunt?"

"No," he said. "I want submissives to be open and honest in their communication."

"So, you are a… a Dom, right?"

"I am," he said. "And you are a submissive."

"Yes. I mean, I think so. No, I am. I definitely am."

He reached out and tugged on a lock of my dark hair. "Have you been spanked before?"

"Yes. Well, no. Not really."

"Define not really," he said.

"I've been with a couple of guys who slapped my butt when I asked them to, but they didn't do it very hard, and you could tell it weirded them out when I requested it."

When he didn't reply, I said, "Have you spanked a woman before?"

Before he could answer, I said, "Oh God, that's a stupid question. Spanking is, like, the least kinky thing you could do here, right? Obviously, you've spanked a woman before. God, sorry. I shouldn't... you know what, I'll stop talking now."

I started biting at my nails, my nerves and embarrassment getting the best of me. The man took my hand, tugging it away from my mouth before running his thumb over my knuckles. "It wasn't a stupid question, and yes, I've spanked a woman before."

I took a deep breath. "Would you be willing to, um, spank me?"

The man's gaze burned me in the most delicious way. "I would very much enjoy spanking you, pretty girl."

The way his voice deepened as he spoke, how his eyes darkened with anticipation and lust, soaked my panties instantly. My nipples hardened against my bra, and I could barely take in enough oxygen to calm my racing heart.

"What's your name?" I squeaked out, my hand going up to my mouth so I could bite my nails.

"Gabriel," he said, his hand retaking mine and pulling it away from my mouth. "And you are?"

"I'm -"

A hard warm hand slid under my hair and gripped the back of my neck. "Her name is Hattie, and you're not playing with her tonight, Gabe."

I glanced up, my jaw dropping wide as I stared into the dark and angry gaze of Finn Whitby.

Finn

"Good evening, sir."

I made myself nod politely to the brunette, despite my immediate irritation. "Good evening, Amber."

She let her slender body brush up against mine, keeping her gaze on the floor. "It's good to see you again."

"Step back, Amber."

She immediately gave me space but arched her back slightly to show off her tits. Like most submissives, she wore very little at the club, and tonight was no exception. Her pussy and ass were covered by a sheer gauzy fabric, but her upper body was naked. She'd painted small pink hearts around her nipples, and she played coyly with one painted nipple as she said, "It's been a long time since we've played together, sir."

"No," I said.

Her smile turned into a pout, and she raised her gaze. She glared at me, and with any other submissive, it would make me itch to spank her. But I had no desire to play with Amber. She wanted more from me, and while she was in her late thirties and had a successful career as an optometrist, I had no urge to date her. Playing with her had given her the wrong idea, even though I'd been honest with her that nothing would go beyond the club. When she'd started texting me outside of the club, I'd immediately cut off all contact with her.

"Please, sir," she said. "I promise not to -"

"I said no, Amber."

The tears welling up in her eyes and her trembling bottom lip didn't bring on a single feeling of guilt. Partly because I was a bastard and partly because we both knew she was faking.

When her tears didn't have the desired effect, they disappeared to be replaced with anger. "Fine. I don't want to play with you anyway. You fucking suck as a Dom, Finn."

I stayed silent, and she sniffed angrily and stalked away. I rubbed my forehead. I thought coming here tonight was exactly what I needed after a shitty fucking week, but I'd been here for hours and hadn't found a single submissive to play with. For the first time, none of the gorgeous women looking to play appealed to me.

Because you want Hattie.

Christ, if my inner voice didn't shut the fuck up about Hattie King, I would strangle it. My current lack of interest in the submissives at the club tonight had nothing to do with my attraction to Hattie. Did I want her? Of course, I fucking did. Who wouldn't? Her dark hair was soft and silky looking, and her light blue eyes had this weird ability to look directly into me as if she could see all of my faults and flaws and imperfections.

I shook off the unsettling thought that Hattie King might be one of the few who could see me for who I really was and thought about her mouth instead. Those perfect full lips of hers that were meant to be wrapped around my fat cock.

Maybe I'd spent every night this week with my dick in my hand jacking off to images of Hattie's perfect tits bouncing as I pounded into her tight wet cunt, and maybe knowing she was submissive brought on more than one fantasy of how she'd look draped over my knee, but that had nothing to do with how I felt right now. This lack of interest in the club submissives was a weird blip due to a bad week and a...

My brain short-circuited as I caught sight of the very woman I couldn't stop thinking about.

Fucking hell. I stared at Gabe talking to Hattie, my shock so great I felt frozen to the damn floor. My gaze roamed over her, taking in the bright blue skin-tight dress that hugged every perfect curve, the black nylons, and - God help me - the 'fuck me' shoes strapped to her feet.

What the hell was Hattie King doing at the club? Even though I'd known she was submissive, this was the last place I'd expected to see her. Not a girl like her. Despite what I knew about her past, there was an inherent sweetness to her, an innocence that shone out of her like a beacon. She was submissive, but I'd bet my left fucking nut she'd never been with a Dom in her life. So, how the fuck did she know about the club?

My questions and confusion disappeared in a wave of irritation when Gabe took her hand. Even from where I stood, I could see the way he caressed her knuckles, the way he gave her a look that practically screamed *mine*.

I loved Gabe like he was my brother, but my immediate intense possessiveness toward Hattie made me forget how important he was to me. I stalked toward the bar, my back tense and my hands wanting to clench into fists.

Despite the club's noise, I had no trouble hearing Hattie when she asked for Gabe's name before chewing on her nails.

"Gabriel," he said, his hand taking hers and pulling it away from her mouth. "And you are?"

"I'm -"

I slid my hand under her soft dark hair and cupped her neck in a possessive grip. "Her name is Hattie, and you're not playing with her tonight, Gabe."

Hattie glanced up, her jaw dropping open as surprise washed over Gabe's face.

"This is your mechanic?" he asked.

"Finn, I... what are you doing here?" Hattie said.

I kept my hand on her neck as I stared at Gabe. "She's not yours to play with, Gabe."

He studied me for a few seconds before standing and nodding to Hattie. "It was nice to meet you, Hattie."

He walked away, and Hattie slid off her barstool, grimacing when she stood. I had no doubt her feet were killing her. The shoes she wore weren't meant for walking in. The thought that she might fuck another man sent another trickle of jealousy through me, enough to make me tighten my grip. She gasped softly, and I dropped my hand and brushed her hair away from her neck, scowling when I saw the red marks my fingers had left. Fuck, she had delicate skin. A Dom would need to be extra careful with her.

She pulled away from my touch, backing up against the bar and biting at her nails.

I tugged her hand away from her mouth. "How did you find out about this place, Hattie?"

"I…" she swallowed hard, "I'm allowed to be here."

"That isn't what I asked." I stepped closer, letting my upper body brush lightly against hers as I placed both hands on top of the bar on either side of her and penned her in. "Answer my question."

I was already going full Dom on her but fuck if I could help that. It'd been hard enough not to be a Dom to her at the damn company barbecue. Here in the club, it was impossible.

"I belong to some… some online groups," she said. "Um, BDSM groups."

Her voice was breathy, her cheeks were flushed, and I had no doubt that her little nipples would be rock hard if I peeled off her dress. I'd turned her on without even trying, and how fucking hot was that? My cock hardened, and if I moved even a little closer, she'd feel precisely what she did to me.

I took a deep breath. "You need to leave."

"What?" She blinked a couple of times, the lust in her pretty blue eyes fading to confusion. "Why?"

"This isn't the right place for you."

"What does that mean?" She gave me the cutest look of indignation as her cheeks went a deeper shade of red. "I'm - I'm a submissive."

"This isn't a little slap and tickle," I said.

"I'm aware," she said. "This is exactly what I'm looking for."

"No, it isn't," I said.

She huffed out a frustrated breath. "Screw off, Finn. You don't even know me."

Her sass made me itch to turn her around, bend her over a

barstool, pull up that dress, and spank her bare ass in front of everyone. She must have seen it in my gaze because her body went soft and pliant, and she gave me a sweetly submissive look. "Will you play with me, Finn?"

"No," I said. "You're leaving, Hattie."

She shoved her way free from the barrier of my arms and stared defiantly at me as she yanked the hem of her short dress down and smoothed it across her flat stomach. "I'm not leaving. You're not the friggin' boss of me, Finn. So, just leave me alone."

She stormed away, and despite my anger, I couldn't keep my gaze from her tight ass and long legs.

"Shit," I muttered before picking up her drink and taking a big swallow. "What the fuck? Is this club soda?"

I waved the bartender over, and he stopped in front of me. "Hey, Finn. You want another whiskey?"

"No, thanks, Thomas. The woman drinking this at the bar? Has she been drinking only club soda?"

"Yep," Thomas said. "Hasn't had a drop of liquor."

"All right, thanks."

I studied Hattie as she walked down the hallway toward the ladies' room. Okay, so she wasn't doing this because she'd had too much to drink. I considered having her escorted from the club, but what if she came back on a different night when I wasn't here? She was brand new to this world, it was fucking easy to see that, and what if she hooked up with the wrong Dom?

I grimaced and muttered another curse. I wouldn't be her Dom, that was too dangerous, but I could keep an eye on her tonight and make sure she went with the right Dom.

Let her go with Gabe. After you, he's the next best one to play with her. At least you know she'd be safe and that he'd make her first time playing with someone a pleasurable experience.

Now the jealousy wasn't just a trickle but a flood. A green wave that washed over me and threatened to drown me. I took a few deep breaths. The idea that anyone other than me would be the first to show her the pleasure of her submission made me want to break the fucking bar in half.

Shit, I was in so much trouble.

CHAPTER 4

Hattie

By the time I found Finn's friend Gabe again, my anger over Finn's belief that he could force me to leave the club still hadn't faded.

Gabe stood near the small stage. The show had ended, and the curtains were drawn. I joined Gabe and gave him my best 'you want to fuck me' smile. I placed one hand on my hip, thrust out my chest, and trailed my other hand down his broad chest.

"Hello, Gabe."

"Hello, Hattie."

"So, um, sorry about earlier, but I'm good to play with you now."

A small smile crossed Gabe's face. "I can't do that."

"Why not? You find me attractive, right?" I let my hand linger on his stomach, close to his belt.

"I do, but Finn is my best friend, and he's made it clear I'm not to play with you," Gabe said.

"So, you let him tell you what to do?" I arched an

eyebrow at him. "I thought you were a Dom, but I guess not?"

His nostrils flared, and I squeaked in surprise when he pulled me up against his body, his hand splaying across my lower back. "Pretty girl, if you ever speak to me in that tone of voice again, I'll turn you over my knee and spank you until your ass bears the marks of my handprint for a week. Do you understand?"

So turned on, I could barely breathe, I whispered, "Yes."

"Yes, what?" His hand slid down and squeezed my ass.

"Yes, sir," I whispered.

"Good girl."

My throat had dried out, and my voice croaked when I said, "Please play with me, Gabe."

He gave my ass a final squeeze before releasing me and stepping back. "Go home, Hattie."

I could have screamed with frustration when he turned and walked away, slipping around a few other people and disappearing from my sight. I took a deep breath and blew it out before turning and scanning the club for Finn. There was no sign of him, and a weird combination of relief and disappointment went through me.

It had taken me almost five minutes of deep breathing exercises in a bathroom stall to get over my shock of seeing him here at the club. Which was stupid because why wouldn't he be? I'd known in my heart he was a Dom, and I was sure Sophie had said he and Liam were originally from Havenport. Was it all that surprising he knew about the Sapphire?

No, but seeing him had still thrown me for a loop. As had the way he'd pinned me up against the bar, the way he'd spoken to me like I belonged to him, and he had every right just to boss me around. Asshole.

Oh, please, it made you so wet, your panties need to be wrung out.

No, what had made me wet was being so close to him. It had nothing to do with him trying to boss me around.

Didn't it, though?

"Good evening."

I turned around, staring at the blond man standing behind me. He was about my height, maybe a little shorter, and he had a stocky, compact-looking body. Hazel eyes studied me from behind thick dark blond eyebrows, and apprehension skittered down my spine. He had a hard look in his gaze, one that promised not just discipline, but pain and plenty of it.

He moved closer, and it took everything in me not to step away as he studied my tits with frank interest. "You're new to the club, yes?"

"Yes," I said.

"You will address me as sir," he said.

I swallowed hard. "Yes, sir. This is my first time at the club."

"How many scenes have you done?" he asked.

"What do you mean by scenes?"

A scowl crossed his face, and when I stared blankly at him, he squeezed my upper arm so hard it made me gasp. "What did I just tell you?"

"I'm not sure what you mean by scenes, sir," I said.

He released my arm and rolled his eyes when I rubbed at the red marks his fingers had left.

"So, you're an absolute newbie."

"Yes, sir. Are you, uh, willing to be with a newbie, um, sir?" Every nerve ending was screaming at me to get away from the guy, but I stood my ground. Maybe this man wasn't the exact Dom I was looking for, but beyond Gabe, he was the only one who'd approached me.

"Very willing." His smile did nothing to ease my nerves. "What are you looking for?"

"Spanking."

His scowl deepened, and I hurriedly said, "Spanking, sir."

"Your manners are atrocious," he said before looking me up and down, "but most newbies' are. Are you open to trying other things?"

"Could I have an example, sir?" I asked.

"Caning," he said. "I enjoy caning immensely, and I think you would too."

"Leave, Steven."

Finn's deep voice sent relief coursing through my body. This time when he put his hand on the back of my neck, I leaned into him, hoping he couldn't feel the way I trembled.

"Do you know the newbie?" Steven asked.

"She isn't for you to play with," Finn said. "She's an innocent."

"I'm well aware," Steven said. "What I wasn't aware of is that you're the only one allowed to play with the newbies."

"I'm not," Finn said, his voice irritated. "But since you believe that caning is appropriate for an innocent, you are no longer allowed to play with them."

"You don't make the rules anymore," Steven said.

"Sylvia will have a new contract written for you by tomorrow," Finn said. "One that states you are no longer allowed to play with new members. Don't sign the contract, and you're out. Break the contract, and you're out. Do you understand?"

"I understand you're an asshole with control issues," Steven said.

Finn gave him a brittle smile. "Just like three-quarters of the Doms in this room. Now get the fuck out of my face before I have you removed permanently from the club."

Steven turned and walked away, but we both heard his muttered, "cocksucker".

Finn dropped his hand from my neck and scowled at me. "You're leaving, Hattie."

"Thank you for your help with that guy, but I'm not leaving," I said. Not until I find a… a nice Dom to play with me."

"Hattie, you will do what I say, or so help me God…."

Finn took a deep breath, scrubbing his hand across his jaw as I grinned at him. "Or what, Finn? You'll spank me?"

My grin turned taunting, and I cranked up the insolent attitude to high. "Ooh, no, please, don't spank me. That's the last thing I want. I didn't come to a BDSM club to get spanked. That's just -"

My taunting grin slid off my face, and I squeaked to a stop when Finn pushed me up against the closest wall. He grabbed my wrists and forced them over my head, pinning them against the wall with one hard hand as he shoved a thick thigh between mine and pressed it against my pussy.

I was one hundred percent trapped, and one hundred percent turned on.

Finn

HOLY FUCK, HAD I EVER WANTED TO SPANK A WOMAN SO badly in my life?

Hattie's fire and cheekiness had me hotter than fucking hell, and I desperately wanted to spank the attitude right out of her. Her soft body against mine made my cock harden, and the way she looked up at me, her chest rising and falling with rapid little puffs of air, the flush in her cheeks, and the desire in her eyes fucking killed me.

"You'll watch how you speak to me, Hattie," I said.

"Or what?" That taunting but *oh so fucking sexy* grin made a second appearance.

I pressed up against her, letting her feel the hardness of my cock against her hip. "Or I'll spank you and give your mouth something better to do than sass me."

Her eyes went wide, and her mouth dropped open, and fuck, she really was trying to kill me. I knew she was. Picturing how she'd look on her knees with my cock sliding into that open mouth was a terrible idea, but there it was, front and center in my brain.

"Finn, please," she said. "Be my Dom for tonight and show me some stuff."

"What kind of stuff?" I asked.

"I… I'm not sure," she said.

"If you're not sure, you're not in the right place," I said.

Frustration seeped into her face. "Fine. I want to be spanked, all right? I know that I want to be spanked."

I studied her flushed face before rubbing my leg against her pussy. Her soft moan and how she arched into me were all the encouragement I needed.

It wouldn't hurt to be her Dom for one night. As long as she understood it was only for tonight, what was the harm in playing with her? I'd get my need for her out of my system, and I'd make sure her first experience as a submissive was a positive one. It was a win/win for both of us.

"Tonight only," I said. "I'll play with you tonight, but that's it. Do you understand?"

"Yes, Finn," she said eagerly. "I understand."

I released her wrists and stepped back, ignoring her disappointed look and holding out my hand. "Come with me, Hattie."

HATTIE

I DON'T KNOW WHAT I EXPECTED, BUT BEING TAKEN INTO A small, dimly lit room that didn't even have a bed was not it. Not that I was opposed to fucking Finn against a wall or something, but, fuck, my feet were killing me. Finn had set a brisk pace to the room, and it was impossible not to limp.

Finn pointed to the only chair in the room - a velvet high back chair with elaborate wood carvings. "Sit."

I swallowed my snarky "I'm not your dog" reply. I wasn't into pet play or anything - at least I didn't think I was - but I *was* here to take orders from Finn, right?

I sat in the chair, watching Finn as he locked the door and crossed to the small bar fridge tucked against the wall. Like his friend Gabe, he wore a pair of jeans with a long-sleeved Henley, only his was navy blue and really made his eye colour pop. I shivered with anticipation as I studied his chest in the tight-fitting shirt.

The wall across from me had thick burgundy curtains covering it, and the three remaining walls were painted a dark gray. A light on each wall provided only the dimmest of illumination, and I squinted at Finn as he joined me at the chair. Maybe I could ask him to turn up the lights when we fucked. If this was my only chance to see his remarkable body, I wanted good lighting for it.

Finn opened the water bottle and squatted in front of me. "Drink, Hattie."

I took the bottle and drank a few swallows to soothe my dry throat. My gaze returned to the curtains. What exactly were they hiding and why -

My gaze whipped back to Finn when his strong hands unbuckled the strap around my ankle, and he eased off my shoe. He kneaded the bottom of my foot, and a moan of pleasure burst from my throat, my free hand gripping the arm of the chair. "Oh, oh God… that feels good."

He released my foot and picked up my right one, unbuckling the strap and removing the shoe before kneading my instep on that foot too. I moaned again, closing my eyes at the sensation and wiggling my poor pinched toes. Holy fuck… was it possible that a foot rub from Finn was better than sex with Finn?

Finn released my foot, and I made a small, displeased sound in the back of my throat. What almost looked like a grin crossed Finn's face before he stood and held out his hand. I took his hand, and he pulled me into a standing position before leading me toward the curtains.

My happiness at no longer walking in those ridiculous shoes faded into the background as I stared at the curtains and sudden understanding washed over me. I stopped immediately, tugging on Finn's hand. He turned toward me with one eyebrow raised.

"I don't want to be watched," I said. I hated the panic I could feel nibbling at my edges, but after years of being in the spotlight, of people watching my every move, I preferred total anonymity whenever I could get it. I was an introvert through and through, and when I'd left Hollywood, I swore I'd do everything I could to protect my privacy.

"Slow your breathing, Hattie," Finn said.

I ignored his solid advice, deciding to continue my panicked breathing and add some babbling to the mix. "Look, I won't agree to being watched, okay? I'm not trying to be difficult, and I'm willing to be open-minded about certain things, but not this." My voice went up an octave, and I felt lightheaded from lack of oxygen. "I will not agree to be watched, and you can't make me, Finn. You can't make me agree to -"

Finn's warm, hard hands cupped my face, and he bent until our noses were only inches apart. "Baby, stop."

I stopped. How could I not when he used that voice on me?

"Take some deep breaths, Hattie."

I took three deep breaths, staring into Finn's gorgeous eyes as his thumbs brushed along my cheekbones. "Good girl," he said. "Take two more."

I took two more and stared mutely at Finn when he released my face. He took my hand, rubbing his thumb along my fluttering pulse. "Better?"

"Yes."

"We're not being watched," he said. "I wouldn't do that to you without beforehand knowledge that you're good with it. In fact," his hand tightened on my hand, "I won't make you do anything, Hattie. Whatever happens between us will only happen if it's something you want and agree to. Do you understand?"

"Yes," I whispered.

"Good. I brought you into this room to watch a woman being spanked. The couple in this room knows others are watching them. All right?"

I nodded, and Finn drew me toward the curtain. He pulled them back, and I stared through the glass at the couple in the room. Their room was larger with a queen-size bed, and the walls were painted a soft blue.

Finn moved behind me, putting one arm around my waist and drawing me back against his body. God, he felt good against my back. His breath stirred my hair when he said, "This is a two-way mirror. They can't see us watching them."

"O-okay," I said. My voice sounded nervous and breathy, and Finn rubbed my hip in an almost soothing manner.

I stared through the mirror. The woman was tall and slender with short blonde hair and multiple facial piercings. She was also completely nude. Her breasts were on the small side with large nipples, each one pierced with a small silver barbell. She was waxed entirely bare, and I stared wide-eyed as the man reached between her legs and cupped her pussy.

The man was short and stocky with auburn hair and tattoos covering his arms. He wore a pair of green joggers and a gray tank top, and his erection was easy to see through the loose-fitting joggers.

The woman clutched at his arm, her head falling back as the man rubbed her pussy. Finn reached over and flipped a switch on the wall, and the woman's soft moans drifted out of speakers fixed to the ceiling.

I clutched Finn's arm, watching as the man sucked on the woman's nipples, tugging lightly on the barbells until she cried out with pleasure. The man reached around her and cupped her ass with his free hand, kneading her cheeks roughly as she rubbed her body against his.

Her hips were rocking back and forth, and her cheeks were flushed with colour. I could feel an answering bite of desire when the man squeezed her ass again before smiling up at her. "Spread your legs."

She spread her legs wide. Wide enough for me to see how he slid two fingers inside of her. She cried out, rising on her tiptoes before clutching at his shoulders.

"So wet, my little one," he said with a satisfied grin. "Are you ready for your spanking?"

"Yes, sir." She moaned her displeasure when he pulled his fingers out of her pussy.

My face flamed red when he pushed his fingers into her mouth. "Suck."

She sucked them clean eagerly. I shifted from foot to foot, my nipples hard and my pussy throbbing as the man led her toward the bed. He sat on the side of the bed and patted his lap. When the woman draped her lower body across his lap, her ass in the air and her cheek resting on the bed, a wave of hot pleasure rolled through my stomach, and my pussy gushed wetness. Holy fuck, this was way better than any porno I'd watched.

I twitched when Finn said into my ear, "Don't cum while you watch, Hattie."

I stared up at him, a little surprised at his comment. I mean, sure, I found this hot, but I wasn't going to cum just from watching. Even if I was super turned on, I still needed my clit rubbed, and it's not like I would start masturbating in front of Finn.

"Do you understand?" he asked.

"Yes," I said. "Why would I cum?"

He didn't reply, and after a few seconds, I returned my gaze to the couple in the room. The man rubbed her ass, squeezing and kneading it while the woman waited patiently. His first spank made my pussy pulse, and I squeezed Finn's arm tightly as the man slapped the woman's ass in a hard and rhythmic pattern.

The woman squirmed on the bed, her hands clutching the covers beneath her as the man's spanks increased in both tempo and pressure.

Her ass was bright red now. I thought about how it would feel to have Finn turning my ass that red, and another wave of pure need went over me. I gasped when Finn's big hand cupped my right breast, his fingers pulling at my erect nipple through my dress and bra.

I moaned as Finn made a low sound of disapproval. "When you're at the club with me, you don't wear a bra. Do you understand, Hattie?"

"Yes," I said.

His hand squeezed my breast, his fingers pinching my nipple until I cried out. "Yes, what?"

"Yes, sir," I said, and the pressure on my nipple eased immediately. It was the first time I'd ever experienced pain while aroused, and I was both a little embarrassed by how much I liked it and hungry for more.

Finn unzipped my dress and pulled it down, leaving it bunched around my waist. Before I could say anything, he had unhooked my bra and pulled it off. I raised my arms to cover my breasts, and Finn took both my wrists and pinned them behind my back with one hand.

I yanked hard against his grip, goosebumps popping up on my skin when Finn made a low chuckle. "Stop trying to free yourself, Hattie. It won't happen until I allow it."

I bit my bottom lip, my back arching when Finn pulled on my nipples again. Fuck, he was right. I was trapped against Finn's hard body, and I'd never been so turned on.

CHAPTER 5

Finn

Watching Hattie struggle to free herself from my grip while seeing her perfect naked tits for the first time was enough to almost make me embarrass myself by cumming in my jeans. When was the last time I'd been this hard just from touching a woman's tits? I couldn't remember.

"Oh, God!" Hattie made a sharp cry when I pulled and pinched her nipples until they were red and hard little peaks.

"Watch the show, Hattie," I said, cupping her tits and playing with her nipples.

She turned her gaze obediently to the mirror again, and I used my grip on her wrists to pull her even closer, pressing my erection against her ass. She ground against it subconsciously as she watched Alex and his sub through the mirror.

Her breath caught in her throat when Alex reached between his sub's legs and rubbed her pussy. The woman moaned loudly, grinding herself against his fingers. She was soaking wet already, and I wondered if my Hattie was just as wet.

There was only one way to find out.

"Look how wet her cunt is, Hattie," I said before pulling on her nipple. "She's dripping all over her Dom's leg."

"Oh God," Hattie moaned as she stared at the wet spot on Alex's leg. Hattie's body trembled when Alex picked up a dildo lying next to him and rubbed it against the woman's swollen clit. I rubbed Hattie's thigh before tugging lightly on it.

"Open."

She spread her legs immediately, and a fresh wave of need made precum drip from my cock. Fuck, she was so responsive to me already. What would it be like to have Hattie in my bed every night? Ready and willing to do whatever I told her to do.

I would rip through my damn jeans if I kept thinking that way. What was happening between Hattie and me could only be for tonight. She was too young for me and too inexperienced. Hell, for all I knew, she could get her spanking tonight and decide it wasn't the kink for her. I knew plenty of submissives who didn't like to be spanked. And I couldn't have a relationship - real or club only - with a woman who didn't want me to spank her.

I pushed thoughts of the future out of my head - after tonight, I'd never touch Hattie King again - and slid my hand up under her dress. She arched her back when I cupped her pussy through her panties. The silk was soaked, and I could no more resist pushing the wet material aside to touch her bare skin than I could stop the sun from rising.

Alex had returned to spanking his sub, and as Hattie watched the woman writhe and beg and moan, I rubbed my thumb across her swollen clit.

"Finn!" Hattie cried out, her hips jerking forward.

"Your cunt is as wet as hers, and you haven't even been

spanked, Hattie," I said. I released her wrists so I could play with her tits again, smiling when she grabbed my arm and dug her nails into my skin.

I rubbed her clit before sucking on her earlobe. Her breath came in harsh pants, and her hips rocked furiously against my hand.

"Are you as tight as her?" I asked.

As Alex pushed the dildo into his sub's cunt, I pushed two fingers into Hattie's sopping wet pussy. She cried my name as Alex's sub made a scream of pleasure. Alex fucked her furiously with the dildo, and I matched his pace with my fingers in Hattie's cunt.

I rubbed Hattie's clit with the ball of my thumb as Alex's sub climaxed with a scream. Hattie's cry was softer, but the way her pussy squeezed around my fingers and the flood of fresh liquid left no doubt in my mind about how hard she'd cum.

Hattie collapsed against me, and I slid one arm around her waist, helping to support her as the last of her climax rolled through her, and her pussy milked my fingers. What I wouldn't give to feel her hot, silky cunt squeezing my dick like that.

But I couldn't fuck her. I knew myself, and if I gave in and fucked her, if I felt that pretty pussy wrapped around my dick, I'd find it nearly impossible to walk away.

Alex was putting his sub on her hands and knees on the bed in the other room. He knelt behind her and entered her with one smooth stroke. Hattie leaned against me, her chest heaving and eyes closed as she recovered from her orgasm. I gritted my teeth and pulled my fingers from her pussy. I wiped my fingers on my shirt before I could give in to my urge to taste Hattie's sweet cream. I reached over and flipped the switch off, cutting out the sounds of Alex and his sub's fucking. I pulled the curtain closed before tugging Hattie's dress up.

"Hattie, put your arms in the sleeves, please." I wasn't taking her far, only a couple of doors down, and I usually wouldn't bother redressing a sub for such a short walk. But based on Hattie's reaction to being watched, I didn't want to leave her exposed for even the thirty seconds it would take to bring her to the other room.

I zipped up her dress, making sure not to catch her silky hair in the zipper, and scooped up her shoes and her bra before taking her hand. "Come with me."

"Can't walk," she said with a cute little smile. "Legs too weak."

I grinned and gave her ass a hard squeeze. "You can walk. Come on."

She followed me toward the door. It was adorable how wobbly she was, and I led her down the hallway to the private room. Hattie glanced around, her gaze seeking out any mirrors on the wall.

"It's a private room," I said before pointing to the camera placed discreetly in the upper right corner of the ceiling. "But you need to know that there is a camera and someone who works for the club watching. It's for your safety, and I can't and won't ask for the camera to be turned off. It's against club rules. You consented to be recorded in the paperwork you signed, but you can walk out right now if you're not comfortable. I won't be upset with you."

"I'm good with being recorded. I knew that I would be recorded for certain stuff, and I understand why. I just - I don't want other random people... I like my privacy," she said.

"The recordings aren't shared with anyone outside the viewing room," I said. "I promise you."

I'm sure she was worried about her former celebrity status. Even after being out of the public eye for as many years as she had, a sex tape would push her right back into the spotlight, and it was clear that she wanted to avoid that possibility.

"Okay." She stared at the bed, and I placed my finger under her chin and tipped her face toward mine.

"I need a safe word, Hattie."

"Flower," she said without any hesitation. "My safe word is flower. But can I use the word yellow if, um, I need you to slow down?"

"Yes," I said. "Yellow means I'll slow the scene, and we can communicate about how you're feeling and what you need, and flower means the scene stops immediately. No questions asked."

She took a deep breath. "Thank you."

I liked that she had done her research.

I took a step back as Hattie glanced at the bed again. "So, I kind of had the fantasy that I would be spanked because I was," her face flushed red, "a bad girl, but, um, I don't know how you feel about doing a fantasy scene."

When I didn't reply, she said, "It's all good. I don't need to make up a fantasy about being punished, so that I deserve the spanking. I'm good with just, you know, a spanking for no reason."

I kept the grin off my face with exceptional willpower. Unlike many of the Doms at this club, I loved working with a new submissive. Loved their combination of willingness and uncertainty. Loved gaining their trust and showing them how beautiful a gift their submissiveness was.

"But you were a bad girl, Hattie," I said as I placed her shoes and bra on the chair in the corner of the room.

"What?" Indignation flooded her face, and her arms

crossed over her chest as she gave me a defiant look. "I was not."

Shit. She was the perfect sub. Willing to submit but making me work for her submission.

"What did I tell you in the room?"

"That we were watching a show," she said.

"What else?" I asked.

Little lines appeared between her eyes. "I don't... oh shit, you told me not to cum."

"That's right," I said. "But you came anyway and broke the rules."

She watched me with wide eyes as I walked over to the bed and sat down on the side of it before pushing up my sleeves. "Strip, Hattie."

Hattie

WATCHING FINN PUSH UP HIS SHIRT SLEEVES TO REVEAL HIS forearms with their sinewy muscle and light dusting of dark hair lit me up like a damn flashlight. My pussy, which should have been perfectly content with the orgasm she'd just had, immediately screamed for more.

"Hattie."

I dragged my gaze from Finn's arms, feeling about three inches tall when I saw the disappointment in his gaze.

"I've asked you to strip," he said. "In the future, if I'm required to repeat an instruction, you'll receive an extra five spankings. Is that clear?"

"Yes, sir," I said. My pussy was now a damn waterfall. Which was stupid because what Finn said was just for show. We both knew he'd never touch me again after tonight.

I pushed away the weird depression that immediately wanted to descend. Now was not the time to feel emotional. This was my only chance to have Finn as a Dom, and I wouldn't wreck the experience by not being fully in the moment.

I took a deep breath and reached behind me to unzip my dress. I pushed it down my body, letting it pool at my feet before stepping out of it. Finn stared at my tits, and I self-consciously slid my panties down my legs and left them on the floor with my dress.

I wanted to cover my pussy with my hands like a shy virgin, which was ridiculous. I may have had a two-year dry spell when it came to sex, but I was far from a blushing virgin.

"Come here, Hattie," Finn said.

Deep breathing like a madwoman, I walked on trembling legs toward Finn. I stopped beside the bed, keeping my hands at my sides, while Finn studied my pussy. His expression gave away nothing, and I hated the insecurity I felt. I didn't wax completely bare like the woman we'd just watched. I kept a patch of hair at the top and waxed the rest because that's what I liked. But did Finn like the completely bald look? I knew from my online groups that some Doms preferred it, but I was a grown woman and the idea of a man wanting me to have no pubic hair had always slightly creeped me out.

Finn still hadn't said anything, and my nerves got the best of me. "I'm not waxing it bare!"

My voice was too loud and had a weird edge to it.

"All right," Finn said.

"Do you want me to wax it?" I asked.

Finn stared up at me. "It's your body and your choice, Hattie."

I flushed a little. That wasn't what I'd expected to hear. "But what's your preference?"

"Why does it matter?" he asked.

"I want to know," I said.

"I prefer a natural look," he said.

"How natural? Like a seventies vibe bush?" I asked.

One of those rare grins crossed Finn's face. "Perhaps not that natural." He sat back on the bed and patted his lap. "Lie down, Hattie."

My nerves went haywire, and I swallowed hard. "Finn, I… I'm nervous."

"I know," he said. "But I've asked you to do something, and you know what will happen if I have to ask again."

The calm quietness radiating from him soothed my jagged nerves. In the past, when I'd asked partners to spank me, any anxiousness I'd shown had immediately made them nervous. That, combined with their inability to spank me in the way I wanted, had ended my spanking requests.

I draped myself over his legs, making a small squeak when Finn shifted me on his lap, and I felt his erection digging into my stomach. It made my lust come roaring back to life, and I moaned when Finn rubbed my ass and squeezed my cheeks.

"Such a beautiful ass," he said.

"Th-thank you, sir," I said, jerking when he pulled my cheeks apart and ran his finger over my anus and down to my pussy. I clutched at the sheets when he brushed over my swollen clit, but he didn't linger, to my dismay. Instead, he slapped my right ass cheek.

I rested my cheek on the mattress, taking in a couple of deep breaths as Finn set up a quick spanking rhythm of my right and then my left ass cheek. I closed my eyes and tried to focus on the moment, but I could already feel disappointment sinking in. My ass was heating up, and Finn's spanks stung, but they weren't what I'd expected or wanted. His spanking wasn't any harder than the tentative slaps that previous partners had given me.

Was this all it was? I had pictured more in my fantasies. More arousal, more need, more... pain. Or maybe I had a high pain tolerance and didn't realize it. Maybe I was -

"Motherfuck!" The screeched curse left my lips before I could stop it as Finn gave me a spank that set my ass on fire.

I started to sit up, and Finn's hard hand pressed down on my lower back, stopping me. "Watch your language, please, Hattie."

I sucked in a breath, crying out when Finn spanked me again, sending another line of fire across my ass. He spanked me hard - *so fucking hard* - twice more before rubbing my burning ass. I wiggled on his lap, clutching at the sheets when his hand slipped between my thighs and across my pussy.

"Oh!" I stuck my ass up eagerly when Finn rubbed my clit. Pleasure washed over me, drowning the burning pain in my ass as Finn teased my clit. "Oh God, Finn, that feels so good."

He gave me a hard slap across the ass. "You'll refer to me as sir during a play scene, Hattie."

"Yes, sir," I gasped out as Finn slid two fingers into my pussy and finger fucked me. I moaned and wiggled and rubbed against his lap as tension and need coiled in my belly.

When Finn stopped rubbing my clit, my soft moan of disappointment was buried under the sound of his hard slaps against my vulnerable ass. They hurt like hell, but underneath the pain was a feeling of contentment and a strange rightness. Like, I'd waited my entire life to be over Finn's knees while he turned my ass a bright red and made me -

"Oh fuck!" I shouted when Finn rubbed my clit in a hard circular motion.

"Hattie," Finn's voice was sharp but calm as he stopped rubbing my clit, "what did I say about language?"

"Please," I moaned, wiggling on Finn's lap. "Please touch me, sir. Please."

"Your cunt is dripping," Finn said. "Your ass is a beautiful deep red, your clit is swollen," I cried out when he rubbed it again, "and your perfect pink cunt is soaking my jeans."

He finger fucked me again, and when his thumb brushed across my clit, it brought me immediately to the edge of that beautiful, wonderful cliff.

"No!" I pounded the bed in frustration when Finn stopped touching me. "Please, sir, I was so close. Please."

"Shh," Finn said, his hand lightly stroking my ass.

"I need to cum. Please, sir," I begged.

"Soon, baby." He rubbed my ass for a few seconds more before spanking me again. I cried out, fisting the sheets as the pain radiated across my ass. Oh God, I couldn't take it anymore. It hurt too much, and I needed my release, and I couldn't play this game any longer. I had to safe word. I fucking had to.

Before I could say "flower", Finn's hand dipped between my legs again, and his beautiful, rough fingers rubbed my throbbing clit.

"Don't stop, please don't stop," I chanted under my breath as Finn pulled me even closer.

"Shh, baby. I'm not going to stop. Show me how pretty you look cumming on my fingers," Finn said.

It was all the encouragement I needed. That, and the way Finn pinched my clit. My orgasm struck me like lightning, sending sparks of pure pleasure through my body. I rode the wave of bliss, my eyes rolling up in my head and my entire body trembling.

"That was the most beautiful fucking thing I've ever seen," Finn said in a low and reverent voice.

My body limp, I didn't protest when he slid out from under me and then flipped me onto my back. I kept my eyes closed, my lungs heaving air in and out, and my fingers clutching weakly at the sheets.

Finn's hard hand slipped under my neck. "Sit up, Hattie."

He pulled me into a sitting position, and I stared at him with half-lidded eyes. "That was so good, Finn."

"Good. Stay nice and still for me, all right?"

"Hmm," I said. I blinked and tried to focus when Finn started to groan.

I looked down, a squeak of surprise falling out of my mouth. Finn had unzipped his jeans and pulled his cock out. I stared at his impressive length and girth, at the wide red head as it glistened with precum, at the way Finn rubbed his palm furiously up and down his length.

I reached for him, and Finn's hand tightened on the back of my neck. "No, baby. Don't touch. Just watch."

I wanted to argue, but Finn made a particularly harsh groan, the cords in his neck standing out as his hand clamped down on my neck and his hips jutted forward. Cum shot out from his dick to land in soft splatters against my tits.

Finn jerked off roughly, moaning my name, his burning gaze trained on my breasts. "Fuck, baby, you look so pretty covered in my cum."

When he was finished, he sucked in a couple of deep breaths before releasing his grip on me. "Don't move, Hattie."

I stayed where I was, watching Finn's jizz drip down my skin as Finn walked to a door I hadn't noticed when we first came in. It opened to a small bathroom, and I heard running water before Finn returned a few minutes later. His magnificent dick was hidden behind his zipped-up jeans, and he carried a washcloth in his hand.

Surprise threaded through me when he sat on the side of the bed and carefully and thoroughly used the warm, damp washcloth to clean his cum off my skin.

When he was finished, he set the cloth on the floor next to the bed. "How do you feel?"

"Good," I said. "Really good. I came so hard. But my ass hurts like hell."

"Put a cold pack on it tonight when you go home," he said. "It will help with swelling." What almost looked like guilt flashed across his face. "I spanked you harder than I should have spanked an innocent."

"I liked it," I said. "Also, I'm not, like, a virgin or anything. You know that, right?"

His low chuckle made me forget about my burning ass. "I don't mean virgin when I say innocent. It's just my term for a new submissive."

"Oh, okay," I said. "I really liked the spanking. A lot."

"Good." He cupped my face, his thumb stroking my cheek, the look in his eyes warm and comforting. "I enjoyed it as well."

I gathered my courage. "I'd like to do it again."

He immediately stood and grabbed my dress, bra, and panties. "Get dressed, Hattie."

"Finn, can we do this again?" I took my clothes from him. "We could meet here next weekend."

"No," he said. "I told you this was a one-time thing."

The warmth had faded from his eyes, and he was back to the usual cold and aloof Finn. "It's almost two, and the club will be closing soon. You need to go home."

He headed toward the door, pausing before opening it. "Take a left in the hallway and then a right. It will lead you to a door that returns you to the elevators."

"Yeah, okay," I said. I was doing a piss poor job of hiding my disappointment.

"Hattie?" Finn's voice was stern. "Don't come here again."

He left the room, closing the door behind him. Probably for the best that he'd left. My disappointment had turned to annoyance bordering on anger.

I might have just let Finn spank me into the best orgasm of my life, but he was in for a massive surprise if he thought I'd let him tell me what to do.

CHAPTER 6

Hattie

"Oh man, this place is so busy tonight," Sophie said as she slid into the seat across from me. "Sorry I'm late."

"That's okay," I said.

"Thanks for meeting me here instead of Taste of Thai. I suddenly had a craving for pasta," Sophie said.

"It's not a problem." It was sort of a problem in that Bello Italiano was more expensive than Taste of Thai, and my limited budget wouldn't let me afford more than an appy, but I wasn't sharing that with Sophie.

She knew that I lived paycheque to paycheque, but she had no idea how tight my budget was, and I intended to keep it that way. If I didn't, she'd insist on buying my dinner every time we went out, or worse - giving me money, and I couldn't stand the idea of being a charity case.

"I can't believe you got us a booth," Sophie said.

"I think I snagged the last one," I said. "Sorry it's so close to the door."

"I don't mind." Sophie grinned cheerfully at me. "I'm glad we could have dinner tonight. Do you feel like I'm neglecting you? I'm worried that I might be neglecting you since I started dating Liam."

I laughed and sipped at my water. "You're not neglecting me, Soph. Besides, you're in a new relationship. You're supposed to want to spend all your time with him. I get it. Where is Liam tonight?"

"He and Finn are having dinner at Alina's place." Sophie perused the menu. "Oh hey, Liam said that Finn said he took his car to you."

"He did," I said. "Thank you for recommending me."

"Are you kidding? Not only are you an amazing mechanic, but I know the Bel Air is your dream car," Sophie said. "Like I wasn't gonna recommend you. Did you figure out what's wrong with it?"

"I think so," I said. "I looked at it today, and I'm confident the float is sticking in the carburetor. It's sticking in the closed position, so there isn't enough fuel in the bowl, and the car stalls."

"Oh, right, of course," Sophie said. Her eyes glazed over like mine did when she talked about lab stuff. "The float is stuck."

I laughed. "Anyway, the guy who restored the car used a rebuilt carburetor and not a very good one. I recommended Finn replace the entire carburetor, and he agreed. I found one, but it'll take a few days to ship to the shop."

"That's great," Sophie said. "Liam will be especially happy to hear that, as will a bunch of people at the lab. Finn has been extra grumpy since his car started having problems. Was he nice to you when you talked to him today?"

"Oh, uh, I didn't talk to him. I called, but he didn't pick up, so I left a voicemail about the car. Then he called back while I was on lunch and left a message with Monica for me to go ahead and order the carburetor."

"Cool," Sophie said. Thankfully, she glanced down at her menu again before seeing the disappointment on my face.

Missing my chance to talk to Finn had put me in a bad mood for most of the day, which was incredibly stupid because I was still pissed at him for thinking he could tell me what to do.

Is that it? Or are you pissed that he won't play with you again?

I shifted on the seat, wincing when it made my butt hurt. Every time I sat, it was a painful reminder that it would never happen again despite how much I'd enjoyed myself on Friday with Finn.

Go back to the club and find someone else then. There's no point in moping around waiting for Finn to change his mind. He's made it clear that Friday night was it for the two of you. And now that you know how good a proper spanking feels, are you really going to deny yourself the experience again?

I didn't want to deny myself, but I could admit that I wanted it to be Finn who spanked me again. No one else would make me cum that hard. I was sure of it.

You have no idea if that's true or not. You haven't even had another Dom spank you. Stop feeling sorry for yourself, go back to that club, and find a Dom who wants to play with you.

"Hey, Hattie? You still in there?"

I stared blankly at Sophie. "What? Sorry, yeah, I'm here. Just up in my head." I shifted on the seat and winced again as pain flared in my ass.

Sophie's eyes narrowed. "Why do you flinch every time you move?"

"I don't." I opened my menu. "What are you thinking of getting?"

"You're flinching and -"

"Sophie?"

Liam's voice made Sophie and I look up in surprise. Liam stood near the restaurant door, and - my face went hot and then cold - Finn stood next to him.

"Liam? Honey, what are you doing here?" Sophie asked.

Liam slipped past the people waiting for a table, and after a moment's hesitation, Finn followed him. Liam stood next to our booth, his hand caressing Sophie's shoulder briefly. "Alina wasn't feeling well, so she canceled dinner. Finn and I decided to grab a bite to eat, and Bello Italiano is his favourite place. Hey, Hattie, how are you?"

"I'm good," I said.

"Hi, Finn," Sophie said.

"Hi, Sophie." Finn smiled at Sophie before giving me a stiff nod. "Hello, Hattie."

"Hey," I said.

"Anyway, we're gonna try someplace else. The wait time for a table is already over an hour," Liam said.

The server stopped by our booth, smiling brightly at Liam and Finn. "Hi there. Will you be joining the ladies this evening?"

Liam shook his head. "No, we were just -"

"Join us," I said abruptly.

Sophie grinned happily and immediately slid over in the booth, patting the seat beside her. "You heard Hattie. Sit down, honey."

"We don't want to interrupt your dinner," Finn said. "We can find another place to eat."

"Don't be silly," Sophie said. "I don't mind, and obviously, Hattie doesn't either. Right, Hatts?"

"That's right," I said. I slid over, only flinching slightly at the pain and smiling at Finn. "Have a seat."

His nostrils flared, and my pussy throbbed with need at the look on his face. I may have only played with Finn Whitby once, but I already recognized his 'you deserve a spanking, naughty girl' face, and it was turning me the fuck on.

I drank half my glass of water as Finn slid into the booth beside me. The booths were on the smaller side, and Finn was a large man. His thigh pressed against mine as the server took his, Sophie's, and Liam's drink orders before leaving.

"It's too bad that Alina wasn't feeling well. I hope it isn't anything serious," Sophie said.

"It isn't," Liam said. "Her leg was sore, and she had a bad headache."

"Does she get a lot of headaches because of the accident?" Sophie asked.

"No. It's a Whitby thing. I lucked out and rarely get them, but Finn gets headaches often," Liam said.

I glanced at Finn, but he didn't meet my gaze. God, he smelled good. A muscle ticked in his jaw, and I really wanted to lick it. I drank some more water instead.

"I wanted to have dinner last night because I was pretty sure Alina might cancel on us tonight," Liam said. "She went swimming at the rec center this morning, and that always makes her leg sore, but Finn couldn't make it last night. He has a long-standing engagement on Friday nights that he never misses, but he refuses to tell Alina and me anything about it."

Finn stiffened and clenched his jaw so hard, I wondered if I'd hear a molar crack.

"Ooh, a mystery," Sophie said teasingly. "Do we think it's a woman?"

"We do," Liam said. "But he won't introduce us to this mystery girl."

"It's not a woman," Finn bit out. The tension radiated from him in thick heavy waves that I could almost see.

So, Liam and Alina didn't know about the club or Finn being a Dom. I can't say I was surprised. Finn came off as a fiercely guarded person, and even if he wasn't, what guy wanted his younger siblings knowing that he liked to spank women for funsies?

I was surprised, though, by Finn's obvious expectation that I was about to spill his personal business. A little offended by it, even. But to be fair, we didn't know each other well.

I leaned forward, ignoring my butt pain, and grinned at Sophie. "Pottery class."

"What?" she said.

"Finn's doing a pottery class."

"How do you know that?" Sophie asked.

"Oh, I don't know it for sure, but he has the look of a guy who's secretly into pottery," I said.

Liam laughed. "Finn is not the creative type."

"Maybe not, but he also looks like a Patrick Swayze fan, and I bet he's seen *Ghost* a thousand times. He's taking pottery in the hopes of recreating that scene - you know which one I mean," I wiggled my eyebrows at Liam, "with some lucky lady who's as into clay as he is."

Liam stared at me with his mouth agape as Sophie giggled and said, "Agreed. But he hasn't found the right woman because there's only one single lady in the class, and Finn's charm isn't working on her."

"Right?" I said to Sophie. "She's a total natural when it comes to pottery, and she's being a snob about Finn's earnestly made, but lopsided bowls that he keeps giving to her."

"Poor Finn," Sophie said.

"Actually," Finn said, "she does find me charming, but she's also seventy-eight years old. My lack of enthusiasm for the early bird dinner is a deal breaker for her."

I started to laugh, and so did Sophie as Liam stared at Finn. "Are you being serious right now? Are you taking a pottery class?"

Sophie laughed even harder as the server returned with the drinks. "Are you ready to order?"

"Do you guys need some more time?" Sophie asked Liam.

"I don't, and I know Finn won't. He eats here all the time," Liam said.

He and Sophie ordered their pasta dishes, and the server smiled at me. "What can I get you?"

"I'll have the mini focaccia," I said. It was the cheapest item on the menu at ten dollars and the only thing available in my fifteen-dollar dinner budget.

"My personal favourite of our appetizers," the server said. "And for your main course?"

"Oh, uh, I'll have that for the main course," I said.

"Of course." The server turned to Finn. "And for you, sir?"

"You need to have more than bread for dinner," Finn said.

I pasted a smile on my face. "I'm good."

"Finn's right, Hattie," Sophie said. "It's not even a very big appy."

"Just the focaccia is fine. I had a big lunch, and I'm not that hungry," I said.

My stomach chose that unfortunate moment to growl. Luckily not loud enough for Sophie and Liam to hear, but

Finn's gaze dropped to my midsection before that muscle ticked in his jaw again. "Hattie, you -"

"Could I also get some more water?" I said to the server.

"Of course," she said before smiling politely at Finn. "What would you like, sir?"

"I'll have the osso bucco," he said.

"Very good." The server took the menus and left.

I could feel Finn's gaze burning into the side of my skull, and I shifted in the booth.

"Why do you keep wincing?" Sophie asked again.

"I'm not," I said.

"You are," Sophie said. "Every time you move, you wince, and you make this face," she scrunched up her face in a little moue of pain, "like you're in pain. Did you hurt yourself at work?"

"Tweaked my back a little," I said. "It'll be fine by tomorrow."

"So, Finn told me the good news about Gretchen," Liam said.

"I knew Hattie would solve the problem," Sophie said. "She's an amazing mechanic."

"It's not fixed yet," I said.

"But it will be," Sophie said. "Finn, did you know that Hattie's favourite car is the Bel Air? You two have so much in common."

I groaned inwardly. I loved Sophie, but her attempts at getting Finn interested in me, while sweet, were also embarrassing. Especially since Finn had made it clear he wasn't interested.

"She mentioned it," Finn said. "Liam, did you hear that Landon's research project at the lab is being shut down?"

"Are you kidding me?" Liam said.

"When did that happen?" Sophie asked.

As the three of them chatted, I sat back in the booth, hoping they would keep talking about work, that my ass would stop hurting, and that my stomach would stop grumbling by the time dinner arrived.

Fifteen minutes later, when the server returned with our meals, only one of the three had come true. Christ, the minute I got home, I was sticking an ice pack on my butt again and treating myself to the leftover rice in the fridge. It was supposed to be for tomorrow's night dinner but screw it. My butt needed calories to heal, right?

I told myself to eat the focaccia slowly and then scarfed it down anyway, leaving only a few wayward crumbs on the plate. I drank some water and eyed Sophie's pasta, wondering if she'd noticed if I stabbed a few noodles from her plate.

"Liam, did you remember to record the new *Chopped* episode?" Sophie asked before eating a forkful of pasta.

I was distracted from Liam's reply by Finn placing some of his Osso Bucco on my plate and then adding some of the fried polenta and a few stalks of asparagus beside it.

"What are you doing?" I asked in a low voice.

"You didn't order enough to eat," he said.

"I'm not that hungry."

"Your stomach's been growling since I sat down," he said.

"So, you're just giving me your dinner?" I asked.

"I'm sharing mine," he said.

"Finn, I can't -"

I forgot what I was saying when Finn's big hand cupped my thigh under the table and squeezed. He stared at me, his voice low and intense. "Eat, Hattie."

My fingers grabbed for the fork before he'd even stopped talking. Using his Dom voice on me at the dinner table was a dirty trick that I couldn't even scold him for. Not unless I wanted to have an awkward conversation with Sophie and Liam.

I ate some of the delicious Osso Bucco before trying the polenta. Finn squeezed my thigh again and, keeping his voice barely above a whisper, said, "That's my good girl."

And just like that, my underwear was soaked.

Finn

BAD IDEA, FINN. SUPREMELY BAD IDEA.

Didn't I fucking know it. Still hadn't stopped me from excusing myself from the booth only a few minutes after Hattie had gone to the ladies' room. Nor had it stopped me from loitering in the hallway outside the ladies' room like a stalker.

The bathroom door opened, and Hattie walked out. She wore jeans and a t-shirt with a *Deadpool* graphic, and her dark hair was in a messy bun on her head. She wore little makeup, and the effects of her late night were noticeable on her face, but she still looked fucking gorgeous to me. I wanted to take her home, tuck her into my bed until she'd caught up on her sleep, and then bury my face between those gloriously firm thighs.

"Finn? What are you doing?" Hattie stopped in front of me.

Instead of answering, I took her hand and studied her chewed and bitten nails. A couple of them were actually dotted with dried blood, and when I ran my finger over them, she hissed out a breath.

"I don't want you biting your nails anymore," I said.

"Oh, well, I'll get right on that then," she said.

I hid my grin. Her sarcasm was adorable and also something I longed to spank her for. "How's your ass?"

"Sore," she said. "But a good sore. Thank you for sharing your dinner with me."

I ran my thumb along her knuckles. "You're welcome. Thank you for not telling Liam about the club."

"You didn't need to be worried about that. I would never tell him or Alina," Hattie said.

"I like my privacy," I said. "It isn't just Liam or Alina. It's also the people I work with and the people in this town who can't keep their mouths shut."

"I get it," she said. "I won't say a word about the club to anyone. Not even Sophie."

"Thank you." I had no reason to believe her, but I did. Maybe it was because she knew better than anyone what it was like to have her privacy invaded.

"We should get back to the table," Hattie said.

"We should," I said. I stepped a little closer, studying her mouth as she made a soft sound that went straight to my dick.

"All day, I've thought about how you looked last night across my knee," I said.

"It was… I liked it very much," she said.

"So did I."

"Then maybe we should do it again. I could meet you at the club next Friday."

My common sense kicked in, and I hardened my voice. "No. I told you to stay away from the club, Hattie. Do as I say."

Her look of defiance made me so fucking hard. "Do you want to be my Dom, Finn?"

"No," I lied. "I don't."

"Then you don't get to tell me what to do." She pulled her hand free from my grip, pushed past me, and walked away.

Hattie

"Excuse me?"

I smiled at the woman standing behind me in the 7-11. A girl of about eight clung to her hand, and she stared shyly at me as her mother said, "I'm so sorry to bother you, but my Delilah is a big fan of your TV show. She watches the reruns every night. Would it be possible to get a picture with you?"

Years of practice made it easy to keep a smile on my face. And honestly, a little kid excited to meet me was the only good thing about my former celebrity status.

I squatted and smiled at the little girl. "Hi, Delilah. I'm Hattie."

She swallowed hard. "I know. I like your show. Julie was really cool."

"I'm glad you're enjoying it," I said as her mom gave her a gentle push in my direction.

"Stand next to Ms. King, honey," her mom said.

Delilah stood next to me, and I said, "Is it okay if I put my arm around you?"

Her eyes widened, and she nodded. "Yeah, that'd be cool."

I put my arm around her narrow shoulders, and we both smiled at her mom, who used her phone to snap a couple of quick pictures.

"Thank you so much," her mom said as I stood up.

"My pleasure. It was nice to meet you, Delilah." I held out my hand, and the little girl shook it. As they walked away, her shyness disappeared, and I could hear her chatting excitedly with her mom.

I headed toward the Slurpee machine. Finn had paid for

my dinner despite my protests, which meant my fifteen-dollar dinner budget was still in play. And I planned to use some of it to buy the biggest freaking Slurpee I could. I deserved it after three whole hours of having to sit practically pressed up against Finn's hard body, right?

I poured my usual concoction of half blue raspberry and half pineapple whip, watching with real happiness as the blue and the yellow combined. I nearly dropped the large cup when Finn's low voice said, "You know that shit is full of chemicals, right?"

"It's what makes it so delicious." I capped the cup with a lid and stuck the straw into it before looking directly at Finn and taking a deliberately loud and noisy slurp off the straw.

The look of disapproval on Finn's face made me kind of hot, and also wish that we were alone so he could spank me for my Slurpee addiction.

Hattie! Get it together, girl!

Right. No more spankings from Finn, no matter how bad I was.

"Are you stalking me?" I asked.

Finn held up a loaf of bread. "Not unless you think stopping for bread is stalking you."

"You know, carbs aren't a great way to start your day," I said. "You should consider eating oatmeal instead."

"Says the girl holding the cup of chemicals."

I took another deliberate sip. "This isn't my breakfast."

"No, it's your dinner," he said.

When I didn't reply, he said, "How often are you asked to take pictures with people?"

I shrugged. "Not that often anymore. Most people in town have gotten over the novelty of the B celebrity returning to her hometown."

"You were more than a B celebrity," he said.

"You stalking me online as well, Dr. Whitby?" I asked.

His cheeks turned red, and I grinned at him. "Holy shit, you are stalking me online."

"No, I'm not," he said. "It's my policy to research any mechanic working on Gretchen."

"Oh, right, of course," I said. "You were researching me because of your car. That is totally a true statement and not at all made up." I made a show of rolling my eyes dramatically before taking another noisy sip of Slurpee.

I was acting like a brat which wasn't like me at all, but there was something exciting about pushing Finn's buttons.

An impudent grin on my face, I said, "You could be a big boy and admit the truth, instead of using some chickenshit excuse like your car to -"

I gasped when Finn pushed me up against the Slurpee counter, his big body pressed against mine and one hard hand gripping my hip. "You are dangerously close to having your ass spanked, Hattie."

The heat of his body and the look in his eyes made my mouth dry up and my pussy gush. I licked my dry lips and said, "You wouldn't spank me here."

"No, but I will take you home, strip you naked, bend you over my bed, and turn that delightful ass of yours a satisfying red." He squeezed my ass, making me whimper with the pleasure/pain.

"Okay," I said.

He blinked, his gaze clearing a little. "What?"

"Take me home." I rubbed against his obvious erection.

He took a step back, looking around before adjusting himself. "Go home, Hattie."

"You're such a tease, Finn Whitby," I said and stalked to the counter with my Slurpee. I paid for it and got the hell out of the store. My mood didn't improve when I slid behind the wheel of my Honda, and it wouldn't start. I smacked my hands on the steering wheel, grunting at the pain. My starter had begun to click and grind, and unable to afford a brand new one, I'd gone to Auto Parts City in Havenport last week and picked up a starter from one of their salvage cars. I'd replaced my dying one and crossed my fingers it was better than my original.

Apparently, I should have crossed my fucking toes too.

I grabbed my bag and my Slurpee and climbed out of the car. I debated whether to call Sophie and beg for a ride home before slinging my bag newsboy style across my chest and walking across the parking lot. There was a bus stop a few blocks from here. It would be two transfers and a couple of hours to get home, but it could be worse. At least our dinky little town had a public transportation system now. Even two years ago, I would have been walking all the way home.

I'd just started down the sidewalk when a silver Benz pulled up beside me, and the passenger window slid down. Finn stared at me from the driver's seat. "What are you doing, Hattie?"

"Walking," I said.

Finn stepped out of his car, staring at me over its roof. "Why are you walking?"

"My car died." I jabbed my thumb back at the gas station. "So, now I'm walking."

"Get in. I'll give you a ride home."

"No, thanks. There's a bus stop a few blocks from here."

"It's dark, and it's late. Get in the car, Hattie," Finn said.

"And if I don't?" I sipped at my Slurpee and grinned at him.

"My car, now," Finn said.

I stomped over to his car and climbed in, setting my Slurpee cup in the pristine looking cup holder and buckling my seat belt as Finn did the same. "Using your Dom voice on me when you have no intention of being my Dom is a dick move, Finn."

"I know. Was that your shitty little Honda back at the gas station?" Finn asked.

"Hey," I glared at him, "don't talk about Mabel that way."

"You named your car Mabel?"

"Do you think it's appropriate to mock me considering you named your car Gretchen?"

He grinned and relaxed in his seat. "So, you get how ironic it is that the mechanic's car broke down, right?"

"I am aware of the irony," I said.

"What's your address?" Finn asked.

"You can drop me off at the bus stop near Hollow Street."

He stared at me, and I sighed. "It's a twenty-minute bus ride from there to my house. I'll be fine."

"Your address please, Hattie."

I grabbed my Slurpee and took a drink to buy myself some time. I lived in a sketchy trailer park in my grandparents' old trailer that was falling apart around me. I didn't want Mr. My Second Car is a Benz to see where I lived.

"Hattie," Finn said in his perfect Dom voice, "stop stalling and tell me where you live."

I recited my address. Finn studied me before saying, "You live in Happy Homes Trailer Park?"

I sucked up another shot of Slurpee. "Yes."

"Wasn't there a murder there last week?" Finn asked.

"A shooting," I said. "Louie didn't die."

"You knew the guy who was shot?" Finn looked like he was about to have an aneurysm. I decided it would be best not to mention the shooting had happened in the trailer right next to mine.

"It's a small trailer park," I said. "Besides, Gina didn't mean to shoot him. It was an accident."

"Gina?" Finn said.

"Louie's wife. She was mad because she missed the final *Jeopardy* question, so she tried to shoot the television but missed and hit Louie instead."

"Jesus Christ," Finn said.

"It was just a flesh wound," I said. "He was out of the hospital the next morning."

"A man was shot in the trailer park where you live," Finn said. "You need to be more concerned about this."

I shrugged. "It was an accident."

"That doesn't make it better."

Finn sighed loudly and pulled out onto the street when I didn't reply. I gripped my Slurpee like a lifeline and stared out the window. Finn didn't say anything, and neither did I, but the closer we got to the trailer park, the more embarrassed I felt.

"You can just drop me off here," I said when Finn drove up to the trailer park entrance.

"So that you can be shot by some pissed-off woman watching *Jeopardy*?" Finn said. "I don't think so."

"Now you're just being dramatic," I said as Finn drove through the park. "It's that one up there on the left."

He pulled into my narrow driveway, parking behind the tarp-covered Lincoln I was restoring and studied my trailer, his hands clenched around the steering wheel. "This is your trailer?"

"Yes." Even in the dark, you could see the ripped cheap plastic skirting, the way the trailer sagged at one end, and the missing pieces of siding torn off during a nasty windstorm last year. My face burning, I said, "Thank you for the ride home. Goodnight."

"You were a successful actress, Hattie," Finn said. "For many years."

"I'm aware," I said.

"You shouldn't be living like this. Even if you blew through the money you made during the show's run, it's on syndication, which means you get royalties. What are you spending your money on?"

Anger and a healthy dose of shame washed over me. My face red and my hands shaking, I fumbled for the door handle as Finn frowned at me. "Answer my question, Hattie."

"It's none of your fucking business," I said and climbed out of the car. I slammed the door behind me and ran toward my trailer, yanking out my keys and stabbing them into the lock. I stepped inside and shut the door, leaning against it with my Slurpee clutched in one hand and my heart hammering at my ribcage.

I didn't burst into tears until I heard Finn's car drive away.

CHAPTER 7

Hattie

"What are you doing here, pretty girl?"

My stomach flip-flopped, and I turned to smile at the man standing behind me. "Hi, Gabe."

Gabe looked me up and down, his gaze lingering on my tits. I wore a tight pair of jeans and an off-the-shoulder top that clung to my breasts and made it perfectly apparent I wasn't wearing a bra.

Feeling bold and a little horny, I brushed my hand along Gabe's arm. "It's good to see you again."

"Does Finn know you're here?" Gabe asked.

"He's not my Dom," I said.

When Gabe just stared at me, I said, "Have you found someone to play with tonight?"

"I'm not playing with you, Hattie," Gabe said.

I pouted, putting one hand on my cocked hip and thrusting out my chest. "Don't you want me, Gabe?"

He laughed. "Pretty girl, you're playing a very dangerous

game. One that will get you a beautiful red ass and a well-fucked pussy when Finn finds out."

"You're wrong. Finn made it clear he won't play with me again," I said. "So, I'm here to find someone who will. I'm hoping that's you."

Gabe shook his head. "It won't be. Do me a favour and go home, Hattie."

"You're not my Dom either, Gabe."

His look suggested he was about two minutes away from spanking me. I gave him a slow seductive smile. "Unless you've changed your mind?"

"I haven't," he said flatly. "Go home."

I shook my head, and without another word, Gabe turned and walked away.

I took a fortifying sip of club soda before making my way across the club. It was much less crowded than Friday night, but I supposed Sunday evening wasn't exactly a bustling club night for most people.

Do what Gabe says and go home, Hattie. You're only here because you're mad at Finn. You don't even want to be with a Dom who isn't Finn.

Totally not true. I was into Gabe, right? I mean, he was no Finn, but he was good looking, and I had a feeling I'd have no trouble getting off with him. I might not even have to close my eyes and pretend he was Finn to make it happen.

Do you hear yourself? Go the fuck home. Please. Even if Finn was interested in you, it was clear how completely different you were last night. It's not just the age thing, Hattie. He's smarter and richer and has his life together. He might want to fuck you, but it wouldn't go beyond that. You're a broke mechanic with grease under her fingernails and a fucked-up reputation as a spoiled former celebrity.

The club soda sloshed in my stomach as the shame made

a roaring comeback. What was I thinking letting Finn drive me home last night? The way he'd looked at my trailer, how he'd looked at *me* like I was a little kid too dumb even to manage her money correctly.

That isn't your fault. Don't feel bad over something you had no control over. Forget about your past and concentrate on your future.

It was good advice, but right now, I was too hurt and too sad over how Finn saw me to care much about my future. Right now, I just wanted to find someone who would make me feel the way Finn had two nights ago at this very club. That's what I would concentrate on and nothing else.

Unfortunately, half an hour later, I was no closer to finding a Dom. I'd spoken with a couple of men and a woman, but I wasn't remotely interested in playing with any of them. Instead, I'd made lame excuses and moved on to a new part of the club. The VIP section was much larger than I'd initially thought, and I wandered through a few different hallways, peeking into rooms that boasted live shows before joining a show already in progress in one of the smaller rooms.

I stepped into the room, my eyes adjusting to the dim light as I joined the thin crowd of people standing in front of a stage. Loud moans and groans were coming from the stage, and I stood on my tiptoes at the back of the crowd to see what the show was about.

My breath caught in my throat, and an involuntary moan squeaked out. The couple standing in front of me shifted to the right, giving me a clear view of the stage. I stared wide-eyed at the bed with the two men and the woman sandwiched between them.

The woman lay on her side facing one of the men, her small body wracked with shudders as he fucked her with long, slow strokes. The second man stretched out behind her, his fingers playing with the end of the butt plug sticking out of her ass.

As the crowd watched, he slowly pulled the plug out and replaced it with the head of his dick. My fingers clenched, and my toes curled when he slid his cock into the woman's ass, and she made a long moan of pleasure.

"That's so hot, honey."

My gaze turned to the couple to my left. The woman leaned back against her partner, staring wide-eyed at the stage. Her skirt was shoved up, and her legs were spread, and I watched her boyfriend rub her naked pussy as she rocked her hips against his hand.

"Honey, we gotta have a threesome," she moaned.

The man kissed the side of her neck. "Whatever you want, sweetie."

"I want to be fucked just like that," she said in a low voice.

I looked away from them and back to the stage. The woman was being fucked by both men, their rhythm slow and steady as she moaned and gasped and pleaded for them to move harder.

My nipples were hard pearls, and my pussy was soaking wet. I couldn't stop staring at how the two men moved so purposefully in her like it was their only job to make her cum all over their dicks.

Finn and Gabe would be like that, I decided. They would know exactly how to move, what to say, how to make me cum from both their dicks. It'd been a while since I'd had anal sex, and I'd never been with two men at once, but the forbidden vision of both Finn and Gabe inside of me had taken up residence in my brain and wasn't going anywhere soon.

"I told you not to come back here." An arm circled my waist, and I almost screamed in surprise when I heard Finn's voice.

I tried to push free of his grip, but he pulled me up against him, his arm like a vice around my waist. When I continued to wiggle, he slapped me hard on the ass. It hurt like hell against my sore butt, and I hissed in pain, glaring up at him when he squeezed my right ass cheek.

"Be still, Hattie," he said.

I slumped against him, staring resolutely at the stage as Finn said, "What are you doing here?"

"What's it look like? I'm watching a show." I could hear the impudence in my voice, and apparently, Finn could too because he immediately slipped his free hand down my top and gave my right nipple a hard pinch.

I cried out at the delicious pain, my hand gripping Finn's forearm. He was already rubbing my nipple with his thumb, soothing the sting away before he palmed my breast and held me even tighter against him.

"I told you not to come back here," he said.

"And I told you you're not my Dom. You don't get to make rules for me."

His hand tightened on my breast, and I stared up at him. He had a heavy five o'clock shadow, and he wore a plain blue t-shirt and a pair of jeans. "How did you know I was here?"

"Gabe texted me," he said.

"That snitch," I said and got another nipple pinch for my impertinence.

As he rubbed away the sting with his thumb, Finn said, "Have you let anyone touch you tonight?"

"That's none of your business," I said.

"Tell me," Finn said.

"Not yet," I said. "But watching this show has got me so

hot, I'm definitely finding someone to touch me after it's finished."

Finn made an honest to god growl that set my panties on fire. I rubbed against his erection as we watched the show in silence for a few minutes. The woman's moans had increased in volume and length, and the men were moving hard and fast now.

The woman beside us being finger fucked by her boyfriend was trying to match the woman on stage in moaning, and Finn looked briefly at her before staring down at me.

"Finn," I begged, grinding my ass against his erection. "Touch me."

He played with my nipples until I could barely stand the ache. "Why should I? You aren't being my good girl."

"I am," I panted as he kneaded my breasts.

"You disobeyed me by coming to the club."

"But I obeyed you by not wearing a bra," I said.

A laugh escaped his mouth, and I wasn't sure what made me hotter - Finn's laugh or the woman being fucked on stage by two men.

"Please, sir," I said.

Finn's gaze darkened, and I moaned happily when he undid my jeans and then slipped his hand inside my panties to cup my pussy.

He slid his middle finger into me, and I squeezed around him, moaning again when he rubbed my clit with his thumb.

"You're soaking wet," he murmured into my ear. "Is it because you like watching other people fuck, or something else?"

I licked my lips, my hips rolling against the pressure of Finn's fingers. I wanted to tell him the truth, but what if he wasn't into it?

"Hattie," Finn prompted, flicking my clit with his thumb.

I made a harsh cry, making the man beside us glance over. He nodded to Finn, his hand working furiously over his girlfriend's pussy as she moaned and panted and stared at the stage.

"Finn, I…"

"Tell me," he said.

"It's something else," I said.

"Tell me exactly what you want," Finn said.

I took a deep breath and threw caution to the wind. "I want you and Gabe to fuck me at the same time."

Finn groaned, and his hand tightened against my breast before he slid his finger out of my pussy and concentrated solely on working my clit with hard, firm circles. I cried out, the need cresting inside me as I watched the woman on stage make one final scream of pleasure before she came hard on the mens' cocks.

"Cum for me, Hattie," Finn said into my ear.

I clutched at his arm and cried his name before cumming against his hand. I shuddered and trembled, my pussy clenching uselessly. I wished that I had Finn's dick deep inside me more than anything.

Finn

I CLIMBED OUT OF MY CAR, STARING AT HATTIE AS SHE exited a dark blue Toyota and joined me at the front door of the east Havenport diner.

"Did you buy a new car?" I asked.

"No. This is Sophie's. She let me borrow it for the evening." She studied the diner with the neon hamburger sign flashing brightly. "A diner? I assumed we were going to a hotel."

"You know what assuming does," I said before opening the door.

"I want you to spank me tonight," Hattie said, balking when I pressed on her lower back, "and I'm not into it being a public event."

I grinned. "Noted. C'mon, Hattie."

"Finn," she said.

I stared down at her. "Your ass is too sore to be spanked tonight."

"It isn't," she said.

"Being my submissive means you accept that I know what's best for you," I said.

"But I really want to play with you tonight," she said.

"I'm aware," I said. "Now, we either go into the diner, or you drive home. Either way, I am not spanking you tonight."

She pouted but walked into the diner. It wasn't busy this late on a Sunday night, and I nodded to the owner, Joe, who stood behind the long narrow counter.

"Take your usual booth, Finn," he called.

I led Hattie to the booth at the far end of the diner. She slid in across from me and stared at the retro furnishings and decorations. "This place is cool."

"It is," I said.

"How did you find it?"

"Gabe and I stumbled onto it one night after leaving the club. It was late, we were starving, and it was one of the few places still open."

"I imagine you work up quite an appetite spanking a woman," Hattie said with a grin.

I rolled my eyes and grabbed the menu from the holder at

the end of the table. "Decide what you're eating, and then we'll talk."

"Oh, I'll just have a glass of water," Hattie said. "I'm not hungry."

"Dinner is my treat," I said.

Hattie bit at her nails, and I pulled her hand away from her mouth. Joe stopped in at our booth. "Good to see you again, Finn."

"You as well, Joe. This is my friend, Hattie. Hattie, this is Joe. He's the chef and owner of the diner."

"Hello," Hattie said. "I love your diner."

"Thanks, little lady." Joe had a tray with two glasses of water and a beer on it, and he set them in front of us. "What would you like to drink, Hattie?"

"The water is good," Hattie said.

"If you're not a beer drinker, they have more than just beer," I said.

"We have a pretty good selection of wine, if I say so myself," Joe said.

"Just water, thank you," Hattie said.

Joe nodded. "I'll give you a few minutes with the menus."

He left, and Hattie said, "You have the owner personally serving you? Is it because you're stinking rich?"

"I'm not rich," I said, "and Joe sends his waitress, Elise, home if it's not busy because she has two young kids."

"Oh," Hattie said.

We studied the menus in silence, and when Joe returned, I ordered the steak sandwich with salad, and Hattie ordered the grilled chicken sandwich with fries.

I settled back in the booth, watching Hattie as she studied the diner, nibbling nervously at her nails the entire time. I didn't say a word, not even when she tore a hangnail and bright blood appeared at the edge of her nail. She grabbed a napkin and held it against her finger. "So, did you meet Gabe at the club?"

"We went to high school together," I said.

"Gabe lives here in Havenport?" Hattie asked.

"He does."

"Is he a biologist as well?"

"Veterinarian," I said.

"Oh." Hattie peeked under the napkin before pressing it against her finger again. "How often do you go to the club?"

"Every Friday night," I said.

"That's it?"

"Yes," I said.

"How often does Gabe go?" she asked.

"More than me."

"Saturdays?" she asked.

I leaned forward. "Gabe won't be your Dom, Hattie. Stop pestering him about it."

She scowled. "Why does he do what you tell him to? What do you have over him?"

"Nothing," I said. "It's called friendship, Hattie."

"But you refuse to be my Dom, so why should Gabe be denied the opportunity?" she asked.

I bit back my "because no one touches what's mine, not even Gabe" retort. It wasn't like me to be this possessive, and I was still trying to come to terms with it myself. Explaining it to Hattie would be impossible. Not to mention, freak her the fuck out. She was looking for a Dom, not a life partner. And even if she was… I was not the man for her. Not with our age difference. Speaking of which.

"Are you twenty-five?" I asked.

"Yes."

Despite her youthful appearance and recent bratty behaviour, which I was confident she was only doing to get under my skin, Hattie gave off a more mature vibe than the average twenty-something-year-old. I'd had high hopes she'd been lying about her age as some actors did and might even be in her early thirties.

"How old are you?" Hattie asked.

"Forty-five," I said. "Too fucking old for you."

Before she could reply, Joe returned with our food. After thanking him, we dug into our meals, eating silently until Hattie said, "This is delicious. Thank you."

"I'm glad you're enjoying it," I said.

She dipped a fry in some ketchup and popped it into her mouth. "You know I'll go back to the club, right?"

I sighed and set down my fork. "If I agree to be your Dom for a couple of weeks, will you agree not to go to the club without me?"

"Two months," she said.

"What?"

"I want you to be my Dom for two months," she said.

I suppressed my grin. "Now you're negotiating?"

She just shrugged, and I said, "Three weeks."

"Six weeks."

"One month," I said.

"Deal." She grinned happily before taking a big bite of her chicken burger.

"Just one month," I said, "and only on Friday nights."

"Could we throw in Wednesday nights, too?" she asked.

"No. I won't negotiate on this, Hattie. As you're aware, my family doesn't know I go to the club, and the more often I go, the greater the risk of them finding out."

"We don't have to go to the club on Wednesdays. We could go to a motel or something," she said. "I'll pay for it."

Considering she couldn't even afford to eat a meal out, I had no idea how she thought she'd pay for a motel, but I wouldn't bring it up. Last night, I'd gone too far questioning her spending habits, and I wouldn't make that mistake again. Forgetting that it was none of my business, I'd spent most of today antsy and feeling bad I'd upset Hattie. Which annoyed me because, generally speaking, I didn't give a fuck what anyone beyond Liam, Alina, and Gabe thought of me.

"No," I said. "Fridays only, and only at the club."

"Sure, okay," she said.

"Will there be issues with your transportation?" I asked.

"No. I picked up another starter at Auto Parts City today before going to the club. My car will be working by Friday."

We finished our meals, and I took a swallow of beer as Joe appeared and removed our empty plates and refilled Hattie's water glass. She smiled at him, and her pretty blue eyes with their long lashes and perfectly straight teeth had Joe blushing like a schoolboy as he walked away. My chest tightened in a weird way that I didn't like when she turned that smile on me.

"The food is so good here."

"It is," I said. "As your Dom, I have four rules you must obey. Breaking them will result in punishment or potentially an immediate end to our agreement."

She nibbled nervously at her nails as I set my beer bottle down and leaned forward, lowering my voice a little.

"Rule one - you don't fuck anyone else without my permission. Rule two - you don't go to the club without me. Rule three - you don't have an orgasm without my permission."

"So, I'm not allowed to masturbate?" she asked.

"You're allowed, but you need to text or call me and ask for permission before you cum. Rule four," I reached out and tugged her hand away from her mouth, "you don't bite your nails."

She stared at her nails. "Because it's a gross habit."

"Because you're hurting yourself, and I don't like it."

"You want to hurt me," she said softly.

"You want me to hurt you too," I said.

She flushed but held my gaze steadily. "I do."

"Do you understand and agree to the four rules, Hattie?"

"Yes. Do I have to sign a contract or something?"

"No, verbally agreeing is enough."

"All right," she said. "So, now what?"

I sat back in my seat. "If we share our medical records, would you be willing to go without condoms?"

What looked like regret crossed her face. "I'm not on birth control."

"I've had a vasectomy."

"Oh, um, okay then. Yes, I'm good with no condoms." She hesitated. "You don't want kids?"

"No," I said. "I don't."

"I don't want them either. I guess we're more compatible than you think, huh?"

Alarm skittered up my back. "Hattie, this is only for a month, and what happens between us are play scenes only. I want to clarify that I am not interested in dating you."

"Why?" she asked.

I admired her bluntness, I really did, but I hated that I had to keep lying to her because of it. "I'm not looking for a relationship, and I'm too old for you."

"Age doesn't mean anything," she said.

"It does to me."

"Why?" she asked.

"Why are you looking for domination and discipline?" I asked.

"Does it matter?" she asked.

"Yes," I said. "I require open and honest communication, Hattie."

She continued to hesitate, and I kept the anxiety off my face with massive willpower. If she weren't willing to share her reasons for looking for a Dom, I would have to end this before it started. Our age difference and my previous relationship validated my concern that Hattie could potentially be looking for a "daddy".

And if she was, I was not the Dom for her, no matter how strong our attraction and connection were.

CHAPTER 8

Hattie

S haring my reason for wanting to be dominated wasn't something I expected Finn to ask me. I fidgeted and squirmed in my seat. I went to bite my nails, snatching my hand from my mouth when Finn said, "No nail biting, Hattie."

"Sorry," I said before clearing my throat. "Can you tell me why you need to know?"

I didn't expect him to answer, but maybe he heard the anxiety in my voice because his expression softened. "Have you heard of the daddy kink, Hattie?"

"Yes," I said. "I don't judge others who are into it, but I'm not interested in it."

Noticeable relief crossed his face, and I said, "That's not your kink either, huh?"

"No, it isn't," he said. "I have no desire to be called daddy by my submissive, and if you're looking for that, we will not be compatible for play scenes."

I swallowed hard. I wasn't dumb. I knew my desire for

discipline and dominance and spanking had a lot to do with my lack of structure and discipline growing up. And while I had precisely zero urge to call Finn 'daddy', maybe what I wanted was a daddy kink, just without the actual term.

"Tell me why you're suddenly anxious," Finn said.

"I'm not," I lied.

"Hattie, this will only work if you're honest with me," he said. "If you keep lying to me, I can't trust that you won't lie to me during a scene. And lying during a scene could lead to you being seriously hurt because you don't safe word when you should. Do you understand now why I need honesty from you?"

"Yes," I said. "Part of my desire for discipline is because I didn't get any growing up. Is that considered a daddy kink?"

"Not necessarily," Finn said. "Tell me about your childhood."

"I was born in Willowdale. My dad died when I was three and left us with a lot of unpaid bills. I was a cute kid, and my mom had a friend who was a talent agent. She got me some modeling gigs, and that money helped make ends meet. From there, she got me into commercials. I did a ton of commercials, and I had some guest appearances on a few tv shows. When I was eleven, my grandparents, who lived in the trailer I now live in, died. Mom immediately moved us from Willowdale to Hollywood. Two months later, I auditioned for the lead role in a new sitcom called "What About Julie" and got the role. Have you heard of it?"

He nodded. "I've seen a few episodes."

I picked at my napkin to distract me from my overwhelming desire to chew at my nails. "I'm an introvert. I never wanted to be an actress, and the immediate popularity of What About Julie and the fame that came along with it, was… a lot for me. After only two seasons, I went to my mom and told her I wanted to quit. She freaked out. She had quit her job when she moved us to Hollywood and acted as my full-time manager. Mom said if I quit, we'd lose everything, our home, our car, the clothes off our backs, because I was the only source of income for us."

"Christ," Finn said, the disgust thick in his voice. "You were thirteen at the time?"

I nodded and started shredding the paper napkin into thin strips. "As What About Julie became more popular, I had a lot of trouble dealing with the fame. To keep me from having a breakdown, my mother started giving me marijuana and liquor."

"What the actual fuck?" Finn said as the disgust turned to anger. "When you were thirteen?"

"Yeah. Mom is an extrovert, and she loved the attention she got just by being related to me. She also was fairly charismatic and knew how to schmooze the right people. The money I earned from the show was a huge motivator for her, but the fame was just as important. She made friends with all the right people, and we started going to parties every weekend. Some of them had some big-name actors too. I once spent an entire Saturday night arguing with Emma Thompson about *The Simpsons* influence on pop culture."

"But you didn't enjoy the partying," Finn said.

"Not at first. But by fifteen, I was doing cocaine at the parties and during the week while filming the show, drinking like a fifty-seven-year-old alcoholic. All with the encouragement of my mother."

Finn stared at me. I had an idea he'd never been shocked into silence before. I didn't love that my childhood was what had brought him to this point.

"Anyway, because of the drinking and the drugs and the partying, I started to get a reputation as a party girl and for being a spoiled princess. Some of that was the drugs. They gave me a major attitude. But Mom also didn't help my reputation. She kept demanding more and more from the producers of What About Julie. I didn't care what my dressing room looked like, my salary, or if the other actors got paid more than me. Again, partly because of the drugs and liquor, but also because I was miserable and didn't want to be an actor anymore. I acted out more and more, trying to get my mom or, hell, anyone in our inner circle to put their foot down and stop my behaviour."

"But they didn't," Finn said.

"They encouraged it. My mom's view of the situation was that the more I was noticed - good or bad - the better it was for my career. I mean, she wasn't wrong. Before I quit, I was in negotiations to star in a movie directed by Steven Spielberg. My mother was over the damn moon about it. I was about to go from small-time television star to legit movie star."

I brought my fingers to my mouth, but before I could chew at my nails, Finn took my hand. He held it in his big one, rubbing his thumb over my pulse point. "What was the catalyst for you quitting?"

I took a deep breath. "I had just turned eighteen, and there was only one season left of filming for What About Julie. It was Friday night and, like usual, I was at some party. Honestly, I didn't even know whose party I was at. I'd done a couple of hits of cocaine and drank a lot of wine. My mom had already left to go to a different party that she said I wasn't invited to. I was making out with some random guy, and we went upstairs to an empty bedroom. Three of his friends were waiting for us."

Finn's hand tightened on mine, but his expression stayed the same, calm and almost soothing.

"They wanted a, well, a gang bang essentially, and I wasn't interested. They kept badgering me to fuck them all, so I locked myself in the adjoining bathroom and called my mom. She answered but refused to leave her party to pick me up. She said I'd gotten myself into the mess, and I could get myself out."

My stomach churned, and I suddenly regretted eating so much food. I swallowed hard as Finn rubbed my pulse again and said, "It's all right, baby. I won't let anyone hurt you."

Even though I knew he didn't mean it, that he was only saying it so I wouldn't freak out in the middle of the diner, I appreciated the gesture. It was easy enough to pretend he was sincere.

"After my mom refused to help me, I stayed locked in the bathroom. Honestly, I wasn't in any real danger. The guys didn't try to open the door or anything, and they were all so high or drunk that they quickly forgot I was in the bathroom. But the fact that my mother didn't care enough to help me from what was potentially a dangerous situation opened my eyes to what she really cared about. After about ten minutes, the guys left the bedroom, and I walked out of the house and went home."

I stared at our clasped hands. "But that was it for me. Any love or affection I still had for Mom died that night. It was finally horrifyingly clear that I was nothing but a cash cow to her. I quit the show that morning and checked myself into rehab by that evening."

"What did the producers of the show do when you quit?" Finn asked.

"By that point, they were so sick of my behaviour and my mother's demands that they were glad to see me go. They put out a statement that they were happy I was getting the help I needed, and they still had great affection and respect for me, blah, blah, blah. Just bullshit Hollywood stuff. For the last season, they focused more on the actress who played my younger sister and had my Julie character move to France for her last year of high school. They wrapped it up in a very neat and tidy bow."

"So, they didn't sue you for breach of contract?" Finn asked.

"No, I don't think they thought it was worth it. They just wanted my mother out of their hair. I stayed in rehab for three months and then moved back to Willowdale and into my grandparents' trailer and became a mechanic. My grandfather loved cars, and some of my happiest memories as a kid were going to vintage car shows with him."

"What about your mother?" Finn asked.

"She freaked out after I quit the show and showed up at the rehab place. She screamed and shouted at me until security escorted her off the premises. I didn't see her again until I finished rehab and returned to our house in Hollywood." I laughed bitterly. "She asked me to go for drinks with her - just one, as if one would be fine for a fresh out of rehab, recovering alcoholic - to chat about my future and how I could fix my mistakes. She said Steven Spielberg was still willing to meet with me. When I refused, she lost her shit and kicked me out of the house with literally nothing but the clothes I wore. Which was fine because I'd already planned to move back to Willowdale."

"Christ," Finn said with a shake of his head. "Do you still talk to her?"

"Occasionally. Mostly when she wants something from me, like to do an interview with her or some shit like that. She's still in Hollywood. For a while, she leeched off of rich boyfriends, and when that stopped working, she started doing interviews and tell-alls about her troubled daughter. That initially paid pretty well, but as I faded into obscurity, so did the public's interest in me."

A small smile crossed my face. "She's become a bit of a D celebrity, and she's currently on a reality show about milf's looking for love. I always know when she's done something noteworthy, though, because the paparazzi show up here to snap pictures and ask me questions about what I think of her latest antics."

Finn studied me quietly and, hating that I sounded defensive, I said, "Also, not that it's any of your business, but I'm not bad with money. Because I was a minor when I started the show, as my manager and guardian, my mother had control over my earnings. She has expensive taste, and as I found out after I quit the show, she'd blown through almost everything I'd earned during the show."

For the first time since I'd met him, Finn looked ashamed of himself. It didn't make me feel any better, but at least now he might understand why money management wasn't my strong suit. I'd never really had any of my own money growing up.

"I had to threaten to sue Mom to get enough of what was left to buy my grandparents' trailer from her, pay for my auto tech schooling, and buy a second-hand car. My lawyer told me to go for all of it, but," I looked down at my hands, "if I'd taken it all, she would have had no choice but to move back to Willowdale with me, and I didn't want her in my life. I wanted to be free, and letting her have what was left of the money was my only way to gain that freedom."

I cleared my throat, my urge to bite my nails a constant drumbeat in my head. "As for the residuals from syndication, there aren't any. Rather than hire someone to help negotiate my contract with What About Julie, my mother decided to do it herself. She did it poorly. Not only did she lock me into a contract that was non-negotiable the entire time I was on the show, but residuals also weren't included in it."

"Shit," Finn said. "Your mother is an idiot."

"She can be. Anyway, I basically had to raise myself because my mom was busy partying. I was allowed to do whatever I wanted for my entire childhood without consequences or discipline. Now, I want that loss of control, and I crave discipline in the bedroom and," my voice turned a little shaky, "occasionally outside of the bedroom, too."

Finn didn't reply, and I said, "I don't mean that I want to be controlled or anything, but sometimes it would be nice to have someone else in charge. I've always had to look after myself, never had anyone worry about me, or make sure I made the right choices. I don't want them making life decisions for me or anything but occasionally having somebody stop me from eating fast food for the third dinner in a row or make me go to bed at a decent time on a work night instead of binging *Friends* until two in the morning, is appealing."

My hand twisted in Finn's grip as my nerves got the better of me. "Do you think that's a daddy kink?"

"No," Finn said, sending relief washing over me. "I don't consider that a daddy kink."

"Okay, good. So, we're good for our month thing then?"

The look on his face made my stomach plummet to the diner floor.

"What's wrong?" I asked.

"You mentioned paparazzi," he said. "I value my privacy a great deal, not only when it comes to my tastes in the bedroom, but in general. If you're still in the public eye, there's a stronger chance of your involvement with the club, and by association, my involvement with you and the club, becoming public knowledge."

I shook my head. "It won't happen. It's been almost a

year since the paparazzi showed up here, and with Mom currently on that reality show, it won't happen over the next month. She's getting enough attention from being on the show. She doesn't need me to keep her relevant right now."

Finn thought this over as I tapped my foot in a quick beat on the floor and told myself not to burst into tears if Finn changed his mind. He had a right to his privacy, and after years of having mine invaded, I could understand how important it was to him.

After what felt like eons, Finn said, "All right. I'll trust that you're reading the paparazzi situation correctly."

"Perfect,' I said as excitement and relief bubbled in my chest. "So, now what?"

"Now," Finn glanced at his watch, "you get in your car and go home." A cute smile crossed his face. "Go straight to bed, Hattie. No binge-watching television shows."

I laughed. "Yes, sir."

As Finn reached for his wallet, I smiled happily at him. "You won't regret this, Finn, I promise."

CHAPTER 9

Finn

W hen Alina didn't answer the door, I let myself into her house with my key. I usually tried hard not to do that, but she hadn't answered any of my texts either, and worry had edged into panic. What if she'd fallen?

"Alina?" I called her name as I walked toward the kitchen. "Hey, you in here?"

The kitchen was empty, and so was the living room. I immediately headed toward the back of the house to her studio. I heard soft music and Alina's voice as I got closer, and my panic eased slightly.

I knocked on her studio door and opened it. "Hey, kid. How come you aren't answering my…."

My voice died in my throat. Alina sat at the long narrow table against one wall of her studio, and sitting next to her was Hattie.

"Hattie? What are you doing here?"

Christ, she looked good. Her dark hair was in a high

ponytail, her face was free of makeup, and she wore a t-shirt with a faded graphic of Thor on the front and dark leggings.

"You know Hattie?" Alina asked.

"She's Sophie's friend. I met her at a company barbecue," I said. "How do you know her?"

"I'm teaching her embroidery," Alina said.

"You decided to start teaching? When?"

Hattie smiled at Alina. "Actually, it's because of Sophie. For my birthday, she bought me one of Alina's embroideries. I loved it so much that Sophie mentioned Alina was open to the idea of teaching embroidery. When I said that sounded cool, Sophie then bought me three lessons. Tonight is our first lesson."

"It's your birthday today?" I asked.

Hattie laughed. "It's not until Sunday, but Sophie is like a little kid giving presents. She has no self-control. She gave me my present last week, then bought me the lessons to give me on my actual birthday and kept it a secret for a whole twelve hours before she spilled the beans. Once she told me about the lessons, I decided to go ahead and set up my first one before my birthday."

Alina grinned at her. "I'm glad you did. This has been so much fun, Hattie."

"I've enjoyed it too," Hattie said.

"Sorry to interrupt," I said. "I just thought I'd drop in and say hello."

"No, you were freaking out because I haven't replied to your text messages in the last hour," Alina said. She turned to Hattie. "I love my big brother, but he's a bit of a control freak. He likes to know exactly where Liam and I are and what we're doing at all times."

"Not at all times," I said, "just ninety percent of the time."

Alina laughed, and I said, "Anyway, I'll let you get back to your lesson."

"Actually," Hattie glanced at her watch, "my hour is up." She picked up the wooden hoop and a small plastic bag that held thread and scissors. "Same day and time in two weeks, Alina?"

"Yes. Work on practicing your French knots, satin stitch, and backstitch on this pattern. If you have any questions, just text me, okay?" Alina said.

"You bet. Nice to see you again, Dr. Whitby." Hattie brushed past me in the doorway, and the scent of her body wash, and the touch of her soft skin against my arm made me want to pull her into the nearest empty room and make her cum until she screamed my name. It'd only been a few days since I'd seen her last, but I'd spent most of my days with the image of her cumming on my fingers lodged in my brain and most of my nights furiously masturbating to the memory of her draped across my knee.

I swallowed hard, following Hattie down the hall before Alina saw the way my jeans bulged at my crotch. My usual iron-clad self-control flew out the damn window whenever I was around Hattie.

The front door opened, and Alina's best friend, Bryce, a curvy woman with a long mass of curly red hair, stepped into the house. She carried a takeout bag from a local Chinese food restaurant in one hand and a tiny Chihuahua in the other. "Yo, Alina, you ready to gorge ourselves on Chinese food and the gorgeous vision of a half-naked Chris Hemsworth in *Thor Ragnarok*? Because I've had the day from hell, and I - oh hey, Finn. How's it going?"

"Hi, Bryce. Good, you?"

"Good." She set the tiny dog on the ground, and it immediately scampered forward to sniff at Hattie's legs. Hattie made a soft squeal and squatted down, petting the dog's head and making ridiculous but weirdly adorable cooing sounds.

"Hi, baby. Hi there. Aren't you just the cutest boy? What's your name, huh?"

The dog licked her face enthusiastically, and Christ, was I jealous of a dog?

"That's Stanley, also known as Stan the Man, Staninator, and He Who Occasionally Pees in the House," Bryce said.

Hattie laughed, and I bent down and petted Stanley when he trotted over to sniff at my shoes. "Hey, big guy. It's been a while since I've seen you."

His tail wagging, Stanley licked my hand enthusiastically before his entire body stiffened, and his ears shot forward. He let out a volley of barks, each more high pitched than the previous, and raced down the hallway, jumping and bouncing off Alina's legs like a brown furry ping pong ball.

Alina scooped him up and pressed kisses against his face as he continued to bark at full volume. "Okay, Stanley. Okay, chill out, buddy."

"Sorry," Bryce called over the barking. "He is obsessed with Alina and shows that obsession by screaming the song of his people at full volume."

"It's no problem," Hattie said with a laugh. "Alina, I'll see you in two weeks."

"Okay, thanks, Hattie!" Alina waved at her as Hattie let herself out the front door.

I waited for approximately two point five seconds before saying, "I gotta go, kid. You two have fun tonight."

I left the house, closing the door against the eardrum-piercing volume of Stanley's barking. Hattie was halfway down the sidewalk, and I called her name. She turned and gave me a polite smile as I joined her. A smile that didn't at all suggest she knew what it was like to have my fingers in her pussy or turn her ass red with my spanking. In fact, she was doing a bang-up job of treating me like an acquaintance and any worry I had that she might spill the beans about us disappeared.

Too bad my worry was replaced by irritation. Did she have to do such a good job of pretending I meant nothing to her?

She's an actor, idiot.

"Hey, how are you?" I said and then cringed at how stupid I sounded.

"Good, thank you." She kept that vague polite smile before rechecking her watch.

"How are you feeling?" I asked.

Confusion washed across her face. "Uh, good. How are you feeling?"

"I meant your ass," I said. "Is the soreness gone from your spanking?"

Smug satisfaction washed over me when she blushed bright red and then glanced around to see if there was anyone close by. "No, it's good. Back to normal."

"Good," I said. "How was work today?"

"Fine. The carburetor hasn't come in yet. According to the online tracking, there's been a slight delay in shipping. But I'm keeping Gretchen safe in the garage tucked under a nice cozy tarp," she said with a small smile.

"Okay, sounds good. What, uh, what car did you work on today?"

Holy fuck, could I sound any more like a moron? But my urge to see her, to keep her with me for as long as possible, was difficult to ignore.

She glanced at her watch again. "I'm sorry, I don't mean to be rude, but the bus will be here in seven minutes, and it's a six-minute walk to the stop. If I miss this one, the next bus isn't for an hour and a half."

"Why are you taking the bus?" I asked. "I thought you fixed your car."

She made a face. "The starter I bought is still working, but the fuel pump crapped out this morning. Luckily, I had just gotten to work, so I wasn't stranded like before."

She started inching down the sidewalk. "Samesh has an old beater that he'll pull the fuel pump out of, and I'll replace it tomorrow during my lunch hour. So, we're still good for," she lowered her voice, "Friday night."

She peeked at her watch and then said in her normal voice, "Nice seeing you again, Dr. Whitby. Enjoy your evening."

"I'll give you a ride home," I said.

She hesitated. "Oh, uh, that's okay. I don't mind taking the bus."

"And I don't mind giving you a ride home. Get in the car."

When she continued to pause, I said, "It's not a request, Hattie." I could hear how my voice had deepened, and when Hattie licked her lips before walking rapidly toward my car, I couldn't keep the smug smile from my face. She was such a sweet little subbie.

Once we were buckled in and driving away from Alina's, I said, "Have you eaten dinner?"

"Not yet. Because I was taking the bus, I didn't have time to eat before coming over," she said.

"Have you been to the Vintage Kitchen?"

The Vintage Kitchen was a casual dining restaurant close to my place.

"Once before," she said. "It was good."

"I'm stopping there for dinner. Why don't you join me?" I said. "I hate eating alone."

That was one whopper of a lie. Eating alone, *being* alone, had never bothered me. But I didn't like the idea of Hattie returning home to that crappy trailer of hers where she was in danger of being shot. That's why I invited her. It had nothing to do with missing her.

"Is it a request or an order," she said with a cheeky smile.

"This is a request," I said. "Unless you say no, then it's an order."

She laughed. "In that case, yes, I'll join you for dinner."

———

"CAN I ASK YOU SOME PERSONAL QUESTIONS WITHOUT YOU reading too much into it or freaking out?" Hattie asked.

"Depends on the personal questions, I suppose," I said.

Hattie poked at her nearly empty plate of pasta. When we'd arrived at the restaurant, she'd tried to order just a bowl of soup from the appetizers. I'd insisted she order an actual dinner because I was paying for it. Her protests that she couldn't constantly let me buy her dinner fell on deaf ears, and she'd eventually given in and ordered the pasta dish.

We'd spent most of the meal talking about our mutual love of cars, and I was impressed by Hattie's knowledge of vintage cars. She hadn't been kidding when she said she loved them, and her knowledge, in particular of the Chevy Bel Air, made me glad I'd brought Gretchen to her.

"Have you ever been married?" Hattie asked.

"Yes. But we divorced nine years ago."

"Do you still talk to her?"

"No," I said, my voice making it clear she'd waded into dangerous waters.

She turned the ship around. "Why does Alina limp?"

"Alina and Liam are my half-siblings. Alina and Liam's mom was my dad's second wife. When Alina was fifteen, she and their mom were in a bad car accident. Their mother died, and Alina was in a coma for two weeks and paralyzed from the waist down for almost a month before the swelling reduced and feeling returned to her lower body. Her leg was shattered, and they recommended it be amputated, but one surgeon was willing to try to save her leg. It took multiple surgeries to keep her leg, and she was left with bad scarring and a pronounced limp, as well as some mental and emotional trauma from the accident. Some days are worse than others."

"Poor Alina," Hattie said. "I'm sorry she went through that."

"Our dad is… he's a fuck up when it comes to being a dad," I said. "Has never had much interest in raising us. After their mom died, he completely fell apart and couldn't even be there for Alina or Liam. So, I…"

"So, you stepped in," she said. "Became the person they needed to get them through it."

I shrugged, a little uncomfortable by the admiration in her voice. "They're my family, and I love them. I spent most of my time with Liam and Alina after the accident. They needed me, but because of that, I wasn't always the best husband to Melissa."

"Is that why your marriage ended?" Hattie asked in her usual blunt fashion.

"We were already struggling, but that didn't help," I said. "About a year after Alina's accident, Melissa gave me an ultimatum. Either I focused on her instead of Liam and Alina, or the marriage was finished. I chose Liam and Alina."

I glanced at her, wondering what I would see on her face

after that confession. To my surprise, the admiration had deepened.

"Good," Hattie said. "She should never have asked you to make that choice, and it serves her right that you chose Alina and Liam."

I blinked at her. "You don't think I should have chosen her? The woman I'd made vows to?"

"She made vows to you too, right? To be there for you in sickness and health, in good times and in bad," Hattie said. "She didn't support you during the bad. She selfishly asked you to toss aside your family when they were going through a genuine crisis and needed you the most because she was insecure and jealous. That's not love or honouring your vows."

"Jesus," I said, "are you sure you're only twenty-five?"

She laughed. "I had to grow up fast, remember?"

"Yes," I said.

"Was Melissa younger than you?" she asked.

"No, we were the same age. Why?"

"I wondered if that's why you don't want to date younger women," she said.

I ate a bite of rice and took a sip of water before admitting, "I did date someone younger who I met at the club. She was a sub, and she also liked being told what to do outside of the bedroom."

"Like me." Hattie had gone still, and I could see the dismay in her eyes.

"No, not like you," I said. "It was more intense than what you want. You liking it when I tell you it's time for bed or not allowing you to do things that might be dangerous are mild in comparison to what she wanted."

"What did she ask you to do?" Hattie asked.

"At first, I was into taking the dominant stuff outside of the bedroom. You might have noticed that I'm naturally bossy," I paused, grinning when Hattie made a fake shocked face before gesturing for me to go on, "so it wasn't a stretch to do it out of bed either. She wanted to try domestic discipline."

"What does that mean?" Hattie asked.

"It's spanking that isn't sexual but more related to pure discipline. So, for example, it was Sarah's responsibility to cook dinners on Thursday and Friday. If I came home from work and she hadn't cooked dinner, she was spanked for not following through on her responsibility."

"But you didn't make her climax or have sex with her after the spanking," Hattie said.

"No, not usually. Sex might happen later, but it wasn't in relation to the spanking she received."

"Did you enjoy that?" Hattie asked.

"Not particularly," I said. "I like to spank, but a big part of spanking is wrapped up in giving my submissive pleasure as well. Luckily, Sarah discovered pretty quickly that it wasn't for her either."

"So, I'm guessing she wanted to call you daddy, and that's why it didn't work," Hattie said.

I nodded. "Not just calling me daddy, but also asking me to treat her like a little."

"Ooh, I know what that is," Hattie said. "It's where you treat her like a little girl. There are variations of its intensity, but it can even mean diaper changing, right?"

"Yes," I said. "I was willing to compromise and have her call me daddy in the bedroom, but that was as far as I would go. It wasn't enough for Sarah. She left me and found a Dom who could give her what she needed."

We were silent for a few minutes as Hattie mulled that over. She ate another bite of pasta before looking at me. "Wait, you don't think I would ever want that, do you?"

"Maybe. I don't know you well enough to say for sure," I said.

"I told you I had no interest in the whole 'daddy' thing," Hattie said.

"Neither did Sarah when we first met," I said. "People can change when it comes to kinks and what they like. Especially when you're new to the world of BDSM."

"I can guarantee you that I will never ask to call you daddy or ask to be your diaper-wearing little," Hattie said. "I find it insulting that you don't trust me on that."

"That's fair," I said. "But if it helps, you've now convinced me you'll never want that."

"Good," she said. "So, do you want to try dating then?"

I laughed and shook my head. "You don't give up, do you?"

"A person doesn't get what they want by giving up," she said. She nibbled at her nails, worrying a hangnail on the corner of her thumb before moving to the ragged nail bed of her first finger. "Look, I get that I'm not exactly a catch with the whole broke, recovering alcoholic drug user, living in a single wide trailer, but I have other qualities that make up for it."

"It has nothing to do with that," I said with a scowl. "I'm not that shallow, Hattie."

"So, it really is just the age difference?" She went to work on her other index finger, nibbling viciously at the edge of her nail.

"After my relationship with Sarah ended, I dated a few other women. A couple were younger, but most were my age or only a year or two younger. They all started off wanting to be dominated, whether I'd met them at the club or not, but as the relationship progressed, they wanted vanilla sex more and more, and I don't do vanilla sex."

"Ever?" Hattie asked.

"Rarely," I said. "There's nothing wrong with it, and when I have it, I enjoy it, but I only want it occasionally."

"Define occasionally," Hattie said.

"A few times a year," I said. "One good thing about my marriage to Melissa was that she always wanted the kink aspect as much as I did."

Hattie stared at her thumb before worrying the hangnail again with her teeth. "So, even if there weren't an age difference between us, you still wouldn't date me because you'd think I'd get less kinky the longer we dated."

"It has been my experience," I said. "Also, I'm not relationship material. I'm independent, moody, and bossy outside of the bedroom and not always in a fun and sexy kind of way."

She grinned. "No one's perfect, Finn."

"True," I said. "But I'm happy with being single, Hattie."

If she was disappointed by my answer, she did a fantastic job hiding it. Why did that bother me so much?

I glanced at my watch as Hattie nibbled at her nails.

"Hattie?"

"Yeah?"

"Would you like to come back to my place?"

Her hand fell into her lap with a soft thump, and her mouth parted in surprise. I had a surprisingly strong urge to slide my cock between those plump lips right here in the middle of the restaurant.

"It's Wednesday," she said.

"I'm aware."

"You said only Friday."

"I've changed my mind," I said.

She grinned happily. "Oh, well, in that case, yes, I would love to go back to your place, Finn."

CHAPTER 10

Hattie

I was beyond thrilled to be at Finn's house. I climbed out of his car and stared at his place. He lived in the ritzier part of Willowdale - no surprise there - and while his house wasn't a literal mansion or anything, it was a hell of a lot better than my trailer.

We met at the top of the driveway, and I smiled at Finn. "Thank you again for inviting me over. I really -"

"What the hell?"

The outraged screech came from Finn's dark porch. I jumped about a foot, and even Finn twitched in surprise.

The small brunette stomping down the porch steps wore a pissed-off expression and very little clothing. "Are you fucking kidding me, Finn?"

Finn stared at the woman. "Amber?"

"Should I go?" I asked. I started to inch backward, stopping when Finn's hand shot out and took my wrist.

"No, stay right here with me," he said as he slid his hand into mine and linked our fingers.

"So, what?" Amber marched right up to Finn, and I gasped when she poked him hard in the chest. "I'm not good enough to bring home and fuck, but this little washed-up celebrity bitch is?"

"Watch your mouth, Amber," Finn snarled.

"Is it because she's younger? I never took you to have a daddy fetish, Finn, but that's gotta be it, right? Because I might be older, but I am twice the woman she is! I saw you at the club with her. I saw the way you fucking looked at her, but to rub it in my face by bringing her to your home when you know that I… that it should be me who…."

"How do you know where I live, Amber?" Finn said in a dangerously quiet voice.

"I would do anything for you," Amber said. "*Be* anything for you, but you won't even give me a chance. You're such an asshole."

"How do you know where I live?" Finn repeated.

Finn hadn't moved, but Amber shrank back at the venom in his voice. "I… I just wanted to see you, Finn. I knew if you and I could be together away from the club, you'd see that I'm everything you need."

"Tell me how you found out." Finn didn't yell, hell, his voice barely rose, but Amber started to shake, and my stomach knotted up tight. I'd never seen Finn so angry before.

"Steven," Amber whispered. "I - he told me your last name."

When Finn didn't reply, she said, "Please don't be angry with me. I came here because I love you. Because we're meant to be together."

Finn shook his head. "No, Amber. We aren't. I made that clear to you both times we played at the club. You need to leave."

"Finn, let me come inside. Tell her to go home, and we can -"

"Leave," Finn said. "And don't bother going back to the club. You'll be banned by tomorrow."

Amber's face paled. "What? No, you can't... you can't do that, Finn. You're not a partner at the club anymore. Sylvia and Javier are the ones who decide."

"You should have stalked me a little better," Finn said. "I'm still a silent partner, and when I tell Sylvia and Javier what you've done, they'll back me up on the banning. You're done at the club, Amber. Forget the club, forget me, and go home."

"You shithead," Amber said as anger flooded into her face again. "You think you can just fuck my life like this?"

"You did this to yourself. Go home before I call the police and have you arrested for trespassing," Finn said.

"Cocksucker!" Amber spat before marching past us. She seared me with a look, and the pure hatred took my breath away.

I leaned into Finn's comforting warmth, clutching his hand as Amber stomped down the driveway and climbed into a Ford Escape parked on the street. She drove away, and I sagged against Finn as he rubbed his forehead.

"That was awful," I said.

He nodded, looking both exhausted and angry at the same time. "Are you okay?"

"Are you?" I asked.

He just nodded again, and after a few seconds, I said, "If you'd like me to leave, I will."

"No," he said. "I don't want you to leave, Hattie."

He started toward the porch, his hand still holding mine tight like he thought maybe I'd just make a break for it. I followed him into his house. Finn locked the front door, set the alarm, and kept the lights off, leading me up the stairs to his bedroom without saying a word.

He turned on the side lamp, and I bit nervously at my nails as he took off his shoes and socks before stretching his neck from side to side. I could still see the anger simmering on his face, and I stepped back when he started toward me.

His face twisted, and he stopped immediately. "Hattie, are you afraid of me?"

"No," I said. "I'm not. But you're angry over what happened, and I'm not sure this is the right time to play."

He studied me with those pretty blue eyes before nodding. "That's fair."

He sat down on his king-size bed, and I sat beside him, smiling tentatively. "If you want to talk about what happened, I'm a good listener."

"There's nothing to talk about. I played with Amber twice at the club. She wanted a relationship. I said no. After that, she approached me numerous times at the club to play, and I turned her down each time."

As bad as I felt for Amber, there was some relief in knowing that it wasn't just me Finn didn't want to have a relationship with.

"I didn't expect her to go this far," Finn said.

"Are you really a silent partner at the club?" I asked.

"Yes," he said. "Sylvia and I started the club together eight years ago. We brought in another partner, Javier, two years ago, and I stepped back from my involvement with the club and became a silent partner."

"Oh," I said. "Will you actually ban Amber from the club?"

"Yes." His voice turned tight. "As well as that fucker Steven. As soon as we're finished playing tonight, I'll contact Sylvia."

We sat in silence for a few minutes before Finn said, "If you no longer want to play tonight, you can say so. I won't be angry with you, Hattie."

"I want to play," I said. "But I wondered if maybe we could...."

"What?" He stared at me, resting one big hand on my thigh.

Feeling a little stupid, I said, "Kiss. We've never kissed, and I like kissing. I like it a lot. I've thought about kissing *you* a lot."

When he didn't say anything, my nerves got the best of me. "Wait, is this like a *Pretty Woman* thing? You don't kiss your submissives? Because that's cool if it is. I mean, I get it... we're not in a relationship or anything, and, if you think about it, in some ways, kissing is even more intimate than fucking, so not wanting to kiss me is perfectly understandable. Actually, forget I even mentioned it. It was dumb, and I won't -"

Finn's mouth on mine stopped my babbling. His hand slid into my hair, and he cupped the back of my skull as his warm lips urged mine to part. I opened my mouth, moaning when Finn slipped his tongue in and explored my mouth with soft licks.

He was gentler than I expected. His kisses were sweet and tender and made me feel cherished. I pulled back immediately, alarm washing over me. Thinking Finn felt anything more for me than lust was a horrible idea.

"What's wrong?" Finn asked.

"Uh, nothing. Sorry," I said before kissing him again. I tried to take control, hoping that might make those tender, soft kisses turn into what I expected from him.

Finn made a low groan. His hand tightened on my skull, and, as I'd hoped, he took immediate control of the kiss, turning it into something urgent and animalistic. He angled his mouth over mine, taking the kiss deep as his other hand cupped my breast through my shirt and bra.

Lust overshadowed my concerns, and I pushed up eagerly against Finn, running my hands over his chest and broad shoulders. I'd never seen him fully naked, and I was determined to make it happen tonight. He lifted his arms when I tugged at his shirt, and I pulled it over his head, staring delightedly at his chest and the dark hair that covered it.

I reached for him, and he caught my hand, shaking his head. "Ask first."

"May I touch you, sir?" I asked obediently.

He nodded and released my hand. I traced my fingers along his collarbone before sliding them into that dark hair. He hissed out a breath when my pinkie grazed his flat nipple. Smiling, I leaned forward and licked around his nipple before sucking on it.

His low groan and how his hand tightened on my breast sent slow beats of lust throughout my body. He pulled me away, a look of hot need covering his features.

"Strip down to your panties," he said.

"Yes, sir." I stood and stripped down to my panties as he'd instructed, trying to look graceful and self-possessed.

"Turn."

I turned for him, gasping when he ran his hand over my ass. I wore a thong, and he stroked and kneaded my bare ass cheeks before saying, "No longer sore, Hattie?"

"No, sir," I said. My whole body buzzed and tingled. I couldn't wait for Finn's spanking. My pussy was already soaked from Finn's kisses and my anticipation for the spanking.

When Finn turned me to face him, he studied my pussy

before staring up at me. "I can see how wet your panties are. Your cunt is soaked for me, isn't it?"

"Yes, sir," I said, my voice breathless with need.

Still sitting on the bed, he leaned forward and kissed my stomach just above my navel, his big hands roaming over my ass and hips. "Tell me which rule you broke, Hattie."

"I didn't," I said.

He slapped my ass hard, and I squealed at the stinging pain. "I mean, I didn't, sir."

"You did." He toyed with my nipples, pulling lightly on them. "Think back carefully, please."

It was hard to concentrate with Finn's fingers tugging on my nipples, but I did my best. "I haven't been with anyone else, and I haven't - ohh, that feels good - I haven't been to the club, and I didn't masturbate last night even though I wanted to. And I haven't bitten my nails since... oh shit."

I stared at Finn as he smiled at me and gave both nipples gentle pinches. "You bit your nails repeatedly during dinner this evening."

"I forgot, sir," I said. "It won't happen again. I promise."

"What did I tell you about breaking the rules?" Finn asked.

I swallowed hard, but truthfully, I was playing up my nervousness about being punished. While I honestly hadn't meant to break the nail biting rule, Finn's spanking wasn't exactly a punishment. I wanted to be spanked by Finn, and it was especially hot for me if I was spanked because I truly deserved discipline and punishment, and he knew that. I appreciated the way he played along with my little fantasy.

"I would be punished, sir," I said.

"That's right." He gave me a gentle push back and stood. "Undress me."

Oof, this punishment was getting better by the damn

minute. My fingers trembling from my eagerness, I unbuckled his belt and unbuttoned his jeans before pushing them and his boxer briefs down his thick thighs. His cock popped out, already hard and thick, with precum slicking its head. My mouth fucking watered at its sight, but I crouched and helped Finn step out of his clothes before tossing them aside.

I wasn't surprised when Finn's hand landed on my shoulder, preventing me from straightening. I moved from crouching to kneeling, staring up at Finn's cock as he fisted it with long, slow strokes.

"Open, Hattie," Finn said.

I opened my mouth, moaning when Finn slid the head of his cock between my lips. I sucked eagerly on the head, cleaning off its tip with slow slides of my tongue. Finn's low moans grew louder as he fed me more of his dick until its head hit the back of my throat.

I gagged slightly, and Finn pulled out. Feeling stupid, I said, "I'm sorry, sir."

"It's fine, baby. Open for me again. I love seeing your pretty mouth full of my cock."

I sucked hard on Finn's cock, bobbing my head up and down the length. He was too big and thick for me to even think about deep throating him, but I took as much as I could and tried to do a variety of tongue movements and sucking techniques.

I'd never had any complaints in the blow job department before, but I wanted to show Finn how eager I was to please him, wanted him to see that I was the right woman - the *only* woman - for him.

Hattie, stop thinking like that.

I ignored my inner voice, leaning forward and pushing Finn's hand away so I could wrap my hand around the base of his dick. He slid both hands into my hair, palming the back of my skull and thrusting his hips back and forth. I opened wide and let him fuck my mouth, staring up at him as he studied my face, his gaze burning with lust and desire.

"Good, baby. So fucking good. Suck harder, yeah, just like that. Fuck, you're so gorgeous with my cock in your mouth." Finn's voice was a low growl that sent waves of need directly to my pussy. I reached between my legs, needing some relief from the unbearable tension.

Finn shook his head, his hands squeezing my skull. "No, baby. No touching yourself. Your job is to make me feel good, not yourself."

I whined my complaint but gripped Finn's thick thighs, sucking his dick hard in the hopes that he would reward me for my efforts by letting me touch myself.

Finn groaned again. "Fuck, baby, you've got me so worked up, I can't help myself. I'm gonna cum in your mouth. Be my good girl and swallow all of it."

He pulled out enough to let me take a few breaths, his hand stroking my hair back from my face. "Will you swallow my cum like my good girl?"

"Yes, sir," I said as he wiped the spit and precum from my chin. "Whatever you want me to do, sir."

He groaned and slid his dick back into my mouth. "Such a good, sweet girl."

His thrusts grew more frantic, and when he let his head fall back and bellowed a curse, I was ready for him. I swallowed his hot seed, the salty sweetness making my whole body shiver with delight. I took everything he gave me and went back for more, licking his cock clean as he shuddered and moaned above me.

When his cock had softened, he took my arms and helped me stand. He studied my face, his thumb rubbing over my mouth. "I fucking love that your mouth is swollen from sucking my cock, baby."

He kissed me hard on the mouth, his tongue diving in to tease mine before releasing me. He turned and pulled back the sheets on the bed before tugging me onto the mattress. I laid down, staring at him in confusion when he stretched out beside me.

His fingers traced along the waistband of my thong as I said, "Finn, aren't you going to spank me?"

He shook his head, dipping one finger into my panties to brush against my pubic hair.

"But I broke a rule," I said. "You're supposed to spank me as punishment."

"Is it your job to tell me when to spank you?" Finn raised one eyebrow at me as his fingers tugged at the hair on my pussy. "Spread your legs, Hattie."

"No," I spread my legs, "but you said you'd spank me and…."

My voice died out in a low moan when Finn cupped my pussy, and his fingers rubbed my swollen and aching clit.

"I never said I would spank you tonight," Finn said.

I didn't reply. I actually no longer cared about the spanking. What I cared about was getting off, and Finn's fingers were getting me there quite nicely. I'd been in a low state of arousal since Finn had given me an orgasm on Sunday night. Not used to denying myself, it'd been a real struggle not to masturbate over the last few days. Especially when all I thought about was Finn and how good it felt when he made me cum.

"Remember," Finn sucked on my earlobe, "you need my permission to cum, Hattie."

"Please may I cum, sir?" I asked immediately, my hand clutching at his forearm as he rubbed a little harder. I was so close, right on the edge, and it would only take a few more strokes to get me there.

"No, you may not," he said and stopped rubbing my clit.

I whined, almost kicking my feet like a toddler having a tantrum. Finn's low chuckle both irritated and delighted me.

"Naughty girls who break the rules don't get to cum," Finn said.

I froze against him when he pulled his hand out of my panties. "What the fuck?"

"Language, Hattie," he said.

"Finn, make me cum," I said.

"No, you broke the rules. There are consequences for breaking the rules."

"Then spank me!" I could hear the desperation in my voice. I sat up, staring wildly at Finn. "Spank me as my punishment."

He sat up, and his little grin kind of made me want to punch him right in his gorgeous face. "We both know that spanking isn't a punishment for you."

"It is," I said. "It hurts like hell."

"Stop trying to argue or bargain with me, Hattie. Denied orgasm is your punishment, not spanking."

"I kind of want to punch you in the face right now," I said.

He laughed so hard, I flushed with embarrassment.

"I didn't know that denied orgasms were on the table as punishments. It's not fair for me to find out now," I said.

"It's not my fault you didn't clarify the consequences before agreeing to follow my rules," Finn said. "Next time, you'll ask more questions."

I pouted and pouted hard, but Finn just leaned forward and kissed my nose. "You can pout all you want, baby. You're still not getting your orgasm."

"Fine." I tried to climb out of bed, and Finn took my wrist.

"Where are you going?"

"Home," I said. "If you're not gonna make me cum, what's the point of staying?"

I was being a bitch, but I couldn't help it. My body was pulsing and throbbing, and I couldn't remember the last time I'd wanted to cum this badly.

"So you can go home and masturbate and break another rule?" Finn asked.

I flushed brightly. "No, I was just going to, um, go home and go to bed."

"Lies will get you punished as well, Hattie," Finn said.

I glared at him, and he tugged and turned me on the bed until I was the little spoon to his big spoon. He cupped my breast with a more comforting than arousing touch and kissed the top of my shoulder. "Go to sleep, baby."

"I can't," I said. "I'm too turned on. I want to go home, Finn."

He nuzzled my neck. "If you're a good girl and sleep in my bed tonight, in the morning, not only will I fuck you until you cum, but I'll eat your sweet pussy as well."

"I have to work in the morning," I said grouchily.

He laughed. "As do I. So, go to sleep, and I'll wake you up early."

"I still want to punch you in the face," I said.

"I know." He kissed the back of my shoulder. "Go to sleep, Hattie."

CHAPTER 11

Finn

I lay on my back, staring up at the ceiling and listening to Hattie's soft and rhythmic breathing. Despite how upset and angry she was at not getting to cum, it hadn't taken her long to fall asleep last night.

After one of the best orgasms of my life, I should have fallen asleep as quickly and easily as she did, but sleep eluded me.

I wanted to fuck Hattie. I could think of nothing else but fucking her. She would never know how close I came to giving in to her pleas last night. But as much as I wanted to fuck her, a bigger part of me wanted - *needed* - her to understand the consequences of not obeying me.

So, I hadn't allowed even a hint of my lust to appear in my voice, had denied myself what I wanted most, and was beyond thankful that Hattie fell asleep before my cock hardened and started pushing against her ass.

I'd eased away from her to lie on my back, smiling when Hattie turned and immediately snuggled up against me. We'd stayed that way all night, Hattie sleeping soundly against me, me and my throbbing cock counting down the hours until we could be buried in her perfect cunt.

I glanced at my alarm clock. It was almost four. Hattie had woken about fifteen minutes ago, sleepily made her way to the bathroom, and then returned to the bed to promptly fall back asleep against me. I stroked her silky hair, the feel of her soft tits against my side and her smooth thigh flung over mine enough to drive me mad with need.

Fuck it. It was technically morning. I needed to taste Hattie, I needed to be in Hattie, and I couldn't wait another fucking minute.

I rolled to face her, smiling when she immediately rolled away from me with a soft mutter. I spooned her and cupped her breast, teasing her nipple into a hard point as she sighed in her sleep before arching against me.

I woke her with soft kisses along her upper back and light pinches and pulls to her nipple. She moaned my name, grinding her ass against my cock. She was still half-asleep when I rolled her to her back and moved between her thighs. I pulled her panties off, tossing them on the floor as I stretched out between her legs and kissed her inner thighs.

She made another soft moan as I pushed her legs wide and studied her perfect pussy. My mouth watered, and I dove in like a man dying of thirst, licking up her slit and teasing her clit with my tongue. Christ, she tasted fucking divine.

She cried out, her body jerking and twitching as her hands clutched at my head. "Finn!"

"Good morning, Hattie," I said before licking her clit again.

"Oh fuck! Oh… oh, good morning to you too," she moaned, making me laugh.

It took barely any time at all before Hattie was dripping. I rubbed my dick against the bed, ignoring my urge to plunge it deep into Hattie's wet cunt. I had promised her a pussy eating, and I wouldn't break that promise.

Besides, I made another long slow lick that had Hattie writhing on the bed, I was confident it wouldn't take long for Hattie to cum on my face. I spread her wet pussy lips with my thumbs and latched onto her swollen clit, sucking hard on it as Hattie cried out and her pelvis arched up off the bed.

I used one hand on her flat stomach to hold her down as her cries grew louder, and she ground her cunt against my mouth. A few more sucks and licks to her clit, and her orgasm exploded through her, sending fresh wetness into my mouth as she screamed my name.

I'd be lucky if my neighbours didn't call in a noise complaint.

I sat up, wiping her sweet cream off my face with the sheet before patting Hattie's thigh. "Turn over, baby."

She turned over, her body still shaking from her orgasm. Usually, I'd let her come down from her high before I fucked her, but my dripping cock demanded relief in the form of Hattie's tight cunt. I pulled her up to her hands and knees, smoothing my hand down her ass as I spread her shaking legs.

Her pussy looked so pretty from this angle I was almost tempted to go down on her again. Instead, I lined my dick up at her entrance and cupped her hips in my hands before sliding into the tightest, slickest cunt I'd ever felt.

Hattie cried out, her hands clawing into the sheets as I bottomed out in her. I probably should have gone slower, given her time to adjust to my size, but, fuck, I was only human. Stopping halfway after months of dreaming about being in her pussy was impossible.

I smoothed my hand over her ass again as my cock throbbed inside her. My urge to spank her was overwhelming.

"Hattie?"

She moaned, and I squeezed her hip with my other hand. "Baby, look at me."

She twisted her head, staring at me through the silky locks of her hair. "Finn, I feel so full."

"You were such a good girl to take all of me like that," I said as I rubbed her ass. "I'm so proud of you, baby."

She wiggled a little on my dick as she tried to get more comfortable. I squeezed her ass and said, "Did you like having your pussy eaten?"

"Mmm," she moaned, making little rocking motions against my dick. "It was so good, Finn. I feel a lot better."

"That's good, baby." I squeezed her hip again when she started to turn her head away. "Did you ask permission to cum?"

She blinked at me, her supple body stilling against mine. "I… yes?"

I grinned and shook my head. "No, you didn't, Hattie. What was rule number three?"

"I don't… I don't cum without your permission."

"That's right," I said.

"Finn," she flipped her hair out of her eyes and licked her lips, "you didn't give me time to ask if I could -"

I slapped her ass hard, groaning when she cried out, and her cunt squeezed hard around me. Without saying anything, I spanked her ten more times, each one harder than the last, gritting my teeth and willing myself not to cum when her cunt clamped around me like a fucking vice with every spank.

"Sir, please!" Hattie cried out.

I rubbed her ass and fucked her hard, driving into her repeatedly as she made a loud cry of pleasure.

I slowed my pace and said, "That spanking was for blaming me for your mistake. This spanking is for not asking my permission to cum this morning."

Hattie cried out when I spanked her ass again. Her ass cheeks were a beautiful bright red, and when Hattie tried to wiggle away, I tightened my grip on her hip and spanked her harder. Her upper body collapsed on the bed, and she buried her face in the pillow, presenting her ass and cunt to me in all their perfect, beautiful glory.

I thrust in and out of her a few times and then spanked her again, enjoying how her body shook, the soft cries she made, and how her cunt practically gushed liquid as I spanked her.

I gave her another ten spanks, enough to make her beg me to stop but not actually safe word. I took her arms, pulling her up onto her knees and resting her spine against my chest as I turned her head toward me and kissed her gently on the mouth.

"Shh, baby, shh. You were such a good girl for your punishment. I'm so proud of you, good girl." I cupped her breasts, lightly teasing her nipples as I pushed in and out of her pussy.

I slid my hand down her flat stomach and between her thighs. She cried out when I rubbed at her clit, her body arching.

"Does my good girl want to cum again?" I asked. I was so fucking close myself. I didn't know if I'd even last long enough for her to cum on my cock.

"Yes," she said. "Yes, please, sir."

"What do you say?" I slid in and out of her, my fingers grazing her clit as her breath caught in her throat.

"May I cum, sir? Please, may I cum?" she asked in her sweet voice.

I pressed a kiss against her mouth. "Yes, baby, you may."

She moaned happily when I fucked her roughly and rubbed her clit. I groaned her name when she came and immediately followed her over the cliff and into pure bliss. Her little pussy milked me, working hard to take all of my cum deep into her body. I stroked in and out, holding her against me until we were completely sated and weak.

I eased out of her, and she fell forward onto the bed with a muffled thump. Smiling, I stretched out beside her, putting my arm around her when she wormed closer and rested her head on my chest.

"That was really great," she mumbled.

"Hmm," I said.

Finally satisfied, I was almost asleep when Hattie said, "Do we have to get up for work now?"

"No," I muttered. "Couple more hours. Go to sleep, baby."

Hattie

"HATTS, ARE YOU GOING TO TELL ME WHAT'S WRONG?" Sophie sat down on her couch next to me.

"Nothing's wrong," I lied.

I glanced toward the front door, and Sophie took my hand. "Liam's out with Nick. He's coming over tonight, but it won't be until later. I know you, Hattie, and there's something wrong. Please tell me what it is."

"I slept with Finn," I said.

Sophie's jaw dropped, and her hand squeezed mine so tight, I lost all feeling. "Soph, ease up."

"Oops, sorry." She released my hand and sat back on the couch. "You slept with Finn. Liam's brother Finn."

"What other Finn do we know?" I asked.

"Good point. Okay, I'm gonna need all the deets - when, where, how…."

"Pretty sure you know how to have sex, Soph," I said.

Sophie laughed and stood up. "I'll get us both iced teas, and then you're telling me everything."

Almost forty minutes and two glasses of iced tea later, I finally stopped talking. Mindful of my promise to Finn, I hadn't said a word about Sapphire's or Finn's involvement in it. It wasn't that I didn't trust Sophie to keep quiet about it. I just couldn't stomach the idea of breaking my promise to Finn.

Instead, I'd told Sophie that Finn had accepted my invitation to have dinner with him the day he brought his car to the shop, and we'd been meeting up at my place.

Sophie studied me thoughtfully. "Okay, so, are you upset because Finn isn't interested in dating and is only giving you a month's worth of," she made finger quotes, "lessons? Or are you upset because you don't like spanking as much as you'd hoped?"

"I like the spanking," I said. "I love it. And last night when he wouldn't let me have an orgasm, even though I was pissed off about it, there was a part of me that liked it."

"That makes sense," Sophie said. "You're looking for discipline, right?"

"Yes." I folded my legs under me and took a sip of iced tea. "I'm upset because I think he regretted taking me to his house last night and letting me spend the night."

"Why do you think he regretted it?" Sophie asked.

"He was quiet and weird this morning and could barely look me in the eye. After his alarm went off at 6:30, he couldn't hustle me out of his place fast enough. I don't think it was in his plans to ever spend the night with me, so things got... weird."

"Sure, but that's on him. You wanted to leave last night, and he wouldn't let you," Sophie said.

"Probably because he was tired and didn't want to drive me home," I said.

"He could have called you an Uber."

"He didn't let me leave because he knew I'd break the rules again," I said.

"Or he wanted to fuck you as much as you wanted to fuck him," Sophie said. "Are you still getting together tomorrow night for your next lesson?"

"I assume so. Maybe not, though. Maybe he's counting last night as the lesson," I said.

Sophie leaned forward. "You like him, Hattie."

"I do," I said. "Which is a huge problem."

Sophie sighed. "Shit, girl. I've been in the exact spot as you. What's with the Whitby boys and their commitment phobia?"

"I don't know," I said. "But at least Liam realized his mistake. That will never happen with Finn. Once our lessons are over, that's it for us."

"Is it? Because he took you for dinner last night and brought you back to his house, even after making it clear it was only Friday night hookups between you too."

"Probably just a moment of madness," I said. "It won't happen again."

Sophie drank the last of her iced tea. "I'm inviting him to your birthday party on Sunday."

"What?" I stared at her. "No, you can't."

"Why not?"

"Because Liam will be there, and Finn doesn't want his family knowing about us," I said.

Sophie scoffed. "As long as you and Finn aren't banging each other on the couch during the party, Liam won't suspect anything. The four of us did have dinner together, and you two have a love of old cars thing in common. Liam won't find it odd that you and Finn are friends."

"He won't come," I said.

"He might."

"He won't." I drank another sip of iced tea. I wasn't outright telling Sophie not to invite him because I knew with utter confidence that Finn would say no.

"Do you need to borrow my car this weekend?" Sophie said. "I can use Liam's if I need to."

"No, it's all good. I replaced the fuel pump in Mabel today, and she's running again," I said.

"Okay, cool." Sophie smiled at me. "Honey, don't resign yourself to thinking this might be it with Finn. From what you just told me, he might be more into you than he'll admit."

"Yeah, maybe," I said. I didn't have the heart to tell her she was wrong. Whatever had happened last night had just been a weird little blip in Finn's brain.

Once the month was over, I'd never be with Finn Whitby again.

"ARE YOU FUCKING SERIOUS RIGHT NOW, CRAIG?" I GLARED at my co-worker, clenching my hands together in a tight fist behind my back so I wouldn't punch him right in his smarmy face.

Craig shrugged. "Look, it isn't my problem. You spent most of your afternoon working on that rich asshole's car."

I bristled at the name calling. "Dr. Whitby is not an asshole, and I worked on his car because the carburetor came in, and he's picking it up tomorrow afternoon. But if I'd known that you told Darren Alderbright that his car would be finished by nine tomorrow morning, I would have worked on it this afternoon."

Craig gave me a shit-eating grin. "Learn to check the fucking schedule, Hattie."

He walked away, and I refrained from kicking the nearest wall. Samesh leaned against the car he was working on, wiping his hands with a rag. "You should talk to Sung-Ho about this, Hattie. Craig did that on purpose."

"Yeah, I know, but Sung-Ho has already left, and he has his kid's recital tonight. I'm not bugging him with this."

"I can stay and help you," Samesh said.

"Don't you have a date with Colleen tonight?"

Samesh's face lit up. "Yeah, I do. But she'll understand."

I shook my head. "It's fine."

"You'll be here until midnight fixing the car," Samesh said. "Don't you have plans tonight?"

"No," I lied. "It's almost five, and you need to get out of here to get ready for your date. Have a good one, Samesh."

"You too. See you tomorrow."

Samesh walked away. Craig had already left, and I was the only one left in the bay. Disappointment made my stomach churn as I pulled out my phone and texted Finn.

Me: Hey, I won't be able to make it to the club this evening. Sorry.

I didn't expect an immediate reply, so I sounded like an excited chipmunk when the three bubbles appeared.

Finn: Did your car break down again?

Me: No, I have to work late. I won't be finished until ten at the earliest.

My heart thumping, I waited anxiously for Finn's reply. Despite what I'd told Sophie last night, I couldn't help but hope that maybe he'd suggest I meet him at his place when I was finished.

Finn: I'll see you next week at the club.

My excitement faded, and I wrote back a quick "sounds good" before shoving my phone into my coveralls pocket. What did I expect? I knew he'd regretted bringing me to his place on Wednesday night.

Swallowing down my bitter disappointment, I tried not to think about Finn at the club with another woman as I headed deeper into the bay.

CHAPTER 12

Hattie

"Oh, this cannot be fucking happening right now." I slammed my hands on the steering wheel as my car sputtered and stalled. I steered it over to the side of the road just as it died completely.

"Goddammit!" I shouted before banging the back of my head against the headrest repeatedly.

I wanted to scream, I wanted to cry, I wanted to burn my fucking car to the ground.

Instead, I took a few deep breaths and stared out the windshield into the darkness. It was just after ten, and I was about halfway home. Despite how late it was, I'd been seriously considering showering quickly and driving to the Sapphire Club.

Why? So, you can watch Finn with another submissive? He'll be playing with someone else by now.

He won't be. We agreed not to sleep with other people. It's the first rule.

No, that's your rule. He made no such rule for himself.

The urge to cry reappeared with a vengeance. My inner voice was right. Finn hadn't agreed not to fuck other women.

I sat for a few minutes, trying to gain the energy to pop the hood and figure out what the fuck was wrong with Mabel now. After only a few minutes, I grabbed my bag and climbed out of the car. Fuck it. I didn't care what was wrong with her. I just wanted to get home, get something into my growling stomach before I passed out from hunger, and then take a hot bath and try not to picture Finn spanking another woman, fucking her, and calling her his good girl in that deep voice of his.

I slammed my door shut and started marching down the dark road. It would take me at least an hour to walk home, but I had no choice. I didn't even have enough money on me for bus fare. What a fucking joke I was.

My phone buzzed, and I yanked it out of my pocket. Finn had texted me, and despite knowing he was probably about to fuck another woman, it still cheered me up marginally.

Finn: Are you at home?

I stopped on the sidewalk and texted back, my thumbs flying over the keyboard.

Me: Just finished work. Halfway home, but my stupid car died on me again, and now I'm walking home. At least it's not raining! How's the club?

I hit send and then smacked myself in the forehead. Did I actually want to know how the club was? No, I fucking didn't. Not that I thought Finn would send me a picture of him with his new submissive or anything, but I wasn't in the mood to hear that he was having a good time.

I quickly put my phone on silent and shoved it into my bag. I would read Finn's reply in the morning when I wasn't feeling so raw and upset.

I had only been walking twenty minutes when headlights

appeared on the road behind me. I briefly considered sticking out my thumb for a ride before telling myself not to be an idiot. Willowdale might be a small town, but that didn't mean hitching a ride with a stranger wasn't a Darwin award winning idea.

The car pulled over and stopped. Despite the lack of light, I recognized the Benz even before Finn stepped out of it.

"Finn? What are you doing here?"

I stared blankly at him as he stormed up on the sidewalk and took my arm. "Jesus Christ, Hattie. What the fuck are you doing?"

"Didn't you get my last text?" I asked. "My car died again."

"I know!" Finn's face was so red I thought he might have a stroke. "Why aren't you answering your phone?"

"I... what?"

"Your phone? Your damn phone, Hattie."

I pulled my phone out of my bag, staring at the numerous text messages and missed calls from Finn. "Oh, sorry, I put my phone on silent after texting you."

"You put your phone on silent? You put your...." Finn made a weird huffing sound before suddenly yanking me into his arms and hugging me hard. "I thought you'd been fucking kidnapped."

"In Willowdale?" I asked. "Finn, are you okay?"

"Fifth rule," he said grimly, holding me out at arm's length so he could stare at me. "You do not put your phone on silent, and you answer my text or phone call within five minutes, or I will spank your pretty little ass until you can't sit down."

"Whoa," I said, "Finn, I think *you* should sit down. I'm pretty sure you're having a stroke or something."

He pinched the bridge of his nose. "You can't just text me

and then put your phone on silent, Hattie. I texted you to stay in your car with the doors locked, and I would pick you up. It took me an extra ten minutes to get here because I didn't know which road you'd taken from the garage because you weren't answering my damn calls!"

He pulled me up against him again, and I awkwardly patted his back. "I'm good. It's not that late, and it's not like I'm out in the middle of nowhere. Also, I thought you were at the club. Why aren't you at the club?"

"Why were you working so late?" Finn asked.

"Craig was being a dick again," I said. "Did you go to the club tonight?"

"What's wrong with your car?"

"I don't know." Sudden weariness made me droop in Finn's arms. "And I don't care at this moment."

"Your car is a piece of shit," Finn said. "You need a new one."

"Thanks for the tip," I said. "As soon as I get a few extra thousand dollars, I'll get right on that."

My mood was ping-ponging back and forth like a four-teen-year-old girl, but I'd had one hell of a long day. I was tired and hungry, and I'd spent most of the evening picturing the man I loved fucking another woman.

Love?

I rubbed my forehead. I could not deal with any of this right now. I was so fucking tired, and my feet hurt, and I just wanted to go home and eat my last package of ramen noodles before my stomach cleaved in on itself from hunger.

"Thanks for checking on me, but I'm fine," I said. "Have a good night, Finn."

I tried to push away from him, but Finn refused to let me go. Instead, he led me toward his car. "Get in, Hattie."

Too exhausted to argue, I climbed into the passenger seat, buckled my seat belt, and closed my eyes.

Finn

I SHUT THE CAR OFF AND RESTED MY HAND ON HATTIE'S thigh. "Hattie, we're home."

Hattie had kept her eyes closed the entire ride home. My intent to lecture her about personal safety had disappeared when I got her in the car and got a good look at her face. She looked exhausted and sad, and I'd had a sudden bout of unexpected guilt for being such a dick to her.

I rubbed her thigh as Hattie opened her eyes and stared out the windshield. "This isn't my house."

"C'mon, baby, let's get you inside."

I slid out of the car and opened Hattie's door when she didn't move. I leaned in and unbuckled her seat belt before taking her hand and tugging her out of the car. She stayed quiet until we were inside my house.

"Why didn't you go to the club tonight?" She took off her shoes and jacket, and I hung her coat in the closet.

"I didn't feel like it," I said.

"But you always go to the club on Friday nights."

I didn't reply, leading her up the stairs to my bedroom and into the attached bathroom. I drew her a bath in the soaker tub as she leaned against the counter and watched silently. She didn't protest when I stripped off her clothes. She just climbed into the hot water and sank to her chin with a soft sigh.

"You soak for a while. I'll get started on dinner," I said.

I ordered dinner from the Vintage Kitchen, staying downstairs and leaving Hattie to her bath until the food arrived. I carried it upstairs and set it on the nightstand before peering into the bathroom. "Food's here. You ready to eat?"

"Yes. I'm starving." She stood, and I handed her a towel, leaving the bathroom before my cock could get the better of me. Hattie needed food, not fucking.

I changed into a pair of athletic shorts and a t-shirt before grabbing another shirt from my closet. When Hattie appeared in the bedroom in the towel, I handed her the shirt. "Put this on."

She slipped it over her head, and I took the towel from her, hanging it on the towel rack before returning to the bedroom. "Sit on the bed, Hattie."

She sat down, piling some pillows between her and the headboard. I sat down next to her, stuffing some pillows behind my back and opened up the bag of food. I handed Hattie her burger and fries, watching with satisfaction when she immediately started eating.

"Sorry," she said after about five minutes, "I'm so hungry, but I'm being kind of rude."

"You're not." I bit into my burger.

"How much do I owe you for dinner?"

"My treat," I said.

She crinkled her nose at me but didn't reply. I watched her eat, my cock twitching at the look of sheer bliss on her face as she ate. Fuck, was there anything Hattie didn't do that didn't make me want to fuck her?

When we were finished eating, I stuffed the garbage into the bag and carried it downstairs to the kitchen, returning with bottles of water for both of us. Hattie took a long drink and leaned against the pillows. "I feel better, thank you."

"You're welcome."

"You really didn't go to the club earlier tonight?" she asked.

"No," I said.

"Why not? You go every Friday night."

"Not always," I said. "What are you going to do about your car?"

I hated the stress that immediately infused her body, but I couldn't have her out there being stranded on the side of the road every other day.

She nibbled at her nails. "Probably junk it and take the bus for a while. Even buying second-hand parts for the damn thing no longer feels worth it. Better to save my money for a new one. Well, a second-hand one, but you know what I... oh, shit!"

She yanked her hand away from her mouth and stared at me. "I haven't bitten my nails since Wednesday night, but I'm tired and a little upset."

She rubbed at her forehead. Weariness was etched into every part of her face as I slid off the bed and ducked into the bathroom. When I returned, she said, "I know I broke a rule, but can we push the punishment to next Friday? I am so not in the mood to be spanked."

I sat cross-legged next to her, rolling the glass bottle between my hands before saying, "Give me your hand, Hattie."

She held out her hand and watched with a small, bemused smile as I carefully painted her nails with the clear nail polish. "You're pretty good at this."

"I used to paint Alina's nails for her after the accident. It cheered her up."

"You're a great brother, Finn," Hattie said.

The admiration in her voice sent warmth rushing through me. I didn't know when Hattie's opinion of me had become as important as Gabe's and my siblings, but I couldn't deny that it was.

"So, this is Alina's nail polish?" Hattie asked.

I shook my head but didn't elaborate. After work today, I had stopped at the drugstore and specifically bought the polish for Hattie, but she didn't need to know that.

I capped the bottle and gently blew on Hattie's fingernails. "This is bitter nail polish."

She made a face. "I hate that stuff."

I blew on her nails again. "Yes, I imagine you do. But it'll help you stop biting your nails and avoid punishment for breaking the rules."

She studied her fingers. "Do I have to be punished tonight, Finn? I know I broke the rules, but I'm not into spanking or denied orgasms right now."

"No punishments tonight, baby," I said.

She relaxed against the pillows as I set the polish on the nightstand. After a few seconds of awkward silence, she sat up again. "Okay, well, I should go. Thank you for dinner."

I pressed my hand on her thigh. "You're staying the night."

"If you have a few bucks I can borrow until I see you again, I can take the bus home," she said. "There's a bus stop only a couple of blocks from here."

I shook my head. "It's almost midnight, Hattie. You're not taking the bus. You're staying here, and, in the morning, I'll drive you to your place for fresh clothes and then drop you off at the garage."

"I don't think I should stay," she said.

My stomach felt like I'd taken a punch and my first reaction was to grab the soft ropes I kept under the bed and tie Hattie to the headboard so she couldn't leave.

That's called kidnapping.

I kept my voice calm. "Why do you feel that way?"

"Because when I stayed Wednesday night, you regretted it the next morning." She lifted her fingers to her mouth before making an exasperated face and tucking her hands under her thighs. "I don't want to see that regret on your face again tomorrow morning."

I hated that she could read me so easily. Typically, I had an excellent poker face, but it went right out the fucking window around Hattie.

"It was a bit strange for me in the morning because I rarely play with subs outside of the club, and I've never had a sub stay the night in my bed," I said.

She blinked at me. "Oh. Yeah, okay, I can see why that would freak you out then. Look, you don't have to worry. I know what this is between us, and I'm not a stalker like Amber."

"I know, but I don't want my actions to suggest that I'm looking for more than we initially agreed on," I said.

My back was sweating, and I had to work to keep my gaze on Hattie's. Could she tell I was lying? I waited for her to ask me why I'd brought her to my house Wednesday night and tonight. Any answer I gave would sound like the lie it was.

To my surprise, all she said was, "I appreciate the clarification."

She slid out of bed, and I said, "Where are you going?"

Christ, now I sounded like a fucking stalker.

"Just to the bathroom," she said.

"You're staying the night," I said. "There's a new toothbrush in the medicine cabinet you can use."

"Thank you." She walked into the bathroom, and feeling awkward and stupid, I turned off all the lights except for my bedside light, stripped off my clothes, and climbed into bed.

I wondered if I should dig out a pair of sleep pants to wear. I usually slept naked, but I didn't want Hattie to feel she had to fuck me. I wanted her - when did I not want her - but she didn't need sex tonight. She needed sleep.

Then why not let her go home? You don't want her to get the wrong idea, but you're allowing her to spend the night without fucking her. You're giving Hattie mixed messages, asshole.

I punched my pillow into a more comfortable position and stared at the ceiling. I wasn't giving her mixed messages. I was letting her spend the night because it was late, and I didn't want to drive her home.

Then why did you bring her back here? Why not just drive her straight home when you picked her up?

Because her trailer wasn't safe, someone was shot there just last week.

Unless you plan to let Hattie move in with you permanently, her living situation isn't your problem.

The bathroom door opened, and Hattie hesitated before crossing the room and climbing into my bed. She curled on her side, staring at me in the dim light before saying, "May I touch you, sir?"

My pulse immediately went haywire, and my dick twitched in anticipation. When I spoke, my voice was hoarse, "Yes."

Her soft hand smoothed across my chest and down my abdomen. The muscles jumped and twitched under her touch as she scooted closer. "You have a great body."

"For my age, you mean," I said.

She scowled, her hand stopping just below my navel. "Did I say that?"

"No," I said.

"Then stop putting words in my mouth."

Her sassy attitude made my dick go from half-hard to fully erect. Hattie had the cutest little scowl on her face, and I reached out and traced the line that appeared on the smooth skin between her eyes. "Before you say much more, know that while I won't spank you tonight, I will keep track of all of your spankable offenses this evening to be administered at a different time. That includes sassing me."

She started to giggle. "Sassing you, is that what I'm doing?"

"Yes," I said with a grin.

Moving quickly, she straddled me. When her pussy brushed against my erect dick, I groaned, and a smug smile crossed her face. "You like it when I sass you."

"I never said I didn't. Only that you'd be spanked for it."

She grinned again, rubbing her soft cunt against my dick with slow and gentle movements as she trailed her fingers over my chest. "You know I don't care about the age difference, right?"

"I know," I said. "But someone your age is better for you."

"Why?"

"Because…"

Fuck, I couldn't think of a single reason.

"Can't even come up with a bullshit reason, I see," Hattie said with a cheeky grin.

I slid my hands to her ass, cupping each gloriously firm cheek and squeezing them. "Your pussy is distracting me."

"Is that right?"

"Yes. I can feel how wet she's getting."

"You do seem to get her wet in record-breaking time," Hattie said. She pulled her shirt over her head and tossed it on the floor.

I stared greedily at her naked breasts before cupping them

and pulling on her nipples. "Lean over so I can suck on your nipples, baby."

"Yes, sir." Her voice was breathless, and she made delightful moans when I wrapped my lips around one stiff peak and sucked. "Oh God, that feels good."

She was rocking against me, using my cock to get herself off, and I reached down and squeezed her hip. Understanding my silent request, she slowed her movements but not without pouting at me.

I released her nipple before tucking her dark hair behind her ears and smoothing my thumb across her lip. "We don't have to have sex tonight, baby. You know that, right? I know you've had a long day and -"

"I want to have sex with you," she said quickly. Her face twisted a little, her body stiffening against mine. "Unless you don't want to? It's fine if you don't. I can -"

I pinched her nipple, making her gasp. There was added wetness on my dick, and Hattie made small rocking motions against my cock again. I fucking loved that she loved a little pain with her pleasure.

"Put my cock in your pretty wet cunt," I said.

"Yes, sir." Hattie straightened and reached behind her to grab my cock. I gritted my teeth at the feel of her soft hand as she guided me into her soaking wet entrance.

We groaned in unison when she took my dick with one smooth downward thrust. I gripped her hips and waited. Sliding into her heat and slick tightness was like coming home after a long trip. I would never tire of being with her, of holding her, of loving her.

Love?

"God, that feels so good," Hattie moaned. She braced her hands on my chest. "May I move, sir?"

"Yes." I held her hips in a loose grip, letting her control

the pace and the depth as she moved up and down. "Does that feel good, baby?"

"So good," she muttered. "I love your dick."

I grinned. "He loves you too."

She stared down at me as she moved, her breath growing ragged and her fingers digging into my chest.

"Come here, baby," I said, tugging on her hips.

She leaned over me, and we kissed, our breaths mingling, our tongues teasing. I kissed her neck before sliding my arm around her waist and anchoring her body against mine. I thrust hard, my body immediately on edge, my balls drawing up and the base of my spine tingling. I never lost control the way I did with Hattie.

Her small cries and soft gasps spurred me to move harder and faster. Her fingers dug into my shoulders as I buried my face in her throat. She made a harsh cry of need before moaning, "Sir, may I cum?"

I lifted my head enough to rasp, "Yes," before burying my face into her throat again.

She cried my name, her body arching against mine as her pussy clamped onto my dick. Her orgasm tipped me over the edge and into mine, and I drove deep into my girl, giving her every bit of me as her pussy squeezed around me.

My body shaking, I eased my grip on her waist and caressed Hattie's quivering back as I listened to her pant softly into my ear.

"Okay, baby?" I asked.

"Hmm," she said before sliding off me in a boneless little heap.

I pulled her up against me, her body notched perfectly against mine, and I smoothed her hair back from her face as she smiled up at me. "Oh God, I feel so much better."

"Good," I said.

"Nothing like an amazing orgasm to make you forget about your problems," she said.

"Happy to help," I said with a small grin.

"Thank you for rescuing me, feeding me dinner, and letting me spend the night," Hattie said before yawning. "Your house is so much better than mine."

"You're welcome. Go to sleep, baby. It's late."

"Okay."

I shut off the light before staring at the dark ceiling. Hattie's breathing was evening out, and her body had relaxed against me.

It felt way too right to have Hattie in my bed.

CHAPTER 13

Hattie

"So, with the new carburetor, you really shouldn't have any more issues." I brushed my hand along Gretchen's hood. "Sung-Ho took it for a test drive, and he said she's running smoothly."

Finn raised an eyebrow. "Why didn't you do the test drive?"

I kept a nonchalant expression on my face, even though I was still pissed that Sung-Ho wouldn't let me drive Finn's car. "Perks of being the boss. Anyway, thank you for your business, Dr. Whitby. I enjoyed working on Gretchen."

Finn nodded and held out his hand. "Thank you, Ms. King."

We shook hands. The formality was killing me, especially since I'd had Finn's dick in my mouth first thing this morning, but we were in plain view of the garage, and most of my coworkers working on cars in the bay occasionally glanced over. Not that I thought any of them were interested in how Finn and I were behaving with each other, but I knew how important it was to Finn that no one knew we were fucking regularly.

Speaking of which… I dropped Finn's hand and gathered my courage. Saturday nights weren't part of our agreement, but neither were Wednesday nights or vanilla sex.

Was it vanilla sex last night, Hattie? You still had to ask him for permission to cum.

True, but the lack of spanking and the tenderness Finn had displayed made it feel pretty vanilla to me.

I kept my voice low. "If you're not busy later tonight, I could come by your house."

Finn hesitated. "I'm spending the evening with Alina and Liam and Sophie."

"Oh, okay." I shoved my hands into my coverall pockets so he wouldn't see my clenched fists. He wouldn't ask me to join them. So, why couldn't I stop the tiny flicker of hope in my belly?

Finn cleared his throat and glanced at his watch. "I need to go. I'm meeting Gabe for lunch."

"Right, of course. Sorry." I was standing in front of his driver's door, and I scooted out of the way, plastering a smile on my face. "Enjoy the rest of your weekend."

He opened the car door before saying, "What's the news on your car?"

I kept the smile on my face like a fucking champ. "Oh, Mable's gone to that great junkyard in the sky. I had her towed to the garage this morning, and Sung-Ho took a look at her for me. Like I suspected, she isn't worth fixing even with second-hand parts."

A muscle twitched in his jaw. "How are you getting home this evening?"

"I've bought a bus pass. I need to get back to work. Bye,

Dr. Whitby." I waved awkwardly before turning and hurrying back to the garage.

"Ouch! Fuck!" I stumbled back and stared at the blood welling up on my knuckle before sticking it in my mouth and sucking it away. The metallic taste made me grimace, and I dropped the socket wrench into my toolbox before kicking the front fender of the Lincoln.

Normally, working on restoring the Lincoln cheered me up, but right now, I only felt frustration and anger. And hunger. I'd spent the last of my cash on a bus pass and getting Mabel towed to the garage and then the junkyard, and payday wasn't until Monday. Which meant I needed to save my last packet of ramen for tomorrow.

I muttered another curse and closed the Lincoln's hood with a harsh bang. Fuck, I hated being broke. I hated that I couldn't make a proper budget. Thanks to a fucked up childhood and a mother who cared more about other people's opinions than her daughter, I barely had any usable life skills, including money management.

Yeah, those things suck, but I think you're actually upset about Finn not inviting you to dinner at his sister's tonight.

I wished my brain would just give it a fucking rest already.

"You okay, Hattie?"

I glanced up to see Louie watering the flowers planted at the front of their trailer. "Yeah, I'm good. How's your arm?"

Louie flexed it a little. "Better now. Still can't wipe my fucking ass without it hurting like hell, but -"

Gina stuck her head out the open kitchen window. "You

barely wiped your fucking ass before I shot you, Louie, so don't start acting like that's why you don't now."

Louie turned red. "Gina, why you gotta say shit like that in front of Hattie?"

Gina rolled her eyes. "Louie, you know I love you and think you're fucking hot, but Hattie don't. She's way out of your league, baby."

Louie blushed even harder. "Ignore Gina, Hattie. She's been into the vodka again."

"Fuck, yeah, I have," Gina said. "Hattie, honey, I'm making some of my famous meatloaf tomorrow. I'll bring some over for you, yeah?"

"Thank you, Gina," I said. "That's really nice of you."

"You're welcome, honey. Louie, get your ass in here. I want my pussy eaten before *Wheel of Fortune* starts."

Still bright red, Louie dropped the hose and, moving pretty quickly for a guy who'd been shot recently, headed into his and Gina's trailer.

Gina winked at me. "See you later, honey."

"Bye, Gina."

She closed the kitchen window, and I hauled the tarp back over the Lincoln, grabbed my toolbox, and headed into my trailer. I closed the door, staring silently at the place I called home. While I had a lot of good memories of my grandparents here, the trailer showed its age with chipped and ragged linoleum, worn carpet, and faded wallpaper. And that was just the external issues. The plumbing was barely functional, with a water heater that gave me a bucket of hot water at a time if I was lucky, the furnace made a weird grinding noise whenever it came on, and if I tried to use the microwave and the toaster at the same time, it blew every fuse in the trailer.

The place was falling apart around me, and in the last

year or so, I'd stopped letting even Sophie visit me here. It was too embarrassing… too depressing.

I took a quick shower, thinking longingly about the large walk-in shower at Finn's house and the glorious amount of hot water it dispensed before making myself the last packet of ramen noodles. At least Gina's offer of meatloaf meant I could eat once today.

I ate the noodles standing over the sink as I stared out the window. I didn't have a television, and last year I'd cancelled all my streaming services in an attempt to better budget. Usually, I didn't care much for watching television, but as the prospect of a boring evening stretched out in front of me, I wished bitterly for the distraction of some mindless binge-watching. Maybe then I could get Finn the fuck out of my head.

I slurped up the last of my noodles and wiped my face before leaving the bowl in the sink. My phone rang, and I glanced at the unknown number on my screen. I debated for a few seconds about answering it before hitting the button.

"Hello?"

"Sweetheart, it's mama."

The noodles in my stomach immediately turned into a mountain of heavy bricks. My jaw clenched, and I had to peel my tongue from the roof of my mouth and force my shoulders down.

"Did you get a new number?" I made my way to the living room, sinking onto the couch.

"Yes. The most dreadful man was stalking me with the other one," my mother said. "Hattie, sweetheart, I need a favour."

That was my mother in a nutshell. At one point in time, shortly after I'd left Hollywood for good, she'd at least attempted to pretend to care about me before she told me what she needed. But that hadn't lasted long. Especially when she realized it didn't help her win me over.

"I don't have any money," I said automatically.

She scoffed in my ear. "I'm not asking for money. God, Hattie, you always think the worst of me."

She'd asked me for money in the past, always getting angry and accusing me of refusing to help because I was still mad about the 'little contract mix up'.

"What kind of favour do you need?" I asked.

"You know I'm on that reality show, 'MILF's in Love', right?"

"Yes," I said. "I haven't watched any of it, though."

"Of course, you haven't. Why would you want to support your mother?" she asked.

I didn't reply, and my mother made an irritated sniff before continuing. "I'm one of the most popular contestants on the show, and the producers want you to be a part of the family segment. You'll have dinner with Thomas and me."

"Thomas… that's the twenty-two-year-old musician?"

"I thought you didn't watch the show," she said.

"Sophie told me about him."

"Yes, that's Thomas. Anyway, the show will pay to fly you to LA and pay for your hotel accommodation. They want to tape the segment on Friday, so you'll need to fly out that morning at the latest."

"I'm working," I said.

"I'm sure your boss will give you the time off," she said. "It's not like your job matters all that much, Hattie."

I bit viciously at my nails, ignoring the nail polish's bitter taste filling my mouth. "My job matters more than some goddamn reality television show."

"You watch your mouth," my mother said. "Hattie, this is important to me."

"I'm not doing it," I said. "I don't want to be on television anymore, and you know that."

"All the other contestants have family members for their segments. I need you to do this for me, Hattie. I haven't asked you for anything in a very long time, and you owe me."

"I owe you?" I said as anger burned bright in my belly. "What do I owe you for, Mom? A raging drug and alcohol problem? A fucked up childhood? Living in poverty now because you spent all of the money I earned as a kid on drugs and vacations and random men?"

"How dare you!" my mother shouted. "I gave up everything for you. I had a successful career, and I gave it up so you could live your dream of being an actress!"

"Being an actor was your dream, not mine." My voice rose. "You used me to live out your fucking dream, and when I stopped being your puppet, what did you do? You fucking walked away from me like I was nothing! Like I didn't matter unless I did exactly what you wanted me to do."

"Don't you speak to me like that!" my mother shouted. "You have no idea what I had to do to keep you on that show! I more than earned that money, and I'm tired of you making me feel guilty. Maybe I wasn't a perfect mother, but I loved you, and I did my best by you."

"No, you didn't," I said. "All you cared about was yourself, which became glaringly obvious when I quit the show."

"You little bitch!" she screamed. "You think my life was so fucking easy? I had to get down on my knees every fucking week and give the producer a blowjob just to keep you on that fucking show! They wanted to fire you after the first week because you were such a terrible actress. If it hadn't been for me, you would be a nobody, Hattie! People know your name because of me! Because of what I did for you! You're nothing without me, and no matter what lies you

303

tell yourself, we both know you only succeeded because of me."

My stomach churning, nails bitten and bleeding, I said, "Don't ever call me again."

"Fuck you, Hattie! Fuck you and your sanctimonious -"

I ended the call and dropped my phone on the couch like a poisonous snake when it rang again. I silenced the call and scrolled through my contacts to call Sophie. I hesitated. I couldn't call her. She was with Liam and Alina and... I swallowed hard, my throat burning... Finn.

My phone rang again, and I could almost feel my mother's rage boiling through the phone. Tears sliding down my cheeks, I turned my phone off before curling into a ball on the couch and chewing at my nails.

CHAPTER 14

Finn

I parked in Hattie's driveway, climbing out of my car and locking it. It was too late for me to be here, but I could see lights on in Hattie's trailer. Relief washed over me. At least she was at home and safe. I'd sent three texts and called twice since leaving Alina's, and Hattie hadn't answered any of them. I hesitated, tapping my fingers on Gretchen's roof. Hattie ignoring me meant this was a bad fucking idea, but the look on her face when I told her my plans for this evening had haunted me for hours.

It took everything in me not to invite her to join me, but what would Liam and Alina think? As much as I enjoyed Hattie's company, we couldn't be a couple. She was too young for me, no matter what she thought, and my failed marriage and past relationships proved that even if the kink factor didn't die off, I was really fucking terrible at being a partner.

You could try. You could do therapy. You could figure out how to be a good partner to her. You love her. Do this for her.

Ignoring my inner voice was getting harder and harder, as was my ability to stay away from Hattie. This was a mistake, but I couldn't stay away from her tonight. But I would keep it less relationship and more dom/sub. I would spank Hattie for ignoring my texts and breaking rule five, eat her sweet pussy, fuck her, and leave.

There was a low whistle from the trailer to the left of Hattie's. I glanced over, staring at the man who stepped into the circle of light from the streetlamp in front of their trailer, a cigarette in one hand and a beer in the other. "That's a damn nice car. What is that, a Chevy Bel Air?"

"That's right," I said.

The man inhaled a drag from the cigarette. "Sweet. That's Hattie's favourite car. You her new man?"

"Who's asking?" I said.

The man shrugged. "I am. A young woman who lives alone needs someone to watch out for her."

My hands clenched into fists at the idea that this man might think Hattie belonged to him or needed his protection when she was mine to protect. "Stay away from her, or -"

"Louie!" A dark-haired woman stuck her head out of a window in the trailer. "Baby, the show's comin' back on. Finish your smoke and get back in here."

"Just a minute, Gina. I'm talking to Hattie's friend," Louie said.

Louie and Gina? My eyeballs nearly bulged out of my head. Hattie lived directly next to the woman who'd shot her husband. Fuck me sideways.

Gina looked me up and down. "Jesus, you're a good looking fucker, ain't ya? You Hattie's new man?"

"Yes," I said. "And you're Gina, the woman who got a little too worked up over *Jeopardy*."

Gina cackled laughter. "Christ, I'm not ever gonna live that down. Louie, hurry the fuck up, baby."

"Be right there." Louie took another drag of his cigarette before butting it out in a large metal can next to the trailer. "You be good to our Hattie. She's a real sweet girl."

I nodded as he walked back into his trailer. I waited for a beat before setting the alarm on Gretchen and then climbing Hattie's front stoop's weathered and splintered steps. I knocked on the trailer door and knocked again after a few minutes.

I clenched my jaw, tempted to hammer on the door, when she still didn't answer. Before I could give in to the temptation, the outside light flicked on, nearly blinding me.

The door opened, and Hattie stared at me. "What are you doing here?"

I held up my hand to block the light. "Can I come in?"

"I was just going to bed."

"It'll only take a minute," I lied.

She sighed. "Fine, whatever."

She walked away, and after a few seconds, I stepped inside and closed the door behind me. She didn't even have a fucking deadbolt on her door, just a flimsy lock on the handle. *Christ.*

"You need to install a deadbolt," I said.

"I'll get right on that." She stood in the tiny kitchen, her back to me as she stared out the window above the sink.

Her kitchen was beach themed with mermaid paintings on the walls, sea turtle salt and pepper shakers, seashell printed dish towels, and aqua coloured accents. A framed picture of Hattie and Sophie standing on a beach with the ocean behind them hung on the wall above the counter.

"You like the beach, huh?" I asked.

"Did you come here to ask me about my vacation habits?"

she said without turning.

"I met your neighbours," I said. "You didn't mention that the woman who shot her husband lived right next door to you."

"It wasn't relevant to the conversation," she said.

"Bullshit. You can't stay here any longer, Hattie. It isn't safe."

Her back stiffened, and her fingers clenched onto the counter's edge. I could see how ragged they were, and the blood caked around her nail beds even from where I stood.

"I'll take your advice under consideration," she said. "Is that all?"

"You broke the fifth rule," I said. "I've texted and called you in the last half hour."

"My phone is off," she said. "And I didn't agree to that fucking rule when we made our arrangement."

I walked toward her, stopping a few inches away. Her entire body vibrated, and her anger and tension were palpable. I'd known she was upset with me when I left the garage earlier today, but her attitude about it was well over the top.

You really think that's what this is about?

No, I really didn't.

"You also broke rule four," I said, reaching out to graze my fingers along her hand.

She snatched her hand away and whirled to face me. "Screw you and your rules, Finn Whitby!"

I stared at her pale face, red and swollen eyelids, and the still visible tear tracks on her cheeks. My feeling that whatever was wrong with Hattie had nothing to do with me deepened. "Tell me why you're crying."

"It's none of your business," she snapped. "I don't feel like being bossed around tonight."

I studied her silently. Her mouth quivered, and she looked

away. The sorrow, anger, and adrenaline radiating from her shaking body made *me* tense and upset. I could only imagine how she felt. I stepped back, and her entire body twitched, her hands reaching out for me before she clenched them into fists and dropped them to her sides.

She didn't want me to leave, despite how she was acting. Every instinct in my body told me something had happened to her tonight that made her desperate for me to be the Dom she needed. I walked to the living room without speaking and sat down on the couch. Hattie stared at me with a mixture of hope and apprehension.

I patted my lap. "Strip and over my knee, Hattie."

"I said I don't want to play," she said.

"Do as I say," I said.

She swallowed hard and joined me at the couch, stripping off the pajama bottoms and tank top she wore. She was naked under them, and I smoothed my hand down her spine when she draped her soft body over my lap.

"That's my good girl," I said.

She made a quiet sob. "Finn, I want… I need…"

"I know what you need, baby," I said and spanked her.

She jerked against my lap, and I cupped her narrow waist, holding her tight against me as I spanked her with firm and rhythmic slaps. I didn't spank her hard, but it didn't take long for her ass to turn rosy and grow warm under my palm.

She was utterly limp against me, her cheek resting against the arm of the couch, and the anxiety and anger on her face gone. In its place was bliss, and when I reached between her thighs and touched her pussy, she was soaking wet.

She moaned, her hands digging into the cushions as I teased her clit with firm circles before sliding my middle finger into her tight cunt. I finger fucked her, watching as she squirmed on my lap, the pleasure growing on her face.

When I knew she was close, I withdrew my finger, ignoring her cry of protest and spanked her again. I'd spanked her much harder in the past, but that wasn't what she needed tonight. She didn't need pain with her pleasure. She needed the freedom of giving up control and allowing me to take away her anger and anxiety.

I took my time, alternating between spanking her and touching her sweet pussy until nothing remained on her face but pure need and desire.

"Sir, please," she finally moaned when I smoothed my hand over her bright red ass. "Please, may I cum?"

"Yes, baby, you may." I rubbed her clit in firm circles, watching with pleasure and pride as Hattie immediately cried out and came hard on my fingers, her body shaking, her well-spanked ass jiggling delightfully.

She collapsed against me, her pussy quivering against my fingers and soft little gasps still escaping her mouth. Ignoring my raging erection, I helped her sit up next to me. "How do you feel, baby?"

"Better. I feel better," she said and then burst into tears.

I pulled her into my lap, leaning back against the couch as she curled into me like a lost kitten and cried. I rubbed her back and rocked her lightly, pressing kisses into her fragrant, silky hair as she sobbed. It took nearly fifteen minutes for the tears to slow and then stop. I handed her some tissues from the box on the coffee table, and she kept her head on my chest as she wiped her face and blew her nose.

I rubbed her back again, shifting her on my lap into a more comfortable position. "Tell me what happened."

She sighed and then, speaking haltingly at first but gaining speed as she went on, told me about her mother's phone call. I pulled her close and hugged her, kissing her on the mouth. "I'm sorry she said those things to you."

"The worst part is, it isn't the first time she's said it," Hattie said wearily. "This time, it was the producer she claimed she had to blow weekly, but in the past, it's been the director, the president of the network, and once when she was completely coked out, she said it was the head of wardrobe she had to blow. It's all lies, but it's upsetting."

"She's a terrible person and a horrible mother," I said.

"Isn't that the truth." Hattie sat up and tried to slide off my lap. I tightened my hold on her.

"Stay with me, Hattie."

She glanced at me before looking down at her lap. "Thank you for spanking me. It helped, and I appreciate it more than I can say."

"You're welcome," I said.

When she reached for the button on my jeans, I covered her hand with mine. "What are you doing?"

"It's your turn," she said. "I can blow you, or if you don't mind that my bed is a double, we can have sex before you leave."

"Stand up," I said.

She stood, and I followed suit, palming her red ass and squeezing gently. "Get dressed and pack some clothes and your toiletries, please, Hattie."

"What? Why?" she asked.

"You're staying at my house for the rest of the weekend."

She raised her fingers to her mouth, and I took her hand before she could bite at her nails. "Finn, I'm fine now. I know you're not comfortable with me staying the night, and I -"

"Hattie," I said, "do as I say or when we get home, I'll eat your pussy until you're begging me to cum, and then I'll make you go to bed without your orgasm."

"You wouldn't do that to me. I've had a terrible day," she said.

"You have. And if you don't get your adorable ass into your room and start packing, it will get worse. A 'you get teased every night but don't get to cum until next weekend' kind of worse," I said.

"You monster," she said, but there was a grin on her face, and she was starting to look more like the Hattie I knew and loved.

"Be my good girl and do what I've asked," I said with another tap to her butt.

"Yes, sir." She paused and then stood on her tiptoes to give me an almost shy kiss. "Thank you, Finn."

"You're welcome, baby."

Hattie

"I don't think I've ever seen you look this happy." Sophie linked her arm through mine and leaned her head against my arm.

"It's my birthday. Of course, I'm going to be happy," I said.

"Sure, but are you happy because it's your birthday or because a certain someone said yes to coming to your birthday party." Sophie gazed at Finn.

He stood at the far end of Sophie's small backyard. He had a beer in one hand and a hot dog in the other, and he was grinning at something Samesh said to him. Monica joined them, and a spark of jealousy zinged through me at how she looked at Finn.

Sophie squeezed my arm. "Don't worry, Hatts. Finn only has eyes for you."

"It's fine," I said. "Monica is close to his age. Maybe

they'll have more in common than Finn and me."

"Keep lying to me like this, and you'll get a birthday spanking," Sophie said, then giggled. "Wait, I bet Finn already gave you one, didn't he?"

"He might have," I said.

"You dirty girl, I fucking love it!" Sophie's gaze turned to Liam, who grilled hamburgers while talking to Sung-Ho and his wife. "I'm going to ask Liam if I can spank him tonight. I bet he'll let me. He's super down with trying whatever I want in the bedroom."

"Good for you, Soph," I said with a grin.

"Good for both of us. We're getting exactly what we want with the Whitby boys," Sophie said.

When I didn't reply, Sophie squeezed my arm again. "Honey, Finn is going to give you more. A man can't look at you like he does and not want more. He just needs some time to adjust to the age difference."

"It isn't just that. He says he's terrible at relationships."

Sophie frowned. "Liam thinks that Finn's first marriage ended because Finn focused so much of his time and energy on Alina and Liam after their mom died."

"There were other issues in the marriage before Alina's accident," I said. "Finn didn't go into detail, but it isn't just his marriage ending. He says he isn't partner material based on other relationships. Throw in the age difference, and I don't have a chance with him. Once our month is up, he'll move on to someone else at the club."

Sophie shook her head. "You're wrong, honey. And I'll be the first to say I told you so when you realize Finn wants more. Because I am just that good of a fucking friend."

I laughed and kissed Sophie on the side of her head. "You're the best fucking friend."

CHAPTER 15

Hattie

I leaned against the Lincoln and wiped the grease from my hands. I'd taken advantage of the warm sunshine and worked on the car for most of the afternoon. It was a gorgeous day, and not only was it Monday and my day off, but Finn was picking me up as soon as he finished work.

I grinned and wiped at a smear of dirt on the Lincoln. The Friday-only rule had gone completely out the window in the last week and a half. Finn and I spent every evening together, and I'd only slept at my trailer once since my birthday weekend.

It was kind of cute all the excuses Finn came up with to justify keeping me at his place every night. They ranged from he was too tired to drive me home and the lock on my trailer wasn't good enough to, it was faster and easier to take the bus from Finn's place to the shop in the morning.

He wasn't wrong about that last one. It was a fifteen-minute bus ride to the garage from Finn's place and nearly forty-five minutes from mine.

We'd gone to Sapphire's on Friday night, and I didn't think I'd imagined the looks of envy from some of the other subs when I'd hung off Finn's arm all night. It made me feel good, to be honest. Knowing I was with the hottest man in the club was a heady rush, and that night had been one of the best of my life. Of course, Finn strapping me down to a spanking bench in one of the private rooms and then spanking me into not one, but two orgasms may also have contributed to the best night of my life feeling.

Yeah, well, don't get used to it. After this weekend, your month is up, and your lessons are finished.

It was easy to ignore my inner voice. I wasn't living with Finn or anything, but what we were doing felt more like a relationship than a month of lessons. I was confident that Finn and I would continue after this weekend. I wanted to be with him, and he wanted to be with me. It was more than sex to him now. If it wasn't, why did he ask me to come over after work last Wednesday when he'd had to leave the lab early with a terrible headache? We didn't even have sex. I'd made him something to eat and then brought him cold packs for his headache while we'd snuggled in bed for the evening.

My smile widened. Finn and I were in a relationship, even if he pretended he couldn't see it. But I was a patient girl. I could wait until he dropped the pretense.

I left the rag on the Lincoln and headed into the house. I grabbed the water jug from the fridge and poured myself a glass, drinking it down in a few large gulps before pouring another half glass. I'd work on the Lincoln for another hour and then shower and maybe pack a small overnight bag. Finn hadn't explicitly asked me to spend the night with him, but no harm in being prepared, right?

Leaving the glass on the counter, I headed back outside,

staring in surprise at the cluster of people standing at the bottom of the front steps. My heart sank when I saw the cameras and the microphones. Fuck, what did my mother do now?

"I have no comment," I said before they could even start yelling questions. "Whatever my mother has done, I have no comment on her or -"

"Is your mother right, Hattie?" A dark-haired reporter in skinny jeans and a sweater climbed the stairs and thrust a microphone into my face. "Do you have daddy issues? Is that why you're into older men and being dominated?"

Thick shock rendered me immobile. I stared wide-eyed at the woman as the reporters surged up the steps and surrounded me.

"How long have you been going to Sapphire?" Another reporter shouted. "How long has Finn Whitby been your Dom? How did the two of you meet?"

"Are you into just spanking or more?" The dark-haired reporter was relentless in her questioning. "Have you been flogged? Does Finn Whitby beat you regularly? Do you call him daddy because you don't have one?"

Cameras flashed, and as the reporters jostled closer and more questions were shouted, my body began to shake. I tried to back up but ran into a man with a camera. His lens smacked into my head, and he huffed irritably. "For fuck's sake, watch where you're goin'!"

I held my hand up, trying to block the glare of the camera flashes as more questions were screamed. I couldn't think, I couldn't move, I couldn't breathe. I was drowning right here in front of my crappy trailer and -

"Hattie! Honey, hold on!"

Sophie's voice sent a surge of relief through me.

I jerked, and a few reporters made startled gasps when

Liam's voice boomed out. "Get the fuck away from her, you assholes!"

"Fucking vultures!" Louie's voice was loud and irritated. "Move, you fucking dickheads!"

Liam's hand pushed through the reporters surrounding me. I grabbed it like a lifeline, and he pulled me through the crowd, down the steps, and into his arms. Keeping one arm around my shoulders, he stared at Louie, who stood beside him. "Once I get her out of here, can you lock up her place?"

Louie nodded. He held his garden hose in one hand, and he patted my shoulder with his free one. "Don't you worry, sweetheart, I won't let them step one foot into your house."

"Can you keep them back long enough for me to get her to the car?" Liam asked.

"Fuck, yes," Louie said. My eyes widened when, with a gleeful grin, he raised the garden hose and depressed the lever, turning it full blast on the reporters. "How's this feel, assholes?"

"Time to go, Hattie," Liam said. He hustled me to his car, where Sophie stood.

"Hattie, oh, honey, are you okay?" Sophie grabbed my hand.

"In the car, both of you," Liam said as the reporters' outraged shrieks and Louie's shrill laughter echoed behind us.

I nearly fell into the backseat of Liam's car. He slammed the door shut behind me and slid behind the wheel as Sophie climbed in on the passenger side. With a squeal of tires, he drove down the street and out of the trailer park, taking a quick left down a side street that led into a subdivision maze of similar looking townhomes.

"Hattie, honey, are you hurt?" Sophie leaned over the seat and touched my shoulder and then my face.

"I'm okay," I said.

I leaned back against the seat as Liam drove aimlessly through the neighbourhood, checking the rear-view mirror from time to time. "I don't think they followed us, but I'll take Bellview Road to get to your place. It's not as well known if you're not a local."

"Thank you, honey." Sophie squeezed his hand before turning her gaze back to me. "Take a deep breath, Hattie."

I did what she said. "What's going on?"

"You haven't been online in the last few hours, huh?" Sophie said.

I shook my head. "No, I was working on the Lincoln, and I... when the reporters showed up, I thought my mom did something, but then they started talking about Finn and Sapphire's and...."

I stopped, staring wide-eyed at Sophie before glancing at Liam. Sophie squeezed my hand. "Everyone knows, Hattie. It's been all over social media and online. You're, uh, trending on Twitter right now."

"Everyone knows what," I said guardedly.

Looking uncomfortable, Sophie said, "About you and Finn and what you do at Sapphire's."

"Oh my God," I said, my stomach threatening to heave up the water I drank. "This cannot be happening. How do they know?"

"A woman named Amber Simpson," Sophie said.

Why was that name familiar? I racked my brain, but I couldn't come up with why I might know her.

"She goes to the Sapphire club," Sophie said. "She had a thing for Finn and -"

"She showed up at his house one night when I was there," I said dully as Amber's face flooded into my head. "She was pissed because Finn wouldn't date her. She'd seen me at the club with him, and she was angry that he brought me back to his place. She was kind of a stalker, I think."

Liam snorted. "She's a full-blown stalker."

Sophie sighed. "She knew you used to be a celebrity, and she told some journalist friend about how you were going to the club. He's been, uh…."

"Spying on you and Finn," Liam said grimly. "For at least the last couple of weeks. There are photos of you going into Finn's house and Finn at your trailer. The journalist even got someone into the club with a hidden camera, and he has footage of the two of you at the club. It's been posted online."

My skin turned ice cold, and my ears rang. Sophie was speaking, but I couldn't hear a word she said. I watched numbly as Sophie quickly climbed over the seat and landed next to me in the back seat with a thump. She pushed my head down between my knees, rubbing my back with one hand.

"Deep breaths, Hattie. C'mon, honey, take deep breaths."

I sucked in a couple of lungfuls of air as the ringing subsided and the world wavered back into focus. After a few minutes, Sophie helped me straighten. "Okay?"

"What did they post from the club?" I rasped.

We'd been in a private room when Finn spanked me on Friday night, but the room had a camera. What if the guy had paid someone to get the footage? What if the entire world had seen Finn spanking me?

"Just some footage of you and Finn walking around in the club," Sophie's face reddened. "But there are a few seconds when you're standing near the bar, and Finn has his hand up your dress. You can't see your hooch or anything, but it's obvious what he's doing to you."

"Is that it?" My voice was still a hoarse rasp. "Was there anything else from a private room?"

"No," Sophie said quickly. "That was the worst of it, honey. But this woman, Amber, gave an interview to the journalist, and she spilled a ton of shit about Finn and what he does to women at the club. She spilled the beans about him, uh," Sophie glanced at Liam, "being a Dom and that he likes to spank."

"Oh God," I whispered.

"There are reporters all over his house and at the lab," Sophie said.

"Fuck."

"I'm sorry, honey, it gets worse," Sophie said. "The journalist contacted your mother and told her about you and Finn, and now your mother is, well, she's…."

"Doing what she does best," I said. "Talking to anyone and everyone who will listen."

"Yeah," Sophie said. "The guy released the story just before noon, and multiple news outlets have already interviewed your mom. She told *TMZ* that she'll be on *Dr. Phil* next week to talk about your issues and why it's your dead father's fault that you like to be spanked. She's been telling anyone who will listen that she's tried for years to get you help but that you're sick in the head and need serious therapy. Which, by the way, she's tried to get you that help numerous times, but you'll barely speak to her because you're jealous of her fame since yours went in the toilet."

Sophie's face was now red from anger. "Your mother is such a fucking bitch. I hate her, and I can't -"

"It doesn't matter," I said. "I don't care what she says about me or what the world thinks of me. It's Finn I'm worried about. He values his privacy, and this is his worst fear. I promised him that no one would know about the club or us and that me being a former celebrity wouldn't be a problem."

"This is not your fault," Sophie said. "This is that crazy stalker's fault."

"If I weren't who I was, no one would have cared," I said. "She only got the story because of me."

Sophie sighed before repeating, "It isn't your fault, honey."

"Can you take me to Finn's house?" I asked Liam. "I need to speak with him."

Liam hesitated. "I don't think that's a good idea, Hattie. He's pissed, and it's best to give him a cooling-off period when he's that angry. Trust me on this."

"Yeah, okay," I said.

Sophie rubbed my back. "It'll be okay, honey. We'll go back to my place for a few hours."

"Why aren't you guys at work?" I asked as I swiped at the tears still sliding down my face.

"As soon as the reporters showed up at the lab and we realized what was happening, I knew they'd be at your place," Sophie said. "I wasn't leaving you to face those fucking asshole reporters on your own. Liam offered to come with me."

"Thank God, I did," Liam said. "They would have trampled you and Hattie into the damn ground if I hadn't."

"Fucking paparazzi," Sophie said. "I hate them."

She slid her arm around my shoulders and kissed my cheek. "It'll be okay, honey. I promise. Finn will cool down, and he'll know it's not your fault. He isn't going to blame you for this."

I nodded and stared out the window. I knew Sophie was trying to make me feel better, but she was wrong. Finn would hate me forever.

CHAPTER 16

Hattie

"Are you kidding me? That's a total dick move by Sung-Ho." Sophie stomped back and forth in her small living room.

"It isn't," I said. "And I don't blame him. The paparazzi are all over the garage, and they mob every customer who tries to drop off their car. I understand why he asked me to take some time off."

"It's only been a few days since it happened," Sophie said. "He could have at least waited a week or so."

I shook my head. "A story this juicy and with my mom still running her big mouth, they'll be sticking around Willowdale for weeks. Samesh told me he saw them talking to people I went to high school with. Apparently, everyone in this fucking town has an opinion about the washed-up celebrity who likes to be spanked."

"Can you afford to go on unpaid leave?" Sophie asked.

"I'll be fine," I said. That was probably a lie, but I was too tired to care. So what if I didn't have any food or my electricity got cut off? What the fuck did it even matter? I had no appetite, and I'd been sitting in my dark trailer anyway for the last few nights in a sad attempt to convince the paparazzi I wasn't home.

"Honey, I'm worried about you." Sophie sank onto the couch beside me.

I stared at my phone. "Finn hasn't texted me back. I've texted him three times and called twice, and he isn't replying. I've said I'm sorry, but I don't know what else to do or say. I just wish I could hear his voice."

Sophie sighed. "Finn's being such a dick right now."

"No, he isn't." I jumped to his defense. "You don't know how hard this is on him, Soph. He's an incredibly private person."

"He's also left you alone to deal with the paparazzi," Sophie said. "That's so selfish. They've completely given up on him and are entirely focused on you now."

"What do you mean?" I asked with a frown. "I thought they were camped out at his place and the lab."

Sophie chewed at her bottom lip. "Uh, they were, I mean they are. Probably. Hey, are you hungry? Why don't I make us something to eat?"

"Sophie, what's going on? What aren't you telling me?"

The door opened, and Liam stepped into the townhouse. "Fuck, the paparazzi are here now too. I just had three different people shouting questions at me about my brother and his sex club."

Sophie rolled her eyes. "I'm surprised it took them this long to find out where I live."

"They probably followed me last night." Liam leaned down and kissed Sophie. "Sorry, honey."

"It's okay," Sophie said. "Hattie, what do you want to eat?"

"I'm not hungry. I want you to tell me what you're not telling me about Finn," I asked.

"He hasn't been at the lab since Monday, and when Liam checked his place on Tuesday, he wasn't there," Sophie said.

"Oh my God." I sat up, tearing at my cuticles with my teeth. "What if he's hurt? What if the paparazzi were following him while he was driving and there was an accident, and he's -"

"Whoa," Liam said. "Hattie, he's okay. I promise."

"Where is he?" I asked.

"He wants to be left alone," Liam said with an uncomfortable look. "If you show up, he'll be angry with you for invading his privacy."

Sophie sighed. "Liam, they're dating. She deserves to know where he is."

"Finn said they weren't," Liam said. "He said it was just a month-long agreement thing so that he could, uh, teach Hattie some stuff."

Liam's face was red, and I couldn't help but feel sorry for him.

"They were spending every night together," Sophie said. "They were dating."

"No, we weren't." I studied my chewed-up nails. "Finn never asked me to date him. He was always clear that this wasn't a relationship."

I swallowed hard and stared at Liam. "I just want to know that he's okay and safe. I'm not going to show up and crowd his space or beg him to talk to me or anything. He's made it clear the last few days that he doesn't want to speak to me, and I'll respect that. But I'm worried about him."

Liam sighed and ran a hand through his dark hair. "He's safe. He went to my dad's hunting cabin outside Havenport first thing Tuesday morning."

I released my breath in a soft rush. "You're sure that he got there, and he's okay? I mean, there probably isn't much reception out there, right? How do you know he made it to the cabin without any issues?"

Could Liam tell that I hoped maybe Finn hadn't replied to my texts because he hadn't seen them? Most likely, because Liam's voice was gentle when he said, "The cell reception is good out there. He's replied to both my and Alina's texts."

I blinked back the hot tears as my last bit of hope took its final ragged breath. "Okay, that's good. I'm glad he's okay. He's probably blocked my number, so the next time you talk to him, can you please tell him that I am incredibly sorry for what's happened and that I promise not to, uh, contact him again in the future or anything like that."

Liam nodded, and I stood up, brushing at my jeans. "I'm gonna go. Sophie, I'll text you later, but I think it's best if we don't see each other for a few weeks."

"Fuck that bullshit," Sophie said. "I'm not leaving you to be eaten by the paparazzi wolves."

"If we keep hanging around together, they'll start digging into your life and Liam's, leading them straight back to Finn or worse - Alina. Do you want them camping out at Alina's house? Shouting questions at her when she leaves, maybe bringing up her car accident? You know how they are. They're relentless about getting what they want."

Liam had gone pale, and Sophie looked like she would throw up.

I took Sophie's hand and squeezed it. "It'll die down faster if I do the hermit thing for a while. You know that, Sophie. We've been through this before. This might take a little longer than usual, but they'll move on eventually. But the less fuel we give them, the better."

"I hate this," Sophie said miserably. "I hate this so

fucking much. You shouldn't have to deal with this alone. It isn't fair."

I hugged her hard. "I love you, Soph. I'll text you later tonight, okay?"

"Yeah, okay," she said. "But you're taking my car. You're not standing at the fucking bus stop waiting for the bus while those assholes shout questions at you."

"You need your car," I said.

"Liam will drive me to work and wherever else I need to go, right, honey?" Sophie said.

Liam slipped his arm around her waist. "Yes. It's not a problem."

"Thank you." I hesitated and said, "Take care of Finn, okay, Liam? I know he usually takes care of everyone else, but he needs you and Alina right now."

"We will, Hattie," Liam said. "I promise."

Finn

I SAT ON THE FRONT PORCH OF MY DAD'S HUNTING CABIN, A cup of coffee in one hand and my phone in the other. I studied Hattie's last text message to me, my stomach already threatening to evict the half a cup of coffee I'd drank.

I'm so sorry, Finn. I never wanted this to happen, and I hate that your life has been blown up like this. This is all my fault, and I desperately wish I could fix it. If I could take it all back, if I could go back in time and never step foot into Sapphire's, I would. I'm sorry.

She'd sent that to me on Wednesday morning. It was now Saturday, and I hadn't gotten a message or a phone call from her since. Why would she? I hadn't said a goddamn word to her since the paparazzi had surrounded me in the lab parking lot at lunchtime on Monday.

I'd been angry. So damn angry. Every secret part of me had been exposed like a raw nerve to the small town we lived in and the entire fucking world. Even worse... to Liam and Alina. I'd texted a few times with both of them since I'd escaped to the cabin, but we hadn't brought up the club at all. And I planned on keeping it that way for the rest of my fucking life.

I reread Hattie's message, my stomach still churning and grinding away. She wished she could take it all back, wished she could change what happened between us, and I hated that she regretted it. Even after what happened, I didn't regret being with her. I never would.

Then why the fuck are you out here? Go home and tell Hattie that it doesn't matter what's happened. That you don't regret it and you want to be with her.

I stood up when I heard the vehicle driving down the dirt road that led to the cabin. My anxiety that the paparazzi had found me changed to an entirely different stress when I saw Liam's car. I took a deep breath, tamping down the urge to simply run into the woods and hide.

Liam parked his car beside mine and climbed out. He stretched, cracking his back with a grimace, before reaching into the car and grabbing his iPad. He joined me on the front porch. "Hey, Finn."

"Hi," I said. "What are you doing here?"

"We need to talk," Liam said.

"I'd rather not," I said.

Liam snorted laughter. "Yeah, well, this time, you don't get to tell us what to do, big brother."

"Us? What do you mean us?" I asked as he opened the cabin door, and I followed him inside.

"What do you think he means?" Alina's voice said. "God, Finn, you live in a cabin in the woods for less than a week, and you lose all of your brain cells."

"Ooh, *Cabin in the Woods*," Liam said as he grabbed a few books from the bookshelf in the living room. He stacked them on the kitchen table and propped the iPad against the book stack. "I love that movie. We should watch it next weekend for movie night."

"Ugh, you know I hate horror movies." Alina peered out at us from the iPad screen.

"I'm not watching another epic fantasy movie, Alina," Liam said as he sat down at the table. "There are only so many times I can watch *Lord of the Rings*."

I sank into a chair next to Liam. "What are you two doing here?"

"What do you think?" Liam said. "We're here to talk some sense into you."

"I don't need -"

"Oh fuck, yes, you do," Liam said.

"It's time to come home, honey," Alina said.

I shook my head. "I can't."

"Yes, you can," Liam said.

I scowled at him. "It isn't that simple."

"Finn," Alina said, "do you really think that hiding in some cabin is the answer to your problems?"

"I'm not hiding," I said. "I'm protecting you and Liam."

"Well, that's some real happy horseshit right there, isn't it?" Liam said.

"If I go back home, if I'm there and keep refusing to answer their questions, they'll eventually go to you and Alina," I said. "Is that what you want, Liam? Do you want them knocking on Alina's door? Crowding her space? Pulling up old news stories about her accident?"

"Of course, I don't," Liam said, his face turning red. "I'm not a fucking asshole, Finn. I love Alina just as much you do, and I will do everything I can to protect her from -"

"Forcing me to come home isn't protecting Alina."

"Letting you hide like a big fucking baby isn't the answer either."

"I'm not hiding!" I snarled.

"The fuck you aren't!" Liam snapped.

"Watch how you speak to me, Liam, or -"

"Or what? Do you think I can't -"

"Oh my God! Both of you shut the hell up, right fucking now!"

Liam and I shut our mouths, staring at Alina as she glared at us from the iPad screen. "Stop talking about me like I'm not even here or don't get a say in my own damn life. I can handle some stupid reporters all up in my business, all right? I'm not a fragile doll. Finn, stop using me as an excuse for why you're hiding."

"I'm not hiding," I repeated.

"You are," Alina said. "You're embarrassed because we know you're a Dom, and you like to spank women."

My cheeks heated up, and Liam grinned and said, "Alina, just throwing it all out there on the table."

"What is the big deal?" Alina said. "We're all adults here, and what you do with other consenting adults is nothing to be ashamed of. Not even with us. Do you think we won't love you because of what you like in the bedroom?"

"Honestly, it's not even that big of a surprise," Liam said.

"What's that supposed to mean?" I asked.

"You're a total control freak, Finn. Alina and I would have been more surprised if you were the complete opposite in the bedroom and liked to be spanked," Liam said.

"Oh my God," I rubbed at my forehead. "I do not want to talk about my sex life with either of you."

"Then we won't," Alina said. "Finn, we don't care that you're a partner in a sex club, nor do we care about what you do in the bedroom, okay? We care that you're happy."

Liam squeezed my shoulder. "Hattie makes you happy."

"We weren't dating," I said hoarsely, refusing to look at either of them. "What happened between us didn't mean anything."

"So, now you're gonna straight-up lie to us?" Liam said.

I glanced at him and then Alina, more heat burning into my cheeks at the looks of disappointment on their faces. "It's complicated."

"No, it isn't," Alina said. "You love her, and she loves you. There's nothing complicated about it."

"She's too young for me, and I'm terrible at relationships."

"No one gives a fuck about age differences anymore," Liam said. "And you're not terrible at relationships. Your marriage ended because of me and Alina, not because of you."

The shock nearly knocked me off the kitchen chair. "No, it didn't."

Alina leaned closer to the screen, her somber face staring at me. "We played a big part in it, and we can never truly tell you how sorry we are."

"It wasn't the two of you," I said. "Melissa and I were having issues before Alina's accident."

"But my grief and Alina's accident didn't help," Liam said.

"Maybe not, but Hattie said...."

"What did Hattie say?" Alina asked with a small smile.

"That Melissa was being selfish and asking me to choose was a terrible thing for her to do."

"Oh my God," Liam groaned. "She asked you to choose between her and us?"

"She did," I said. "But it wasn't a choice. I love you and Alina, and I will always be there for you. Always."

"We know that," Liam said.

"All for one and one for all," Alina said.

"You've done so much for us, Finn, and we can never thank you enough. But it's been ten years, and we're good. We want you to stop living for us and do what makes you happy," Liam said.

"What if it doesn't work out?" I asked. "What if I fuck it up, or what if she eventually wants something I can't give her?"

"You have to take the risk, buddy," Liam said. "And not to sound like a walking cliche, but love is worth the risk."

"He's right," Alina said. "Don't spend your life alone because you're afraid. Don't be like me."

I frowned at her. 'You're not afraid, Alina, and you're not alone. You have Liam and me."

"I know," she said. "And now I have Sophie and Hattie too if you'll stop being a dumb-dumb and fix things with her. I called her yesterday, and we talked for over an hour. She feels terrible about what happened."

"It isn't her fault,' I said.

"Yeah, well, you're acting like it is," Liam said. "You won't talk to her, and you abandoned her to face the paparazzi all by herself. She had to take unpaid leave from work because reporters kept harassing customers at the shop."

"What?" I stood and paced back and forth in the kitchen. "She's not working?"

"No. She won't let Sophie visit her either. She's holed up

in that awful trailer of hers all alone because apparently, it's the fastest way to get the paparazzi to leave. Of course, if her asshole of a mother doesn't stop doing interviews and fueling the fire, they're never going to leave Hattie alone," Liam said.

"Fuck!" I ran my hand through my hair.

"She needs you, Finn," Alina said.

"She does. So, will you keep hiding out here at the cabin, or will you man the fuck up and go to Hattie?" Liam asked.

I stared at him and Alina. "I'm gonna man the fuck up."

CHAPTER 17

Hattie

I took a deep breath before turning into the trailer park and driving slowly toward my trailer. It was Saturday afternoon, and after five days of hiding in my trailer, boredom and lack of food had driven me out into the real world and straight into the paparazzi cameras.

They'd followed me from the trailer to the grocery store, and after only ten minutes of them trailing behind me in the aisles, snapping photos and shouting questions, I'd grabbed the bare necessities and got the hell out. The looks from other shoppers, the flashing lights of the cameras, were all threatening to take me back to a dark time in my life, and the memories made it feel impossible even to breathe.

I parked in front of my trailer, preparing myself for the barrage of questions from the reporters who'd followed me back home and were already climbing out of their cars. I didn't know if their stalking and intrusion into my life really were worse now or if it just felt that way because I was no longer used to it. Either way, I was over it, and if my mom didn't stop fucking talking to the media, I'd fly to California and strangle her into silence.

My hands were clenched in tight fists, and I had a tension headache. I rubbed my forehead as the paparazzi stood behind Sophie's car like poisonous snakes waiting to strike. For a moment, I was tempted just to drive away, find an even smaller town where nobody knew me, and fade into obscurity.

You think hiding from your problems like Finn's doing will solve them?

Just thinking about Finn made me want to cry. I'd spoken with Alina last night, and I couldn't help but ask if she'd talked to him and did she know if he was doing okay. She said she'd been texting with him but hadn't given any details. I'd asked her to tell him again that I was sorry before forcing myself to change the subject. I loved Finn and would spend the rest of my life loving him, but I had to stop hoping that he would just show up on my doorstep and announce that all was forgiven. His biggest nightmare had come true because of me, and that wasn't something a person just forgave and forgot.

I climbed out of the car, grabbing the grocery bags from the back seat and plastering a stoic look on my face as the reporters surrounded me.

"Ms. King, are you into BDSM because of trauma? Is your mother's statement that you're into spanking because she didn't believe in corporal punishment true?"

"Ms. King! Ms. King!" A camera flashed in my face. "How often do you go to the club? Are you and Finn Whitby in a relationship?"

"No comment," I said as I pushed past them toward the front door.

Like the relentless jackals they were, they surrounded me again. "Do you call Finn Whitby daddy?"

"No, she doesn't." Finn's deep voice sent my heart into overdrive, and I nearly dropped the grocery bags I carried.

The reporters turned, staring up at Finn as he stepped out of my trailer and walked down the steps toward us. He pushed through them and put his arm around me before taking the grocery bags with his free hand. He pressed a kiss against my mouth and smiled at me before turning to the people around us.

"Hattie and I are in a committed relationship. I love her, and what we do in the bedroom is no one's business but ours."

Keeping me tucked up against him, he started toward my trailer. His big body easily pushed past the flood of reporters, and he led me into the trailer, shutting the door against the sound of their shouted questions and their clicking cameras.

He set the bags on the counter before smiling nervously at me. "Hi, Hattie."

I stared silently at him before asking, "Did you break into my trailer?"

Really, Hattie? He just told the paparazzi he loved you, but that's the question you're going to ask?

"No, Louie told me where you hid your extra key." A look of disapproval crossed his face. "Hiding it in a fake rock in the flower bed is the first place a thief would look, Hattie."

"It's a good hiding spot," I said.

Hattie, that's not freaking important right now!

"I love you," he said. "I love you, and I'm so sorry that I abandoned you to face the paparazzi alone. It was a real dick move."

"It was a cowardly move," I said. "I never thought you'd be a coward, Finn."

He didn't flinch. "I know, and I'm truly sorry. My behaviour was inexcusable, and the only thing I can do is say I'm sorry and promise that I will never do that to you again. I love you, Hattie."

"Since when?" I asked. "You told me repeatedly that -"

"I was an idiot. I was afraid and," he grimaced, "acting like a coward because I didn't want to be in love with you, Hattie. I didn't want to fall in love and watch the relationship die because we no longer wanted the same things."

"Comparing me to your other relationships wasn't fair," I said. "Just because they stopped wanting you to be dominant with them doesn't mean I will."

"I know. I shouldn't have compared you to them, and I'm sorry I did."

"Three sorries in a row," I said. "Alina told me you never apologize."

"It's not something that comes easy to me," he said.

"What does?" I asked.

"Loving you," he said. "I love you, Hattie, and I'm asking you to forgive me even though I probably don't deserve it because I can't imagine my life without you in it. No matter how our relationship changes or evolves, it doesn't matter. What matters is that I love you, and I can't live without you."

"Even if that means vanilla sex for the rest of your life?" I asked.

"Yes," Finn said.

I stared at him for a few seconds before smiling. "Vanilla sex is boring."

The corners of his lips turned up. "With the right person, it can be exciting."

I walked toward him, wrapping my arms around his waist and staring at him. "I love you, Finn Whitby."

"Thank Christ," he said.

We kissed, our tongues touching delicately as I inhaled his delicious scent. He pulled back. "I've missed you."

"I missed you too." I rested my forehead on his chest. "But you need to know that I can't guarantee that your life won't be exposed again if you're with me. That you won't have reporters following you around again at some point because of something my mother has said or done."

"I know," he said. "I don't care. As long as I'm with you, that's what matters."

I studied him, warmth washing over me. "You mean that, don't you?"

"Yes," he said, "I do. I love you, Hattie. Will you forgive me?"

"Yes," I said. "If you let me drive Gretchen."

He laughed. "You can drive Gretchen whenever you want."

"Seriously?" I asked said.

"If you move in with me, yes. If you don't, I'll only let you drive her on the third Sunday of every month and only if you've been my good girl," he said.

"You drive a hard bargain, Dr. Whitby," I said.

He grinned and kissed me again. "Are you in, Hattie?"

"All the way," I said.

Keep reading for "The Physicist", Book Three in the Sexy Scientists Series.

THE PHYSICIST

VOLUME THREE

THE PHYSICIST

He understands energy matters.

Alina

I'm a cliché. I'm in love with my brother's best friend.

But it doesn't stop me from pining after Nicholas Campbell like a love-struck kitten. Can you blame me though? He's deliciously sexy, a brilliant physicist, and the kindest man I know.

Which makes him the perfect person to help me lose my v-card.

Only he's never looked at me as anything other than my brother's kid sister. He's off-limits… or is he?

When he needs a place to stay for a few weeks, I come to the rescue. And it's the perfect opportunity to show him that I'm all grown up.

Nick

I can't have Alina. Not only is she my best friend's sister, but she's sweet and innocent and I'm… not.

But physics has taught me that opposites attract, and now

that we're roommates, our attraction grows stronger. To her, my past doesn't matter.

And even though my ability to resist her magnetism weakens each day, there is no happily ever after for us.

Can we find our happiness, or are we on a collision course to heartbreak?

CHAPTER 1

Alina

"You can do this, Alina," Liam said. "I know you can."

My shaking hands, upset stomach, and urge to flee straight back to my house suggested I didn't, but I gave my brother a tight smile and nodded.

Liam opened the front passenger door of his car. I stared at the interior like it was a predator about to drag me into its lair as Liam touched my shoulder. "You need to try, Alina. It's been weeks."

"I know," I said. Ignoring the constant drumbeat of fear in my head, I sat down in the car, using my hands to help pull my bad leg in before clenching them in a tight fist in my lap.

A squeak escaped my lips when Liam shut the door, and I jerked as fresh fear washed over me. I started to hyperventilate, and I clutched Liam's hand when he slid behind the wheel.

"Can't breathe," I said. "Liam, can't breathe."

My throat was closing up, and I could barely hear Liam over the ringing in my ears.

"Yes, you can." His voice was kind but firm. "Slow your breathing, Alina. You can do this. Remember what your therapist said - the fear doesn't have to control you. Take slow, deep breaths in."

I closed my eyes, keeping hold of Liam's hand as I breathed in and out as slowly as I could. The ringing in my ears subsided, and the terrible sensation of choking faded as the constriction in my throat eased.

"Better?" Liam asked.

"Yes."

"Good. Can you put your seatbelt on, or do you want me to buckle you in?"

"I can do it." I released Liam's hand, ashamed of my sweaty grip, and buckled the seatbelt.

"Good. You're doing great, Alina."

"Thanks," I whispered.

"I'm starting the car now," Liam said.

I made an approximation of a nod, but another low moan of fear escaped my throat when Liam started the car. I clutched at the seat belt, my heart knocking against my ribcage so hard I wouldn't be surprised if it cracked a rib.

My bad leg pulsed and ached. The pain that never really went away always got worse when I was upset or afraid.

"Deep breaths, Alina," Liam said. "We'll just sit here until you're ready."

I didn't know how to tell him I would never be ready. Liam and our older brother, Finn, tried so hard and spent so much time doing what they could to help me get over my trauma. Admitting defeat and telling them it was pointless made me so ashamed I wanted to throw up.

But the guilt I felt over wasting their time, especially now that they were both in relationships, ate at my stomach.

We sat in silence for nearly ten minutes. Liam didn't turn

on the radio or play music on his phone. The car accident that had taken my mother's life and nearly mine had been accompanied by my mom's favourite radio station playing. Now, any music or noise from the radio made my panic at being in the car exponentially worse.

"I'm ready," I said.

Liam didn't ask if I was sure. He just put the car into drive and pulled out onto the street. Immediately, my heartbeat went into overdrive, the thudding boom of my pulse echoing in my ears as my chest tightened unbearably and sweat covered my body.

My vision shimmered as I gasped for air before I finally made a strangled cry of defeat and croaked out, "Enough, please. Enough."

Liam immediately pulled over, and I fumbled for the seat belt clasp, starting to cry when my shaking hands wouldn't allow me to depress the button. Liam's hands pushed mine away, and he freed me from the belt's tight grip. Still gasping for air, I clawed at the door handle until the door popped open, and I nearly fell out of the car.

I staggered a few feet up the sidewalk before I bent over with my hands on my knees and waited to see if I would vomit or pass out. I'd done both in the past.

My leg throbbed, and I shook so much that it was in danger of collapsing under me. Before I could fall, Liam's arm circled my waist. I leaned against him, gasping and trying not to cry as sweat slid down my face and into my eyes, making them sting.

"You're okay, Alina. You're okay. I have you," Liam said. "Deep breaths, okay? Take deep breaths."

I sucked air in and out in a steady rhythm, Liam holding me patiently as the breeze dried the sweat on my forehead and brought the soothing scent of honeysuckle. When my vision cleared and my chest no longer felt like it had an elephant sitting on it, I straightened and gave Liam a smile of shame.

"I'm sorry, Liam."

"Don't apologize," he said. "You did great, Alina."

I barked harsh laughter as, walking slowly, Liam and I headed back toward my house. "I made it, what... half a block, this time?"

"A full block," he said, "and I was driving slow. It's better than the last time."

He made a fair point. Last time, I had freaked out when he put the car in drive. Liam didn't even get to step on the gas pedal.

"We can try again next week," he said.

I shook my head. "I can't, Liam."

"Your therapist said it's better to have shorter periods between attempts," Liam said.

"I know, but I... I need Finn here too."

Usually, when I tried what I thought of as my 'car therapy', I had Liam and Finn in the car. But Finn was currently on vacation with his new girlfriend, Hattie, in Hawaii.

Liam didn't say anything, but I knew he thought I was making an excuse. I wasn't, though. Having Finn drive with Liam in the back seat, leaning forward and holding my hand, did make it more tolerable, if not easier. Once, Finn had even driven around the entire block before my panic attack forced him to pull over.

Of course, that had been last year, and I hadn't managed to do better than that since then. The shame deepened in me. Finn and Liam had been so excited that day. They were sure it'd been a breakthrough, positive that my years-long inability to drive in a car would soon be a thing of the past. When it had proved wrong, when my fear and panic attacks worsened after that, they did a fantastic job hiding their disappointment.

But I knew it was there, lurking behind their smiles and belief that I would overcome my trauma.

"I'm so sorry, Liam," I said as we walked up the sidewalk to the house. "I wish I could get better. I wish I didn't disappoint you and Finn over and over and -"

"Hey, stop that." Liam pulled me to a gentle stop and frowned at me before kissing my forehead. "Alina, we are not disappointed in you, I promise. We're proud of you and how you never give up, even with how scary this is for you. When Finn returns, we'll try again, okay?"

"You and Finn don't have time for this now," I said. "You're in relationships and -"

"Both Sophie and Hattie understand," Liam said. "They already love you, Alina, and want you to get better as much as Finn and me. Sophie volunteered to come with us today, but I wasn't sure if you would be comfortable with that."

"She's a wonderful girl, and I like her a lot," I said.

Liam had the same adorable look on his face whenever Sophie was mentioned. "She's amazing, and I love her."

I hugged him briefly before limping my way into the house. "I'll be right back."

"Sure." Liam headed into the kitchen as I made my way to the bathroom. My leg throbbed and burned, and after I'd used the bathroom, I shook out a pill from the bottle in the medicine cabinet and swallowed it. I tried not to take the prescription pain relief very often, but I'd whacked my leg on the side of the bed frame last night, leaving it even sorer than it usually was.

I returned to the kitchen, inwardly cursing when I realized what Liam held in his hand.

"Alina, why do you have an overdue notice on your utility bill?" He brandished the paper at me.

"Why are you snooping through my stuff?" I asked.

"I wasn't snooping. It was right here on the counter," he said.

Okay, he had me on that one. But forgetting to hide the overdue notice meant I was about to get a huge lecture from my brother, and I was so not in the mood.

"Why didn't you tell us you couldn't pay your bills?" Liam asked.

"I'm so not in the mood for this," I said.

"Too bad," Liam said. "I'm texting Finn and -"

"Don't you dare!" I glared at him. "Butt out of my business, Liam."

"If you can't afford to pay your bills, Finn is perfectly fine with you skipping a few rent payments. You know how much it pisses him off that you even pay rent to him."

"I'm not paying rent. I'm paying a mortgage to him so that someday this house will be mine," I said. "And I'm not skipping some payments, so stop bringing it up."

"You can't go without electricity," Liam said, his face turning red.

"Oh, for heaven sakes, it's one overdue notice," I said. "I'll pay it next month."

"Next month!" Liam's face was almost purple now. "Alina, if you're having money trouble -"

"I'm not having money trouble," I said. "Sales have been a little slow the last couple of months, that's all. It'll pick up, it always does, and I'm starting to make some income from teaching embroidery. I'm fine, Liam."

"Look, I get if you don't want Finn to know, he'll blow a fucking gasket, but I can give you a loan," Liam said. "It's not a problem."

It was a problem in that the loan would be not so much a loan but rather a gift. And as much as I loved my brothers for wanting to help, making my own money and paying my bills was one of the few ways I felt even remotely independent in a life where I spent too much time depending on others. Adding money to the list of what I needed from my brothers was a horrifying prospect for me.

"Thank you, but I don't need a loan," I said.

Liam's hand clenched around the overdue notice. "This would suggest you do."

I didn't reply, and Liam made a noise of frustration. "I want to help you, Alina. It's ridiculous that you're scrimping and going without when both Finn and I are more than capable of helping. But you won't let us. Why won't you let us help you?"

"Because," I nearly shouted, "I want to be independent in just one area of my life, Liam! Don't you get that? So often, I feel like a burden, and it kills me that I'm twenty-five years old and have to rely on my brothers like I'm a helpless child. Supporting myself financially feels like the only independence I have, and I don't want that taken away from me. Not when I've already lost so much."

I blinked back the hot tears before sinking into a chair and rubbing at my leg. Fuck, it hurt. The adrenaline rush from being in the car, the walk back to the house, and the fight with Liam had drained my energy, and I drooped in my chair like a wilted sunflower.

Liam crouched beside me. "You're not a burden, Alina. You're our sister, and we love you."

He tipped my chin up until I stared at him. "We're the Three Musketeers. All for one and one for all. Remember?"

I nodded, and Liam stood and grabbed a tissue. He handed it to me for my watering eyes before sighing. "Look, I can't say that I understand it because I don't, not really. But I will try to honour your wishes for now. But if I come over here next month and you're living by candlelight, I'm telling Finn on you, and you're gonna get in so much trouble."

"Tattle-tale," I said with a small smile.

"Fuck, yeah, I am," Liam said before grinning at me. "Are you sure you won't take a small loan?"

"Positive," I said.

"Yeah, okay." Liam sighed.

When he casually walked over to the fridge and opened it, I rolled my eyes and said, "I can afford to buy food."

"I wasn't looking to make sure you had food," Liam said innocently. "I'm feeling peckish and wanted a snack."

"Right," I said. "Promise me you won't say anything to Finn, okay?"

Looking like he'd rather eat a bug, Liam grudgingly said, "I promise. For now."

Nick

"I AM FUCKED, LIAM. I AM COMPLETELY FUCKED." I STORMED into my best friend's living room and collapsed on the couch.

Liam came out of the kitchen and handed me a beer. "I don't know what's going on, but you look like you could use this."

"Fuck, yes." I tipped the bottle to my mouth and drank half the beer before staring at Liam. "Where's Sophie?"

"Over at her parents. Tell me what's going on."

I stared moodily at the football game playing on the TV. "I came home from work to a notice on the apartment building. Mold. We got a fucking mold problem."

"How bad?" Liam asked.

"Bad enough that they have to gut the entire lobby, exercise room, and first-floor laundry room. All of our apartments have to be checked for mold, but even if they're mold free, they still have to shut the building down while cleaning out the mold and renovating. The building manager said it would probably be at least eight weeks, maybe twelve before we could move back in."

"Well, that's one hell of a way to start your weekend," Liam said as he sat down in the recliner chair.

"I've had better Friday nights." I drank some more beer. "I know you're in a new relationship, but would you be cool with me crashing here while the renovations happen?"

"It's not a problem," Liam said.

"Maybe check with Sophie first," I said. "She spends enough time here that she should get a say in it."

Liam laughed. "Good point. I'll talk to her, but I'm positive it won't be an issue."

"Cool, thanks."

"You need me to go with you tonight to pack up your shit?" Liam asked.

"Nah. I packed a quick overnight bag for tonight, but the building is giving everyone until tomorrow night to pack what they'll need. They start gutting the lobby Sunday morning."

"Sorry, man. That sucks."

"It does, but at least I don't have to live in a motel for the next three months," I said. "And, listen, I'm happy to pay you rent and help out with groceries, utilities, etc."

"Shit, that's it," Liam said.

"That's what?" I asked.

Liam muted the television and leaned forward in his chair, an excited look on his face. "Alina."

"What about her?" As always, whenever I even thought about Liam's sister, my idiot dick perked up like Pavlov's dogs hearing the bell.

"You can stay with Alina," Liam said.

"What? Why would I do that when you have a perfectly good guest room I can use?" I could hear the panic in my voice. Two months in the same house with a forbidden woman whose face and perfect body I jerked off nightly to was the stuff of fucking nightmares.

"Alina is having some cash flow issues," Liam said. "Her Etsy shop sales have been slow for a couple of months, and earlier tonight, I found an overdue utility notice at her place. But you know how stubborn she is. She won't take any money from me, and she begged me not to tell Finn."

"She can't go without heat and electricity," I said. "She's gonna have to accept help from you or Finn."

"She won't," Liam said. "She… look, it's not my place to share her reasons she doesn't want money from us, so I won't. But if you move in with her even for a couple of months and pay rent and help with groceries, it'll help her a lot. And she won't consider it charity because she'll be helping you out. Right?"

"I guess," I said slowly.

Liam frowned. "What? Why don't you want to help? This is the perfect solution, Nicky."

"It isn't that I don't want to help your sister, but…."

"What?" Liam repeated.

"She may not want me living with her," I said.

Liam scoffed and took a drink of beer. "She won't have a problem with it. You're like her third brother, Nicky."

I bit back my urge to snap that I was not Alina's fucking brother. But what would be the point? Liam did see me as her brother, and so did Finn. Which was for the best because if either of them had a clue about my filthy fantasies starring Alina, my body would never be fucking found. Finn would make sure of it. And as much as Liam loved me, he had the protective vibe dialed up to a hundred when it came to Alina. Which meant he'd be right there with Finn helping to dig my grave.

Liam studied me, a glimmer of awareness in his gaze. "Wait, you aren't, like, interested in my sister, right?"

"Of course not," I lied.

"Good, because, dude, that's disgusting. She's basically your little sister."

"Yeah, and she won't want to live with a brother," I said.

"It won't be a problem." Liam hesitated with his beer bottle near his mouth. "But can you do me a favour and not bring your sex buddies to her place while living there? Alina doesn't need to be around that sort of thing."

Liam's comment stung more than he would ever know, but I got what he was saying. I did have a reputation for fucking anything that moved, and just because I hadn't slept with a woman in over a year didn't change the fact that I'd come by my reputation honestly.

"It won't be a problem," I said shortly.

"So, you'll do it then?" Liam asked. "You'll move in with Alina?"

"If she agrees to it, which I still think she won't," I said.

Liam sat back in his chair and hit the volume for the television. "She will. Her leg was sore tonight, and the car therapy did not go well, so I know she went to bed early. But I'll call her tomorrow, and then you can move your stuff in on Sunday."

He grinned at me and held up his beer bottle. "This will be great, Nicky. Thank you. You have no idea how much better I feel. I was freaking out about Alina."

"Yeah, don't mention it," I said.

I stared unseeingly at the television. Everything would be fine. Even if, and this was a very big if, Alina said yes to me living with her, it wasn't like she lived in a tiny apartment. We wouldn't be directly in each other's faces all the time. I could avoid her during the week with some late nights at work, and on the weekend… well, I'd figure something out.

CHAPTER 2

Alina

"So, did you practice your breathing techniques when the panic attack happened in the car yesterday?" Dr. Wilson leaned back in her chair.

I could see the big bay window behind her through the iPad screen and even catch a glimpse of her golden retriever, Marion, lying in a patch of sunlight at the far end of the yard.

"I tried." Holding the iPad steady on the lap tray, I shifted on the bed and eased my left leg up. I rested my chin on my knee, keeping my bad leg stuck straight out in front of me. "It didn't really work. I can't control my breathing or think past the fear. And Finn wasn't there, which seemed to make it worse."

Dr. Wilson nodded. Since the accident, she'd been my third therapist and, honestly, my favourite. She was thoughtful and kind, and she'd made plenty of helpful suggestions over the last two years. Because of her, I could sit in a car for even a short period.

"How far did Liam drive?" Dr. Wilson asked.

"A block," I said.

"That's better than last time."

"Yes, but still terrible. I managed not to vomit all over his car, but it was a close call," I said.

Dr. Wilson smiled sympathetically. "I know it feels like this is taking forever, but the trauma you experienced as a teenager was severe. It can take many years to heal."

"It's been a decade," I said. "I should be over it by now."

"Beating yourself up about your progress will not aid in improving it," Dr. Wilson said.

I smiled at her brisk, no-nonsense tone. She often reminded me of a female version of Finn, and I suppose that's why I connected so well with her. "You're right."

"I have a suggestion for you in regards to your therapy. It's a little unconventional, but I think we're ready to try unconventional, don't you?"

"Yes," I said.

"You've mentioned before that the loss of control during the accident was incredibly," Dr. Wilson paused, "unsettling for you. Knowing the crash was about to happen and being helpless to stop it is a recurring theme in your nightmares. Correct?"

I swallowed hard, my guts already churning and my fingers icy cold. "That's right."

"Well, perhaps if you're in control when you're in the car, it may help. By being in the driver's seat, literally and figuratively, you may find it easier to be in the vehicle."

I stared at her, nausea fading away as confusion washed over me. "Wait, you mean actually drive the car?"

"I do," Dr. Wilson said.

"I don't know how to drive," I said. "I don't have a driver's license."

"You could learn to drive," Dr. Wilson said. "You'll know

pretty quickly if being in the driver's seat helps with your panic. If it does, one of your brothers can teach you to drive."

"I don't... I mean, I'd have to take a driver's test, and I could never pass that or -"

"You're looking too far into the future," Dr. Wilson said. "Right now, let's focus on the present and whether my idea will work. Next time, sit in the driver's seat, feel the wheel in your hands, start the car, put it into drive, and see how it feels. Okay?"

I nodded, although I was confident Dr. Wilson could see my skepticism.

A rare smile crossed her face, and she said, "Think of it as an experiment, Alina."

"Okay," I said. "I'll try it when Finn comes back from vacation."

"Good. Now, let's chat about the other topic we discussed last month. How is that going?"

"Um, okay, I think. I've been on two dates with Ethan, and they've gone well."

"Define well, please," Dr. Wilson said.

"I believe he's someone I could have sex with," I said. I was proud of myself for not blushing. When I first brought up the topic of my virginity with my therapist, I'd been bright red the entire time and could barely stop myself from giggling like a little kid.

"That's good. Developing a relationship with another person, whether that's a sexual or romantic one, is an important step in furthering your independence," Dr. Wilson said. "Have you put any thought into my suggestion that you look for not just a sexual relationship but a romantic one as well?"

"I have," I said slowly, "but I don't think it's the right decision. My trauma and everything that goes along with it is a lot for a person to deal with. I need more time to heal first."

"Normally, I would agree," Dr. Wilson said. "But in your case, I think having a romantic partner would be beneficial in helping you heal. You've spoken of your guilt about relying on your brothers so much. This guilt and belief that you are a burden to them forms and shapes your trauma in ways that are not conducive to healing. Finding a romantic partner, someone with whom you support and receive support in return, would obviously ease the guilt you carry regarding your brothers, and in turn, help with the healing process."

What Dr. Wilson said made perfect sense, but I'd never told her my true reason for not looking for a boyfriend, and today was not that day to confess. Not after Liam's phone call to me this morning where I'd agreed to let the *true reason* live in my damn house for two months.

Always incredibly perceptive, Dr. Wilson leaned closer to the camera and said, "Is there another reason you don't want a romantic relationship, Alina?"

I couldn't lie to her. I had promised her when we started therapy that I would never lie to her. So, I took a deep breath and said, "There is, but I need some time to get it straight in my head before I discuss it with you."

She sat back and nodded. "All right. When you're comfortable, we'll discuss it. But I will note to ask you about it in a future session if you don't bring it up again."

"Okay, that sounds good," I said.

"And have you told your brothers about these dates?" Dr. Wilson asked.

I laughed. "Oh God, no. And I never will. Especially since they're only about sex. One - they would freak out if they knew I was having sex with random guys just for the sake of having sex, and two - they would insist on interrogating each guy I met. No guy will be willing to face down

was a doozy of a project. A new mall was being developed on the outskirts of Willowdale. There was a lot of buzz about it, especially as there would be no big box department stores like Walmart or Kohl's in the mall.

The mall development was a passion project for a wealthy businessman named Arnold Waters, who wanted to shine a spotlight on businesses and artists in Willowdale. Every store in the mall would be rented to local business owners only. According to Bryce, the concept was already creating a buzz in the business world. The mall would not only directly help local artists, but it would undoubtedly make a positive impact on tourism in Willowdale.

A lot was riding on the project, and because of the interest, Arnold had hired Bryce's PR firm to handle media relations and hype the concept's uniqueness to potential investors.

Bryce made a face. "Arnold told me today that they're bringing in a geologist to survey the ground before they begin building. There's some question about it potentially being too unstable."

"Uh, oh," I said.

"Yeah." Bryce poked at her noodles with her chopsticks. "Once the geologist arrives, Arnold wants me to babysit him."

"Why? You can't do anything if the ground is too unstable to build on."

"I know, but Arnold is a complete control freak," Bryce said. "He wants daily reports on what the geologist finds and has tasked me with delivering those reports."

"You're his PR firm, not his assistant," I said.

"That's what I said!" Bryce tossed a noodle to Stanley, who caught it and slurped it up. "But Arnold is our biggest paying client, and Carol will do whatever is necessary to keep him happy. Including making me babysit a geologist."

"Jerk move, Carol," I said before taking a drink of water.

Bryce laughed. "Carol's a great boss, and I love her, but what I thought would be my dream assignment is turning into a nightmare. Arnold is a nice guy but insanely controlling and demanding. We don't even know if we can build the mall yet, and he's already got me writing up press releases about the mall opening."

"Sorry, Bryce," I said.

"I'm sure it'll all work out. Hopefully, the geologist is a nice guy who doesn't mind if I shadow him. Anyway, how are you doing? How did last night go?"

"Not great," I said. "Liam drove a block before he had to pull over."

"A block is better than last time," Bryce said.

"Yeah, I know. Nick is moving in with me tomorrow."

Bryce spit out the mouthful of noodles she'd just put in her mouth. They landed on her legs with a wet splat, and Stanley hoovered them up in seconds before settling in to lick the noodle landing spot on Bryce's jeans.

"Nick is moving in with you. Nicholas Campbell... your brother's best friend, super smarty pants physicist, and the man you've been in love with since you were seventeen?"

"Yep," I said.

"Girl, you give me every detail right this minute before I throw the rest of my noodles at you," Bryce said.

I laughed. "His apartment building has mold, and they have to gut and renovate it. He needs a place to live for at least two months."

"Okay, but why here? I get not wanting to live in a motel, but Liam has a guest bedroom he can use."

I grimaced. "Liam saw an overdue notice yesterday when

he was here and is freaking out about my lack of money. He didn't come right out and say this, but he wants Nick to live with me because Nick will pay me rent and help with grocery and utility costs."

"Are sales with your shop that low?" Bryce asked. "Because, honey, I'm happy to lend you a bit of money until they pick up again."

"I appreciate that," I said, "but I can't. I'm already so dependent on my brothers and you, and -"

"We want to help you," Bryce said. "Besides, you haven't heard my loan interest rates yet."

I laughed. "Nick living with me is the perfect solution. I'll have some extra cash for the next two months, which will give me some breathing room to promote embroidery lessons to make extra income."

"Sure, but what about your attraction to him?" Bryce asked.

"What about it? It's never going to go anywhere."

"Um, what about how he touched you while half-naked in your kitchen. Grabbed your hips and gave you a *look* were the exact words you used. He was hot for you that day, and you said he would have kissed you if Liam and Sophie hadn't interrupted."

"Okay, he was only half-naked because the plumbing repair went wrong, and his shirt got soaked. And I was wrong about what might have happened. I misread the situation," I said.

"Why do you think that?"

"Because I've seen him numerous times since then, and he's back to how he always is with me. A brother looking out for his kid sister." Just saying the words made me feel nauseous.

Knowing Nick looked at me like I was a sister to him

made my dirty thoughts about him feel even more inappropriate than they already were. What would Nick do if he knew I masturbated to fantasies of him on an almost nightly basis?

He'd freak the hell out and definitely not move in with me, that was for sure.

Bryce frowned. "Are you sure about that?"

"Yes. You've been around Nick and me how often, Bryce? Has he ever looked at me like he's remotely interested in sleeping with me?"

Bryce hesitated, and while I appreciated her unwillingness to hurt my feelings, I already knew the truth. "You can say it, Bryce."

She sighed and set her empty noodle container on the coffee table. "No, I've never seen him look that way at you."

"Exactly," I said. Stanley climbed into my lap, and I gently rubbed his ears. "Anyway, it'll be fine. I'll spend most of my time in my studio, and I know Nick is busy at work. We'll probably barely see each other. Liam said Nick's been working some long hours lately."

"What exactly does Nick do for Hudson Automobiles anyway?" Bryce asked.

"He's the head of their research and development team for the new electric car that Hudson is producing," I said.

"He really is a smartypants, huh?" Bryce said.

"He is. He's brilliant. He has a degree in engineering physics and a master's in physics. Liam says he's wasting his talents working for an automotive company, but Nick is passionate about earth sustainability practices, and Hudson Automobiles is one of the leading manufacturers in creating hybrid and electric vehicles."

"Cool. A guy who cares about the environment, and he's a total hottie. I love me a dark-haired, dark-eyed man, and I'm pretty sure he's totally ripped under his shirt, yeah?" Bryce said.

"He is," I said a bit morosely. "His body is incredible."

"So, you still going ahead with your plan even with Mr. I've Got an Eight Pack living here?"

"I am," I said.

I could almost feel Bryce's surprise. "You're really going to give up your v-card to some rando while Nick is sleeping in the bedroom next to yours?"

"We'll be quiet," I said.

"Girl, if you can be quiet during an orgasm, he's not doing it right," Bryce said.

I laughed. "I'll pick a night that Nick is out or something. Look, I'm tired of being a virgin, okay? I want to have sex. It sounds like a lot of fun."

Bryce grinned. "It's ridiculously fun."

I scratched under Stanley's chin. "Hey, Bryce?"

"Yeah?"

"I want to say thanks for not judging me for deciding to sleep my way through a roster of Willowdale men. I appreciate it."

"I will never judge you," she said with a somber look. "I mean that. You want to have sex, I'm gonna support you however you go about doing it. As long as you're safe."

"I am," I said. "Ethan seems nice, and he's not pushy. Our third date is coming up, and I think that'll be the date we have sex."

"Good for you," Bryce said.

I studied her. "Do you mean that?"

"I do," Bryce said. "But I want you to be certain that you're doing this for the right reasons."

"I am," I said. "I don't want a relationship. I have too much baggage and trauma for a guy to deal with. At least right now. Maybe in another decade or so... but waiting until I'm thirty-five to have sex is not happening. So, casual sex-only hookups are what I'm after."

"Or are you not looking for a relationship because you're in love with Nick?"

"That isn't it," I said.

Bryce looked like she wanted to argue, but thankfully her phone buzzed, and she got distracted. I sat back against the couch, rubbing my sore leg with one hand and Stanley's belly with the other. I hadn't just lied to Bryce. At least not entirely. I really did believe that it was unfair to saddle a romantic partner with the baggage I carried.

But you also know that you'll compare every guy you try to fall in love with to Nick.

I sighed inwardly. Yeah, I would.

CHAPTER 3

Nick

"So, this is your room." Alina opened the door, and I followed her into the room. It was small and sparsely decorated with just an Ikea dresser and a single bed covered in a blue checkered quilt.

"Sorry, I think the bed might be a little on the small side for you." Alina eyed my frame, and I had to think about Liam busting up my face to stop me from getting an erection. This was such a terrible fucking idea.

"It's fine," I said. "I appreciate you giving me a place to stay. I know it's a pain in the ass to have me here."

She smiled her perfect, beautiful smile. "It isn't. It'll be nice to have some company for a couple of months."

"Anytime you need my help, just let me know," I said as I set my two suitcases on the floor near the bed. "I'm happy to run errands for you or pick up stuff you need."

"You're not here to be my errand boy," Alina said with a frown.

"It's my way of saying thanks," I said.

"You're saying thanks by paying rent and helping with groceries." Alina limped her way to the closet. "I have some of my clothes stored in the closet, but there's still at least half the space left. But if it isn't enough room, I can move my clothes out."

"More than enough space," I said.

"Okay. Well, the guest bathroom is yours to use. Towels and extra toilet paper are in the linen closet just down the hall, and here's a house key for you."

She handed me a small silver key, and just the brush of her fingers against mine sent my cock into overdrive. Christ, I was in so much fucking trouble.

"I'll let you get settled in," Alina said. "I'm making Parmesan chicken for dinner, and I'd love it if you joined me. I don't expect you to eat dinner with me every night or anything like that, but I wanted to do something special for your, uh, first night here."

"I'd love to, thanks, Alina," I said. "And thanks again for letting me stay here. You're really helping me out."

"Yeah, I think we both know you're helping me out, but I appreciate the sentiment," Alina said as she limped to the door. She paused in the doorway, a weird look on her face. "Hey, um, I'm okay with you having overnight guests, but I would appreciate it if you could give me a heads up by text or whatever."

"I won't be having overnight guests," I said as a stupid blush heated my cheeks.

Alina's cheeks were red as well, and she looked supremely uncomfortable. Her bedroom was next to this one, and I suppose the thought of potentially hearing a guy, the equivalent of her brother, banging a chick grossed her out.

"Right, okay, well, I just wanted to let you know that you

don't have to change your lifestyle just because you're living here," she said.

"I'm not." My voice was harsher than I intended, but while Liam alluding to my man-whore past just made me resigned, Alina bringing it up brought on intense shame.

"Right, sorry, I didn't mean…." Alina's face was bright red now. "Dinner will be ready at five."

She limped out of my room, closing the door behind her. I groaned and sank onto the bed, staring up at the ceiling. Fuck me. I was an idiot.

Alina

I HELD MY BREATH AS I LIMPED PAST NICK'S DOOR. STEPPING over the creaky floorboard just outside his room made my bad leg burn, and I gritted my teeth and released my breath in a harsh sigh as I headed toward the kitchen. Stupidly, I'd left my prescription pain relief in the kitchen earlier tonight. Probably because I was distracted by Nick. He wasn't as big as my brothers, and he was on the quieter side, but I was hyper aware of him. My entire body was on edge whenever he was close, and, extra money or not, I was starting to regret agreeing to let him live with me for two months. I'd never survive. At least not without masturbating twice a day. Except I was loud when I came, and the walls were thin. Man, I should have practiced cumming without moaning so loudly before Nick moved in.

I ran my hand along the counter in the darkness. I could turn on a light, but it was almost one in the morning, and I didn't want to risk waking up Nick. My fingers skated across the pill bottle, and I grabbed it and popped the lid off, shaking two pills out into my hand. Two pills would knock me off my ass, but it was what I needed. The pain was terrible tonight. Bad enough that I wouldn't sleep without the pills, and I had a custom embroidery that I had to finish by tomorrow. I needed sleep.

I grabbed a glass and turned on the tap, all by touch alone, before taking the pills with a few swallows of water. I left the glass on the counter and headed out of the kitchen. I'd only taken a few steps when the muscle cramp shot through my leg with unbearable pain, locking up my entire leg and dropping me to the floor like a stone. My flailing hands caught a chair as I went down, and it tipped over with a loud clatter.

Whimpering, the tears already sliding down my cheeks, I rubbed at my thigh, but it was like trying to knead stone. I bit down savagely on my inner cheek as sweat slid down my cheeks to mix with the tears. The cramp went on and on. I tried to breathe through the pain, but it felt impossible. I was hyperventilating, and I would pass out at any minute. I gave up trying to knead out the cramp and immediately laid down flat on my back, the breath whistling in and out of my lungs. The last time this had happened, I'd fainted and whacked my head a good one on the floor. Luckily, it'd been on the back of my head, and I could hide the goose egg from Liam and Finn with my long hair pulled into a strategically placed bun.

It hurt worse to lie on my back, but I didn't fancy having to ride my bike to the doctor tomorrow to check for a possible concussion, and I was going to pass out. I knew that as easily as I knew my name. The pain was too bad, the cramp too -

"Alina? Baby, what's wrong?" Nick's voice came from a distance as he hauled me into a sitting position and sat behind me on the floor. I collapsed against his chest, my voice sounding weirdly muffled.

"Leg cramp, thigh... bad," I muttered.

"Okay. Hold on."

I cried out, and the room came back into sharp focus when Nick reached around me, and his strong hands kneaded my thigh just below my pajama shorts. I clutched at his muscled forearms, making another harsh cry as Nick's low voice said, "I know it hurts, baby. I'm sorry. Be strong."

A wave of intense nausea washed over me, and I stopped my gorge from rising with gritty determination. I would die of humiliation if I vomited all over Nick. The pain grew worse - agonizingly so - and I dug my nails into Nick's forearms as the world wavered in and out of focus again.

Nick kept working the muscle, and I sucked in a gasping breath when the cramp's excruciating grip eased a little. Enough for me to relax my grip on Nick's arms, enough for me to breathe almost normally. Nick continued to knead and rub until the cramp had loosened entirely.

"Better," I gasped out.

Nick released my leg but kept one warm hand resting on the thick scar that twisted its way from the middle of my thigh down to my ankle. I sprawled against him, sucking in breath after breath as the grueling pain lessened to a more tolerable level.

Nick reached up and snagged the dishtowel that hung from the stove handle. He used it to blot away the sweat on my forehead and the tears on my cheeks.

"Thank you," I said. "I'm so sorry I woke you up."

"It's okay," he said.

"It isn't. You have to work in the morning and -"

"I don't need much sleep." His other hand rubbed my arm. "You're cold. Do you want to try to get up?"

I shook my head even though I was chilled to the bone from the cold tile, and I wanted nothing more than to be in my bed. "I can't, not yet. If I try to walk on it, my leg will cramp up again."

My whole body trembled, and goosebumps had broken out on my skin. Probably more from the adrenaline despite the chill I felt.

Nick hesitated briefly before easing me away from him and into a sitting position. He hopped up and put his hands around my waist. "I'll carry you."

He lifted me easily to my feet, and I stared wide-eyed at him as I balanced on my good leg. "Nick, I…"

"Arm around my shoulders," he said.

I slid my arm around his broad shoulders, registering for the first time that he wore nothing but a pair of athletic shorts. I'd seen him without a shirt a dozen times before - probably more - but this was the first time I'd been pressed against his naked chest. Too bad the pain in my leg had completely killed my libido.

Nick slid one arm around my back and the other under my knees and scooped me up with a soft grunt. Walking carefully so that he didn't bang my legs against the walls, he carried me to my bedroom, lowering me onto the bed before turning on the bedside lamp.

"Thank you," I said.

"Where are your pain meds?" he asked.

"I took some in the kitchen before the leg cramp. They'll kick in soon." I massaged my leg again.

He frowned. "Is it cramping again?"

"A little," I said, "but not as bad as before."

Nick climbed into the bed beside me and sat cross-legged by my leg, his big hands pushing mine away. "Here, I'll do it."

As he rubbed and kneaded, he studied me in the dim light. "Does this happen a lot?"

"More often than I'd like," I said.

"You almost fainted in the kitchen," he said.

"It's a particularly bad one this time."

"Do Liam and Finn know this happens?" he asked.

"They know I get leg cramps. My doctor said there isn't much that can be done about it," I said.

"Do your brothers know they're so bad you pass out?"

"No, and they don't need to know." I tried to pull my leg from Nick's grip, crying out when it sent a bolt of pain shooting down to my toes.

"Hold still, Alina," Nick said as he continued to rub.

"If you tell Liam about this, I'll never forgive you," I said.

He sighed. "Alina, what if it happens in the shower and you pass out and hit your head?"

"It won't," I said. "If I'm having a bad leg day, I minimize the risk. I don't shower and try to rest it as much as possible. Look, I appreciate your help tonight, but I've been living with this for over a decade, and despite what just happened, I promise I can take care of myself."

"They should know," he said.

"So that, what? They make me move in with them or hire a nursemaid to live with me 24/7? I don't want that, Nicky. I'm an adult, and I need independence in my life. I don't want to be a burden to anyone anymore."

He frowned. "You're not a burden, and you never were, Alina."

I didn't reply, lying back on the bed instead and staring at the ceiling. "I've been a burden to my brothers for nearly a decade, Nick. You think I don't know why they drop in to say hello nearly every night? They put their needs aside for me every day, and it doesn't seem to matter what I say or do, they won't stop."

Nick stretched out beside me, resting his head on the pillow beside mine. "Because they love you."

"Yes, they do, and I love them too," I said. "But I have a lot of guilt over what they've had to do for me. They uprooted their whole lives and left our dad and the city they grew up in to make my life easier. They knew I hated the city and knew that I loathed taking the bus and having people staring at me because of how I walked. So, they moved here where I could bike to places, where I could have the quiet life I craved, even though they both loved living in the city."

Nick shook his head. "They're happy here, Alina. Even more so now that they're in relationships. Liam would have never met Sophie, and Finn wouldn't have met Hattie if it wasn't for you."

I made a sound that was almost a laugh. "You're just trying to make me feel less guilty for ruining my brothers' lives."

"No, I'm not." Nick made himself more comfortable on the bed, tucking his arm under the pillow as his dark eyes regarded me solemnly. "Liam is happier now than he ever was in the city. Besides, it's not like Havenport is hours away. If they want a taste of city life, it's only twenty minutes away."

"Why did you move here, Nicky?" I asked. "You loved city life."

"I wanted to work with Hudson Automobile, their new electric car prototype will be one of the best when it's built, and I saw how content the three of you were here in Willowdale. It seemed like a good idea. Especially since I missed…."

"Missed what?" I asked when he didn't continue.

"Liam," he said, his cheeks turning a little red in the faint light. "I missed my best friend a lot."

"I wish you were closer to your family," I said. "I hate that they don't see you and appreciate you for who you are."

He shrugged. "My dad wanted me to follow in his footsteps and become a cop. He hates that I took a 'sissy' job, as he puts it."

"He's an idiot," I said. "He should be proud of how damn brilliant you are."

"Dad values street smarts more than intelligence, and he is very vocal about my lack of street smarts."

"Don't let him get in your head that way," I said. "He's just jealous of how smart you are."

The pain meds had kicked in. My leg only throbbed dully now, and it was hard to think past the fuzziness in my brain. "You're the smartest guy I know, Nick, and," I groped for his hand, squeezing it tight, "I'm so proud of all the work you do to save the environment."

He made a low chuckle, his thumb rubbing against mine. "Thanks, Alina. I think you're a little bit high."

"Oh, I'm a lot high," I said before squinting at him. "You're the best, Nicky. I'm gonna make you massage out all my cramps from now on."

He laughed again. "Sure. Whatever you need, Alina."

I wanted to tell him that what I needed was his dick in my pussy, but that seemed inappropriate, even if I was high as a kite. I pulled on his hand until his arm was across my waist and then yawned. "Will you stay with me for a while, Nicky? I don't want to be alone tonight."

Nick's hand tightened against my hip, and he snuggled closer, his voice low in my ear. "I'll stay, baby."

CHAPTER 4

Nick

I let myself into Alina's house, closing the door and checking the kitchen and the living room. Alina wasn't in either room, and I headed toward her studio at the back of the house, shifting my sports bag on my shoulder.

Alina's studio used to be the deck that ran the length of the house. A year and a half ago, Liam, Finn, and I had closed it in to give Alina a space for her embroidery. I'd always been good with renovating and shit like that, and while I wouldn't call Liam or Finn 'handy', they knew how to swing a hammer and take orders. At Alina's request, we had done floor-to-ceiling windows along the back wall. It had given her less space in the studio for storage, but I knew why she'd requested it. The light was gorgeous in this room, and the windows gave the area a bright and cheery vibe that was perfect for her, especially since she spent so much time here.

I stopped in the doorway, my hand raised to knock lightly on the open door, the breath knocked out of me. Alina sat in her chair at the narrow table, studying the hoop on the wooden stand. Sunlight streamed through the window, high-lighting the red tones in her dark hair and making her pale skin glow. God, she was so fucking beautiful.

My heart set a frantic beat, and I studied the curve of her breast as she reached for some thread that sat on the table. I'd woken up this morning a little before six with my hand cupping that breast and my body the big spoon to Alina's little spoon.

I hadn't meant to fall asleep in her bed. I'd only meant to stay with her until she was sleeping, and I was sure the pain in her leg wouldn't wake her again. But I was tired, and her double bed was more comfortable than my single and the last thing I'd remembered before waking this morning was how good it felt to sleep next to her.

It had felt good, all right. So good that my dick had been at full mast and pressing hard into Alina's soft ass. Thank fucking God, she'd still been asleep. I'd eased out of her bed and returned to my own without her waking.

Staring at Alina and remembering how perfect her breast felt in my hand would give me another fucking stiffy if I didn't stop thinking about it. I quickly knocked on the studio door, smiling at Alina when she stared up at me. "Hey, how are you?"

"Good. How was volleyball?"

"We won," I said. "How's your leg today?"

"Better, thanks again for your help last night."

"You're welcome."

There was an awkward silence, and then Alina said, "Did you eat dinner?"

"Nah. I'm gonna have a quick shower and then make a sandwich."

"There's leftover stir fry if you want it," she said.

"I don't want to eat your leftovers," I said.

"There's plenty."

"You sure?"

She smiled at me. "Positive."

"Okay, thanks." I left her studio, heading back to my bedroom and stripping out of my clothes. I was sweaty and a bit sore from volleyball, and I spent longer than usual in the shower, letting the hot water ease the aching in my back muscles, deliberately keeping my mind clear of thoughts of Alina. Not that I thought she'd hear me masturbating in the shower, but it didn't feel right to jerk off with Alina just down the hall.

Of course, I needed to get over that particular phobia because going two months without masturbating while living with Alina was a grim and, frankly, impossible prospect.

Once I'd finished showering, I toweled off and threw on a pair of gym shorts. I grabbed a t-shirt and headed out into the hallway, pausing in putting it on when I heard a loud clunk drifting down the hallway from Alina's studio.

Alarm swept through me. Had she fallen again? Dropping my shirt, I took off at a dead run to her studio. My blood ran cold, and my stomach dropped to the fucking floor when I saw Alina standing on the much too fucking tall stepladder in the middle of her studio, balancing on her good leg with her bad leg stuck out behind her.

"What the fuck are you doing?" My panic made my voice too loud.

Alina let out a soft scream, her body jerking as she turned to look behind her. Her foot slipped, and I darted forward as she fell off the ladder, catching her before she could land on the floor. The lightbulb in her hand fell to the floor and broke with a jagged cough, spraying glass shards along the wood floor.

She clutched at my shoulders, her eyes wide with alarm. "Nick, you scared the crap out of me!"

"I scared you?" To avoid the glass, I carried her over to a second table that held some of her supplies. I sat her in an empty space on top of the table, glaring at her as I crowded between her thighs. "What the hell are you doing on that ladder, Alina?"

She glanced at the ladder and the light above it. "Changing the light."

"Changing the light?" I was gonna have a fucking stroke. I raked my hand through my wet hair. "You cannot stand on a fucking ladder, Alina. Why didn't you call for me?"

"Because it's not your job to change my light bulb," Alina said. "I'm not helpless, Nick."

"You could have hurt yourself badly," I said. "You fell off the ladder!"

"Because you scared me," she said. "I wouldn't have fallen if you hadn't come in here yelling your head off."

"I was not yelling my head off," I said through gritted teeth. "Alina, I will do shit like that, okay? You don't need to be climbing ladders or -"

"I don't need a babysitter, Nicky!" Alina scowled at me. "Also, why are you half-naked again? Do you ever wear a damn shirt?"

"I'm half-naked because I thought you'd fallen, and I didn't want to waste time putting on a shirt," I said.

She pushed on my chest. "I said I was fine. Move, Nick."

"Not until you promise me you won't do something like this again."

"You're not my boss," Alina said, but her voice had lost her anger. She sounded... weird. Out of breath and, if I didn't know better, she sounded like how I imagined she would if she was turned on.

I became aware of two things at once - Alina's hand had moved from my chest to my abs, and my cock was rock hard and incredibly noticeable against the thin fabric of my gym shorts.

"Nicky," Alina breathed as she stared at my dick.

I tried to back away, I swear to fucking God I did, but Alina wrapped her good leg around my waist, pulling me up against her as her fingers traced my stomach muscles. They jumped and twitched under her touch, and when she looked up at me, and I saw the lust in her gaze, that was it for me. I couldn't fucking resist her any longer.

I dropped my mouth to hers, swallowing her gasp of surprise as I took advantage of her parted lips and slid my tongue between them. She tasted sweet, like strawberries, and I explored her mouth with long slow licks as I cupped her face and held her still.

Her hands clutched at my waist, and she pulled me even tighter against her, rubbing her pussy against my aching dick as she boldly explored my mouth with her tongue. Her kissing technique was awkward and unsure, but it lit me up like a fucking firework.

I cupped her tit, rubbing my thumb across her nipple until it hardened. When I kissed her neck and lightly bit at her collarbone, she moaned my name and arched her back. I shoved my hand up her shirt and wormed it under her bra, growling in satisfaction when I felt her tight nipple against my palm. I kneaded her breast, kissing her again as she rocked against me.

"Nicky, please," she moaned against my mouth.

Her hand cupped my dick, and I sucked in a harsh breath. What the fuck was I doing? I yanked my hand out from under her shirt and backed away, breaking free of her grip on me.

"Nicky?" Alina's face was flushed, her lips were swollen

from my kisses, and those beautiful blue eyes radiated desire and confusion. "What's wrong?"

"I can't do this," I rasped. "Alina, this is… wrong."

"No, it isn't," she said.

"I'm practically your brother."

She made a face. "Don't say that to me after you just had your tongue down my throat. You don't think of me as a sister. Admit it."

I blew out my breath and adjusted my throbbing dick. "No, I don't. I've wanted you for a long time, Alina."

"I've wanted you too. But you knew that, didn't you? Because of that moment in the kitchen when you fixed my sink. If we hadn't been interrupted by Liam and Sophie, we would have kissed then."

"I convinced myself that I only saw what I wanted to see that day," I said.

"Me too," she said. "But we both felt the same thing for each other, didn't we?"

"Yes," I said.

"Then come back here," she said with a soft smile.

"I can't," I said. "Just because we don't see each other as siblings doesn't mean that… other people don't."

"It's none of Liam and Finn's business," she said. "It's not our problem they think we have that type of relationship."

"They would kill me," I said. "They don't think I'm good enough for you."

"Stop that," she said. "You're more than good enough for me, and besides, they're not in charge of who I date. I am. And I want to date you, Nicky."

"I'm not the settling down type," I said. "You know my reputation, Alina."

"So, what? Because you like to sleep around, you'll never be interested in a relationship?"

"That's exactly what it means," I lied. "I like variety, and I don't do commitment."

Hurt flashed across her face for only a few seconds before she slid off the table, landing on one leg before gingerly putting weight on her other leg. "All right. Thanks for letting me know you're not interested in dating me. I won't touch you again."

"Alina, it's not you. It's me."

"Oh my God," she said as she limped past me. "Are you serious right now, Nick?"

"Okay, that was a stupid thing to say, but that doesn't make it any less true." I followed her out into the hallway. "My lack of interest in a relationship has nothing to do with you, Alina."

"So you've said." Her back straight and her shoulders stiff, she walked toward her bedroom. "It's been a long day. I think I'll go to bed early. Good night, Nick."

"Alina...."

She slipped into her bedroom and shut the door. I slumped against the wall. Could I have fucked that up any harder if I'd tried?

Alina

"THE BLUE DRESS, DEFINITELY THE BLUE," BRYCE SAID. SHE lounged on my bed with Stanley, her fingers brushing over the mountain of clothing strewn across it. Stanley had made himself comfortable on one of my sweaters, and he stared at me with his tiny tail wagging as I crossed the room and lowered myself onto the bed.

I rubbed my leg, and Bryce said, "How bad is it today?"

"Not bad," I said. "I've been resting it a lot this week because Ethan wants to meet at the Vintage Kitchen for dinner, and it's a bit of a bike ride to get there."

"Why didn't you ask him to have dinner somewhere closer?" Bryce said.

I shrugged. "I didn't want to inconvenience him."

Bryce's scowl deepened as she sat up and crossed her legs. "Please, he should be falling all over himself just for the chance to get into your pants. You're a stone cold fox."

"Yeah," I said dryly. "Every guy is dying to bang me except for -"

Shit! I immediately changed the subject, hoping Bryce hadn't noticed my mistake. "So, you think the blue dress and not the red one? I'll be losing my virginity tomorrow night. That feels like it calls for dressing up a little more."

"The blue one," Bryce said. "The red is too fancy for Vintage Kitchen. Which guy isn't dying to bang you?"

"Hmm?" I said, pretending to play dumb before leaning over and kissing Stanley's forehead. "You are just the best baby, Stanley. Yes, you are."

Bryce poked me in the back. "Hey, what aren't you telling me?"

I sighed and straightened. "Nick and I made out on Tuesday night."

"What the eff, Alina!" I thought Bryce would fall off the bed as she grabbed my arm. "Start talking, now."

It only took ten minutes to explain what happened. When I was finished, Bryce grabbed her wine glass from the bedside table and took a sip. "Wow... that was unexpected."

"What? The kissing or the part where he rejected me and has avoided me for the last two days?"

"All of it," Bryce said. She took a good look at me and sighed. "I'm sorry he's being a dick now."

"He isn't," I said. "I appreciated his honesty. At least now I know I'm not wasting my time with Ethan, right? And there's a weird kind of comfort in knowing that Nick doesn't think of me as his sibling. The thought that he might while I was daydreaming about having sex with him really messed with my head."

"I get it," Bryce said. "But I wish it had worked out for you."

I kept the smile glued in place. I'd cried enough the last couple of days, and it hadn't solved the problem. I didn't want to cry anymore.

"You okay, honey?" Bryce asked softly.

"Yes. I don't want to talk about Nick. I want to talk about how I'm finally going to have sex tomorrow night."

"You sure you want Ethan to be the dude?" Bryce asked.

"I'm sure," I lied. "He's nice, polite, and he looks like he'll be good in bed."

"You sure about that? You said his kiss at the end of the second date didn't light any fires in your lady garden," Bryce said.

"Only because I was still stuck on this idea of Nick," I said. "Now that I know it's never going to happen, I can fully concentrate on Ethan. And he wasn't a bad kisser or anything. It just wasn't fireworks like...."

"Like with Nick," Bryce said.

I sighed and grabbed a shirt off the bed, folding and refolding it. "The date is going to go wonderfully tomorrow night. I know it."

The front door opened and then shut, and Stanley perked up, his eyes going wide and his ears pricking forward. He jumped off the bed with a high-pitched bark and ran out of the bedroom at full speed.

"Looks like Nick's home from work," I said.

Bryce glanced at her watch. "It's almost nine. That's a long-ass day."

"Yeah, well, as I said, he's avoiding me."

Stanley's barks turned pterodactyl in volume and length, and Bryce grimaced. "Oh man, Stanley's barking is just getting more shrill with age."

I laughed as Stanley's barking died down, and we heard Nick's footsteps in the hallway. I took a deep breath, resisting the urge to smooth my hair or maybe quickly run into the bathroom and slap on a full face of makeup. Nick wouldn't sleep with me, so what did it matter what I looked like?

Nick stopped in the bedroom doorway, a genuine smile lighting up his face when he saw Bryce. "Hey, Bryce. How are you?"

"Good, Nicky. I hear you have a mold problem," Bryce said.

"Yes." Nick held Stanley in one hand, stroking his ears with the other. "Hey, Alina. How was your day?"

"Good," I said. "Finished a hoop for a client and had an embroidery lesson with a new client. How was yours?"

"Busy," Nick said with a polite smile.

Man, I hated how formal and weird we were now. Almost enough to make me wish we'd never kissed. At least then, there wouldn't be this awkward tension between us, and Nick wouldn't feel obligated to spend as much time as possible away from the house.

"What's all this?" Nick pointed to the mountain of clothes on the bed. "You cleaning out your closet?"

"Figuring out clothes for a date, actually," Bryce said cheerfully.

I glared at her, and she winked at me as Nick said, "A date, huh? Who's the lucky guy, Bryce?"

"Oh, not me," Bryce said before I could tackle her to the

bed and smother her with a pillow. "Alina. Alina's going on the date tomorrow night."

"What?" Nick stared at me, his hand stilling on Stanley's back. "You're what?"

"She's going on a date with Ethan," Bryce said.

"Who the fuck is Ethan?" Nick said.

"Her date," Bryce said.

"Do your brothers know about this?" Nick asked.

"Do they need to?" Bryce raised an eyebrow at him. "She's a grown woman, Nick."

Nick's face was bright red as he walked into the room and handed Stanley to Bryce. He glared at me. "How did you meet him? How much do you know about him?"

"I met him on a dating app," I said, "and I know a lot about him."

"How? You can't get to know someone over a damn app," Nick said.

"She's had plenty of time to get to know him," Bryce said. "It's her third date with Ethan. You know what they say about the third date."

"Bryce," I said, giving her the stink eye.

She grinned and slid off the bed, kissing my cheek as she grabbed her phone and shifted Stanley to her other hand. "I gotta go. Have fun tomorrow night, honey. And wear the blue dress. It's sexy as fuck on you."

She grinned at Nick and left the room. Nick looked like he was about to blow a gasket, but I tamped down the small part of me that enjoyed his obvious jealousy. Nothing would come of it.

"I want to meet this Ethan guy," Nick said.

"No way." I stood and started to hang clothes back in the closet as Nick glowered at me.

"Yes, Alina. If you won't let Liam meet him, then I have to. What if he's a serial killer?"

I laughed. "He's not a serial killer, Nick. He's a lawyer."

"Even worse," Nick snapped.

I laughed again. "He's a nice guy. I like him, and I'm having dinner with him tomorrow night, and no, you can't meet him, and don't you tell Liam about this, or I'll light a bonfire in my backyard and burn all your clothes."

"What restaurant are you going to?" Nick asked.

"Why?"

"I'm curious," Nick said.

"Like I'm going to tell you so that you can show up there in the middle of my date." I reached past Nick for a sweater, going still when he grasped my wrist.

He was distractingly close, and my pussy did this weird tingling thing when he rubbed his thumb over my pulse. "Tell me which restaurant, Alina."

"Stop that," I said. "Don't distract me with your touching and your ridiculously good smelling aftershave."

He leaned down and brushed his mouth against mine. "Tell me, baby."

"Vintage Kitchen," I said, my body swaying toward his. "We're having dinner at Vintage Kitchen."

He released me and stepped back. I glared at him as the fog of lust lifted a little. "That's playing dirty, Nicholas."

"I know," he said without a hint of shame. "How are you getting to the restaurant?"

"I'm riding my bike. How else would I get there?" I asked.

"It's too far," he said. "Why aren't you taking the bus?"

"Because I hate taking the bus. It's hard for me to get up the bus steps with my leg and everyone stares at me, and…

you know what, I'm not talking about this with you. Promise me you won't show up at the restaurant, Nick."

He hesitated, and I glared at him. "Promise right now, or I'll ask Ethan to meet me at a different restaurant, I swear to God."

"Fine." He crossed his arms over his chest. "I promise."

"Thank you." I glanced at the clothes on my bed. "I need to get this cleaned up to go to bed. Good night, Nick."

With a muttered curse, Nick turned and stomped out of my room.

CHAPTER 5

Alina

"Thank you for buying dinner, Ethan." As we stepped out of the restaurant, I smiled at him and didn't object when he took my hand.

"You're welcome." He squeezed my hand, but his touch didn't affect my pussy one bit the way Nick's touch did.

Disappointing, but I'd work with it. A qualifier for sex wasn't pussy tingling when they grabbed your hand, right?

Ethan led me into the parking lot, even though my bike was locked to the bike stands close to the restaurant. I smiled at him as he leaned against his car and then brushed a lock of my hair back from my face. "You look beautiful tonight."

"Thank you," I said.

Ethan bent and kissed me. It was a perfectly nice kiss that didn't send a lick of lust through my body. I parted my lips when he probed at them with his tongue. Ethan stepped closer, backing me up against the car as his tongue - his admittedly very large and suddenly very wet tongue - invaded my mouth. He tasted like beer and the shrimp he'd had for dinner, and I pulled my head back before doing something unladylike, like gagging in his mouth.

"What's wrong?" Ethan asked.

"Nothing," I said before taking a deep breath. Okay, so my sexual attraction to Ethan was minimal -

Minimal? Is zero considered minimal?

I ignored my inner voice. Once we were in my bed, it would be fine. I'd be turned on, I was sure of it. Ethan was a nice guy.

Ethan, the nice guy, smiled at me. "So, what do you think about heading to your place to…."

"Netflix and chill?" I asked.

Ethan laughed and caressed my arm. "Something like that. I don't want the night to end yet, Alina."

I smiled before I could blurt out that I did. "Sure. Um, but…"

My plan to bring Ethan back to my place and just be really quiet while we boned finally loomed large as the ridiculous plan it was. I couldn't have sex with a guy while Nick was in the next room. I just couldn't. And I knew for a fact that he wasn't out tonight. He was at home waiting sullenly for me to return from my date with Ethan, the potential serial killer.

Although to give him credit, Nick hadn't shown up at the restaurant, and I'd really expected him to despite his promise.

"Alina? What's wrong?"

"Nothing," I said, "but, um, I have a friend staying at my place, so maybe we could go to your place?"

"Sure. But I live over on the north side, so it's too far for you to bike."

I frowned. "But you matched with me. Your profile said you were only a few miles away."

He grinned at me. "Oh, yeah, that was my old place. I

moved a few months ago but forgot to change my location in the app. It's no big deal, I'll just throw your bike in the trunk, and you can drive with me. I'll drive you home later, I promise."

"It's not that," I said. "You know that I have issues with cars."

"Yeah, I get it," he said as he opened the passenger door. "It's a little scary for you because of that car accident you were in as a kid, but I promise I'm a really safe driver. Get in the car, and I'll go grab your bike for you."

"I can't," I said, resisting when Ethan tugged on my elbow. "It's more than just being scared, okay?"

Annoyance flickered across Ethan's face before he smoothed it out. "I promise, sweetheart, it won't be that bad. And when we get to my place, I'll make you forget all about the big, bad car ride."

He leaned down to kiss my neck, and I jerked out of his grip. "No, I can't, Ethan."

"Are you fucking kidding me?" The annoyance was back.

It changed his face from something blandly appealing to mildly dangerous, and my heart rate kicked up a notch. I looked around, but the parking lot was empty.

Ethan took my elbow again. "C'mon, just try it. Okay? Don't be such a baby."

"Let go of me before I kick you in the nuts," I said.

He sighed impatiently. "You fucking chicks are all the same.

His hand squeezed tighter, and I glared up at him. "You're hurting me. Stop it now, or I'll hurt you."

"You're barely five feet, and you've got a bum leg," Ethan laughed. "You actually think your threats even -"

"Let her go now, or I'll rip your fucking head off."

Nick's voice sent fresh adrenaline roaring through me and

a rush of relief. Ethan dropped my arm and turned around, staring at Nick. "Who the fuck are you?"

Ignoring him, Nick stared at me. "You okay, Alina?"

"Yes," I said. "Ethan was just leaving."

Ethan stared at me and then at Nick before rolling his eyes. "Whatever. This cold bitch isn't fucking worth it."

Nick started toward him, his hands clenched into fists, and I immediately pushed my way between them, wincing at the pain in my leg from the sudden movement. I grabbed Nick's arms and said, "Please don't, Nicky."

Nick slipped his arm around my shoulders and pulled me into him as Ethan walked around the car. He opened the driver's door as Nicky said, "Lose her number, asshole."

"Fuck you," Ethan said. "I wouldn't call this bitch again if you paid me."

Nick's body stiffened, and I tightened my hold on his waist, pulling him back as Ethan got into his car and flipped us the bird before driving away.

I sagged against Nick, the adrenaline making my body shake. Nick pulled me even closer, cupping my face and stroking my cheekbone with his thumb. "You're all right, baby. He's gone."

"What are you doing here?" I asked.

He flushed. "I didn't break my promise. I didn't show up at the restaurant. I stayed in the parking lot."

I stared at him before bursting into laughter. "Oh my God, Nicky. Have you been sitting in the parking lot my whole date?"

"Maybe."

I leaned against him, resting my forehead on his chest as he rubbed my back. After a minute, I said, "Aren't you going to tell me I told you so?"

"No," he said. "C'mon, let's go home, Alina."

"I'll meet you at the house," I said.

He shook his head. "You can double me on your bike, and I'll pick up my car tomorrow."

I frowned. "Nick, that isn't -"

"No arguing," he said gently before kissing me on the forehead. "It's late, and I need to make sure you get home safely. Okay?"

"Okay," I said.

"Good. You comfortable with me riding double?"

I smiled up at him. "Yes, but I think it might be illegal, so you're paying the fine if the police pull us over."

He laughed and took my hand. "Deal."

Nick

"ALINA? I'M BACK!" I SHUT THE FRONT DOOR AND KICKED off my shoes before heading toward the kitchen. Alina sat at the table typing on her phone, and she smiled up at me.

"Hi there. How did it go with the car?"

"Fine. I picked it up from the restaurant, and it was all in one piece." I grinned.

"Good." She sipped at her coffee as I poured myself one.

"You didn't have to pay for the Uber," I said as I sat in the chair next to hers.

"Yes, I did," she said. "Your car was only at the restaurant because of me."

I wanted to keep arguing, but I knew it was pointless. Alina was stubborn as hell.

"What are your plans for the day?" Alina asked.

"Not sure yet. Might go for a run," I said. "What about you?"

"Not much. I have a new embroidery pattern I want to design, and I need to go to the grocery store. Liam and Sophie are coming over for dinner tonight. Will you join us?"

I should say no. Spending time with Alina, especially when Liam was there and could potentially pick up on the sexual tension between his sister and me, was dangerous. But the prospect of sitting in my room or at some restaurant alone wasn't exactly appealing. I could behave myself for an evening. I'd been pretending for years that I didn't see Alina as anything but a little sister.

Yeah, but that was before you kissed her. Before you knew how it sounded when she moaned and how tight her nipples got when you touched them. How wet do you think she was that day? Wet enough to take your dick?

"Nick?" Alina said.

"Sorry. Yeah, I'd like to join you. If you give me a list, I'll run to the grocery store for you and save you a bike trip."

"You sure?" she asked.

"I am." I drank some coffee as Alina stood to refill her cup. I watched the sway of her firm ass in her leggings, adjusting my semi under the table. Christ, her ass was amazing. Her whole body was amazing, and watching that fucking douchebag Ethan manhandle her last night had made me see red. The only thing that had stopped me from breaking his nose was Alina's soft voice.

Her phone dinged, and I glanced idly at the screen, my eyes widening when I saw the message. "What the hell, Alina?"

"What?" She joined me at the table again, the steam from her coffee rising in the cool air. "What's wrong?"

"You just got a message from some guy named Royce," I said.

"Oh, perfect." She opened her phone and scrolled across the screen. "I matched with him earlier this morning."

"You matched... you're still on that dating app?" I said in outrage.

"Yes." She glanced at me. "What's wrong?"

"What's wrong? The last guy you matched with turned out to be an asshole," I said.

"True. But not a serial killer." She grinned at me.

"This isn't funny," I said. "Look, I get that you want to date someone, but this is not the app for that, okay? You need to try E-Harmony or some shit like that. This app is for people who are only looking for sex."

"I know." Alina was still typing on her phone and missed my bug-eyed look of surprise.

"Alina, are you... are you just looking to get laid?" I asked.

She set her phone down. "What if I am?"

"That's not you," I said.

"You don't know that," she said.

"Yes, I do," I said.

She made another infuriating shrug. "I want to have sex without commitment. There's nothing wrong with that."

"Your first time shouldn't be with some random hookup," I said.

She froze, her pretty blue eyes studying me intently. "How did you know it's my first time?"

A shudder of awareness washed over me. I'd assumed it was her first time but was also well aware of what assuming did. To find out that it would be her first time sent a wave of unexpected emotion over me. I was a little ashamed to realize that emotion was excitement. I was immediately annoyed with myself over my patriarchal response to her virginity. It was sexist *and* pointless since it wasn't like I would be her first.

Nope, some asshole like Ethan will be her first. Is that what you want?

Jealousy flamed to life. Its fire so intense it threatened to melt my bones into ash.

"How did you know, Nick?" she asked as her chest went blotchy and redness crept up her neck.

"Just a lucky guess," I said.

She laughed, the sound a little bitter. "An easy guess, I suppose. I've basically been a damn hermit since the accident."

"That's not your fault," I said. "But I don't think a random hookup is the best idea for your first time."

"I'm tired of being a virgin," she said. "I want to have sex, Nick."

"I get that," I said. "But the right guy is out there. You'll find him."

She laughed again, and this time the bitterness was unmistakable. "That's complete bullshit. We both know I'll never find someone to deal with all of my trauma and my baggage. It's not fair to them to have to deal with that."

"The right guy won't have a problem with it," I said.

She brushed off my comment. "Maybe, but the odds of me finding him are slim. But that doesn't mean I have to live the life of a nun. So, I'm finding someone to have sex with. And this Royce guy has potential."

She turned back to her phone, and with my jealousy a roaring, raging, rolling inferno burning me alive, I said, "I'll do it."

She glanced up at me. "Do what?"

"I'll have sex with you."

CHAPTER 6

Alina

The last thing I ever expected was for Nick Campbell to volunteer to have sex with me. A myriad of emotions swept through me - surprise, excitement, embarrassment... lust. The lust overpowered everything else, which probably explained why I quickly blurted, "Okay."

Nick twitched slightly, muttering a curse when hot coffee sloshed over the cup rim and onto his hand. "That was quick. Maybe you should think on it overnight."

"Why?" I asked. "You know I'm attracted to you. You know I want to have sex. Why should I wait another twenty-four hours to make my decision?"

"I don't want you doing something you'll regret," he said.

"Why would I regret it?"

"Because I can't give you anything more than what I'm offering - only sex. But I'm Liam's best friend, which means we'll be required to socialize even after the sex stops. It could be awkward and uncomfortable."

"Maybe," I said, "but life is full of awkward and uncomfortable moments. You can't avoid them all."

"Sure, but you also don't need to create those moments deliberately," Nick said.

I sipped at my coffee. "Are you worried that I'll go all psycho weird when you eventually fall in love with someone else, and I have to spend time with her?"

Nick set his coffee down, then stood and paced the kitchen, his lean body tense with nervous energy. "No. I told you - I'm not relationship material. I won't be dating anyone."

"You've dated in the past," I pointed out.

"Nothing serious for the last five years," he said.

"Why?"

He answered with a question of his own. "Are you sure you're good with this being a one-time thing?"

"Can we make it a weekend event?" I asked. "I imagine the first time won't be that good for obvious reasons, so I'd like to have at least one other shot at it where it isn't going to hurt."

He sat in his chair and reached for my hands, staring earnestly at me. "Alina, I promise I'll do everything I can to make your first time feel good."

God, he was so sweet. It was a real shame he was so determined to stay single. He'd make a fantastic boyfriend.

Yeah, to another woman. Alina, this is a mistake. You know it is. You love him, and if you sleep with him -

I shut inner Alina out before she could really hammer home how stupid I was being. I'd been in love with Nick Campbell since I was seventeen years old. I wouldn't turn down the chance to have sex with him, no matter how much it hurt later.

"I appreciate that," I said, squeezing his hands.

He smiled at me. "That being said, I'm good with a weekend event."

"Fantastic," I said cheerfully, making him laugh. "When do you want to start?"

"How about right now?" he asked. "Unless you need to finish that embroidery pattern first?"

"I'll do it Monday," I said.

"Are you sure?" he asked.

I stood up, tugging on his hands. "Hmm, let's see... have sex with a super hot guy for the first time or work on an embroidery pattern. It's *such* a hard choice, Nicky. However will I decide?"

He laughed and stood up. "You're cute even when you're being a smartass."

"I know." I led him toward my bedroom, my excitement level growing by the second. I was about to have sex with the man of my dreams. It didn't get any better than this.

Sure it could. The man of your dreams could want more than just a few rounds of hiding the bishop.

Yeah, well, that was never gonna happen for me. Besides, Nicky wasn't the only one determined not to be in a relationship.

I stopped by the bed and turned to Nick. He studied me for a few seconds, a frown marring his forehead. "Hey, you okay?"

"Yes, why?" I asked.

"You look a little worried or... sad," he said.

"I'm not." I plastered a grin on my face. "Let's get naked, Nicky."

He caught my hands when I tugged at his shirt hem. "Alina, you know if you want to stop at *any* point, all you have to do is say so, right? I won't be upset or angry if you change your mind."

"I know," I said. "I want this, Nick."

He studied my face again before nodding. "Okay. I'll grab a condom from my room and be right back."

"Already taken care of." I opened the bedside drawer and grabbed the condom box, taking one out and setting it on the nightstand before shoving the box back inside the drawer. "We're good to go, Houston."

He laughed and pulled me up against him, running one hand down my back to my ass. He squeezed it, and I rubbed against the hardness I could feel rising against my belly.

"I love your ass," he said. "It's great."

"Thank you. Isn't this the part where we get naked?"

"So impatient," he said but put his arms up so I could take off his shirt.

"Can you blame me?" I ran my fingers over his chest and down his stomach. He hissed out a breath when I traced my finger along his belt, but he shook his head when I reached to unbuckle it.

"Not yet, baby."

I scowled at him. "I want to see you naked, Nicky."

"You will," he said before tugging my shirt over my head and dropping it on the floor with his, "but not yet, impatient girl."

I snorted in frustration, and Nick laughed before kissing my neck. "I promise it'll be worth the wait."

"Someone thinks highly of their dick," I said, arching my back when Nicky cupped my breast.

"It's a very nice dick, and I'm positive you and he will be excellent friends," Nick said before nipping at the soft spot where my neck and shoulder met.

I moaned when he circled my nipple, turning it into a stiff peak that strained against the cotton material of my bra.

His other hand cupped the back of my skull, and we

kissed, Nick's tongue teasing mine with gentle strokes. Kissing Nick was a heady rush and something I would never grow tired of. When his hands slid behind my back and unhooked my bra, I helped him take it off. Unexpected shyness washed over me, and I crossed my arms over my chest as Nick added my bra to the growing pile of clothing.

He smiled and put one arm around my waist before nuzzling my throat. He kissed me again, angling his mouth over mine and taking the kiss deep with a possessiveness that made my shyness disappear.

I slid my arms around his shoulders, pressing my breasts against his chest. He groaned and immediately cupped one breast, his thumb circling my nipple as he sucked on my bottom lip. He stepped back, staring at my naked breasts with a hot and glittery gaze of need that I felt to my toes.

"So beautiful," he said before leaning down and sucking my right nipple into his mouth. The pressure and the warm wetness of his tongue made the coil of need tighten in my belly. My pussy was growing wetter by the second, and I'd never once dreamed that having Nick's mouth on my nipples would feel this damn good.

I arched my back when he kissed his way to my left nipple and sucked and teased it until I cried his name and pulled on his hair.

"Okay, baby?" he asked with a small grin.

"Nick," I panted, "I need… something."

"Is that right?" He guided me to the bed, helping me lie back and lift my sore leg onto the bed before he stretched out beside me. He ran his fingers lightly over my stomach and across my ribs before teasing the underside of my breasts.

"Nicky!" I grabbed his hand, pushing it onto my breast and glaring at him. "Don't tease."

He just grinned again, then leaned down and kissed one

throbbing nipple before sucking on it. I moaned and reached to palm his cock. He sucked in a breath, his hand tightening almost painfully on my breast before he pulled my hand away and kissed the palm. "Not yet, baby."

"I want to touch you," I complained.

"I know, and you will," he said. "But this is all about you right now."

"I know I'm new to this, but I'm pretty sure that's not how sex works," I said. "It's a give and take."

He smiled and brushed a lock of hair away from my face. "That's true. But I'm determined to make your first time special, and cumming in my jeans because you touched me isn't the special I had in mind."

I grinned and reached for his dick again. "I don't have any experience, but I know it takes more than a few rubs over clothing to make a guy cum, Nicky."

He pulled my hand away, a pained look on his face. "Yeah, normally, but when you're in bed with the woman you've fantasized about for -"

He stopped abruptly, and I shook my head. "Oh, don't you dare stop now. How long have you wanted me like I've wanted you?"

He cleared his throat. "Five years."

"Five years?" I stared wide-eyed at him. "You've wanted to have sex with me for five years?"

Red tinged his cheeks. "Yes."

"I never knew," I said. "You hid it so well."

"I didn't know you wanted me either," he said. "Unless this has been a more recent thing?"

"No. Eight years for me," I said, and Nick made a small sound of surprise. "I was seventeen, and I'd just been discharged from the hospital after one of my surgeries. You and Liam put me on a lounge chair by the pool so I could get some sun while you two swam. You were half-naked and wearing a wet bathing suit. My lady parts went zing."

He laughed. "I remember that day. You really wanted to go in the pool, but you couldn't get your surgery site wet. So Liam and I put you on a floatie and pushed you around the pool until Finn came home and freaked out. We got in so much trouble from him later."

It was my turn to laugh. "I don't even remember Finn freaking out."

He circled my nipple again with his thumb. "So many years of wanting to be with each other and neither of us having any idea."

I smiled but didn't reply. I hadn't lied to Nick, I told myself. That day by the pool, I realized that I wanted to sleep with him. But I'd fallen in love with him two weeks before that. I'd still been in the hospital, and while the latest surgery mainly had been a success, I'd been having a difficult time emotionally and mentally. Being alone in the hospital depressed me to the point of crying. Liam and Finn had made sure that one of them was with me at all times so that I wouldn't be sad. There'd been a day where neither could miss work, and they made my dad promise to stay with me instead. But he bailed at the last minute, as usual. Nick had arrived at the hospital within the hour with flowers and my favourite candy bar, and he'd sat in that stupid hospital room with me all day, making me laugh with his silly jokes and watching *The Lord of the Rings* with me on my tablet even though we'd both seen it a dozen times.

I'd fallen in love with Nick Campbell on that day and never stopped.

"Hey, you okay?" Nick stared down at me with concern etched into his face.

"I am," I said, tracing my hand down his chest.

"If you want to stop, we can," he said. "I won't be upset or -"

"I don't want to stop," I said. "In fact, I'm a little annoyed that you haven't even tried to explore my lady garden yet."

Nick burst into laughter. "Lady garden? Please don't ever use that term for your pussy in front of me again."

I giggled. "What? It's cute."

"If you say so." Nick bent and sucked on my nipple again. Hot desire slammed into me, and I moaned his name, my body tingling when he slid his big hand down my stomach.

He slipped his hand inside my yoga pants and into my panties before exploring the patch of hair at the top of my sex.

"Nicky, please," I gasped, widening my legs.

He smiled against my breast and then nipped at the underside before licking my nipple. "Still impatient," he said but slid his hand further down and cupped my pussy.

He lifted his head to stare at me, the same hot need I felt stamped all over his face. "You're so wet for me, baby."

"Oh!" I clutched at his arm when he rubbed my throbbing clit. "Oh, God, that feels good."

"I like making you feel good." Nick studied me intently as he caressed my wet pussy lips before concentrating on my clit again. "I want you to cum for me, Alina."

I rocked my hips, looking for that perfect friction and crying out when Nick pressed more firmly and gave it to me. "Oh, right there. So good, Nicky... so good."

He leaned down and kissed my nipple again before sucking lightly on it. He circled my clit, using just the right pressure and rhythm to get me off. Fuck, this was so much better than my own hand. I clutched at Nick, closing my eyes and reaching for my orgasm. I was so close. So damn close.

I cried out when Nick stopped touching me. He yanked

his hand out of my pants and shook his head when I started to speak, pressing his finger against my lips.

I stared at him in confusion as he glanced at my bedroom door.

"Nick," I said in a low voice, "what's wrong? Why did you stop?"

"Alina?" Liam's voice from somewhere in the house made my eyes widen. "Hey, where are you?"

I sat up in a hurry as Nick slid off the bed and grabbed his shirt. I limped to the open door and shouted, "Hey, Liam. Just in my room. Give me two minutes."

I shut the door and dressed in record time as Nick pulled his shirt over his head. Without looking at him, I left my bedroom and walked down the hall to the kitchen. Liam and Sophie were sitting at the table, and Liam frowned when I limped into the kitchen.

"What is going on with your hair?" he asked.

I smoothed my hair as Liam said, "Dude, brushing your hair is basic hygiene."

"Shut up, Liam," I said.

Liam laughed, but Sophie gave me a considering look that made me nervous. I rubbed my hand across my mouth self-consciously as if she could see Nick's lip imprints on them before making my way to the coffee pot.

"Where's Nick?" Liam asked.

I shrugged, keeping my voice nonchalant. "Not sure. His room, maybe. What are you two doing here?"

My tone sounded a little accusatory, but could you blame me? I'd been right on the edge of an orgasm with the man I loved, and Liam had interrupted it.

"Sophie had a great idea," Liam said.

"But you don't have to do it if you don't want to," Sophie said. "Absolutely feel free to say no."

"Say no to what?" Nick strolled into the kitchen, looking calm and collected and not at all like he'd had his fingers in my pussy not five minutes ago.

"Hey, buddy," Liam held out his fist, and Nick bumped it.

Nick smiled at Sophie. "Hi, Sophie."

"Hi, Nick," Sophie said before turning to me. "A new farmer's market opened up. It's smaller than the usual one on Jade Street, but it's only, like, a ten-minute bike ride from here. You've mentioned before that you've wanted to go to a farmer's market. Liam and I have our bikes, and we thought the three of us could bike over and check it out."

She glanced at Nick. "If you're not busy, you should join us."

I had to work very hard not to kiss Sophie in gratitude for inviting Nick.

"Sure," Nick said, "if Alina doesn't mind doubling me again. My bike is back at my place."

"Again? What do you mean again?" Liam asked.

I groaned inwardly as a look of panic flashed across Nick's face. "Um, the other day, I...."

"The other day, you what?" Liam looked at me and then at Nick. "What is going on with you two?"

Sophie stood and plopped herself into Liam's lap, "Honey, I forgot to tell you that *Commando* is on Netflix now. I saw it the other day."

"Seriously?" Liam's face lit up. "We have to watch it tonight."

He squeezed Sophie's waist and, in a bad Arnold Schwarzeneggar impression, said, "I eat Green Berets for breakfast. And right now, I'm very hungry!"

I rolled my eyes as Nick laughed. "Seriously, dude, you have the worst Arnold Schwarzeneggar impression."

"It's better than your Sean Connery impression," Liam said.

"He's lying," Nick said to Sophie. "I do an impeccable Sean Connery impression."

"Do you, though?" I asked.

Nick gave me a look of fake hurt. "Such betrayal, Alina."

I laughed as Sophie pressed a kiss against Liam's mouth before smiling at me. "Well, what do you say? Are we farmers marketing it, or what?"

"We are," I said.

CHAPTER 7

Nick

"Honey, we should get going." Sophie nudged Liam. "Alina looks tired."

It was close to eight, and we'd spent the entire day with Liam and Sophie. It'd been fun, and I loved how excited Alina was to be at the farmer's market, but the trip to the market and then making dinner, despite how much the three of us had helped with it, had worn her out.

I studied Alina as she struggled to stand up from the armchair. Liam jumped up from the couch and hurried over, helping her out of the chair and steadying her when she swayed slightly. A stupid bout of jealousy washed over me. I wanted to be in Liam's place and be the one she turned to when she needed a little extra help.

"You okay, Alina?" Liam asked.

She nodded, but her face was pale, and little pain lines were etched around her mouth. "Yes. Just tired, and my leg is aching."

"I'm sorry," Sophie said. "The farmer's market was too much."

"It wasn't," Alina said. "I loved it, and I had a lot of fun. Thank you for suggesting it, Sophie."

Sophie gave Liam a worried look who said, "Maybe we should spend the night, in case you need -"

"I can help her," I said.

Liam glanced over. "You don't mind?"

"Why would I?" I asked.

Before he could reply, Alina said, "I'm fine. I don't need anyone helping me tonight."

"Do you have a headache?" Liam asked.

She glanced away. "No."

She was lying, it was obvious, but Liam just nodded and said, "We'll get out of your hair so you can rest. Nick, take good care of our baby sister, yeah?"

I winced inwardly but nodded. "I will."

"Alina, stay in the chair," Liam said.

Alina shook her head. "I'm fine, Liam. Stop fussing." She followed them to the door, and my concern for her grew. I hadn't seen her limp this badly in years.

Liam kissed Alina's cheek. "I'll come over around ten tomorrow, and we'll try car therapy, okay?"

Alina paled but nodded. "Yes. I'll see you then."

We said our goodbyes and as soon Alina shut and locked the front door, I carefully picked her up and headed toward the bedroom.

"Someone's impatient to pick up where we left off." Alina smiled at me, but it looked forced and unnatural. I carried her into her bedroom and then into the attached bathroom. I used my foot to close the toilet lid before setting her down on it.

"Nick, what are you doing?" she asked when I started the water in the tub.

"Drawing you a hot bath." I turned around to catch her rubbing at her forehead, a sure sign she had a headache.

She dropped her hand and smiled at me. "Will you be joining me? I'm good with that. Although with my leg, I can't actually have sex in the tub, but we can do other stuff, right?"

"You're having a bath, taking some meds for your leg and your headache, and going to bed," I said.

"I don't have a headache," she argued.

"Baby, don't lie to me, okay?" I said.

She sighed and rubbed her forehead. "It's not that bad. Besides, I read somewhere that orgasms can help headaches."

I squatted in front of her, placing my hands lightly on her thighs, feeling the thick scar on her right one even through her yoga pants. "Your leg is too sore for sex tonight, Alina."

A stubborn look crossed her face. "No, it isn't. As long as you don't want me to ride you or get on my knees, it'll be fine."

"It's not a good idea," I said.

"I want to have sex with you, Nicky." Her cool hands cupped my face. I turned my head and kissed her palm.

"I want to have sex with you, and we will. Just not tonight, baby."

I straightened and reached for the pill container on the bathroom counter. "One or two pills?"

She hesitated. "Two."

"That bad, huh?" I shook out the pills, filled a glass with water and handed both to her before leaning over and turning off the water in the tub.

"Pretty bad," she finally admitted before swallowing the pills. "While making dinner, I tweaked my leg when I got the pot out of the bottom cupboard."

She sighed, a look of frustration on her face. "I hate that even the simplest chores can do this to me."

"I'm sorry." I kissed her forehead. "I wish it wasn't like this."

"Me too," she said before smiling at me. "But Finn always says that feeling sorry for myself isn't going to change the past. All I can do is move forward."

"You're doing amazing," I said. "I'm going to help you undress and get in the tub, okay?"

"Thank you, Nicky." She caught my hand and squeezed it. "I appreciate your kindness. I'm sorry we can't have sex tonight."

I brushed my lips against hers. "You don't have to apologize. We have plenty of time, baby."

"YOU READY, ALINA?" LIAM HELD ALINA'S HAND AS HE opened the car door with the other.

Alina nodded, but her face was white, and she looked close to vomiting. My stomach was nauseated, just feeling the tension pouring from Alina.

"Maybe this isn't a good idea," I said. "Didn't you say you'd wait for Finn to get back before trying again?"

"We did, but I think it's important that Alina not wait that long between attempts, and she's agreed," Liam said patiently.

"Because she doesn't want to disappoint you," I said. "Not because she wants to try again."

Liam scowled at me over Alina's head. "Hey, why don't you go wait in the house. Alina and I are good on our own here."

Before I could say no fucking way, Alina grabbed my hand and said, "I want him here, Liam."

Liam's gaze flickered between us, but I didn't let go of Alina's hand. I didn't care what Liam thought or what he figured out. I wasn't leaving Alina when she needed me most.

"Sure, okay. Whatever you want, Alina." Liam gave me another look over Alina's head that I had no trouble reading.

Don't say another word, Nick.

Alina let go of my hand, and I smiled encouragingly at her as she sat down in the passenger seat. Liam helped her ease her bad leg into the car as I climbed into the back seat, buckled my seat belt, and leaned forward. I reached over the seat, ignoring the way the belt dug into my shoulder and chest. Alina latched onto my hand with a death grip, her fingers cold and clammy against mine.

Liam settled in the driver's seat. "Do you need help with your seat belt, Alina?"

She shook her head and released my hand long enough to buckle her seat belt before grabbing my hand again.

"I'm going to turn the car on," Liam said, his voice low and gentle. "You let me know when you're ready."

Alina nodded, her eyes closed and her face pinched. Liam started the car, and Alina's body jerked wildly. I squeezed her hand. "It's okay, baby. You're okay."

Liam gave me a look, and I cursed inwardly. I needed to remember to watch what I said around him. It was so easy to forget, though, especially after last night. I'd helped Alina into the bath, left her to soak for a half-hour and then helped her out. She'd started to be drowsy from the pain meds, and after brushing her teeth and putting her pajamas on, she'd asked me to carry her to the bed.

I'd been happy to help and even happier to stay with her in the bed when she asked. We'd fallen asleep together with her soft body nestled against mine and the feel of her slow and even breaths against my throat. I'd slept like a rock, not waking up until close to nine. After a quick shower, I'd brought Alina a muffin and coffee in bed.

She promised her leg was better, but I could almost see the nerves and anxiety leaking out of her in steady waves as she prepared for Liam's arrival. I'd never been with Alina when she tried car therapy, and her obvious fear tore a hole in my chest, reached in, and clamped onto my heart until I could barely breathe.

"I'm ready," Alina said.

Her hand tightened on mine, and her face lost what little colour was left in it when Liam put the car into drive and pulled out onto the street. Immediately, Alina's breath turned short and shallow, and blotchy red patches developed on her chest.

We hadn't even driven half a block when Alina gasped out, "Stop. Liam, please stop!"

He pulled over immediately but put his hand over hers when she reached for the seatbelt. "Take a couple of deep breaths, Alina. Don't leave yet."

"Can't breathe," Alina gasped. "Not enough oxygen."

"There's enough," Liam said firmly. "You can do this, Alina."

I couldn't take it any longer. "She wants to leave, Liam. Let her."

"Be quiet, Nicky," Liam said without taking his gaze off Alina. "Deep breaths, Alina."

"Can't," Alina gasped.

"You can." Liam kept his hand over the seatbelt.

"Liam, enough," I snapped. "Unbuckle her."

"Nick, stay out of it," Liam said.

"I said unbuckle her!" I yanked Liam's hand away and

unbuckled Alina's seat belt, freeing her. She clawed the door open and stumbled out of the car to stagger a few feet away.

I climbed out of the car and hurried toward her, glaring at Liam when he pushed past me and put his arm around Alina. "What the hell, Nick?"

"She needed to stop, Liam," I said.

"You didn't help the situation," he said. "You have no idea what we do or how this works, okay?"

"You think forcing your sister to stay in the car when she's having a panic attack and begging to be let out is a good fucking idea?"

Liam released Alina and walked forward until his chest brushed mine. I refused to back down as he got in my face and said, "What I think is that I know my sister better than you. That it's been Finn and me doing car therapy with her and that you need to mind your own fucking business, Nicky. I have this handled."

"I care about Alina just as much as you and Finn," I said. "And it was obvious that what you were trying to do wasn't helping her. Are you so anxious for her to get better that you'd put your own needs ahead of hers or -"

"What the fuck did you just say to me?" Liam shouted before shoving me hard in the chest.

I stumbled back, catching my balance before I fell on my ass. "Keep your hands off of me, Liam."

"Stop insinuating that what I'm doing isn't for Alina then," Liam said. "All I fucking care about is helping her, and if that means a little tough love, so be it."

"Tough love or torture?" I snapped. "Maybe until you figure out the difference, you should leave Alina's car therapy to Finn and me."

"You?" Liam said. "You live with my sister for a fucking week, and now suddenly you're the best person to make decisions for her? Get the fuck out of here with that bullshit, Nick."

"I know what's best for her and -"

"No, you don't," Liam said. "I'm her brother, Nick. Not you. So butt out before I -"

"Stop it!" Alina's voice was sharp and angry. "Liam, be quiet. Nicky is only trying to help."

Liam turned to her as she joined us. "Alina, he's acting like I'm abusing you, like I'm forcing you into this."

"I am not," I said.

"Yes, you are," Alina said, bursting my smug bubble with a loud pop. "Liam is trying to help me too, Nick, and while I get that it's hard to watch me in the car, I can assure you that everything Liam did was under the advice of my therapist. He's only doing the things she suggested he do. So, back off."

She turned to Liam before he could say anything. "And stop acting like Nick doesn't have the right to speak up when he's worried for me. He's a part of our family, and in this family, we're allowed to voice our opinions. Isn't that what Finn always says?"

"Yes, but -"

"Nick is allowed to feel how he feels," Alina said. "But both of you are being assholes to me and each other, and this is the last thing I need right now."

Shame nearly bowled me over, and from the look on Liam's face, he was having a hard time standing under the weight of his shame as well.

"Fuck," I said. "Alina, I'm sorry."

"I'm sorry too," Liam said.

"Thank you," Alina said. "Now apologize for being assholes to each other."

My anger deflated. I stared at Liam, seeing not a guy who was hurting the woman I loved but the man I'd called a best friend since I was sixteen years old. "Shit. Liam, I'm sorry. I just… it upset me to see Alina upset, and I took it out on you. I shouldn't have."

"I get it," Liam said. "The first time we tried car therapy, I cried like a fucking baby when Alina had her panic attack. Finn had to calm both of us down."

"It's true," Alina said with a soft smile. "He bought us ice cream to get us to stop crying."

I laughed, and Liam grinned before pulling me in for a hard hug. "I'm sorry, man. I was being a dick. I love you."

"I love you too," I said.

We broke apart, and Liam took Alina's hand. "We'll wait until Finn comes back before we try again. I'm sorry I pushed you."

"I know why you do it," Alina said and hugged him. "I love you, Liam."

"I love you too." Liam took a deep breath. "You got any ice cream?"

Alina laughed. "Yeah. Rocky Road - your favourite. Come in the house."

CHAPTER 8

Alina

"Hey, how are you feeling?" Nick poked his head into my bedroom.

"I'm fine," I said. I folded the last of my shirts and slipped it into the drawer before setting the laundry basket on the floor. "What happened in the car isn't anything new for me, Nick. I know it's tough to watch, but you shouldn't have lost your temper with Liam."

I limped to the bed and sat down on its edge, massaging my leg. Nick joined me, easing down beside me, his thigh resting against mine. Despite my annoyance with him, flutters of anticipation appeared in my stomach. God, I wanted him.

"I know," he said. "I'm sorry I lost my temper. It won't happen again."

"Why have you avoided me since Liam left?"

Nick cleared his throat. "I'm not."

"Oh yeah? Because Liam left three hours ago, and you've been hiding in your bedroom ever since."

"I haven't been hiding," Nick said. "I've been…."

I stared expectantly at him, and Nick sighed. "I've been hiding."

"Nicky," I took his hand, "if you don't want to have sex with me anymore, you can just say so."

"Trust me, I still want to have sex with you," he said. "But after my behaviour in the car and with Liam, I wasn't sure you'd be into the idea of having sex with me."

"Sex with you is all I can think about," I said.

He squeezed my hand, his gaze roaming over my face. "Me too, baby."

I leaned toward him, pressing my mouth against his. The kiss started with sweet, soft brushes of our lips that made me feel cherished. But when Nick took the kiss deeper, when he cupped the back of my skull and held me tight as he explored my mouth, the sweetness disappeared. Our kisses grew more urgent, and when I pulled at Nick's shirt, he broke the kiss to yank his shirt over his head.

He helped me pull off my shirt and unhooked my bra, tossing everything to the floor.

"Lie back," he said.

I scooted back, smiling my thanks to Nick when he helped me lift my leg onto the bed before stretching out beside me. He wore just a pair of shorts, and I couldn't stop staring at the obvious bulge at his crotch. I was itching to touch him, itching to see my first dick in real life, but before I could ask him to strip, he bent his dark head and captured my nipple in his mouth.

I slid my hands into his hair, closing my eyes and concentrating on how good Nick's mouth felt on my aching nipple. He toyed with my other nipple, his fingers plucking and pulling until it was as hard as the one in his mouth.

He lifted his head. "I love your tits, baby. They're fucking gorgeous."

"Thank you," I said. I gasped when he pinched my nipple, and he smiled up at me.

"Too much?"

"No," I moaned. "I, um, I liked it."

He nuzzled my neck, tasting my skin with slow licks before sliding his hand down my stomach to my yoga pants. "You good with me taking these off?"

"God, yes," I said.

He grinned and sat up, patting my leg lightly. "Hips up."

I lifted my hips, and Nick dragged my pants down. They took my panties with them, and he made a soft little growl of need when he saw my pussy. He removed my pants and underwear from my legs and dropped them over the bed with infinite care.

"Your turn," I said.

"In a minute." He stared at my pussy like it was a glass of water, and he was dying of thirst.

"I want to see your dick," I said.

He grinned up at me. "I know, and you will. I want to taste your pussy first."

I swallowed hard. "You do?"

He raised an eyebrow at me. "Did you think I wouldn't?"

"We said sex, not sex adjacent things."

Nick laughed so hard that I blushed from embarrassment. "Oral sex is a pretty intimate act. From what I've read, not every guy is into it."

"If they're not, they're idiots," Nick said before leaning over and kissing the small patch of dark hair at the top of my sex. "I plan on being tongue deep in your sweet pussy as often as you'll let me."

I laughed, but I knew he didn't mean it. Today was it for us. It was the last day of our agreed weekend of sex, and after this, I'd never get to touch or be touched by Nick again.

Sorrow wanted to fill me up, but I pushed it away. I wouldn't ruin my time with Nick by thinking of the future. I would concentrate on this moment and only this moment.

Nick pressed a kiss against my hipbone before stroking my thigh. "Can you spread your legs for me, baby, or will it hurt your leg too much?"

"It won't hurt," I said. "But we'll probably need to have sex missionary style. I know that's boring, but I'm not sure my leg can handle me being on top or doggy style. Sorry."

I could feel the heat rising in my cheeks as I spread my legs, but Nick settled his body between my thighs and said, "We'll do whatever you're most comfortable with, Alina. Don't stress about that, and don't apologize, okay?"

"Yeah, okay." I grabbed the sheets when Nick kissed my inner thigh before using his big hands to spread them apart even further.

"This still okay?"

"Yes, other than that you can see straight up my lady gard - I mean, straight up my pussy," I said.

He laughed again, and warmth washed over me. I loved how easy and relaxed it felt with him. Sure, I was nervous and unsure and even a little worried about the potential pain, but being with Nicky swept away any awkwardness I felt about my first time.

He leaned in, and at the first gentle press of his lips against my pussy, I had to stop myself from moaning like an idiot. One kiss shouldn't have made me feel so -

"Oh my God!" I nearly shrieked, my hips bucking upward when Nicky's tongue brushed across my swollen clit. "Oh, oh holy fuck!"

Nick laughed again, but I barely heard it. I was too busy grabbing the back of his head and trying to push him face first into my pussy. "Do that again, Nicky!"

"Yes, Alina," Nick said. He held my hips down and licked my clit repeatedly. I squirmed on the bed, not the least bit embarrassed as I ground my pussy against his mouth. Had I ever felt anything so good? His tongue was warm and wet and -

"Fuck!"

Nick had stiffened his tongue and thrust it into my opening. I moaned at the sensation, my lungs already heaving for air and my fingers scrabbling for purchase against the sheets.

"Baby, be careful of your leg," Nick said as he licked my inner thighs and then nibbled my pussy lips.

"I don't care about my fucking leg," I said. "Nicky, please, I need you to do the tongue licking again."

His low chuckle washed over me, and I felt the light pressure of his hand against my right leg, holding it steady, so I couldn't thrash it around as he licked my clit. Tension coiled in my belly, and I moaned Nick's name repeatedly. When he sucked on my clit, I shrieked again, my orgasm hitting me so hard and fast that my body shook wildly. I finally collapsed on the bed, my legs sagging wide as I gasped for air, my body still trembling from little aftershocks of pleasure.

Nicky stretched out beside me, rubbing my right thigh lightly as he smiled at me. "You okay?"

"Better than okay," I gasped out. "That was the best orgasm of my life."

He laughed. "That's awesome to hear, but I meant your leg. How does it feel?"

He traced the thick scar with his fingertips as I worked hard to catch my breath. "It's good. It helped to have you holding it."

"Good." He kissed my rock hard nipple. "Do you need a break?"

"God, no," I said and pulled impatiently at his waistband. "Show me that dick, Nicky."

Nick

ALINA CUMMING ON MY FACE WAS HANDS DOWN, IN THE TOP three most beautiful moments of my life. How she tasted, moved against my mouth, and let go of all of her inhibitions made me want to eat her sweet pussy every fucking chance I got.

My dick leaking precum like a fucking fountain, I hissed out a breath when Alina pulled at my waistband again. "Nick, get undressed."

I didn't need to be told again. I climbed off the bed and dropped my shorts and briefs, smiling at the way Alina's gaze immediately arrowed in on my dick. I was impossibly hard. The skin stretched thin and the head slick with precum.

I ignored my urge to roll on the condom and bury myself in Alina's wet pussy. I was confident it was her first time seeing a dick in real life, and while I was only a little above average in width and length, I didn't want her to feel overwhelmed or nervous. I would give her the chance to touch me first before I allowed myself to do what I wanted most in this fucking world.

I stretched out next to Alina, smiling when she turned to face me, her warm breath mingling with mine. She studied my cock, her hand tracing back and forth over my chest before she finally said, "It's bigger than I expected."

"Thanks," I said with a grin.

She blushed. "Can I touch it?"

"Yes," I said. I mentally prepared myself for her soft

touch, but my hips jerked forward, and a groan escaped my throat when Alina ran her fingertips along my shaft.

She pulled her hand back, licking her lips nervously. "Was that wrong?"

"No," I said. "I've just had an enormous number of fantasies of this very moment, so it's difficult not to cum all over your fucking hand."

Her smug grin made me laugh, and I pressed a kiss against her lips. "You won't be so smug if you have to wait longer for me to fuck you because I cum when you - fuck! Oh, fuck, baby."

Alina had wrapped her long fingers around me and tentatively stroked me a few times. "Does this feel good?"

"So fucking good," I groaned.

Gritting my teeth, I let her jack me off with soft and tentative movements for a few minutes before I folded my hand over hers. "Tighter grip, baby, I won't break."

I showed her the motion I liked best, my hips pumping with the movement of her hand. "Rub your thumb along the head," I said.

She did what I asked, another smug grin lighting up her face when I groaned a curse and fresh precum spurted out from the tip. She varied her grip and the pressure, her gaze switching between my dick and my face until I couldn't take the torture. I'd cum all over her perfect tits and flat stomach if she kept touching me.

I filed that fantasy away for another time and pulled away from Alina's touch, gripping the base of my cock and squeezing hard. "Baby, give me a minute."

She pouted but relaxed on the bed, running her fingers across my chest, exploring my flat nipples and the tiny scar just below the hollow of my throat. "What's this from?"

"I don't remember," I said. "I've had it forever. Baby, are you ready for me?"

"Yes," she said.

"We can wait if you aren't," I said. "There's no rush."

She turned and grabbed the condom from the bedside table. "I don't want to wait any longer."

I ripped open the packaging and rolled the condom on as Alina turned onto her back again and spread her beautiful thighs. I leaned over and kissed the scar on her right thigh before kneeling between her legs.

She shifted slightly and smiled at me. "I'm ready, Nicky."

I leaned down and kissed her until she clung to me and made those soft sounds of need that made my dick feel like it might explode. I brushed my nose against hers. "I'll go slow, baby."

"I know. I trust you, Nicky."

Alina

NICK PRESSED THE HEAD OF HIS COCK AGAINST MY entrance, and to my surprise, I didn't feel a lick of nervousness. How could I when Nick was so sweet, careful, and loving?

He pushed, and I bit my lip at the strange sensation of his cock sliding into my pussy. He paused, his gaze assessing as he said, "Still good?"

"Yes," I said. I gripped his forearms as he braced his body above mine. "Nicky, I think one hard push is best."

"You sure?" His voice was tight with control.

"Positive," I said.

He continued to hesitate, and I lifted my head and pressed

a kiss against his mouth before whispering, "Make me yours, Nicky."

With a hoarse groan, he thrust deep into my pussy. A pinch of pain subsided quickly, leaving a weird feeling of fullness. Nicky hadn't moved after his initial thrust, and I admired his restraint as he hovered above me, his arms trembling lightly and his need for me written all over his face.

"Okay?" he rasped.

"Yes," I said. "It didn't hurt."

"Good." He swallowed hard before making two slow and measured thrusts. "Fuck, you're so tight, baby. You feel so fucking good on my dick. I'm gonna move again, okay?"

I nodded, and keeping his gaze on my face, Nick moved in and out of me with long, slow pumps of his hips. I watched the play of emotions on his face, smiling in delight when I did my best to match his rhythm, and another low groan of pleasure fell from his mouth.

"Fuck, that's so good," he muttered. "Gonna go faster, 'kay?"

"Yes," I said. "Whatever you need, Nicky."

He closed his eyes and thrust in and out in a hard fast rhythm. To my surprise, tiny sparks of pleasure lit up my pelvis, and I squeezed my pussy around him in response.

"Oh fuck!" He made a hard and out of control thrust that tore a gasp from my throat. "Baby, don't squeeze. Christ, don't fucking squeeze. I'm barely hanging on as it is."

"I want you to cum," I said.

He barked out harsh laughter. "That won't be a fucking problem. Touch your clit."

"Right now?" I asked.

He nodded. "Yeah, rub it for me."

Feeling a little self-conscious, I pushed my hand between our bodies and rubbed at my clit. My fingers brushed against

Nick's dick as he surged forward, and he groaned out another curse before looking down. "Does that feel good?"

"Yes." I rubbed harder. Nick's cock and my fingers had turned those tiny sparks of pleasure into an out of control fire. "I think I might cum again."

"That's the idea." A sound that was half-laugh, half-groan fell from Nick's mouth. "I want you to cum on my cock if you can."

I didn't reply. I was too busy concentrating on how good it felt to rub my clit. I stroked and teased the little bundle of nerves as Nick moved harder and faster. I slid my free hand around his waist, clutching at his back as I teetered on the edge of my climax.

"Nick, oh, Nicky," I panted. "I'm so close."

"Good. Cum on my cock, baby. I need you to cum for me right now," he growled out.

I cried out, his hot words pushing me over the edge and into pure bliss. Nick shouted my name, surging forward and shaking wildly as he came hard.

He collapsed against me, his leg pressing against mine and sending pain radiating down my thigh. "Nick," I gasped. "My leg."

"Fuck!" He immediately moved off me, staring anxiously at me as he gently rubbed my leg. "Baby, I'm sorry. I didn't mean to hurt you. Do you need to go to the hospital?"

"I don't know… do I need a hospital visit for a freshly fucked pussy?"

Nick's jaw dropped, and I burst into loud laughter. "Oh my God, the look on your face right now, Nicky."

I continued to laugh as Nick shook his head before leaning over and kissing my chest. "You scared the hell out of me."

Holding the condom, he walked to the bathroom and

returned to climb into the bed beside me a few minutes later. He pulled the blankets up around us and smiled at me when I snuggled into him. "Seriously, Alina, is your leg okay?"

"It is," I said. "It just hurt at the end and only because you accidentally pressed on it."

"Are you sure?" he frowned.

"I am. But I'll warn you now, so you don't freak out... it'll probably be sore tomorrow, and I'll limp more than I usually do."

He scowled, and I smoothed away the lines on his forehead with my fingertips. "It was worth it, Nicky. So worth it."

He kissed me before relaxing against the bed, and I rested my head on his chest, listening to the comforting beat of his heart. After a few minutes, he said, "What are you thinking about?"

"Isn't that supposed to be my line?" I asked.

He stroked my back. "Tell me what you're thinking."

"I'm thinking that my therapist was right, and I'm glad my first time was with someone who knew it was my first time and who...."

"Who what?"

I took a deep breath. Saying 'who loved me' was beyond presumptuous. Nick cared for me a great deal, and just because he'd done everything he could to make sex good for me didn't equal love.

"Who made it so special," I said.

He kissed my forehead, his hand stroking my back. "It was special for me too, Alina. I'll never forget it."

"I won't forget either, Nicky. Ever." My throat tightened and burned, and I blinked back the hot tears. I'd known this was it for us, so why did it hurt so much?

CHAPTER 9

Alina

"Oh my God, Alina! Where are you?" Bryce called as she slammed the front door shut.

"I'm in my studio," I hollered.

Two minutes later, Stanley came tearing into the room, followed by Bryce. Her curly hair was a red tornado around her head, she carried two computer bags, and the look on her face was a combination of excitement and dread.

I picked up Stanley, petting him and letting him lick my face for a few seconds before settling him on my lap. "Hey, what's wrong?"

Bryce dropped her computer bags and collapsed in the chair across from me. "I found out who the geologist for the land survey is today."

"Okay. Who is it?" I asked as I picked up my embroidery hoop.

"Griffin Morris."

I immediately dropped my hoop on the table and gave Bryce my full attention. "Wait... *the* Griffin Morris?"

"Yes," Bryce said.

"I thought you said he and his brother would never come back to Willowdale," I said.

"I didn't think they would. No one did." Bryce yanked hard on a lock of hair. "Do you think I could find another job if I quit this one?"

"Bryce, you are not quitting your job," I said.

"I can't face him, Alina. Not after what happened."

"It was almost a decade ago, and you were a teenager. Teenagers do dumb things," I said.

Bryce's face turned as red as her hair. "I'm still embarrassed by it. I won't be able to look at him, let alone shadow him all fucking day. That's it. I have no choice. I have to quit."

"You don't," I said. "Bryce, he probably won't even remember it. You've turned it into this huge deal in your head because you're embarrassed. But from what you've told me about high school, all the girls hit on Griffin or his brother. You were probably just one little fish in a sea of girl fish who tried to kiss him."

"Yeah, but I'm the only fish who barfed on him," Bryce said sadly.

I didn't want to laugh, I really didn't, but my face twitched, and a small snort escaped. Bryce glared at me. "It's not funny, Alina."

"It's kind of funny," I said.

"There is nothing funny about vomiting on the hottest guy in high school," Bryce said.

"There is if you had just eaten a big bowl of Lucky Charms," I said.

Bryce groaned and slithered off her chair to lie on the studio floor. Stanley hopped off my lap and wandered over to lick her face consolingly as she said, "There were Lucky Charm marshmallows stuck to his cheek, Alina."

"Which ones?" I asked. "You've never said."

"Clover and heart."

"At least one of them was a heart," I said.

Bryce stared at me before laughing so hard she had to hold her stomach. Stanley danced around her, barking and play bowing as I picked up my embroidery and resumed working on it.

After a few minutes, Bryce's giggles finally died down, and she stared at me from her spot on the floor. "What am I gonna do, Alina?"

"You're going to be the amazing, awesome PR person you are, and you'll be a professional and talk to Griffin Morris like you have never vomited Lucky Charms all over his face," I said.

"Right," Bryce said. "Be professional. I've got this."

"You do," I said. I added some more blue to the piece I was working on. The sound of the needle in the fabric and the precise way I lined the thread up were always soothing, even with my emotions as messed up as they currently were.

Bryce sat up, leaning against the storage unit that held my extra floss, and petted Stanley when he climbed into her lap. "How did therapy with Dr. Wilson go today?"

"Fine," I said.

"You sure?"

"Yes, why?" I cursed when my thread knotted and carefully picked at the knot.

"Because you have that look on your face when the appointment has been difficult."

"It wasn't," I said.

"Then what's wrong?"

I sighed and gave up on the knot, placing my WIP on the table and folding my hands in my lap. "I had sex with Nick."

"Good God, woman. You have got to stop announcing shit like this in the same way you'd mention cheese is on sale at Walmart," Bryce said. "When did you decide to sleep with Nick?"

"After my date with Ethan went so horribly, I started trying to connect with other guys on the app the next morning."

"Right," Bryce said. "You sent me that one dude's profile... Roy or Troy or something."

"Royce," I said. "He seemed nice, and I was all set to message him when Nick asked why I was still on the dating app."

"Is that really any of his business?" Bryce asked.

I shrugged. "He was worried, and I couldn't blame him. I mean, he did just have to help me with Ethan the night before."

"Good point," Bryce said. "Go on."

"Anyway, once he realized that I was only looking for sex, he volunteered. He knew it would be my first time, and he said it should be with someone who would make it good for me."

"And he just happened to be that guy," Bryce said with a roll of her eyes.

"He wasn't wrong," I said. "It was amazing."

"Good for you, honey," Bryce said approvingly. "I'm glad you enjoyed yourself."

"I did, but now I'm sad because we agreed to it being the weekend only and thanks to Liam and Sophie unwittingly cockblocking me, I only got to have sex with Nick once on Sunday."

"Ooh, tough luck," Bryce said.

"Yeah. Honestly, I thought I could tempt Nick into sleeping with me again this week, but it's Thursday, and I haven't seen him once since Monday morning. He's avoiding me again. He leaves for work before I even wake up, and he doesn't come home until after I'm in bed. I've tried staying awake, but I'm not a night owl."

"Tell me about it," Bryce said. "I can barely keep you awake past ten on our movie nights."

"Anyway, I had great sex with Nick, and now I'll never have it again, and I'm bummed about it. I told myself to move on, to look for someone new on the dating app to expand my sex knowledge with, but I couldn't. I don't want anyone but Nick."

"Shit," Bryce said. "That's not good."

"Yeah. I'll get over that, though, right? Eventually, I'll meet someone I want to sleep with, even if I'm in love with Nick?"

"Sure," Bryce said, but she didn't sound confident.

I stared at my embroidery, trying not to sound as dejected as I felt. "I don't know how to stop loving him."

Bryce leaned forward and patted my knee. "I think it'll take time, Alina. Time and maybe some space. You should ask him to move in with Liam until his apartment is livable again."

"I can't do that," I said. "Liam would badger us both about the reason why, and I'm not up for that kind of interrogation. Besides, Nick is doing a fine job of avoiding me. I've got all the space I need."

Nick

I SET MY COMPUTER BAG ON THE FLOOR AND HUNG MY jacket in the closet before heading toward the kitchen. I was bone tired and starving, but my excitement to see Alina overrode them. It'd been a very long fucking week, and while I loved my job, the stress and the long hours this week had left me craving Alina's soft voice and touch. I'd only lived with her a week and slept with her once, but I was already addicted.

Yeah, well, you don't get to fuck her anymore, so let that dream die.

That was true, but I needed to be around her anyway. Would it be difficult to be with her and not touch her or kiss her? Fuck, yes.

But I needed Alina like a flower needed the sun. She was my everything and always would be.

I walked into the kitchen, my stress drifting away when I saw Alina standing at the stove. She stirred a pot of stew that smelled mouth-wateringly delicious.

"Hi," I said.

She glanced at me over her shoulder, surprise on her face. "Hi. What are you doing here?"

"I live here?" I said with a small grin.

Her smile lacked its usual warmth. "I meant, why are you home so early? You've been working late all week."

"Not tonight," I said. "That smells great."

"Thanks." She turned back to the stew. "You're welcome to have a bowl if you don't have supper plans."

"I don't." I joined her at the stove, frowning at the stiffness in Alina's back and how she wouldn't look at me. "I wanted to say thank you for all the leftovers this week. It was great of you to share your meals with me. It made a huge difference not having to come home at eleven at night and cook."

"Anytime," she said as she stared at her ceaselessly stirring spoon.

"What's wrong?" I asked.

"Why would anything be wrong?" she said.

"You're angry with me, and I'm not sure why," I said.

"You're not sure why?" She set the spoon on the counter and turned to face me. Her face was red, and her eyes were spitting sparks, and, fuck, she'd never looked more beautiful. "You can't possibly begin to understand why I'm angry with you, Nick?"

When I stared blankly at her, she made a small snort. "You've avoided me all week. You've left early and come home well after I've gone to bed, all because you think I'm some sex fiend who won't honour our agreement to only have sex last weekend. Look, I get that I've been clear about my attraction to you and how much I enjoyed our time together, but that doesn't mean I'll try to seduce you, even if all I think about is having sex with you again. But I never once decided to avoid you as a way to solve the problem because I'm an adult who knows she needs to handle her own wants and needs. Avoiding me this week was a really immature thing to do, Nick."

She crossed her arms over her chest, glaring at me as I tried not to grin. Not that I was happy Alina was pissed at me, but knowing she was having as hard of a time as I was made me feel a little better.

"Are you smiling?" Alina squinted at me. "Swear to God, if you smile, Nicky, I will replace your shampoo with Nair."

"Damn, Alina," I said with a grin. "That's harsh."

"I'm so mad at you right now," she said, but she looked close to tears.

I pulled her into my arms, resting my forehead against hers. "Don't cry, baby. I wasn't avoiding you this week. I mean, I was, but not on purpose. Work has been a shitshow this week. On Monday, we discovered a huge problem with our electric car prototype's battery, and the entire week has been putting out one fire after the other. I really did have to go in early and work late every day this week."

"Really?" she sniffed.

"Yes. It had nothing to do with thinking you couldn't control yourself around me."

She sighed, and I kissed the tip of her nose. "But I will admit that the work stuff made it easier for me not to seduce *you* this week."

"Do you mean that?" she asked.

"Yes. I want to be back in your bed and in your pussy on a level of desperation that's embarrassing," I said.

"I want that too," she said.

We stared silently at each other for a few minutes before she said, "We really didn't get a full weekend of sex. It was only once on Sunday."

"That's true," I said.

She put her arms around my shoulders and pressed her body against mine. "Maybe we could have a do-over weekend."

"Sounds intriguing," I said. "Would this do-over weekend involve the two of us naked and my tongue in your pussy?"

"Most definitely," she said. "Although, I will have to insist some time be devoted to having your dick in my mouth."

She grinned when she felt my erection against her stomach. "Feels like you might be willing to consider that."

"Baby," I rasped, "you have no idea how often I've thought about my dick in your mouth."

"Hmm, maybe we should turn that fantasy into a reality."

She reached over and turned the stove burner off before taking my hand. "Unless you're starving for food?"

"I'm starving for you," I said.

"Cheeseball," she said, but she had a pleased smile, and she laughed when I squeezed her ass as we headed toward her bedroom.

We helped each other undress, both of us too eager to do it slowly. When we were naked, I pulled her close and cupped her ass. "Get on the bed, and I'll eat your sweet pussy."

She shook her head and took my cock in her hand, stroking it lightly. "I meant it when I said I want to give you oral sex."

I groaned, my hips already moving with the rhythm of her touch. "If you're sure…."

"Very sure," she said. "Lie on the bed, Nicky."

I stretched out on the bed, smiling at Alina when she sat carefully next to my hip. "Does that hurt your leg?" I asked.

"Nope, all good." She leaned over, and her soft hair brushed against my thighs. I groaned, my hands clenching the sheets when she held my cock in her hand and licked a path around the head. She cleaned the precum off the tip before sucking on the head.

I groaned again, my hips rising when she took more of me into her mouth, and I watched my dick disappear between her plump lips. "Oh fuck," I said. "This was a very bad fucking idea."

She laughed and pumped my dick slowly with her hand. "I think it's a great idea. Tell me if I do something wrong, okay?"

"Mmm," I said before reaching up and pressing on the back of her head. "Suck me again, baby."

She leaned over, and I tucked her hair behind her ear so I could watch as she sucked my cock. Her movements were a little awkward and sloppy, but her sheer enthusiasm for it made up for her lack of experience. Not that it mattered. I was so gone for Alina, she could do anything to me, and I would believe it was perfection.

"That feels so fucking good," I praised when she hollowed her cheeks and sucked hard. "That's good. Keep sucking, baby. Can you take more? I want you to take more of me."

She slid her lips further down my shaft, gagging a little when I hit the back of her throat. "Sorry," she said, rubbing at her swollen mouth.

"It's fine, baby. You're doing great."

She giggled. "Thanks for the pep talk."

My laugh turned into a loud moan when she took me to the back of her throat again and sucked hard, using lots of tongue. She bobbed her head up and down, driving me crazy with the heat and the suction. When she cupped my balls and lightly tugged them, I pulled her mouth off me with a loud pop.

"Enough," I rasped.

"Did I do something wrong?" She licked my precum from her lips, giving me a worried look.

"No, God, no. I was just close."

"You can cum in my mouth," she said. "I don't mind."

I groaned loudly and sat up, yanking open the bedside table drawer and grabbing a condom. "Fuck, you're trying to kill me."

"What?" she asked. "What did I say? Don't you want to cum in my mouth, Nicky?"

"You need to stop talking about me cumming in your mouth if you want to be fucked, sweetheart," I said.

She paused and then made a zipping motion across her lips. I grunted out a curse as I tore at the condom packaging. I finally got it open and rolled the condom on before turning on my side and patting the bed next to me. "Lie on your side away from me, Alina."

She carefully eased onto her right side. She braced her injured leg against the bed, and I smoothed my hand over the curve of her hip. "How's your leg?"

"Good. This position doesn't hurt it at all," she said.

I pushed her hair aside and kissed the back of her shoulder as I cupped her breast and played with her nipple. She moaned and leaned back against me, thrusting her chest out to give me better access. I teased her nipples until they were hard and their usual pink had deepened to a dark red.

Alina ground her ass against my cock, and I pressed my dick between her ass cheeks, groaning at the sensation. I slipped my hand between her thighs and cupped her pussy. She was so fucking wet, it made my cock harden to the point of pain. If I didn't get inside her soon, I'd lose my mind.

I rubbed her clit, smiling at how it made her moan and squirm. "Oh, oh, I'm so close, Nicky."

I stopped immediately, giving her shoulder a little nip when she tried to push my hand away to touch herself. "No, Alina. You don't get to touch, only me."

"Nicky," she pouted at me, "I need to cum."

"I know you do." I shifted down on the bed and lifted Alina's left leg. "Hold your leg up for me, baby."

She did what I asked, and I guided my cock into her wet opening, both of us groaning when I slid right into her slick, wet heat.

She lowered her leg, and I rubbed her ass and then her hip before rocking in and out of her. She met my thrusts, already more confident about how to move to get what she wanted. Her soft moans and low cries spurred me on, and I gripped her hip and pushed harder and faster. Our bodies grew slick with sweat, both of us gasping for air as we fucked.

On the brink of my orgasm, I reached around and cupped Alina's pussy again, my fingertips finding her swollen bundle of nerves. It only took two strokes of my fingers to tip Alina over the edge. She cried out, her body going stiff against mine as her pussy clamped around my dick. I shouted her name, rubbing hard at her clit as my orgasm washed over me and my body shook against hers.

She pulled my hand away, gasping out a "too much," and I circled her waist with my arm and buried my face in her throat through the last pleasure drenched shudders of my orgasm. When I came back to my senses, Alina still panted and trembled against me. I smoothed away her hair and kissed her shoulder. "That was so good, baby."

"Hmm," she said, keeping her eyes closed. "Amazing."

I eased out of her and went to the bathroom to dispose of the condom. When I returned, Alina hadn't moved an inch. I crawled in behind her and spooned her again. "You hungry, baby?"

"Not enough to get out of bed yet," she said.

I hugged her close. "I'll bring you dinner in bed."

She turned to smile at me. "Yeah?"

"Yeah," I said. "I'll be right back."

I left her in the bed and threw on a pair of shorts in my room before heading to the kitchen. When I returned ten minutes later holding a tray with two bowls of stew and two beers, Alina wore my shirt and had sat up in bed, leaning against the headboard.

I set the tray on the bed, and she held it steady while I got myself situated next to her. I handed her a beer and held up my bottle. "To a delicious dinner."

She grinned. "To a delicious dinner and outrageously good fucking."

I laughed, and we clinked bottles before taking a drink.

"So, did you get the battery problem solved?" Alina asked.

I swallowed my bite of stew. "We did, thank God. But it took us a while to figure out the issue, and there was a lot of pressure coming down from the top to fix it quickly."

"I'm sorry it was so stressful and that I was a bitch when you came home tonight," Alina said.

"You weren't," I said. "I should have texted you and told you what was going on. I guess I'm too used to living alone and not having to check in with anyone."

"You don't have to check in with me," Alina said. "We're not dating."

I immediately lost my appetite, but I forced myself to eat a few more bites. "I know. How was your week?"

"Good. I had two more people sign up through my website to take classes on embroidery. Both want online classes, so yesterday, I spent most of my day setting up my workspace to teach them online. Liam and Sophie came by a couple of evenings and hung out with me."

She grimaced. "I feel bad because Liam feels like he has to do more with me since Finn is away, but I wish he wouldn't feel that obligation. I'm fine being by myself."

"I don't think he sees it as an obligation," I said. "Him or Finn."

"Maybe." She poked at her stew before taking a drink of beer.

"When do Finn and Hattie get back?" I asked.

"Next week," she said.

"That's a long holiday."

She smiled. "It is, but Finn had a lot of vacation days

banked at the lab, and Hattie was still on leave at her job because of the paparazzi. I guess Hattie loves the beach, so Finn decided Hawaii was the perfect place to take her."

"The paparazzi didn't follow them?" I asked. Hattie was a former celebrity who had returned to Willowdale to live a quiet life as a mechanic. She'd mostly succeeded until her and Finn's involvement with a BDSM club had been exposed to the paparazzi. They'd been hounding her and Finn relentlessly for nearly two weeks when Finn had finally had enough and taken Hattie to Hawaii.

"Nope," Alina said. "But I think that had a lot to do with the fact that a new celebrity scandal involving Brad Pitt had hit social media and the focus shifted immediately to him."

I shook my head. "Christ, I would not want to be a celebrity."

"Me either," she said. "Anyway, I video chatted with Finn and Hattie last night, and they'll be back next weekend. At least then he and Liam can share the burden of their sister."

"Stop it," I said. "You're not a burden to them, Alina."

"I feel like one," she said. "It's hard not to when I don't drive and can barely pay my bills. Add in the trauma and how both of them are determined to heal me from it, and I feel like they'll never be able to stop looking after me. Sometimes I think I'm selfish in not looking for a relationship, you know? I'm so determined not to drag some guy into my messed up life, but all that means is that my brothers have to do more, be more for me than they really should. And now that they're in relationships, I feel even worse about it."

She set her half-empty bowl of stew on the tray and drank some beer. I cleared away the tray, took it down to the kitchen, and put the leftover stew in the fridge before returning to Alina. I climbed into the bed beside her and took her hand.

She studied our linked fingers before smiling at me. "My therapist says I should try driving."

"A car?" I said stupidly.

"Yes. A big chunk of my trauma from the accident is the loss of control I felt when the accident happened. Mama had her heart attack and passed out, and the car veered into oncoming traffic. I could see the semi coming toward us, knew what was going to happen, but I couldn't grab the steering wheel to turn it. Mama had slumped over it, and I couldn't push her back in time to grab the wheel and turn it before we were hit. It all happened so fast and so slow at the same time. It's weird."

She shuddered, and I put my arm around her shoulders, pulling her up against me. "I'm so sorry, Alina."

She nodded, her face pale and grave looking. "Anyway, Dr. Wilson thinks that if I drive, if I'm the one in the driver's seat and in control, it might help. It sounds weird, I know, but apparently, I'm at the stage in my recovery where it's time to try unconventional methods."

"Will you try it?" I asked.

She nodded. "I think so. It can't hurt, right?"

I kissed her gently. "I think it'll be good to try."

She leaned against me, and I said, "Hey, I know it's early, but what do you think about staying in bed, maybe binge-watch something silly for a couple of hours, and then…."

"Then we fuck again," she said.

I laughed and kissed her. "Then we fuck again."

CHAPTER 10

Alina

"You're going to teach me to drive?" I stared up at Nick and then at his car.

His smile was patient and warm. "I am."

"Is this why we're up before five on a Saturday morning?" I asked.

"There will be fewer people around," he said. "Even if we just end up driving around the block, there shouldn't be anyone else in the neighbourhood driving."

"What if we get in an accident?" I asked. "What if I drive us into a tree or something?"

Panic bit at my insides. Nick stepped closer, pulling me into his embrace and dropping a kiss on my mouth. "I know it's scary, but I think you should try. We don't even have to drive today. You can do what your therapist suggested and sit behind the wheel. Okay?"

I took a deep breath. "Okay."

"That's my girl." Nick kissed me again and opened the

driver's door. "Get in, and we'll figure out where the seat needs to be for you to reach the pedals."

My stomach churning, I sat behind the wheel, making a soft squeak when Nick crouched and pushed a button beside the seat, and it moved forward with a low hum.

"You're okay, baby. Just moving the seat. Touch the pedals with your foot for me."

I touched the gas pedal and then the brake and Nick said, "How does that feel?"

"Uh, good, I think. Easy to reach the pedals."

"Doesn't hurt your leg?"

"No," I said. "Not yet."

"Good. I'll get in the passenger seat, and then we'll go over everything on the dashboard and steering column, okay?"

"Okay."

Nick shut the door and walked around the car to climb in beside me. I reached out and gripped the wheel, and it weirdly eased the panic I felt. Maybe my therapist was right. Maybe being in control would help.

"Okay, baby?" Nick asked.

I nodded and listened as Nick explained every button and lever on the steering column clearly and calmly over the next fifteen minutes.

"You ready to try starting the car?" Nick asked once I'd repeated back to him what he'd taught me about the controls.

"Yes." I reached for the seatbelt and clicked it in place, hesitating at how weird it felt to be on this side of the car.

"Take as much time as you need," Nick said as he fastened his seatbelt.

I took a deep breath, and my hand, only shaking a little, pressed the brake and pushed the start button. The car started with barely a sound. "Shouldn't it be louder?"

"It's a hybrid," Nick said. "Electric cars, even hybrids, are quieter than a standard gas-powered car."

"Oh, okay. It's on, though, right?"

"It is," Nick said. "You feeling okay about that?"

"Weirdly, yes." I gripped the steering wheel and took a deep breath. "Okay, the first thing I do is adjust my mirrors."

"That's right," Nick said.

I peered in the rearview mirror and pretended to adjust it before doing the same with the side mirrors. We had adjusted them earlier when Nick talked about the controls. He'd even gotten out of the car and demonstrated exactly where my blind spots were.

I took another deep breath. The panic and the worry were still there, but it was dampened by the concentration I needed to follow Nick's instructions.

"Foot on the brake, shift it into D for drive," I said.

"Good," Nick said when I did both. "Remember, a soft, gentle depression of the gas pedal. Don't stomp on it."

"Right," I said. I gripped the steering wheel hard enough to turn my knuckles white, but I didn't feel short of breath or like an elephant sat on my chest as I gingerly pressed the gas pedal. The car moved forward a few inches, and I immediately stepped on the brake, wincing when we both pitched forward, our seat belts locking tight.

"I'm sorry," I said.

"You're doing great," Nick said. "Everyone does this when they're first learning to drive."

I glanced over at him. He was sitting in his seat, his body language relaxed, and nothing on his face indicated any anxiety. His lack of nervousness calmed me, and I flicked on my indicator, stepped on the gas again, and steered the wheel carefully to the left to lead us out onto the road.

"Good," Nick said. "Straighten your wheel, just a little.

Good. Turn off your indicator. Perfect. Now, the speed limit is thirty-five, but there's no one on the road, so if you'd like to go slower, do it. Don't feel any pressure to go faster. There are no cars behind us."

"Okay," I said. I concentrated on keeping the car centered in my lane and steady and even pressure on the gas pedal.

"Great job, baby," Nick said. "Let's turn right up here at the stop sign. We'll drive around the block."

I nodded, biting my lip in concentration as we pulled up to the stop sign. I pressed the brake pedal too hard and fast again and muttered a curse when the seatbelts locked up. "Sorry! Sorry about that."

"You're doing great," Nick said again. "Check both ways for traffic, use your indicator, and when it's safe, turn right."

I did what he said, my heart beating faster when we turned onto the new road. I was too busy concentrating on driving to take stock of my physical reaction to being in the car, but I knew I was nowhere close to having a panic attack. I had to stay calm and relaxed. Nick was counting on me to keep him safe.

Under Nick's tutelage, we drove around the block five times before I carefully pulled up in front of my house. The wheels went up over the sidewalk and back down, and I winced. "Ooh, sorry."

"It's fine," Nick said with a slight grin. "I haven't taught you how to park yet."

I put the car into park and shut it off before glancing at the clock on the dashboard. I'd been in the car for nearly twenty minutes without a panic attack.

"How do you feel?" Nick reached for my hand.

"I feel… I feel great," I said. I unclicked my seatbelt and leaned across to kiss Nick on the mouth. "I did it. Nicky, I did it!"

"You did," he said. "I am so fucking proud of you, baby."

"I am so fucking proud of myself," I said.

Nick laughed, and I kissed him again. "I am really happy and weirdly horny right now."

"Is that right?" Nick said with a grin.

"Yes. And I can't think of a better way to celebrate that I just drove a car *and* didn't have a panic attack than having sex with you," I said.

He laughed and opened his car door. "Well, then you'd better get that perfect ass into the house because it sounds like the perfect celebration to me too."

"OH SHIT," I SAID WHEN THE BACK TIRES WENT UP ONTO THE sidewalk.

"You're fine. Just try again," Nick said.

"I don't like parallel parking," I announced as I pulled forward and turned the wheel for my fourth attempt.

Nick laughed. "No one does, baby."

"I'm never gonna parallel park," I said. "Why do I even need to learn to do it?"

"You have to parallel park to get your driver's license," Nick said.

I maneuvered the car into the parking spot, staring expectantly at Nick when he opened the door and studied the space between the car and the curb.

"Well?" I asked.

"Better," he said. "But not perfect."

I stuck my tongue out at him, and he grinned before stroking my thigh. "I can think of so many better uses for that tongue, Alina."

"I am not giving you road head," I said.

He laughed hard, and, as always, the sound of his laugh made pure joy infuse my body. It'd been a week since Nick had given me my first driving lesson, and we'd practiced every day since then. I'd driven all over town, and yesterday, Nick had come home early so I could practice driving in rush hour traffic. Well, as rush hour traffic-y as Willowdale could be.

My confidence had grown with every lesson, and I hadn't even blinked when Nick had me drive him through downtown this morning to a suburb I'd never been in before. I'd driven down the unfamiliar streets with a confidence I hadn't felt in a long time and was even feeling semi-good about my parallel parking attempts.

"Do you really think I could get my actual license?" I asked.

"I know you can. You haven't had a panic attack once in the car since you started driving."

"I know, but…."

"But?" Nick said.

"I guess I'm worried that maybe you're my talisman against the panic attacks. That without you, I'll turn back into a shivering, crying mess even if I'm driving."

"You won't," Nick said confidently. "I was of absolutely no use the first time I sat with you in the car, remember? It didn't stop your panic attack."

"True," I said.

"You've got this, baby," Nick said. "You can get your driver's license. I know you can."

I smiled at him. "I love how confident you are in me."

"You make it easy," he said before leaning over and kissing me. "It's a beautiful day. Why don't you drive to Willowdale Park, and we'll sit by the lake for a while."

"We could do that," I said. "Or we could go home, and I could bang your brains out."

Nick laughed again as I wiggled my eyebrows at him. We'd spent most of last weekend in bed together, and while we'd both agreed Monday morning that we wouldn't have sex again, Nick had been home roughly four minutes on Monday night before we were all over each other.

We'd had sex every night this week, and Nick spent each night in my bed. We both knew what was happening between us couldn't last, but we didn't talk about the future by unspoken agreement. And that suited me just fine.

"Very tempting," he said, "but you're limping more than usual today. I knew I shouldn't have let you ride me last night."

"I wanted to try it," I said.

"It hurt your leg."

I shrugged but didn't argue with him. Although not as much as I feared, it had hurt my leg, but I so wanted to be normal in bed for Nick that it was worth the extra pain today.

"I think it's good if we use today as a sex break day," Nick said. "Give your leg a chance to rest."

"Saturday doesn't feel like a good sex break day," I said. "That feels like a Monday thing."

"Nice try," he said. "Now, put that car in drive, baby, and take me to the park."

I rolled my eyes but shifted into gear and pulled out onto the street.

Nick

HER FACE FULL OF FIERCE CONCENTRATION, ALINA PULLED into a parking spot and shut off the car. In front of us was a cement walking trail that circled the park. A barbecue area with a scattering of picnic tables was to the west. A children's playground was next to the picnic section, and the lake shimmered in the distance, vast and an almost impossibly bright shade of blue in the sunlight.

Not surprisingly, the park was busy, but I paid no attention to the people walking along the trail as I smiled at Alina. "I'm so proud of you."

She laughed. "Are you going to say that every time I successfully park the car?"

"Fuck, yeah," I said, unbuckling my seat belt. "C'mere and give me a kiss."

She unbuckled her seat belt and met me over the console. I kissed her perfect lips, letting my mouth linger on hers despite the people walking back and forth in front of the car. I flicked her bottom lip with my tongue, loving her soft moan and the way her lips parted in response. She was perfect in so many ways, and I could spend the rest of my life -

Alina's door yanked open, and we broke apart, both of us staring in surprise at Liam as he leaned down and said, "What the fuck?"

My stomach churned, and I took a deep breath as Liam said, "Alina, are you - what the fuck is happening right now?"

Sophie appeared, her small hands gripping Liam's arm and pulling him back so that Alina could slide out of the car. I climbed out, jogging around the car to join Alina, putting my arm protectively around her shoulders as Liam stared wide-eyed at us both.

"What are you doing here, Liam?" I asked.

"What am I doing here? I'm going for a run with my girlfriend," Liam said. "The better question is - what the fuck are you doing, Nick?"

"I can explain," I said.

"Can you?" Liam asked. "Can you explain why I just watched my sister drive your fucking car into the parking lot? My sister, who doesn't have a license and could have a panic attack at any minute?"

"I've been teaching her to drive," I said. "And she's -"

"Does teaching her to drive include making out with her like a horny fucking teenager?" Liam shouted.

"Liam!" Alina glared at him as a few people in the picnic area looked our way. "Lower your voice, please."

"You and Nick were kissing, and you want me to lower my voice?" Liam said.

"That's exactly what I want," Alina snapped.

Sophie rubbed Liam's arm. "Take a few deep breaths, honey."

He sucked in some oxygen. "Explain to me what the hell is going on."

"I told you -"

"Not you!" Liam glared at me. "Don't say another word, Nicky. I love you, I fucking do, but I am so close to punching you in the face right now. Do you know how much danger you put Alina in? Do you even care?"

I opened my mouth to tell him how fucking wrong he was, but Alina squeezed my hand. "Nick, let me explain it to him."

I pushed down my caveman's urge to protect Alina. She was a grown woman who could take care of herself without my help.

"My therapist suggested that I try driving," Alina said. "She thought being in control might help the panic attacks, and she was right, Liam. It has helped. Nicky started teaching me to drive last Saturday, and I've driven every day, all over town, without a single attack. I can't explain it, I don't know exactly why it works, but it does."

"You don't have a license," Liam said. "What if the police had pulled you over?"

"It's a fine, nothing more," I said. "Which I would have paid."

Liam ignored me. "What if you have a panic attack and lose control of the car?"

"I won't," Alina said. "For the first time in nearly a decade, I'm not afraid when I'm in the car. I feel like myself again."

Liam swallowed hard, his eyes watering. "Alina, I... "

"This is a good thing," Alina said. "I promise you, Liam."

"Are you and Nick having sex?" Liam asked.

"Liam," Sophie said. "Honey, that's none of our business."

"If my best friend has been lying to me and having sex with my baby sister, I have the right to know," Liam said.

"Yes, we're having sex," I said.

Liam's face twisted. "She's like a sister to you, man."

"No, she isn't," I said. "I haven't felt that way about her for a very long time. I'm sorry I didn't tell you, but -"

"You should have told me," Liam snapped. "But you didn't because you knew what I would do to you if you admitted that my sister was another one of your fucking conquests."

"It isn't like that," I said.

Liam snorted angrily. "Stop lying to me. You've told me how many times you don't want a relationship. You use women. That's who you are, Nick. Alina deserves better than you."

"Liam, stop it!" Alina stepped forward and took his hand.

"This is Nick, your best friend. I know you're angry that we didn't tell you but stop saying shit you will regret."

"Am I wrong?" Liam said. "Are you and Nick in a relationship?"

"No," Alina said, "but -"

Liam pulled away from her, his face stark and his eyes accusatory as he stared at me. "I will never forgive you for this, Nick. Stay the fuck away from me and stay the fuck away from my sister."

He stomped away, and Sophie said, "He'll be okay. He just needs a few days to cool down. I'll text you later, Alina."

She hurried after Liam, taking his hand and rubbing his back as they walked to their car. I stared at Alina. She was pale, and her lips trembled, and I had no doubt that she was as close to vomiting as I was.

"Alina, I'm sorry," I said.

She took a deep breath before opening the car door and sliding behind the wheel. "I want to go home, Nick."

CHAPTER 11

Nick

I followed Alina into the house, dropping my jacket on the kitchen chair as Alina went straight into the bathroom. When she returned, I'd made her a cup of tea and was mentally preparing myself to break her fucking heart and mine.

"Sit down, Alina," I said.

She sat down, and I took the chair next to her. I wanted to hold her hand but folded mine into a tight fist instead. Everything I needed to say would be even more difficult if I touched her.

"Are you okay?" I asked, then scoffed. "Sorry, that was a stupid question."

She studied me quietly, her face drawn and body tense, like she knew what I would say. She probably did. "Alina, I can't -"

"I love you, Nicky," she said. "Do you love me?"

Happiness flooded through me, followed by sorrow and

regret for what I could never have. "We can't be together, Alina."

"That isn't what I asked," she said.

"Yes, I love you."

She smiled radiantly and took my hand, uncurling my fingers from the tight fist and linking them with hers. "I know what happened was awful, but Liam will come around. He just needs time to process."

"Alina, I don't do relationships," I said.

"Neither do I," she said. "But we've been in a relationship this past week, and it seems to be working okay."

"We can't base our future together on a week," I said. "Relationships are…"

"They're hard," Alina said. "They require work and commitment and love. I'm not saying this will be easy or even work. I'm saying that I want to try because I love you."

Every part of me wanted to shout my love to her from the fucking rooftops, but the look on Liam's face kept shoving its way into my brain. My best friend hated me now.

"You said you didn't want to be in a relationship," I said.

"I know. I've changed my mind," Alina said. "Being with you, Nicky, made me realize that my fear of being a burden to the man I love didn't have to be true. Being with you actually makes me more independent. It showed me that I could do anything with the right person by my side. I drove a fucking car, Nicky! Because of you. You help me be the best version of myself because you love me, and you will never think of me as a burden."

"You're not a burden," I rasped. "You're… perfect."

She smiled and swiped at the tears running down her cheeks. "I'm far from perfect, but I'm perfect for you, Nick. Admit it."

"You are," I said. "You're everything I want and need, Alina."

"Life's too short not to be with the person you love, Nicky." She leaned forward and cupped my face. "I don't want to be alone anymore. Not when the man I love is right here before me."

"Liam and Finn," I said. "They'll never believe I'm good enough for you because of my past."

"It doesn't matter. I love my brothers, and I value their opinions, but you're the man I love, and I know exactly who you are and how special you are. I know fighting with Liam is hard, and I know it feels like I'm asking you to choose between Liam and me, but I'm not, honey. Because I know without a doubt that Liam will come around. He loves you. You are a good man, Nicholas Campbell, and my brother knows it. Give him a few days to process, and he'll remember how amazing you are and be happy for us."

"What if he doesn't? What if he and Finn never approve of us?" I asked.

"I don't need their approval to be happy with you. Do you?" she asked.

"No," I said. "I just need you, Alina. For the rest of my life."

More tears slid down her cheeks, and she kissed me hard. "The rest of our lives, Nicky."

Alina

I OPENED THE DOOR AND SMILED AT MY BIG BROTHER. "Hello, Finn."

"Hey, kiddo." He stepped inside and pulled me to him for

a hug. I wrapped my arms around his waist and hugged him hard before releasing him.

"Come into the kitchen."

It was Sunday afternoon, and I wasn't surprised to see Finn on my doorstep. He and Hattie had gotten home last night, and, honestly, I was shocked it had taken him this long to come over. I didn't doubt that Liam texted him the minute Finn stepped off the plane.

I set a cup of coffee in front of him and sat at the table. "You look good. Very tanned."

He grinned. "We spent most of our time on the beach or in the ocean. Hattie loves the water."

"Is she at home?"

He nodded. "Well, my place, but it'll be her home soon. We're moving in together."

"Good for you. I'm happy for you, Finn."

"Thanks, kid." He took a sip of coffee before glancing out the kitchen doorway.

"Nick is at the store," I said. "I assume Liam texted and told you everything."

"He called," Finn said. "He's really upset, Alina."

"I know he is," I said steadily. "And I'm sorry that he's upset, but I love Nick and want to be with him."

"Does he love you?" Finn asked.

"Yes." Nick walked into the kitchen, setting the grocery bag on the counter. "I love her."

He sat in the chair next to me and took my hand. "I love her, Finn, and I will do everything in my power to make her happy."

Finn studied us both. "Okay."

I blinked at him as Nick made a shocked sound.

"Okay," I echoed.

"Okay," Finn said. "I'm not super happy about you breaking the law and driving without a license, though."

"Forget the license thing," I said. "You're really okay with me and Nick dating?"

"Yes, why wouldn't I be? Nick's a good man, and it's obvious you two love each other," Finn said.

"Who are you, and what have you done with my brother?" I asked. "Finn, hang on, buddy if you can hear me in there. I'll find an old priest and a young priest."

Nick snorted laughter as Finn rolled his eyes and took another drink of coffee. "I'm your brother, not your keeper, Alina. If you want to date Nick, I'm happy for you."

"Why aren't you freaking out like Liam is?" I asked.

Finn hesitated. "Maybe I freaked out a little when Liam first told me the news, but the woman I love is exceptionally good at calming me down and pointing out when my control tendencies wander into asshole territory."

"God, I love Hattie so much," I said.

"As do I," Finn said. "You and Nick love each other, and you're happy. That's good enough for me."

He took another sip of coffee before smiling pleasantly at Nick. "Unless you hurt her. Then they'll never find your body, Nick."

"Finn!" I snapped.

Nick laughed. "There's the Finn we know and love."

"I'm kidding, Alina," Finn said. "Mostly."

"I love you, Finn," I said.

Finn grinned at me. "I love you too, kid. Now, let's talk about this driving without a license thing."

CHAPTER 12

Nick

I stepped onto the back deck of Sophie's townhouse. Liam stood near the grill with his back to me, a set of tongs in one hand and a beer in the other.

It'd been a week since our fight, and Liam hadn't spoken to Alina or me. Alina insisted he would come around and to give him time and space, but I knew Liam almost as well as she did. The longer I waited to talk to him, the harder it would be to repair the friendship.

"Grill isn't hot enough for the steaks yet, Soph." Liam turned around. "But I can start grilling the veggies if you… Nick, what are you doing here?"

"We need to talk," I said.

"Now isn't a good time," Liam said.

"You can't avoid me forever," I said.

"I can give it one hell of a try." Liam pushed past me and reached for the sliding door, glaring at Sophie when she locked it from the other side. "Sophie, open the door."

"No, honey. I love you. Talk to Nick." She blew him a kiss and walked away.

Liam scowled and took a long drink of beer before staring at the yard like he was contemplating just walking out the back gate and into the alley.

"Five minutes," I said. "That's all I'm asking for, Liam."

"I'll give you two," he said without looking at me.

"I know you don't think I'm good enough for her," I said.

Liam winced. "It isn't that. My sister needs stability and someone who will be there for her no matter what. But you've never wanted to settle down. Your last serious relationship was nearly six years ago."

"Because I've been in love with your sister for the last five years," I said.

Liam stiffened, his knuckles turning white around the beer bottle. "Five years?"

"Yes. I told myself I wasn't. I denied that I felt anything for her because I didn't believe I was good enough for her, and I knew you didn't either. I didn't want to ruin our friendship, Liam, and I didn't want Alina to be with someone who didn't deserve her."

Liam's eyes watered, and he compulsively swallowed as I said, "But I was wrong. Alina showed me I was wrong. She believes I'm worthy of her despite my flaws and my past, and I will spend the rest of my life proving to her she's right. I love her, Liam."

"You lied to me," Liam rasped, his voice breaking. "We're best friends, and you lied."

"I'm sorry I lied. I shouldn't have done that, and I regret it. I love you, Liam. Your friendship is one of the most important relationships of my life, and I don't want to lose it. But if loving Alina means losing you, then I choose her because a life without Alina isn't a life at all."

Liam stared at me in shock. I squeezed his shoulder before walking down the deck stairs and across the yard to the gate, letting myself out and walking a few feet down the alley before leaning against the neighbour's fence.

My stomach was so knotted up that I could barely breathe, and I wanted to start sobbing right there in the damn alley. The idea of losing my best friend made me want to vomit, but I'd said what I needed to say. I could only hope that, with time, Liam would forgive me.

Alina

I STUDIED THE HOOP IN MY HAND. THE COLOURS WERE ALL wrong, the thread wouldn't stop knotting, and my frustration level was at an all time high. I knew it had nothing to do with my WIP and everything to do with my worry that Liam would never forgive Nick and me, but that knowledge didn't help my mood any.

Nick had spoken to Liam yesterday evening, but he'd refused to share exactly what he'd said to Liam, and he'd been quiet and withdrawn since. He'd gone for a run this morning, and I'd retreated to my studio, hoping that working on my embroidery would relax me.

I dropped the hoop on my worktable and rubbed my fore-head. I said all the right things to Nick, and I put on a happy face, but I was a complete mess inside. The idea that I had destroyed Nick and Liam's friendship ate at me like acid on a penny. I knew how important Liam was to Nick. What if, over time, Nick grew to resent me for ruining their friendship?

I looked up at the soft knock on the studio door, relief and trepidation trampling for space in my body when I saw Liam. "Liam! Hi, honey."

"Hi, Alina." He sat in the chair across from me, leaning forward and resting his forearms on his thighs. He looked tired and sad, and my heart ached for hurting him.

I took a deep breath. "I didn't hear you come in."

"Nick was just getting home from his run. He let me in."

"Oh." I glanced at the doorway.

"I asked him to give us a minute before joining us," Liam said.

I knew I should just let Liam speak, but he looked so sad and upset that I was sure he was here to tell us he could never accept Nick and me together. Speaking so rapidly, my words ran together, I said, "Nick has been nothing but good to me, Liam. He accepts me for who I am, and that includes my limitations. He makes me stronger when I'm with him. I feel like the old me and not like a burden."

Liam reached out and took my hands, squeezing them tight. "I know. I'm sorry for what I said and for my behaviour. I've been a real asshole. I love you both, and I want the two of you to be happy."

Nick stepped silently into the room. He smiled at me, and I felt a wave of love for him that threatened to crush me with its intensity. I turned back to Liam. "What changed your mind?"

Liam glanced at Nick before facing me again. "Nick told me yesterday that he would choose you over me."

I stared wide-eyed at Nick as he winced. "I probably should have thought of a nicer way to get that point across."

Liam shook his head. "No, it's exactly what I needed to hear. It's how I knew you were the right person for my sister, Nicky. I want someone who will put her ahead of everyone else."

He squeezed my hands again. "You deserve to be the most important person in Nick's life, Alina. I'm happy for you both, and I'm sorry for how I reacted."

I leaned forward and wrapped my arms around Liam's shoulders. "Thank you, Liam. I love you."

He leaned back and brushed away the tears on my cheeks. "All for one and one for all, Alina."

"Always," I said.

Liam cleared his throat and stood. He and Nick hugged, and fresh tears slid down my face. "We're having dinner at Finn and Hattie's tonight. Finn said you and Alina are to be there, no arguments."

"We'll be there," Nick said.

Liam studied him for a few seconds. "I love you, man."

"Love you too," Nick said.

Liam clapped him on the shoulder. "Welcome to the Three Musketeers, D'Artagnan."

He left the studio, and Nick waited until the front door closed before joining me and lifting me to my feet. He slid his arms around my waist and pulled me close as I smiled happily at him. "Hi, Nicky."

"Hi, baby." He pressed a kiss against my mouth.

"Can I say 'I told you so' now, or should I wait until after you screw my brains out?" I asked.

Nick burst into laughter before picking me up and carrying me out of the studio and toward my bedroom. "Definitely after."

He set me on the bed and stretched out beside me, running his fingers over my damp cheeks. "You're so beautiful, Alina."

"So are you. Will you move in with me permanently?" I asked.

"I can't think of anything I want more," he said. "And it isn't just because of your house's remarkable lack of mold."

I laughed and pulled him close, resting my forehead against his. "I love you, Nicky."

"I love you, Alina."

Keep reading for an excerpt from "The Geologist", Book Four in the Sexy Scientists Series.

THE GEOLOGIST EXCERPT

SEXY SCIENTISTS SERIES, BOOK FOUR

Bryce

"Bryce? Why are you still here?" My boss Carol stuck her head into my office.

Well, office may have been too strong of a word. I had taken over an unused storage closet that had no windows and barely enough room for a desk, but it was still infinitely better than working in the bullpen. I loved my fellow PR specialists, but trying to concentrate in a sea of voices, ringing phones, and clicking keyboards made my teeth itch.

"I work here?" I said with a raised eyebrow.

"Smartass." Carol rolled her eyes and leaned against the doorway, her blonde hair in a perfect chignon and her magenta-coloured suit tailor made for her slender figure. "You're supposed to be meeting Arnold and Griffin Morris at two."

I put on my *you love me the best* smile and said, "Can't you tell Arnold that me shadowing Griffin while he does his geo survey thingy, is a waste of Arnold's money? Does he really want to pay for me to babysit the geologist?"

Carol sighed. "One, Arnold Waters is our biggest client, and you promised me you would be committed to doing whatever he asked if I assigned you as his PR specialist."

"I know, but -"

Carol carried on without stopping. "And two, you knew walking into this assignment what a control freak Arnold is. He has a lot riding on this mall project, and he's paying our firm a great deal of money."

"To write media releases, help him communicate with the public, and manage the flow of information for the mall development," I said. "Not to babysit. It's a waste of his money and my time."

"Honey, when you have as much money as Arnold Waters does, what he pays us in fees is only a drop in the damn bucket. But that's not the point anyway. The point is, he's our largest client, and we're going to do what he wants because my firm promises results. Do you want to lose your first big assignment before writing your first press release?"

"I've already written two press releases about the mall," I said.

Carol stared at me until I looked away like a little kid chastised for overeating candy.

"You know as well as I do that Arnold building this mall in Willowdale will revitalize our town. The buzz around building a local vendor-only mall is making waves not just here in the US but in Canada and Europe too. It's the first mall of its kind – not a single franchise or big box department store allowed in the mall - just vendors and creators from right here in Willowdale. Our little town is on the map because of Arnold's idea, and we owe him a lot. Disappointing him is not an option," Carol said.

"I know," I said.

"You're one of my best specialists, and I want to know that I can count on you not to fuck this up," Carol said. "If we lose Arnold as a client because of something you say or do, I will fire you."

Yikes. Usually, I loved Carol's total bluntness even when it was aimed my way, but the prospect of losing my job sent the proverbial icy shivers down my spine. There weren't a lot of opportunities for PR work in my hometown of Willowdale which, if I lost this job, left my options limited – move to Havenport, a midsized city about half an hour away, or find a different job.

Neither appealed to me. I couldn't imagine leaving Willowdale, or more accurately, leaving my grandparents, and I loved my job.

"Why are you so against shadowing Mr. Morris?" Carol asked. "You'll be getting paid to be out of the office and in sunlight for a change."

I pointed to my pasty white skin. "Oh yes, because as a redhead, sunlight is definitely my friend."

Carol laughed. "You can expense the sunblock you'll need to use. Seriously, Bryce, why is this a problem?"

I picked at a file folder edge. "Griffin Morris is from Willowdale."

"I'm aware," Carol said. "It's one of the reasons Arnold picked the firm Griffin contracts with. He wanted a geologist who knew Willowdale and the area.

"I knew Griffin in high school," I said.

"Makes sense. You're around the same age, right?"

"He was a grade ahead of me," I said.

"Still not seeing the problem," Carol said with a touch of impatience.

"He and his older brother Ben were very popular in high

school. They both played football, and they left town on football scholarships because of how good they were. All the girls in my high school had a crush on Griffin or Ben. I was no different."

"Okay, you had a high school crush on Griffin, so what?" Carol said. "That was a few years ago. Neither of you are teenagers anymore."

"I tried to kiss him," I said.

"All right," Carol said. "But again, that was a few years ago and -"

"I threw up on him," I said.

Carol winced. "Oh God. Seriously?"

"Yes. I went in for the kiss and instead vomited Lucky Charms all over him."

I had to give Carol credit. She struggled hard to hold in the laughter. Sure, she failed miserably, but I couldn't blame her for it. If it hadn't been me who threw up on the most beautiful man in existence, I would see the humour in it too.

"You seriously barfed Lucky Charms into his mouth?" Carol said.

"He turned his head so, no," I said. "It hit his cheek and down his neck." My face was bright red, just remembering the moment.

"Well, that's slightly better, right?" Carol said.

I glared at her. "There is no way to turn 'I vomited Lucky Charms on the man of my dreams' into anything slightly better, Carol."

She laughed hard, leaning against the doorway and pressing one hand against her flat abdomen. "Okay, yeah, I guess not."

"So, can we talk to Arnold about me not babysitting Griffin?" I asked.

Carol gave me a sympathetic look but shook her head.

"Nope, sorry, Bryce. Vomit or no vomit, you will be Griffin Morris's shadow for however long the geotechnical survey takes."

I slumped in my chair, rubbing my forehead. "I kind of hate you right now, Carol."

"I know," she said. "Hey, what did you have for lunch today?"

My stomach was in too many knots about seeing my high school crush again to eat anything today. "I skipped lunch. Why?"

"Just wanted to make sure it wasn't Lucky Charms," Carol said.

"When you leave work one evening and find your car toilet-papered, it was one thousand percent me," I said.

She laughed and glanced at her watch. "That's fair. Now get your butt in your car and head over to Brilliant Beanz before you're late for the meeting with Arnold and Mr. Morris."

I stared at Arnold's text and then tossed my phone into my purse, trying not to scream my frustration right there in the Brilliant Beanz parking lot. Of course, Arnold was called into another meeting and couldn't make this one. Facing Griffin Morris without the buffer of Arnold, where he would undoubtedly bring up the humiliating Lucky Charms vomit incident, was the perfect cherry on top of the shit sundae that was currently my day.

I climbed out of my car with a heavy sigh, straightened my navy blue power suit, and walked toward the coffee shop. I'd smoothed and tucked away my crazy curls into a severe bun on top of my head, and while it wasn't my cutest hairstyle, it made me feel more professional. My makeup was impeccable, and I'd chosen my most flattering suit.

I looked good, and while that gave me a confidence boost, my nerves were still rattling around like one of those old-school wooden roller coasters, and I could only hope that Griffin Morris wouldn't bring up the past.

I stepped inside the coffee shop, inhaling the good scent of roasted beans. The shop was pretty busy, but Griffin Morris wasn't the type of guy to blend in in high school, and eight years hadn't changed that.

My mouth went dry, and my steps faltered. Griffin stood at the counter, all six foot five of him, wearing a pair of jeans and a dark green shirt with a grey striped tie. His dark hair was cut shorter than in high school, and his jaw sported a dark shadow of scruff that hadn't been there in his teens. But it wasn't the facial hair that had turned my panties into a soaking wet mess.

Griffin had been muscular back in high school – you couldn't spend as much time practicing football as he did and not be muscular - but apparently, he'd taken up a side hobby of bench pressing small cars and tiny houses because I was pretty sure his muscles had muscles at this point.

Griffin grabbed his coffee and walked toward a table near the window. I stared at his beautiful ass and thick thighs. Was it weird to be jealous of denim? Because I wanted to be the one clinging to those powerful thighs.

My formerly dry mouth now salivating so much I was in danger of drooling all over my power suit I considered turning around and walking back out. Griffin hadn't seen me yet, and time had not lessened my crush on him as I'd assumed. Apparently, my unrequited love for him still burned as brightly as ever, and there was no way I could be near him without climbing him like a fucking tree.

I spun around but only took two steps before stopping. What was I doing? I loved my job, and I would be damned if I lost everything just because I couldn't keep my libido in check around a man who would be less than pleased to see me.

I straightened my back, lifted my chin, and marched toward Griffin with a bright and welcoming smile plastered on my face. I stopped at his table and said, "Griffin?"

He stood and smiled politely at me. "Hello."

Now that I was up close, I could see a few lines around his eyes that hadn't been there before, and his nose had definitely been broken in the past. His dark eyes were the same, though, guarded and just the tiniest bit sad.

Say something, girl!

I cleared my throat, trying not to blush. "Hi, it's so great to see you again. You look wonderful. How was your trip? Does it feel strange to be back in Willowdale? I bet it feels a little strange."

Jesus. Stop saying something, girl!

I made myself stop talking as Griffin gave me another one of those polite and vague smiles. "It's nice to see you again as well, Ms...."

"Bryce. Bryce Watson," I said.

Not a flicker of recognition crossed his face, and hope blossomed in my belly. Holy shit. Could it be possible? Did Griffin Morris not remember me? I didn't know whether to be insulted or elated. Elation won by the narrowest of margins.

I cleared my throat again. "I'm the PR specialist working with Mr. Waters on the mall development project. I'm meeting with you and Mr. Waters today."

"Oh," he said. "My apologies. Arnold didn't mention you'd be joining us. Please, have a seat."

He pulled out the chair next to his, and my stupid heart

went all a titter. I couldn't help it. I loved a man with manners.

I sat down, and Griffin returned to his seat, taking a sip of coffee. I hadn't gotten a coffee, but my stomach churned so much that I was terrified even to consider it. I'd already barfed once on Griffin Morris. I would walk barefoot across hot coals before I did it again.

"Mr. Waters texted me, and unfortunately, he's been held up in another meeting and won't be able to make it today," I said.

A flicker of irritation crossed Griffin's face. "Why didn't he just cancel then?"

"He's asked me to chat with you about the geological survey in his place," I said.

One thick dark eyebrow raised, and he looked me up and down. I resisted the urge to fidget or pull at my clothes. "It's called a geotechnical survey, and why would he ask his marketing rep to talk to me about it?"

"I'm not in marketing," I said, swallowing down my annoyance. "I'm a PR specialist."

"Is there a difference?" he asked.

"A huge difference," I said icily. My crush on Griffin was melting away with every sentence he spoke. I didn't remember him being this ornery and dismissive in high school.

Griffin took a sip of his coffee and said, "Okay, so why is a PR specialist," the slight emphasis he put on specialist made me grit my teeth, "chatting with me about my survey?"

"As I'm sure you're aware, the mall development project is incredibly important to Mr. Waters. He's asked me to accompany you as you do your development site survey."

"No," Griffin said.

I stared at him. "No?"

"No," he confirmed.

"What do you mean no?"

"I'm sorry, is there another way to say no in PR speak?" he asked.

I held onto my temper with the thinnest of threads. "Perhaps I didn't make myself clear. Mr. Waters, the man paying you to do your job, has asked me to accompany you on the survey."

"I don't need a babysitter," Griffin said.

"And I have better ways to use my time than babysitting, but here we both are."

"I work alone," Griffin said. "End of story."

"Fine," I said and stood up. "You can let Mr. Waters know that you'll be turning down the job. I'm sure you have his cell number."

I turned to leave, hoping like hell that Griffin didn't call my bluff. If he called Arnold and said he wouldn't let me shadow him during the survey, I'd definitely lose my job, even if I explained it was Griffin's choice, not mine. Arnold wasn't interested in excuses. He only wanted results.

"Wait," Griffin said.

My heart thudding so loudly, he could probably hear it over the buzz of the espresso machine, I returned to my seat and gave him a polite smile.

Griffin scowled, his thick fingers drumming against the table with an impatient beat. "Why is he assigning me a babysitter? If he thinks I can't do the job, why the hell did he specifically ask for me?"

"Mr. Waters is…" I paused, trying to find a way to say 'he's a damn control freak' politely and coming up empty.

"He's got control issues," Griffin said.

"Yes. Mr. Waters purchase of the property is dependent on what you find in your survey. The property is the only spot in

Willowdale that will work to develop a mall this size. Can you blame him for wanting to ensure everything goes smoothly?"

"He could try trusting that I'll do my job properly," Griffin said.

"He does trust you. Honestly, he wants me to accompany you to make your life easier." I hit him with the smile that worked on even the most difficult clients. "I promise I'll be an asset, not a liability, Mr. Morris."

He looked me up and down again, barely able to hide the contempt in his gaze. "I doubt that very much, Ms. Watson."

That thin thread holding my temper snapped like an over-strung violin. "What exactly is your problem with me assisting you while you conduct your testing, Mr. Morris?"

"Oh, I don't know," he growled. "Maybe I'm just worried I'll have Lucky Charms vomited all over me again."

My stomach landed on the floor with an audible thud, and heat flashed across my face.

I was wrong. Griffin Morris not only knew who I was, but he remembered exactly what I'd done to him.

Shit on a motherfucking cracker.

ABOUT THE AUTHOR

Ramona Gray is a Canadian romance author. She currently lives in Alberta with her awesome husband and her super cute dog. She's addicted to home improvement shows, good coffee, and reading and writing about the steamier moments in life.

For more information about Ramona, check out her website at

www.ramonagray.ca

facebook.com/RamonaGrayBooks
twitter.com/RamonaGrayBooks
instagram.com/ramonagrayauthor
amazon.com/Ramona-Gray/e/B00OD26SAM
bookbub.com/profile/ramona-gray

ALSO BY RAMONA GRAY

Individual Books

The Escort

Saving Jax

The Assistant

One Night

Sharing Del

Filthy Appeal

Forbidden Bliss

Shadow Security Series

Dead of Night

Edge of Night

Dark of Night

Undeniable Series

Undeniably His

Undeniably Hers

Undeniably Theirs

Undeniable Series Boxset

Working Men Series

The Mechanic

The Carpenter

The Bartender

The Welder

The Electrician

The Landscaper

The Firefighter

The Cop

The Paramedic

Working Men Series Bundles

Working Men Series Books One to Three

Working Men Series Books Four to Six

Working Men Series Books Seven to Nine

Sexy Scientists Series

The Chemist

The Biologist

The Physicist

The Geologist

The Paleontologist

The Botanist

Sexy Scientists Series Box Set

Sexy Scientists Series Books 1-3

Sexy Scientists Series Books 4-6

Other World Series

The Vampire's Kiss (Book One)

The Vampire's Love (Book Two)

The Shifter's Mate (Book Three)

Rescued By The Wolf (Book Four)

Claiming Quinn (Book Five)

Choosing Rose (Book Six)

Elena Unbound (Book Seven)

Other World Series Box Sets

Other World Series Books One to Three

Other World Series Books Four to Six